Joss Wood loves books, coff___ ___ ___
to the wild places of southern ___ ___
She's a wife and a mum to two young adults, two cats and
a dog the size of a small cow. After a career in local
economic development and business, Joss writes full-time
from her home in KwaZulu-Natal, South Africa.

THE TROUBLE WITH LITTLE SECRETS

KEEP YOUR ENEMIES CLOSE…

JOSS WOOD

MILLS & BOON

First Published in Great Britain 2023
by Mills & Boon, an imprint of HarperCollins*Publishers* Ltd
1 London Bridge Street, London, SE1 9GF

www.harpercollins.co.uk

HarperCollins*Publishers*
Macken House, 39/40 Mayor Street Upper,
Dublin 1, D01 C9W8, Ireland

The Trouble with Little Secrets © 2023 Joss Wood
Keep Your Enemies Close... © 2023 Joss Wood

ISBN: 978-0-263-31766-4

0823

This book is produced from independently certified FSC™ paper to ensure responsible forest management.

For more information visit: www.harpercollins.co.uk/green

Printed and Bound in the UK using 100% Renewable Electricity at CPI Group (UK) Ltd, Croydon, CR0 4YY

THE TROUBLE WITH LITTLE SECRETS

One

I, Lady Avangeline Forrester-Grantham have been caught out before, have found myself in tight situations, but never as this bad. But if my grandsons continue to treat as if were stupid, I will knock some heads together. I know as much as they do. Probably more.

Jack Grantham was comprehensively pissed off with his brother.

He'd thought he'd been angry with Fox before—both of them were strong-willed, determined guys, and they'd had more than their fair share of rumbles—but this was next-level.

He was beyond livid, and he didn't know if their relationship was salvageable. Right now, if he never saw his brother and business partner's face again, he'd consider that a win.

Jack rested his forehead against the cool window of his office, with its incredible view of Central Park, his head throbbing. He'd had a headache for days, and he didn't see it going away anytime soon.

Hearing a sharp rap on his barely open door, he didn't bother to turn around. "Go away, Fox. I'm not ready to talk to you yet. I'm not sure if I ever will be."

"Wrong brother."

Jack turned around and pulled a small smile onto his tight-as-hell face. Merrick Knowles had grown up with him, his cousin Soren and his two brothers—Malcolm and Fox—at Calcott Manor after the death of his and Soren's parents in a plane crash when he was eight. Their grandmother, Avangeline, the billionaire hotel and restaurant entrepreneur, had sold her empire to raise four boys under the age of eleven with the help of her beloved housekeeper and trusted friend, Jacinta Knowles, and they'd all decamped to Calcott Manor, Avangeline's vast estate outside Hatfield, Connecticut. One of those boys had been Jacinta's eight-year-old son, Merrick. Merrick wasn't only his non–blood brother; he was also his best friend.

Merrick walked over to the coffee machine in the corner, jammed two cups under the dual spouts and banged the back of his fist against the button to dispense espresso. Picking up the tiny cups, he walked across the room and handed one to Jack.

It was his sixth this morning, and the caffeine in his system had yet to penetrate his anger. He felt gutted and betrayed, and couldn't believe it was his barely older brother who'd made him feel this way.

"You know that Fox was just trying to protect you, Jack," Merrick said, sitting down on the couch and stretching out his long legs. They were all big guys, but Merrick was the tallest of them all, topping out at six four.

"I am thirty-three years old; I don't need protecting," Jack growled, dropping into his custom-made leather chair.

A week ago, when Fox invited him, Soren and Merrick for dinner in his hotel-suite apartment, right next to his own living space, Jack thought that Fox wanted to update them about his time spent at Calcott Manor, to inform them whether he'd made any progress to get their intractable grandmother to write a will. At eighty-plus, Avangeline was standing in God's waiting room, a woman with the assets and spending power of a third-world country. If she died without a will, it would mire her heirs in red tape, domestic and international, for years, and he'd hoped Fox had an explanation for her illogical streak of stubbornness.

He'd also expected Fox to tell him, Merrick and Soren whether he'd discovered why Alyson Garwood, Avangeline's guest and the recipient of their brother's liver after his death, was ensconced in Avangeline's manor house. He'd expected answers as to why she'd taken a sabbatical from her job as a lawyer specializing in social media and escaped to Calcott Manor, and what she wanted—cash? A property?—from Avangeline.

But no, instead of an update, his world had been shattered. While staying at Calcott Manor, Fox discovered that their grandmother was being blackmailed. The blackmailer was threatening to expose the identity of Avangeline's long-term lover—why would that be an issue?—and, more worryingly, the fact that his parents had used an underground, on-another-level S-and-M sex club they owned as their personal playground. The very parents he'd adored, respected and, yeah, worshipped.

The knowledge of their dangerous, secret lifestyle shocked him, and that Fox had kept it from him for so many years rocked him to the depth of his soul.

Merrick put his cup on the coffee table and leaned forward, resting his forearms on his thighs. "Jack, from the time I met you, you have had an extremely unrealistic view of your parents. In your mind, they have always been as close to perfection as two people could be. All your life, you've held them up to this impossible standard of perfection. It's been a point of pride with you that your parents got life, *did* life, right."

Jack ran his hands over his face. "And it was a lie of epic proportions. And Fox knew. He let me carry on believing that."

"So, what are you really angry about? That your parents had a nonvanilla attitude toward sex or that they weren't perfect?"

"I'm angry that Fox didn't tell me!" Jack yelled back.

"Sure, and you have a right to be," Merrick replied, being as reasonable as ever. He was their self-appointed protector, the glue bonding them together. Jack hoped that glue was super strong, because the sticky strands connecting them were on the verge of snapping.

"But I get why he didn't, Jack. It's always been incredibly important to you that your parents' legacy of being America's perfect couple—stunning, successful, crazy about each other—remains intact."

"Bullshit!"

Merrick raised a dark eyebrow, the same color as his black hair. "Dude, you sued a newspaper for defamation a few years back for a two-line paragraph when the journalist vaguely suggested that your father used his political contacts to land a government contract."

"I didn't win."

Merrick ignored his hot reply. "You issued a statement when Vance Kane, in his tell-all memoir, alluded to having an affair with a blond, gorgeous East Coast socialite, a thinly veiled reference to your mom. By insisting your parents were insanely happy and didn't cheat, you amplified a story that would've skimmed under the radar otherwise. Your parents' reputation is your trigger point. I've always wondered why."

Jack stared down into his empty coffee cup, recalling the last conversation he'd had with his dad on the morning of his death. He'd finally found the courage to show his dad his report card, a mixture of A's and B's. His father had perused his grades, looked at him with his cool gray eyes and uttered the seven words that came to define life.

Is that the best you can do?

Everything, his appearance, his work ethic, his relationship and his business successes, were judged by those words. And no was the answer to the question he frequently asked himself. He could always do better, be better, run harder and work smarter.

The next project, date, relationship and business had to be better than the one before. He was always chasing the next goal and making a new plan. He frequently felt like a hamster on a fast wheel going nowhere.

In his eyes, his parents had been perfect and he needed to be as well.

Except that they weren't, and he had no concept of how to process that information. It felt as if Fox had cut away the bedrock of his beliefs, and he felt adrift.

And angry. Had he mentioned angry?

Merrick drained his coffee and leaned back, placing his ankle on his knee. "You need to get over this, Jack, and you need to forgive Fox. He was trying to protect you. You guys didn't survive the deaths of your parents and then Malcolm to let this wrench you apart."

"You're putting the blame where it doesn't belong," Jack snapped. "I wasn't the one who kept important information about my parents from my brother."

"But you are the one who idolizes them, who won't ever hear even the mildest criticism against them. You are the one who has arranged fundraisers and benefits in their memory, who rants and raves when you read or hear anything that contradicts your Pollyanna version of your family. You can still love them while accepting they had their faults."

"Owning a sex club wasn't a fault. It was—" Jack shouted before pulling his words back. He linked his hands behind his head and closed his eyes. "This has rocked me to my core, M."

"Sure it has," Merrick agreed. "Bro, you've been around the block enough times to know that sometimes people like a little kink—"

Sure, hearing about his parents' sex lives was gross, but he was old enough and experienced enough to accept their lifestyle choices and push them aside. It was the rest of it that bugged the hell out of him.

"I can handle that, but that they hired young, barely legal sex workers freaks me out. And the fact that my mom met a dangerous group on the dark net and wanted to—God—bring them into her world makes my blood run cold. That's just insanity. And stupid."

His parents had not been stupid people, so what the hell had they been thinking?

"And how do you feel about the fact that they, apparently, hated each other and were on the point of divorce?" Merrick asked.

Stupid. He felt stupid. He'd always thought they were the happiest couple alive. "It's a good reminder that I shouldn't trust the obvious, that people lie all the time."

Merrick winced. "Yep, even the gods among us are prone to failure and foibles." His eyes slammed into Jack's. "Just be careful that you aren't shooting the messenger because of the message, Jack. You've lost enough. You can't afford to lose another brother too."

Intellectually, he understood that. Emotionally? He wanted to rip this building apart with his bare hands. "I just need some time to wrap my head around everything that's happened."

"You do. And we haven't even talked about who is black-mailing Avangeline," Merrick said.

Jack groaned. He hadn't forgotten about that, he'd just temporarily pushed it aside. Grabbing a notepad, he jotted down a few points.

- Avangeline has a long-term lover and they corre-spond via coded postcards.
- No one in the family knows who the lover is.
- Why is this blackmail material? Why is this enough to make her change her will?
- She's paid millions in cryptocurrency already—des-tination untraceable—and refuses to contact the po-lice.
- The blackmailer has given her six weeks to draw up a new will, have it filed and notarized.
- Avangeline—thank God—does not know about the secret sex club.
- There are too many secrets!

He pushed the list across the table to Merrick, who nod-ded after reading it. "That sounds about right," he replied before frowning and asking for a pen. Jack threw him one and Merrick balanced the paper on his knee and scribbled on it before pushing it back across the desk.

Why is Aly Garwood at Calcott Manor, and what the hell does she want?

"Do you think there's anything to her theory that she's inherited some of Malcolm's thoughts and memories, tastes and quirks?"

"Seriously?" Jack scowled at Merrick. "Please tell me you don't believe her?"

Merrick rolled his eyes. "Of course I don't—it's BS. But Soren and Fox do."

"Falling in love has rattled something loose in their brains," Jack snapped. How could smart and sensible men believe such unadulterated crap?

His headache worsened at the thought, and he felt as if his brain was trying to squeeze its way out of his skull.

"You need to get up to Calcott Manor and sort this out, Jack," Merrick said.

Jack glared at him. "Isn't Fox leading the charge?" he asked sarcastically.

Merrick didn't rise to the bait. "Fox, as you'd know if you were talking to him, has flown to Malaysia to interview a new group accountant for that region."

Yeah, he remembered that. Ru, his world-wandering fiancée, was meeting him in Kuala Lumpur.

"If I leave, there won't be anyone here at the head office," he told Merrick, desperate for an excuse to not return to Hatfield.

"There's nothing you can do from here that can't be done from Calcott Manor," Merrick told him. "You employ excellent managers, Jack, let them do their jobs. They can cope without your micromanaging and perfectionistic ways."

Jack thought about disputing Merrick's statement but couldn't. While he had high standards for his staff, he aimed for flawlessness in his own life by working exceptionally hard and demanding more from himself. It was hard work, but his constant need to be better resulted in him being named, like his father before him, one of the most brilliant businesspeople of his generation.

Besides not wanting to leave the hospitality empire Malcolm had dreamed up, and he and Fox built, for their managers to run, he didn't want to return to his childhood home for an extended time. Not only were his memories of his parents strongest at Calcott Manor, but being in Hatfield reminded him of a violet-eyed redhead who haunted his dreams.

Peyton Caron had been Malcolm's fiancée, but they'd called off their wedding just a few weeks before his death ten years ago. Was sleeping with your dead brother's ex a violation of the bro code? Jack didn't know.

And there was no one he could ask, not even Merrick.

But what he did know was that his one-night stand with Peyton two years ago had been the best sexual encounter of his life, and that the memory of her and the night they spent together was almost overwhelming in Hatfield. No wonder he spent as little time there as possible.

"With Fox overseas, someone has to pick up the investigation into who is blackmailing Avangeline and why. I can't. I'm launching a diner in Cancún this week and another in Seattle the week after," Merrick said.

Soren and Fox had each spent time in Hatfield at their grandmother's luxurious estate, and it was—Jack reluctantly conceded—his turn.

Shit.

"So, when are you going?" Merrick asked.

Jack picked up one of his many squeeze balls and clutched it in his fist before throwing it against the opposite wall. It flew past Merrick's ear and back at him quickly, and he snatched it out of the air.

He looked at Merrick, who didn't blink. Cool bastard. Always had been.

"So? When?" Merrick asked again.

Jack looked at his dark computer, which he'd yet to turn on today, and his empty desk. He hadn't accomplished anything yet, had done little yesterday and absolutely nothing in the two days before that. If he was going to be useless, he could be useless at Calcott Manor.

"I'll drive down this morning," Jack said in concession, feeling a hundred years old.

Merrick slapped his hands on his thighs and stood up. "Excellent—my work here is done," he said, giving Jack a satisfied smile. He was halfway to the door when he stopped abruptly and spun around. Merrick placed his hands on his hips and glared at Jack.

"And, for the love of God, don't fall in love as Soren and Fox did. If I'm the only single man left standing, Mom will nag me to death."

Jack shook his head. Jacinta, his second mother, wouldn't be nagging him. Thanks to his one-foot-out-the-door strategy, his romantic relationships were doomed to fail. Maybe his fear of intimacy and opening up to someone had something to do with his inability to commit, but he didn't have the time—or interest—to figure out why he always bailed. It was easier to remain single, to have shallow encounters with women who expected nothing more than a night of fabulous sex.

Desire he understood, but love?

No, love didn't exist.

Peyton skipped down the steps, her long braid bouncing as she jogged down the steep stairs from her apartment to the ground floor of Clancy's, the bar Simon and Keene, her best friends, owned. Keene had collected Noah from her shortly after six, telling her that he and Simon were taking him to the beach, and she'd gratefully returned to her bed and slept until eight. Then she took a leisurely shower, washed her hair and shaved her legs, reveling in the gift of time. On the West Coast as a single mom, she never had the luxury of taking it slowly.

It was a stunning day in early August, and her summer vacation was coming to an end. In the final days of the month, she would relocate to Chicago to take up an assistant curator position at the Museum of Contemporary Art, and these long, lazy summer days would be a distant memory. It would be her and Noah again, a team of two.

After a trip into the bar's kitchen to pour herself a mug of coffee, Peyton walked into the public area of the bar and bistro and immediately spotted her two best friends and her baby sitting at the corner booth. Noah had fallen asleep on Simon's broad shoulder, and Peyton sucked in a breath. It was the strangest thing; sometimes she caught mental images of Noah when he was an adult and, God, he looked like his dad.

A Grantham through and through.

She'd met Fox, the middle brother, a few weeks back, and it had felt weird to reconnect with the man who'd almost been her brother-in-law. Fox looked the most like Malcolm, while Jack, the youngest Grantham brother, was a blue-eyed blond. Unlike Malcolm and Fox, Jack didn't try to control his curly hair by cutting it short; he just styled it off his face and let it fall to brush the collar of his shirt. Jack's beard was, or had been, when she saw him, longer than Fox's stubble.

You've seen two out of the three Grantham brothers naked...

Dear God, where did that thought come from, and why now? It had to be because she was back in Hatfield, the scene of all her man-related crimes. It was her hometown, where she'd fallen in love with and gotten engaged to Malcolm, and where she'd slept with Jack eight years later.

Had she cheated on Malcolm with Jack? No; she was being ridiculous. There had been eight years between Malcolm and her encounter with Jack. And, *crucially*, you couldn't cheat on a dead man.

Annoyed with herself for revisiting the past, Peyton walked through the empty bar area—they'd be opening in only a half hour or so—and dropped a kiss on Noah's head. Her boy didn't sir.

She slid into the booth next to Keene and mock-glared at his husband, also her fitness-obsessed oldest friend. "Did you make him do one of your high-intensity training routines, Simon?" she said teasingly.

"Yes, it's called chasing seagulls. It's his favorite game," Simon told her, his free hand coming up to cover Noah's back.

On hearing that she had the summer free, Simon and Keene had begged her to come to Hatfield, and not knowing when she'd be able to visit next, she'd accepted their offer to stay in their above-the-bar apartment. They'd scooped Noah up and given her plenty of breaks, time to relax and catch up on her reading, her sleep and me time. Maybe spending the summer in Hatfield hadn't been her brightest idea, as she now knew exactly what she'd be missing when she moved to the Windy City.

What she wouldn't miss was the memories of her father, Harry, of Malcolm and of the way Jack made her body sing.

It was too beautiful a day to think of Harry and his deception, of Malcolm, Jack and the past. The sun was high and hot, the sky was a brilliant blue, and Peyton was with her best friends.

People who loved her. And, more importantly, loved her boy.

She smiled at Simon and then at Keene, thinking that life couldn't get better than this. God, if only she could find a decent job in Hatfield, she wouldn't hesitate to stay. Unfortunately, the tourist town, busy in the summer and empty in the winter, didn't have much call for art experts.

"You guys are looking very serious," she said, noticing their somber faces and worried expressions.

Simon and Keene exchanged a long look, and Keene nodded at Simon, as if encouraging him to speak. Oh, this wasn't going to be good.

"We heard some news today, and you need to decide how you are going to deal with it," Simon said.

He looked so serious that Peyton thought he was about to tell her Harry was dead. She didn't know how she'd feel about that. Relief? Sadness? Indifference? She didn't know.

"Jack Grantham is back in Hatfield, and we've heard, via a reliable source, that he plans to stay for a while."

Jack. Jack was back. In Hatfield. Dear God, Simon had to be pulling her leg; this couldn't be true. She'd only agreed to come home to Hatfield for the summer because Simon, who was a cop and knew everything about everyone, reassured her that Jack seldom visited Hatfield. When he did, it was to make quick, in-and-out visits to see his grandmother, Avangeline, at Calcott Manor. Being in the hospitality and leisure trade, summer was his busiest season, and the hotel empire he co-owned with Fox needed all hands on deck—specifically his.

"Peyton, this is ridiculous. You have to tell him," Simon insisted, pulling her attention back to their worried faces. "Apart from the fact that you could do with some financial help, he has a right to know that he is Noah's dad. It's not fair that he doesn't know."

Peyton knew that Simon and Keene were desperate for a child and were investigating the process of egg donations and surrogacy. She knew they felt strongly about Noah knowing his dad, but they didn't know her entire history with the Grantham family, why she and Malcolm had split up and why Avangeline blamed her for his death.

"I can't tell Jack," she told them, shaking her head. "That's not an option."

Malcolm is dead because of you, and I will never forgive you. I can't stop you from staying in Hatfield, but you will stay away from my grandsons. You may attend Malcolm's funeral, but you will not play any part in the proceedings or speak to any of his family. You will never have any contact with a Grantham again. If you do, I will destroy you and anyone you love.

Avangeline's warning had been delivered in a cold, hard voice, and Peyton understood it wasn't an idle threat and that the billionairess had the power and influence to do exactly as she promised. She'd been nineteen at the time and scared to the soles of her feet. Ten-plus years later, she hadn't forgotten one word of the warning. And she hadn't lost any of her fear.

If Avangeline heard that she'd had a one-night stand with Jack, she'd lose her marbles. God knew what she would do if she heard Noah was her great-grandson.

Peyton could hardly hear herself think over the sound of her thunderous heartbeat. Her hand shook as she placed her coffee cup on the table, and she bit her bottom lip so hard that it left tooth marks. She tried to tell herself that she was overreacting, but she couldn't make herself believe it. At one point, Avangeline had been considered one of the most powerful women in the world, and she hadn't gotten to that point by smiling sweetly.

Peyton wasn't prepared to take a chance on what she might, or might not, do, and whether her threats had an expiration date. Avangeline had the wealth and power to make Peyton's professional life hell too. The billionairess was the owner of one of the best art collections outside of major museums and was a force in the art world. With one telephone call, she could decimate Peyton's reputation and have her offer of a curatorship rescinded. If she was spiteful enough, Avangeline could make sure she never worked in a museum or gallery again. If Avangeline went nuclear, Peyton doubted that she'd even be able to sell touristy souvenirs by the time she was finished with her.

And Peyton had no idea how Avangeline would react to hearing that Jack had a son. Knowing how deeply protective she was of her family, she might persuade Jack to seek custody of Noah, and Peyton didn't have the financial resources for a court battle. She was a good mom—a great mom—but sometimes being a good mom wasn't enough when you went up against a family who had the operating capital of a small country at their disposal.

Avangeline had also threatened to destroy anyone she loved and cared about, and that meant that Simon and Keene, the family of her heart, were at risk. Simon was employed as a detective by the Hatfield Police Department, which was funded by the town of Hatfield. Avangeline made regular and generous donations to the city and also to the campaigns and causes of the politicians who ran the town. One call, and Simon would be out of a job, and at Avangeline's behest, the city officials could make life so difficult for Keene—health and safety inspectors, tax audits, general red tape—that he'd find it difficult to operate Clancy's. They'd be run out of town.

To Avangeline, Peyton was a bug who could be easily squished. Money bought power and influence. Lots of money bought control.

"I'm not going to divulge the identity of Noah's father," Peyton stated.

"Well, you're going to have to," Keene said, his Irish accent becoming more pronounced. "Because the rumors are flying around town that he is Noah's father. He's going to hear them at some point, and he'll demand some answers."

Peyton's heart plummeted, hit her feet and bounced back up again. *"What rumors? What do you mean?"*

Simon shrugged. "That's what we heard this morning. Someone knows, and that somebody is talking."

"Not us," Keene said.

Of course not. Simon and Keene would no more sell her out than she'd hurt Noah.

She rubbed her jaw with a shaking hand. "Nobody knew—nobody!"

Keene placed a hand on the middle of her back. "Well, somebody does, and they're talking."

Simon's brown eyes narrowed. "But why now? Peyton's been back for two months already. Why are we suddenly hearing these rumors the day of Jack Grantham's return to Calcott Manor? The timing is suspicious."

"Definitely," Keene said in agreement.

Peyton couldn't think about that now. She was concentrating on hauling air into her lungs to keep breathing. The urge to grab Noah and run was strong, and she shot to her feet. Keene stood up and wrapped his arms around her, rocking her from side to side. "What's got you so scared, pet? What aren't you telling us?"

Peyton wrapped her arms around her waist and held on, feeling as if she were dancing on the edge of a hurricane. The cat was out of the bag, so maybe she could tell them about Avangeline and her threats.

But keeping her own counsel about her past was a habit so deeply ingrained that she couldn't get the words to form, couldn't put them into sentences. And right now, she should be concentrating on the fact that Jack would soon hear—probably via Jacinta, Calcott Manor's housekeeper and one of Hatfield's most popular residents—that he was the father of her child.

"I'll deny the rumor and tell everyone that Noah's dad is a surfer I met in LA," Peyton said, pulling back from Keene. She linked her hands behind her neck and tipped her head back to look at the ceiling. "If I deny it, then it will die quickly, and people will just think that someone is making up nasty stories."

Simon looked up at her and grimaced. "You could try to do that," he stated, not looking convinced.

"But you don't think it will work." Peyton tipped her chin up defiantly. "Why not?"

"There are a couple of problems with your plan, Peyton," Simon replied. "Apart from the fact that you are perpetuating the lie and denying Jack and Noah the chance to know each other, Jack can do the math. Noah's conception and birth dates are a perfect match to when you were together, and Jack will figure that out very quickly. Also,

Noah looks like a Grantham. He has Jack's coloring, the Grantham nose and the Grantham chin. Jack Grantham's eyes. You can say he's not his until the cows come home, but anyone with a brain in his head will think that he is— it's too obvious to miss."

Shit. Shit. Shitshitshitshit.

What the hell was she going to do?

Two

Jack swam behind the back line, the salt water burning his eyes. Although he wasn't Olympic medal–winning good like his cousin-turned-brother Soren, he was a strong swimmer, and it had always helped him relax. After a shouting match with his grandmother, he needed to burn off some excess energy.

While his brothers, especially Fox and, back in the day, Malcolm, frequently lost their tempers and raised their voices, he always remained calm, thinking that someone had to wipe up the blood at the end of a fight, and it might as well be him. And he found that icy anger was frequently a lot more effective than screaming and shouting. The people he employed, from Shanghai to Stockholm, knew that when his eyes turned an icy blue, it was time for them to run.

He never yelled, so raising his voice at his grandmother was an anomaly, and he wasn't proud of himself. She was nearly eighty-two years old, and she'd raised him and his brothers, so she deserved his respect. Sure, Avangeline had yelled back, but that didn't change the fact that he'd lost control, that he'd allowed his emotions to rule. And damn it, despite their heated back-and-forth, he hadn't made any progress. He still didn't know anything more about Avangeline's blackmail situation than he did yesterday.

Control was important to him, and he hadn't lost it since he was a kid...no, that was a lie. He hadn't done that since he led Peyton away from the country club and took her to bed. He'd been consumed by the need to have her, to taste her pink mouth, to spread her pale red-gold hair across his pillow and to watch her gorgeous purple-blue eyes darken as he slid into her. It had been, despite numerous sexual encounters before and since, the best night of his life.

And it had been with his brother's fiancée, the woman whom Malcolm had professed to love more than life itself.

Out of breath, Jack stopped swimming and lay flat on his back, looking up at the blue sky.

Jack, Soren and Merrick had mocked Mal relentlessly about Peyton, but he never had. Partly because something about Mal's obsession with Peyton hadn't rung true and partly because, if he had been so in love with her, he wondered how Malcolm had had the guts to love someone so much after all the loss they'd experienced. With his bold and brash attitude, their tragic past had never seemed to affect him. He'd barreled into situations, laughed hard and long, loved with passion and enthusiasm, and gulped at life, taking huge swallows of it.

Maybe he'd suspected or somehow sensed that he only had a limited time on Earth and knew he had to pack as much living in as quickly as possible.

In contrast, Soren chose to retreat from people, spending as much time as possible in the pool to avoid relationships.

Fox avoided commitment, and he, well, chased perfection, unable to embrace failures or foibles.

Jack dropped his legs, trod water and looked toward the beach, his eyes caught by a slim figure standing on the path that led to Calcott Manor. Long reddish hair glinting with fine gold strands blew in the wind, and Jack's heart thu-thumped in his chest. Peyton was here, and she was look-ing in his direction.

Was she watching him? Waiting for him?

Why?

He started to swim to the rolling breakers, wondering what had brought his one-night stand—his brother's ex-fi-ancée—to his door. Or, more accurately, his beach. She'd made it very clear two years ago that sleeping together was a once-and-done deal, that she wasn't interested in taking it further. If he called, she would ignore it, and if he wrote, she'd delete his emails, unread. One night, take it or leave it.

He wasn't stupid, so he took it.

As he moved into the shallows, he wondered why he hadn't been able to resist her, to walk away from her. There was a bro code, and had Malcolm lived, he would've ripped his head off for sleeping with Peyton. It just wasn't...cool. Not cool at all. And it was still something he felt guilty about. Silly, since Malcolm was long dead, and nobody cared about or even remembered the so-called Caron-Grantham feud.

He and Peyton, as clichéd as it sounded, had talked with their bodies, not with their mouths. And their bodies had had a lot to say.

Jack put his feet down, his toes digging into the sand, and walked onto the beach, water streaming from his hair and body. He pushed the excess water from his hair, keeping his eyes on Peyton, who sat on the wrought iron bench at the start of the path leading back to Calcott Manor.

She wore a pretty dress that reminded him of mint juleps, that dipped low to show a hint of her modest cleavage, that was tight in the waist and flared out to end above her knees, showing off tanned and toned calves. A punch of want hit him, and need entered his bloodstream, potent and addictive. He'd envied Mal but loyalty to his brother instantly made him shut down any I-think-she's-hot thoughts. But two years ago, desire ambushed him, and the lust he'd suppressed—the same lust coursing him through him now—almost dropped him to his knees. And, yeah, his legs were feeling damn unsteady.

"Peyton." It was only one word but all he could manage. She was the last person he'd expected to run into after his swim. He'd genuinely believed that he'd never see or speak to her again. And what was she doing back in Hatfield, as he'd last heard she was living on the West Coast. LA, maybe?

And why was it that all he wanted to do was lower his mouth to hers, feel her tongue wind around his? He wanted to place his hands on her slender hips and jerk her to his wet body, to feel her breasts pushing into his chest, her hands on his bare skin.

"Hello, Jack. There's something I need to tell you." Her voice was the same as he remembered, a slightly raspy lilt suggesting French roots, not a surprise since she'd been raised by her French Canadian father, who'd been born and raised in Montreal. Harry Caron had come to the US as a young man, but he'd never lost his accent. Peyton was raised by him, so it made sense that his accent would affect hers. But what did she have to tell him that couldn't wait?

He sat down on the bench, keeping a healthy amount of

distance between them, and dripped water onto the dune grass beneath the bench. "So, do you want to tell me your important news here or do you want to go up to the house?"

She winced and shook her head. "Here is fine."

Yeah, he thought that would be the case.

"How do you know what I have to say is important?" she asked him, her lovely mouth just a little pursed.

"I recall you telling me that I'd never hear from you again," Jack said, leaning back and lifting his face to the sun. He knew he looked relaxed, but inside he was as jumpy as a meth addict. He wanted to shake an immediate explanation out of her, demand to know why, after two years, she'd broken her own rules.

He heard her heavy sigh, opened his eyes and turned his head to look down at her. Fear skittered across her face, and he fought the urge to sling an arm around her shoulder and ask what he could do to help.

Fox's scathing words bounced around his brain. *You're such a goddamn white knight, Jack. You do not need to heal every broken-winged female you pluck from the sky, dude. It's not your job to fix the world, to make it perfect.*

"Rumors are flying around town. I don't know if you've heard them…" Peyton said, trailing off.

He didn't give a rat's ass what people said about him, and he couldn't think of anything anyone could say that would cause him a moment of lost sleep. He didn't pay attention to what people said or thought; he walked his path and marched to the beat of his own drum. It was a Grantham trait; they were an independent group of guys. Avangeline had raised them that way.

"I couldn't give a shit what anyone has to say," he told Peyton, his voice diamond hard.

"You will about this."

He very much doubted it, but since she'd made the effort to make the drive to Calcott Manor, to ring the doorbell and to walk down to the beach, he'd let her say her piece. "Okay then, surprise me."

"I have an eighteen-month-old son, and the town gossips are saying it's yours."

He was about to laugh, but then he caught the fear in her eyes. He did a couple of mental calculations, quickly establishing that if she got pregnant the night they were together, then the kid could be his. But they'd used protection—he always used protection—so...*no*. Not possible.

"What are you trying to tell me, Peyton?"

"That there are rumors you fathered my son." Peyton dropped her face into her hands, and he had to strain to hear the next words out of her mouth. "And the rumors are true. Noah is your son."

When Jack didn't say anything, Peyton slowly raised her head and forced herself to look at him. His face was slack with shock, his bold blue eyes a little unfocused. Behind the blue, she saw his mind working a mile a minute, trying to process her words and what they meant. Any second now, he'd start yelling, either denying her accusation or demanding to know why she didn't tell him.

Or both.

Jack did neither. He just sat up and leaned forward to rest his forearms on his thighs, staring at the ground. A muscle jumped in his rigid jaw, and she suspected he was grinding his teeth. Looking at his profile, she could see why people wouldn't believe her denials about Noah being his son. When he lost his baby fat, her son would be the spitting image of his father.

While he pondered his new reality, she took in Jack's

details—how could she not? As always, he looked fit and strong, and he didn't carry any excess weight. His shoulders were wide and muscled, and his arms were bigger than she remembered. His chest was covered in a fine layer of blond hair, darker because it was wet, arrowing down into a thin line bisecting his spectacularly defined eight-pack. He had long muscled legs and great feet, big but still elegant. His hair was blonder, as if he'd recently spent some time in the sun. His beard was shorter, and the lines at the corners of those thickly lashed eyes were deeper.

Hotter. Sexier. Grumpier. She wanted to jump him right then and there, and she cursed her libido. What the hell was wrong with her?

Jack Grantham still had it all, damn it. She'd watched him walk up the path and fought the urge to fly down and launch herself at him, plastering her mouth on his, boosting herself up his strong body and winding her arms around his neck. She'd wanted him just as much as she did before.

What madness was this? Why couldn't she get him out of her mind?

Jack sat up, then stood up, and placed his hands on his narrow hips. Every muscle in his body seemed tense, and she couldn't help that her eyes dropped to his ridged stomach. Gorgeous. *You are having a conversation about his son, Caron. Do try to concentrate.*

Maybe she should have opted to have this discussion with his clothes on, but then she would've run the risk of seeing Avangeline. Confronting Jack was one thing; she didn't think she could handle a dustup with Avangeline as well.

"Firstly, how did this happen? We used condoms. They are effective."

She wondered the same thing. "I can't tell you, Jack. Maybe one had a micro tear or a hole." She lifted her chin, looking defiant. "Are you going to insult me by demanding a paternity test?"

"Why didn't you tell me?" he asked, ignoring her question and lobbing another conversational bullet instead.

How much to tell him? All of it? Some of it? Nothing at all? "That's a long and complicated story," she answered truthfully. When he refused to drop his eyes, she knew that he'd wait as long as he needed to for her to answer his question. "I was scared," she admitted.

"Of what?"

Of what your grandmother might do if she found out. No, she couldn't tell him that. "Of how you'd react, of what you'd do."

Jack's face turned granite hard. "What did you think I'd do?"

He was a megarich, famous, socially and politically connected businessman from a top-tier family. Maybe he didn't realize or consider how much power he wielded and forgot how money could change power balances.

"You could've sued for custody. You could've taken Noah away from me," she told him.

Jack looked horrified, then insulted. "You are his mother—I would never have done that to you! Do you not know me at all?"

No, she didn't. She'd spent one night with him, and they hadn't shared any pertinent information. She knew nothing more about him than what Malcolm had told her, and he hadn't spent a lot of time discussing his pesky younger brothers. "All I know is that your family hated mine and that you all—especially your grandmother—blame me for Mal's death."

"I've never blamed you for his death!" Jack roared, and she was surprised to hear the anger in his voice. But she knew that it wasn't directed at her. "I was sad and angry that he was dead—he was taken from us too young—but I blamed nobody except Malcolm for his death. He craved speed, and he pushed the envelope far too often, and we all knew it."

Well, his grandmother blamed her. It embarrassed her that Avangeline thought so little of her, that she'd judged her so easily and dismissed her so quickly. She'd never been in favor of their marrying, and her disinterest in Peyton turned to dislike after Mal's death.

"Did you ever stop to consider, just once, that I lost my parents when I was a kid and that I would never, not ever, put another child, whether he was my blood or not, in that position of not having his mother in his life?"

Peyton felt as if she were drowning in embarrassment. No, she hadn't thought that.

Lifting her head, she nodded and winced. "No, I didn't. Sorry. Anyway, I've told you about Noah. And now I need you to do something else for me…"

"I wasn't aware that I'd done anything yet, but, sure… what?"

"I need you to deny that we had an affair and deny that he's yours."

He'd just heard that he was a dad, that they'd made a tiny little person when they last met, and now she was asking him to pretend that something momentous hadn't occurred?

What fresh hell was this?

And why did he think that there was something he was missing, that he'd skipped an entire chapter in a very convoluted book? Why come here and tell him that he was a dad and then expect him to do nothing about it? What game was she playing?

He didn't think she was the type to jerk people around, and he was irritated at his disappointment. He'd been raised by a strong, forthright woman—two of them, actually—and he hated women who played mind games.

Was she telling him the truth? Could he believe her? Was she setting him up? Jack looked into her eyes and couldn't see any hint of deceit. Her eyes didn't skitter away from his, and she wasn't fidgeting or shuffling her feet. Her body language told him she was telling the truth.

"Yeah, well, that's not going to happen."

Peyton stood up and crossed her arms, hugging her slim body. Her hair blew in the wind, and beneath the stubbornness in her eyes, he caught a glimpse of fear and more than a little anxiety. He was definitely missing a few chapters.

But unlike Fox, who had all the finesse of a dozen elephants in a flower patch, he knew better than to thunder in and demand answers. That would put her back up and he wouldn't get the answers he needed. No, he needed to tread softly, to take some time.

"What's going on here, Peyton?" he asked softly. "What aren't you telling me?"

"Lots," she answered, shocking him with her honesty. She stared out to sea and kept her eyes on a container ship on the horizon. After a couple of minutes, she turned to look at him. "It really would be better if you just walked away, Jack."

Not going to happen. He didn't run away from his responsibilities, and he lived with the consequences of his choices.

"That won't happen, so deal with it." Sighing, he pushed his hand into his hair and raked it back. He had so many questions and they tumbled over each other on his tongue. There was so much he wanted to know—what she'd been doing since he saw her last, whether her hair still carried the smell of an orchard of lemons, how she supported herself and Noah—but first, he wanted to know about his son. "Tell me about Noah. How old is he, exactly?"

"Seventeen and a half months," she answered, and by the flash of love he saw in her eyes, he knew she adored him. "He's part angel, part thug, all boy and simply delicious."

He wanted to meet him. Now, immediately. Did he have his blond or Peyton's red hair, his blue eyes, or were they touched by violet? "Where did you have him? And why did you come back to Hatfield?"

"Noah was born in LA, and I came back to Hatfield because I'm between jobs. Simon Reed, he grew up in Hatfield, and is my oldest, best friend…" She gabbled on, and he watched as a hint of pink touched her cheeks. She took a breath and tried again. "Anyway, he and his husband, Keene, invited me to spend the summer in Hatfield, and they offered us the apartment above Clancy's pub for the duration of our stay. Simon and Keene are joint owners of the pub."

"The Irish one down by the harbor?"

"That's the one. I said yes, and we've been here since the beginning of June."

"And your new job, where is that? And what do you do?" He had apparently fathered a child with this woman, but he didn't know anything about her. That felt weird. And wrong.

"I have a postgrad degree in art history, and I specialize in twentieth-century American painters. I've been offered a curatorship at the Museum of Contemporary Art Chicago—it's my dream job."

Chicago. God. That was halfway across the country, and he hated its brutal winters. "When are you supposed to start?"

"At the end of the month—September first, to be exact."

Right. How the hell was he supposed to see his son when

she lived in Chicago and he in Manhattan? God, was he already thinking of establishing a relationship with his son and how to have visitation rights? He hadn't even met the kid yet! But, yep, he was. Knowing about Noah but not having him in his life, ignoring his flesh and blood, was inconceivable. But Peyton wanted him to walk away. Why?

"It's a lot to take in, right?" Peyton asked, looking, for the first time, slightly more approachable, more like the warm, sexy woman whose bed he'd shared two years ago.

So much. And he was used to dealing with a crisis; he knew how to handle them. But those were work problems, not something that would affect his personal life.

He had a son. Noah was the first Grantham born of the next generation. Avangeline was going to be beside herself with excitement. Then again, would she? Jack bit the inside of his cheek, his mind working at a frenetic speed.

Avangeline hadn't been shy about expressing her dislike of Peyton, and Peyton had been right when she'd said that Avangeline blamed her for Malcolm's death. Before today, he'd often wondered if his grandmother had had words with Peyton sometime between Malcolm's death and his funeral, because Peyton had sat on the opposite side to the Granthams in the church and in the second row, obviously trying to downplay her role in Malcolm's life. Her father, the man who'd tried to fleece Malcolm in a business deal that went wrong, hadn't attended the funeral, and Jack remembered that he'd never seen someone look as alone and fragile as Peyton had looked that day.

Did Avangeline have something to do with why Peyton wanted him to ignore Noah's existence? Did his grandmother, who had a sharp tongue and could be cold, do or say something to Peyton that made her want to keep her distance from him?

He wouldn't put it past her.

"What did Avangeline tell you?" he asked, keeping his tone casual.

"That she'll destroy everyone—" she slapped a hand to her mouth and winced "—Damn it!"

He loved his grandmother, he did, but when she thought that someone was attacking her family, she turned rabid very quickly indeed. "And when did she tell you this?"

Peyton met his eyes and shook her head. "I should never have told you that much!"

"Well, you did," Jack said, shooting back. "When did she say that to you?"

Peyton sighed. "Shortly after the funeral. She made it clear that she blamed me for Mal's death and that if I ever came within shouting distance of any of you, she'd rip my head off. Or she'd ruin me. And ruin anyone I cared about."

He pulled a face, easily imagining Avangeline in the throes of a tantrum. Like him, she didn't lose her temper often, but when she did, demons took cover. "She was devastated when Malcolm died. He was the best of us and her heir apparent. She was looking for someone to blame, and she found you. I very much doubt she would've carried out any of her threats."

Avangeline had a very impressive bark, but her bite wasn't as ferocious as people thought.

"I was nineteen years old, Jack, and she was my ex-fiancé's powerful, rich grandmother. Of course I believed her, and I *still* believe her! If she knew you and I slept together, if she knew I gave birth to Noah, she'd have my new job whipped away—and she'd make sure that I never worked in the art world again."

No, she was wrong. Yes, Avangeline probably said all that and more, but her family was her biggest priority. She hadn't liked Peyton back then, and he suspected she hadn't approved of her and Mal's relationship, but that was ten years in the past. Hopefully, they'd all moved on. On hearing she had a great-grandson, Jack had no doubt that Avangeline would pull Peyton into the family fold and that she'd dote on Noah, and he explained this to Peyton.

She didn't look convinced. "You weren't there—you didn't see the anger on her face."

No, but he did remember how Avangeline was when Malcolm died, exhibiting rage instead of grief, yelling and throwing things instead of crying. His grandmother preferred action to tears, anger to grief. He was the same. After his parents died, unable to cry, he'd broken every window in the glass greenhouse out of sheer rage. "Trust me on this, Peyton."

Peyton shook her head. "I don't trust anybody on anything, Jack. And especially not a Grantham."

Right. Hmm. He might think that the Caron-Grantham feud was dead, but Peyton didn't. That was going to be tricky since he wanted to meet his son.

And see her again.

Peyton still fascinated him, damn it, more than any other woman he'd ever met. She looked fragile and wispy, but underneath her ethereal looks was a woman with a steel-rod spine. She hadn't had an easy life growing up—being Harry Caron's daughter had distinct disadvantages—and losing Malcolm had to have put some scorch marks on her soul. She'd had her baby alone across the country and was raising him by herself...

That took guts. And determination.

"I want to meet Noah. I want to get to know my son," he told Peyton, his hard tone telling her that he wasn't playing games.

"Yeah," Peyton said, dragging the tips of her fingers across her forehead. The blue smudges under her eyes betrayed her exhaustion. "Have you thought about how weird this is, Jack?"

"Finding out that you are a father isn't for the faint-hearted," he agreed.

She sighed audibly. "Not that!"

"If not that, then what?" he snapped back.

"I'm talking about the timing of the rumor."

Then why didn't she say so? "I don't understand what you are getting at, Peyton."

She seemed annoyed that he wasn't following her train of thought. But he'd just heard that he was a father; he was allowed to be a little off his game. "I've been in Hatfield for two months, but you've been home…what, two days? You've barely had time to settle in, and then the rumors start? Why now?"

Right. He was all caught up, and, damn, that was a very good question. Jack stared at her, then transferred his gaze to the horizon, noticing that the container ship had disappeared from view.

Hmm…

He was the third Grantham grandson to arrive at Calcott Manor to be with his grandmother over the summer, and someone who had more than a passing interest in their lives, such as a *blackmailer*, might wonder what had brought three of Avangeline's grandsons home in quick succession. Finding out their grandmother was being extorted would—and did—make them return to Hatfield, and the blackmailer had to be cursing their knowledge and involvement.

It made sense to assume that whoever was extorting Avangeline had done a deep dive into all of their lives, looking for dirt, an edge, an angle. Someone, *somehow*, knew that he and Peyton had slept together and, after doing the math, assumed that Noah was his son.

Someone smart would believe he was here to help Avangeline, and a great way to distract him would be to drop a kid into his life. It could be assumed that he'd turn all his focus onto his son, a very normal reaction, hopefully neglecting his duties to his grandmother, thus allowing the blackmailer to carry on with his nefarious scheme.

Clever, Jack conceded. Very clever indeed.

But Noah notwithstanding, these machinations just made Jack more determined to unmask whoever was messing with his family. And when he did, God help them.

He looked back at Peyton, thinking that she was the woman who was going to be in his life for the rest of it. Strangely, despite her keeping his son from him, he was okay with that. "I'll agree to keep this quiet for a few days. I need to think it through, take it in. But I won't keep it a secret forever."

That bright head, the color of old rose gold, bobbed in agreement.

She turned away, and he reached out to hold her upper arm, making sure to keep his touch light. He was a strong guy, and she had pale skin that would bruise easily. When she focused her attention back on him, he frowned at her. "I'm not happy about you not telling me, Peyton. That was way out of line."

Her lips firmed and her cheeks bloomed with embarrassment. "I know, but I thought I was doing the right thing."

He thought about saying more, but her blush deepened, and he knew that humiliation, hot and uncomfortable, was coursing through her. He'd made his point—he didn't need to belabor it. "I'll be by in a day, maybe two."

"There's a door around the back of the restaurant, and there's a hidden intercom under the letter box."

"When will you be in?"

She shrugged, looking wry. "If I'm not helping out behind the bar, then I'm upstairs with Noah. Eighteen-month-old babies don't lend themselves to having a hectic social life."

He usually worked until after eight most nights, and five out of seven, he joined friends for dinner or went out with his brothers to a bar or club. He rarely spent any time at home, and if he did, he worked. Her lifestyle was alien to him. But, he thought, if he wanted to make space for Noah in his life, and he fully intended to, then some things would have to change.

And quickly.

As he walked Peyton back to her car, he thought that for someone who didn't like change, he was finding it remarkably easy to wrap his head around his new circumstances. Strange.

Three

Peyton sat at the table on the minuscule balcony of her apartment, which overlooked the busy street below and the tiny harbor across the road. Below her, revelers enjoyed the warm night, and laughter and shouts drifted on the brine-tinged air.

In contrast to the bonhomie below, Peyton felt as if she'd gone ten rounds with a sumo wrestler. And lost.

She placed her feet on the railing and tapped her finger against her empty wineglass. Jack knew about Noah; the proverbial cat was out of the bag. There was no going back now. He'd been pissed that she didn't tell him about Noah before, probably still was, but she'd genuinely been con-cerned—okay, scared—about how Avangeline would react.

But because she tried to be honest as she could with her-self, she'd wanted to keep Noah's paternity quiet. After a lifetime of kowtowing to her father, then being yanked along by Malcolm's forceful move-at-the-speed-of-light person-ality, Noah was all hers. She called the shots and made the decisions; she didn't need to consult anybody about anything. And unlike all the other men she'd loved, she knew that Noah needed her, loved her. She knew that he wouldn't abruptly yank his love away and leave her feeling desolate.

That was a hell of a lot to put on the shoulders of her baby boy.

Simon and Keene were right; she should've told Jack earlier, and it was wrong to keep Noah from him. But, she argued with herself, the circumstances were different for them than they were for the run-of-the-mill noncouple who found themselves unexpectedly pregnant.

Her father, Harry Caron, operated on the fringes of Hatfield society. Thanks to ripping off a couple of the better-known businesspeople in town, he had a reputation for being shady and less than honest. Deeply unreliable, he was tolerated but not accepted.

In comparison, the Granthams were an East Coast dynasty of national fame. Avangeline was not only minor royalty in the truest sense of the words—she held the title of Lady Forrester—but she'd also been on tea-taking terms with the late Queen Elizabeth. Jesse and Jason Grantham, Avangeline's twin sons, had been the country's most eligible bachelors back in the eighties: fabulously rich, smart and stunningly good-looking. They'd joined their mother's wildly successful empire, helping her establish fine-dining restaurants and exclusive hotels all over the globe. They'd married blue-blooded, moneyed American heiresses, and the brothers and their respective wives had been the most envied couples in America.

Of course, after they died in an airplane crash, they were touted as being tragically unlucky. Peyton's sympathies rested with their sons because she knew what it was like to lose one parent—devastatingly horrible—but to lose two was pain she couldn't comprehend.

She'd always been fascinated by the family, and through a waitressing job at Hatfield's exclusive country club, she'd met Malcolm. Bold, brash, exciting, tempestuous, he'd swept her eighteen-year-old self off her feet. By nineteen, she was engaged and had planned on marrying before her twenty-first birthday.

With Malcolm's arrival in her life, her relationship with her dad improved exponentially, and she suddenly had the connection with him she'd always craved. After being ignored and emotionally neglected for most of her life, she and Harry had daddy-daughter dinners, enjoyed family meals and went on outings together. Harry had started hugging her, sending her cute text messages, and once, surprisingly, he'd even told her he loved her. Peyton had blossomed, completely convinced that this was the dawning of a new age and that her life, from that point onward, would only be champagne and roses.

It was amazing how stupid one could be at nineteen.

Not once had it occurred to her that the only reason Harry was paying her attention was that, without her, his access to Malcolm and his rich friends would be ripped away.

Then, just a few months before their wedding, her world imploded. Malcolm and Harry had a falling out, and Malcolm demanded that she choose between him and her father. She couldn't have both, he told her. She'd lost her mom at the age of five and couldn't lose her dad too. She finally had the dad she wanted and needed, and she hadn't prepared to let him go. So she'd chosen Harry, completely convinced that after the dust settled, after Malcolm and her dad stopped snorting and stomping and locking horns, they'd reconcile, and she'd have her fairy-tale wedding.

Six weeks later, Mal was dead—and Avangeline, blaming his accident on Peyton, issued her stay-away-from-me-and-mine warning. Jack's grandmother also told anyone who would listen that Harry had stolen money from Malcolm and that Mal was heartbroken from their split and had become more reckless. His brothers hadn't publicly agreed with her, but the fact that they never visited Peyton after his death and barely talked to her at the funeral had spoken volumes.

The Granthams had mourned Malcolm together and had each other to lean on when the grief and pain became overwhelming. She'd had no one, because, the day after Malcolm's death, Harry returned to being the cold, distant, unaffectionate father she'd always known.

Mired in grief and confusion, it took her a year, maybe a little more, to realize that, to her father, she was a tool, someone to be used and wielded, then put away and forgotten about. She rode out the next six months, and when she turned twenty-one, she took the small trust fund left to her by her grandmother and used it to pay for college. She'd called Harry at Christmas and on his birthday.

He'd never bothered to call her.

Eight years after Malcolm's death, she returned to Hatfield for the first time to be the maid of honor at Simon and Keene's wedding.

Everybody who was anybody in Hatfield had been at the Hatfield Country Club that night, if not for the wedding, then to dine at the club's fine-dining restaurant or socialize at the bar. Her father had been there, as had been the entire Grantham clan, out for a meal. When she unexpectedly met them in the lobby on her way to the bathroom, Avangeline had sent her a death stare and turned her back on her, lifting her aristocratic nose in the air. Fox had ignored her and escorted his grandmother out, and Merrick and his mom, Jacinta, had given her a polite but pained smile.

But she'd found Jack in the lobby when she returned from the bathroom—Jack who'd bluntly told her that life was too short to feud, who'd invited her to come on a drive with him to clear the air. Simon and Keane had left and, knowing she wouldn't be missed, she'd followed him out into the night. Stunned and surprised and swept away by his confidence and charm, she'd slid into his arms and stayed there the rest of the night.

And into the early hours of the morning.

Now Jack knew about Noah and they had new challenges to face. Who was trying to cause trouble by leaking the rumor of Noah's paternity, and why? And what would happen when that rumor reached the ears of an intrepid local reporter?

When the story broke, she would be judged for sleeping with both brothers—eight years apart, but would they care about that? —and her nonrelationship with Jack would be analyzed and dissected. They'd dig into her life and discover that she was estranged from her dad and would wonder why. But on the plus side, she had the social life of an agoraphobic nun, so there wouldn't be any ex-boyfriends putting their oar in. She couldn't say the same for Jack's exes…the man had quite the social life, or so she'd read.

Hearing the buzz of her intercom, Peyton walked over to the front door and looked at the black-and-white screen above the phone. Jack stood at the bottom of the outside steps dressed in a pair of shorts, a loose button-down shirt and flip-flops.

Although she'd been expecting him, her stomach still did a long, low swoop, and her breath caught in her throat. He was taller, older, tougher and far sexier than she remembered. He also seemed quieter and possessed a great deal more control than Malcolm.

Malcolm had been impetuous and tempestuous, a volcano in the throes of an explosion—loud and impressive and breathtaking. Jack, somehow, was equally impressive but in a completely different way. He was a wide, powerful river, seemingly calm, but she knew that there were dangerous currents below the surface. Mysterious, intriguing and unexplored.

So very sexy.

Her intercom buzzed again, and Peyton pushed the button to let him in.

After unlocking her door, she walked over to the dining table and, using one arm, scooped the laundry into the basket and kicked a pair of her sneakers under the table. Her place was messy, but she defied anyone to keep on top of housework when they had an active, energetic toddler to keep entertained.

Jack knocked. She called for him to come in, and he stepped inside. Their eyes collided, and Peyton was swept into a storm of fierce blue. His eyes were incredible, the deep blue of old-fashioned ink. They lightened when he was angry and warmed when he felt affection. They were a bit flat tonight, and she knew that he was trying to hide his nerves.

He was about to see his son for the first time, so he was allowed to feel a little anxious.

"Hey," he said, sliding his hands into the pockets of his khaki shorts.

"Hey," she replied.

He glanced at his expensive watch and grimaced. "I hope it isn't too late for a visit?"

"For me, no. For Noah, I'm afraid so," she told him, smiling at his whispered words. "He's asleep, but you don't need to whisper—he'd sleep through a bomb blast."

"I can too," Jack told her. He glanced toward the hallway, then looked back at her. "May I?"

She followed him down the hall, admiring his shapely butt and long, long legs. At the door to the small second bedroom, he hesitated, then took a deep breath, and Peyton realized how consequential this meeting was.

For the first time, he was going to look at the baby they'd made together. For him, this was the equivalent of Noah's birth. She bit her lip, ashamed that she'd kept Noah from him, and wished she had been braver.

Hauling in another deep breath, Jack walked into the room and stood next to Noah's bed. Noah had rolled onto his back, and one hand was tucked behind his head. His cheeks were round, his mouth pursed and he looked like an angel, completely and staggeringly wonderful.

Her beautiful boy...*their* beautiful boy. Peyton felt the lump in her throat and looked up at Jack, who ran a gentle finger over Noah's blond hair, down his round cheek.

"He's beautiful, Peyton," Jack said, and she heard the thrum of emotion in his voice, the rasp to his tone that suggested he was fighting back...well, not tears but something close. "He looks like me."

He did. They had the same blond hair, and Noah had Jack's brilliant blue eyes, the Grantham nose and his stubborn chin. Malcolm once told her that the Grantham boys had too much energy and not enough sense, and she suspected that Noah would follow in their footsteps. He wanted to taste and try everything, preferably all at once.

It would be a miracle if she didn't turn gray by the time she was thirty-five.

Noah stirred in his sleep, and Peyton placed a hand on

Jack's warm arm. The touch sent a spark skittering up her arm and through her body, finally landing between her legs. Perfect. She was dealing with a lot right now, and she didn't need to add out-of-control attraction and horniness to the list.

"Do you want some coffee?" she offered, dropping her hand.

"Yeah, thanks." Jack gestured to Noah. "Do you mind if I watch him for a minute or two?"

"Take your time. I'll be in the kitchen."

Ten minutes later, Jack walked into the kitchen section of her open-plan apartment and pulled a barstool away from the counter, which served as a breakfast bar. He sat down, and Peyton pushed a cup of coffee across the counter. "I have whiskey, if you prefer."

"No, I'm good." Jack stared down into his cup, and Peyton noticed the blue stripes under his eyes and the way his skin was tightly pulled across his cheekbones. He'd had a stressful day and looked wiped out.

"I am sorry I didn't tell you about Noah, but…"

"But Avangeline scared the shit out of you," Jack said, continuing her sentence. His eyes met hers, and a wry smile touched his mouth. "She can be damn intimidating."

That was an insufficient way to describe Avangeline in a rage. "Terrifying" would be better.

"I spoke to her about what she said to you," Jack said, running a finger around the rim of his cup.

"You did?" Peyton demanded, surprised. "Why?"

"Because I always, always get both sides of a story," he replied. "You tend to get closer to the truth that way."

Peyton swallowed, nervous. "And what did she say?"

Jack's eyes were steady on hers. "It was as I thought. She was consumed by grief and looking for someone to blame, an action to take, and she lashed out. She got it into her head that Malcolm was heartbroken, and that was why he was flying down the highway, why he lost concentration and control and crashed his Ducati."

"He always drove fast," Peyton said, a little irked that she was being blamed when Malcolm had always been intensely reckless.

"I told her that and reminded her that, before you, she'd had many conversations about him driving too fast and taking unnecessary risks. And even if he was heartbroken, it was his choice to get on that bike, to speed. It wasn't fair to blame you, not then and not now."

Peyton felt a weight she hadn't known was there lifting from her shoulders. She closed her eyes. "Thank you for that."

"I told Avangeline that you were a convenient target for her anger and that she was very out of line for what she said to you and how she treated you."

Wow. Jack had gone to bat for her. She was grateful and surprised, especially since she'd kept his son from him. She barely knew him, and she wondered if he was ever anything but calm and even-tempered or whether, like Malcolm, he could lose his temper. She sensed that under that steady surface, there was a lot of turbulence and unexpressed emotion.

"She agreed."

Uh…*what*? Peyton gripped the back of the chair on the opposite side of the island and stared at him, not sure if she'd heard him properly. She hadn't thought that Avangeline Forrester-Grantham had it in her to backtrack or admit she was wrong.

Jack smiled at her astonishment. "Yes, I know. When she said that, I looked to see if pigs were flying past." He shrugged. "She sounded genuinely remorseful and said that she was out of line when she spoke to you. She never believed that you'd take her words so seriously."

"I was nineteen. How else would I take them?" Peyton asked.

His eyes remained steady on her face. "That's what I told Avangeline. Anyway, she's genuinely remorseful, and she'd like to apologize to you in person. She's wanted to for a long time."

Peyton felt a spurt of irritation. "I'm sure she could've tracked down my email address or cell number over the years."

Jack didn't respond to her cutting comment. "She's invited you to tea with her tomorrow. Will you meet with her?"

Peyton pulled the band from her hair and shook out her strands so they fell to her shoulders. As she raked her hair back again and secured it in a fresh ponytail, she considered his question. Did she want to rake up the past, or should she just let sleeping dogs lie?

She couldn't do that, not now that Jack knew about Noah. At some point, she'd have to interact with Noah's great-grandmother, and those interactions would be easier if they cleared the air. She didn't think Avangeline would ever be her favorite person, but being civil to each other would be a good first step.

Also, knowing that Avangeline wouldn't tank her career for some past transgression was such a relief. She wasn't nineteen anymore; she was a proper adult with a son to raise. She could handle Avangeline...

Maybe.

"Have you told her about Noah?" Peyton asked him, resting her forearms on the counter, her hand just a couple of inches from his.

"No. I thought we'd try and mend your relationship with her before we spring a great-grandson on her." They were thinking along the same lines. "And I'd like to meet my son properly before anyone else does."

Fair enough.

Peyton resisted the urge to stroke the frown lines off his forehead with her thumb, to skim her fingers over his thick eyebrows. He had a headache; she could see it in his eyes, in the tension in his neck and shoulders. He was living with some high-grade stress and was trying not to show it.

"Malcolm once told me that your brothers called you 'White Knight,' that you are the family troubleshooter, the one everyone runs to when there's a problem to solve. Is that still true?"

He thought for a moment. "Yes. Soren has been focused on his Olympic swimming career, and Fox is too abrupt and impatient, so he normally makes the situation worse. Merrick tends to be too overprotective, so I usually step up and sort things out. I don't overreact."

"I can believe that. I was expecting you to scream and shout at me for not telling you about Noah, but you were incredibly calm. I appreciate that."

Something flashed in his eyes, and she hesitated, cocking her head. "You're still mad at me, aren't you? You just don't show it."

He didn't respond immediately, taking his time to find the right words. "I am angry that I missed out on knowing Noah from the beginning, and that you had to cope—financially and emotionally—with a baby on your own. I'm angry I missed his birth and his first birthday, seeing him crawl and walk and say his first word—what was it, by the way?"

She knew he expected to hear her say "Mama"—wasn't that what all babies said first? "Cookie."

"Cookie?" Jack raised his eyebrows, obviously amused.

"It wasn't the great bonding experience I imagined," she said admittedly. And because she didn't want Jack to think that she regularly fed him sugary snacks, she told him that cookies were a rare treat. "I have no idea where he learned the word."

Jack's smile faded and he looked down into his cup. When he met her eyes again, all humor was gone. "Anyway...yeah, I'm pissed, but how is me losing my shit, screaming and shouting, going to help the situation? It's not going to change anything. I'm not going to be able to rewrite the past."

Jack was a philosopher and a thinker, someone who tried applying his big brain to a problem instead of letting emotion swamp him. Having lived with Harry, who used emotions—love, anger and jealousy—as weapons, she appreciated his thoughtful approach to their situation.

And, honestly, Jack knowing about Noah was such a relief that it was a weight off her shoulders. And after she met with Avangeline, the low-grade but constant fear she lived with would be gone. It was so much better to stand in the light of truth than to hide in the shadows.

"And there's something else I can't ignore. You are still so incredibly beautiful..."

Despite his conversational tone, Peyton's head whipped up, and she suddenly felt tense, but in the best way possible. The room felt electrified, and blue fire burned in Jack's eyes. He looked from her eyes to her mouth and back up again, and she knew, without him saying a word, that he wanted her, that the attraction that burned so hot two years ago was now an out-of-control wildfire.

"I saw you standing on the dunes, and I thought, yeah, *there* she is."

She knew she should stay where she was, to keep the

island a barrier between them, but her feet carried her to him. Her brain asked her what she was doing, but she still stepped between his legs, and his knees pressed her thighs, locking her in. His big hand curled around her hip as she lifted her mouth to meet his.

What was she doing? Why was she opening this door? She was the sexual equivalent of the dumb girl in horror movies who went down into the basement where a serial killer lurked with an ax. But Peyton couldn't resist finding out whether his taste had changed, whether his muscles were as hard as they looked, whether he still smelled of a walk in a forest or whether she still felt herself, but better, when she was in his arms.

It was just sex. She was a normal woman in her late twenties, and she had urges. Peyton ignored the thought that she'd only experienced these urges with Jack.

Jack stood up, and his hands cradled her face as his lips rediscovered hers, strong and sure and oh-so-confident. He tipped her head slightly, and his tongue flirted with the seam of her lips, begging for admittance. Peyton opened her mouth and sighed when his tongue met hers in a long, hot slide. She wrapped her arms around his back and couldn't help sliding her hand up and under his shirt to run her fingers over his broad back, down the deep valley of his spine. She pushed her fingers under the small gap between the band of his shorts and his skin, wanting to stroke his buttocks.

Jack was also on a journey of need and exploration. He kept one hand on her head, melding her mouth to his, feeding her dizzy-making kisses. His other hand stroked her neck, her collarbone, and his fingers tap-danced down her ribs before his thumb connected with her already-hard nipple. He stroked her through the fabric before pulling her shirt and bra aside to have skin-on-skin contact. She groaned and pushed her stomach into his steel-rod erection, phrases such as *Take me now* and *Yes, please* tumbling through her head and landing on her tongue. But she managed—how?—to keep them behind her teeth.

She wanted him, wanted to experience the rush of pleasure, the hot orgasms she'd only experienced with him. He made her burn, fly, shatter, scream. She wanted that again, she wanted it all. It had been so long since she'd last been touched, since she'd felt like a woman and not a stressed-out single mom. It had been two years or so, and his hands had been the last to touch her. He'd been the last and only person to rock her sexual world.

She wrenched her mouth off his and reached for her shirt, needing it off, wanting to feel her skin against his. She dropped her shirt to the floor and realized he wasn't making any moves to pull off his shirt or to drop his pants. He just stood there, as still as a statue, breathing heavily.

Jack linked his fingers behind his head and tipped his face to the ceiling. "Put your shirt back on, Peyton," he told her, his voice raspy but his tone oh-so-determined. "We're not doing this."

Needing to catch her breath, Peyton bent her knees and grabbed her shirt, putting it over her head and yanking it down her chest. Her face and body flamed with a combination of frustration and humiliation, while need and want still pulsed between her legs, making her womb ache.

She wouldn't be getting lucky tonight. Her brain said that was a good thing, but her body howled its disagreement.

Jack had slammed on the breaks so hard that there were tire marks on her psyche, scorch marks on her libido. She forced herself to think: she wanted him, and he, judging by his still-tented shorts, wanted her. There was a bed just down the hallway, and they were alone. Why had he stopped? Why weren't they kissing and touching and—

God. The thought slapped her with all the force of a bullet train. He was in a relationship. Disappointment, cold and brutal, washed over her, and she closed her eyes, trying to get air into her lungs. He was a good-looking guy in his midthirties; of course he'd have a lover, a significant other. He hadn't been hanging around waiting for her...

Peyton whirled away from him and walked to the picture window across the room, looking for some air to cool her burning face. Why was she so upset? Even if she wanted a partner—and she didn't, because she'd lost her trust and faith in men and what they said—she couldn't expect Jack to wander back into her life and fill that role.

She was being an idiot, and she was embarrassed and humiliated. But she'd started this and she needed to apologize. "Sorry. That got a little out of hand. I shouldn't have pushed so hard, and I should've read the room better."

"Peyton..."

She flinched at his voice, so calm.

"Will you please look at me?" Jack asked.

Peyton sucked in a long breath, prayed that her face wasn't still fire-engine red and slowly turned around, keeping her hands locked behind her. "Yes?"

"Why do you think I stopped?"

She shrugged, wishing he would just go so they could pretend this didn't happen. "Probably because you have a partner waiting for you somewhere."

The inscrutable look in his eyes was replaced by surprise. "No partner."

The relief she felt was indescribable, intense. And that was bizarre, because she had no claim on this man. He was just someone she spent one night with two years ago, a man who'd given her the gift of Noah. Yes, he was going to be part of Noah's life, a part of her life, but their connection stopped and ended with their son.

"Stop thinking, Peyton," Jack commanded. "You're jumping to conclusions, and all of them are wrong."

She cocked her head, silently asking him for an explanation.

"I stopped because I've had a very long, very stressful day. It started with an argument with Avangeline—about something else—then I met you again, found out about Noah and ended the day with another intense conversation with my grandmother. It would be easy to push away my crappy day with mind-blowing sex, but I think doing that would complicate a situation that is already way too complicated."

He was right—of course he was—and he was being super sensible, thoughtful even. Her brain got it. Her body most definitely did not.

Jack walked over to her, put his hands on her shoulders and gently, so gently, kissed her temple. Keeping his head resting on hers, he spoke again. "We've got to keep our heads, Peyton. This road we're suddenly on is tricky. One wrong move and it will crumble."

Aarrgh! He was being so...so *adult* about everything. Maybe it was time to show him that she could be mature too. She stepped away to put some distance between them and went to stand in the open doorway leading to the balcony, hoping the night air would cool her flaming-with-embarrassment-and-frustration face. To her relief, a cool breeze blew off the sea, a natural fan. After a moment or two, she spoke again. "You need to meet Noah when he's awake. When do you want to do that?"

He rubbed his jaw. "I think that depends on you."

Peyton forced herself to think. They might as well get

this first, awkward meeting over with as soon as possible. "Noah is an early riser, and after his breakfast, I normally take him for a walk on the beach so that he can run around and get rid of some of his excess energy."

God knew what she was going to do in Chicago, especially in winter, with an overexcited toddler in what she knew would be a small apartment. She was going to miss the beach and the sea, being able to let Noah run as free and fast as his little legs could move.

"Can you meet us tomorrow morning on the main beach at seven forty-five?" she asked.

Jack nodded. "Sure." He jammed his hands into the pockets of his shorts and glanced at the door. He raked his hands through his hair and rolled his shoulders. He glanced down, clocked her beaded nipples and swallowed. Desire flickered in his eyes and across his face, and Peyton thought he might've swallowed a low groan. "I should go."

He should, especially since he was looking at her like he was reconsidering his decision to take her to bed. "You're too damn tempting, Peyton Caron, more than you were two years ago."

"Were you attracted to me ten years ago?" Peyton asked, curious.

She'd noticed him, she'd noticed all the brothers, but it was Malcolm, hot and wild, who'd captured her girlish heart. She'd been so young and so naive, caught up in her relationship with a much older guy. Sometimes, when she couldn't sleep and the ghosts of the past came back to haunt her, she wondered what a guy six years older than her had been doing with an inexperienced nineteen-year-old. What had Malcolm seen in her, and why had he been so in love with her? She couldn't figure out why a guy who'd had experience and a reputation for being a playboy had wanted a virgin with no experience in men at all.

It was a question that still kept her awake at night.

"No," Jack replied curtly. "You were too young, Malcolm's, and I don't poach."

Four

It was embarrassing that she had only discovered great sex in her early fifties. By Jacinta's reckoning, she'd missed out on thirty-five-plus years of fantastic orgasms, and she couldn't help feeling a bit peeved about that.

Could her previous lovers not have put a little more effort in and done some research into how to please a woman? And she was also to blame for not demanding more but, in her defense, it took Pasco falling into her bed and life itself to show her that there was more to making love than a vague hint of pleasure.

How long could she keep this up? How long could she keep up with him? The older they got, the more those twelve years would make a difference. Her energy levels would flag and her ass would start stalking her. Her boobs had already dropped, damn them...

"And she's off," Pasco murmured.

She turned her head to look at him, his long black eyelashes resting against his tanned skin. He hadn't shaved for a couple of days, and his jaw was rough with black stubble.

There was a hint of gray in his beard, and she liked seeing that indication of maturity.

"What do you mean?" she asked, rolling over to place her hand on his wide chest.

"I can tell when you are indulging in your I'm-too-old-for-him crap," he told her, sounding a little irritated. Her obsession with their age difference annoyed him; he couldn't understand why it was a big deal. She liked him, he liked her and they had amazing sex...

But she had sons—the Grantham boys were as much hers as Merrick was—just eight years younger than him, and with Fox and Soren now engaged, grandbabies might not be that far off.

She tensed and rolled away, sliding out of his bed and picking up his T-shirt from the floor. She pulled it on and went to stand in front of the picture window that looked out to the guesthouse's perfect gardens and, from there, out to the sea. The guesthouse was a fair distance from the main house and was out of sight, and she was glad. She didn't want anyone knowing that she regularly met Pasco here for morning and afternoon sex and that she'd spent many nights in his arms and his bed.

She wasn't ready for anyone to comment on their relationship, to judge their age difference, to spoil what they had.

She heard Pas leave the bed, the rustle of him pulling on a pair of shorts and his footsteps as he walked over to where she stood. His arms snaked around her waist, and he pulled her back into his chest and rested his chin on the top of her head. "I wish you could enjoy what we have and not get all caught up in the age difference and the what-people-will-think crap."

She heard the sadness in his voice and realized she was tainting the moment, diluting his pleasure. She would try to be better, to do better and to not get so caught up in her thoughts.

"What else is bothering you, Jace?" Pasco asked her, tugging her over to the window seat and pulling her down so that she sat between his thighs, the back of her head on his chest. While he was implacable and unreadable, Pasco had no problem reading her and knew when she was upset, worried and needed to talk. He also knew when she didn't need to talk, and on those days, she frequently found herself naked against a wall or on a desk or on the floor...

He was a truly excellent lover. And a helluva nice guy.

She could stay like this forever, surrounded by his strength, but that wasn't possible. As soon as his oversize sculpture was finished—that was why he was here at Calcott Manor; he'd rented one of the estate's largest barns, as his New York City studio was too small for his biggest-ever work—he'd be returning to the city, and their relationship would fade away.

He wouldn't, couldn't stay here, and Calcott Manor was her home, the Granthams her family. This was where she belonged.

"Jace? What's going on?"

She angled her head back and up to look at him, wondering how he'd become her closest confidant in such a short space of time. And, as he was not a part of the Grantham family, she appreciated his intelligent and unemotional take on their recent dramas.

"I heard a rumor in town today," Jace told him, her gaze back on the sea. "There's this girl, Peyton—"

"Mm-hmm, I know her—she sometimes helps out behind the bar at Clancy's."

Of course Pas would've noticed her, Jace thought. Peyton was gorgeous, and crucially, she was the same age as many of his previous girlfriends. She also, as Jacinta found out, had an art history degree. She and Pasco would get along like a house on fire—

"What about Peyton?"

"She has a little boy, and there's talk that Jack is the father of her kid."

Pasco was quiet for a minute. "Hold on, let me get this straight... Peyton was engaged to Malcolm, right? The one who died?"

Jace wrinkled her nose. "Mm-hmm. Neither Avangeline nor I were happy about the engagement at the time."

"Why?"

"It just seemed to us that Malcolm wanted a family more than he wanted a wife. He was desperate to have kids, to be the first to start the new generation of Granthams. Peyton was too young for him, and I sometimes think that he wanted her just to carry his kids." She waved her hands around. "Maybe I'm being too harsh. He said he loved her and was gutted when they broke up."

"Why did they break up?"

"Something went wrong between him and Peyton's father, Harry—I think it was a business deal, but I'm not sure—and Mal demanded that Peyton choose between them. Peyton chose her dad, and Mal lost it."

"Did they not get along?"

"I thought they did until that fight. Maybe Malcolm was right, as Harry has a reputation for questionable deals and for being a bit of a con man. Avangeline hates him with every fiber of her being, but I kind of like the guy. He can be funny and charming."

"Did you date him?"

Jace's lips quirked at the jealously she heard in Pas's voice. "No, I didn't *date* him. But I won't cross the road when I see him coming either. I've spoken to him, and he once gave me a lift when my car broke down." Pasco's arms tightened around her waist, and his hand came up to hold her right breast, a subconscious but possessive move. And damn, if it didn't make her feel all squirrelly.

"Has there been any progress with discovering who is blackmailing Avangeline?" Pasco asked, his Australian accented voice a deep rumble in her ear. It was Pasco who deciphered the code on the postcards Avangeline received from her secret lover and her blackmailer. Without him, the family wouldn't know that Avangeline was being extorted.

"No, but Avangeline and Jack had an enormous fight yesterday. God, I'm surprised you didn't hear them yelling. Long story short, Jack got nothing out of her."

Pasco leaned forward to peer down at her, frowning. "She won't tell him who her lover is?" he asked.

"Nope. And she told Jack to butt out, that she's handling everything."

"She should go to the police," Pasco stated.

Jace patted his arm. "You try telling her that," she muttered. She looked at her watch and winced at the time. "I need to—how did you put it?—get a wriggle on. I've got things to do, and you have a sculpture to finish."

"Yeah. My agent keeps telling me that it should've been finished weeks ago."

A cold hand gripped her heart at the thought of him leaving. But that was going to happen, and the sooner she wrapped her head around it, the better. The famous sculptor and the housekeeper didn't have a future, and she wouldn't be stupid enough to imagine that they did.

She slipped out of his grip and started to walk to the en suite bathroom. She'd take a shower and then she'd return to the real world.

As she walked away, Pasco gripped her wrist, and she turned back to look at him. "Try having a little faith, okay? It'll all work out."

"Jack and his brothers will get to the bottom of it," she told him, deliberately misunderstanding him.

Because, really, there was no way they could work out. The deck was stacked against them, and Jace, practical to her core, knew that their relationship had a time limit.

And they were in the second half, rapidly counting down the clock.

Peyton followed Jack down the hallway of Calcott Manor, her eyes darting from artwork to artwork, an impressive—and probably priceless—collection of sculpture, ceramics and furniture. There was a Dalí in one space, and a Frida Kahlo opposite, and farther along, she thought she saw an unsigned Degas sketch.

A pair of perfectly matched antique chairs—eighteenth century and, she suspected, rare—stood on either side of tall double doors, and on the small table sat a collection of nephrite jade, carved by a master sometime in the seventeenth century. Peyton knew that Avangeline had one of the greatest private art collections in the world, but she hadn't expected anything like this. She could spend days in this house; it was an artist's and art lover's dream.

"Ready?" Jack asked her, looking over his shoulder and sending her a reassuring smile. He had a hand on the handle of one of the double-volume doors, and she pushed back the urge to turn around and run.

She shook her head. "No."

Jack grinned, and her stupid heart, the one that insisted on reliving every second of their very hot kiss last night, flipped over and bounced off her rib cage. His smile was wide and sexy, and the right side of his mouth tipped up a fraction higher than his left. Her insides felt as if they'd taken a dip in a warm pool of golden light. Peyton snorted. She was being a tad fanciful, and she should stop that. Immediately.

"It'll be fine," Jack assured her.

She wasn't so sure. But she had to do this, so she squared her shoulders, pushed steel into her spine and took a deep breath. Jack opened the door, and Peyton looked around the room, instantly falling in love with the huge windows looking out to a rose garden, the expensive squishy white couches and the art on the walls. Oh God, that couldn't be… no way was that a Turner on the wall above Avangeline's snow-white head. Peyton stormed up to it, falling into the colors of the sunset, ocher and browns with a hint of red. It was one of his later works, more abstract than his earlier paintings and more powerful for it.

She loved it. She wanted to fall into the painting and roll around in it, feel the waves pounding her body, the wind whipping her hair. How did he manage to get so much emotion in just a few square feet?

Feeling a presence next to her, Peyton turned to look into Avangeline's lined face. "It's fabulous. No, it's more than that, it's exceptional," she said, her voice sounding as if it were coming down through a tunnel.

"I'm very lucky to own it," Avangeline said in her aristocratic English accent. "It's my favorite piece today."

"Today?" Peyton asked, confused.

"My favorite depends on my mood. Some days it's the Turner, some days it's the Basquiat. Freud, Kahlo or an Ansel Adams photograph."

Peyton placed her hand on her heart. *She owned a Basquiat. Dear God.*

Jack's low rumble of laughter broke their immersed-in-art spell. "I knew that if I could just get you two talking about art, you would be firm friends in two seconds," he said.

With that, Avangeline's expression changed and so, Peyton supposed, did hers. They both stiffened, as if reminded of why she was here and what had happened in the past.

Avangeline gestured for her to take a seat. The old lady sat opposite her, tucked her ankle behind her calf and rested her linked hands in her lap. She inclined her head and looked Peyton dead in the eye. "I was wrong to threaten you, wrong to imply that I would meddle in your life. Jack tells me that you took my words very seriously indeed."

"I was young and scared," she said, wondering how many more times she'd have to explain.

"And I was wrong. I apologize," Avangeline reiterated, sounding as though she were giving birth to every word. It was obvious that she wasn't in the habit of saying sorry and that she hated being in this position. But Peyton didn't doubt her sincerity.

"I was grieving Malcolm, but I had no right to blame you for his death," Avangeline explained.

Peyton nodded, her thoughts racing. While she was here, discussing the past, she might as well try to get some answers to the questions that still kept her awake at night. "You were always against our relationship, and you and Mal had words when we got engaged. Why?"

Peyton felt Jack sit down beside her, but she was unable to pull her eyes off Avangeline's face. The older lady sighed and looked away through the tall windows, studying her rosebushes, lost in thought. It took her a little time to refocus.

"Malcolm was only six years older than you, but it felt like so much more. The experience and education gap between you was even bigger. You were naive, young, innocent, and Malcolm was not. He was so much more experienced than you, so much more a man of the world."

"And I wasn't enough for him?"

"I didn't say that." Avangeline shook her head. "There was a power and experience imbalance, and Malcolm held all of it. I warned him about it, told him he was out of line." She sent Peyton a challenging look. "I suppose you're going to take umbrage with me about that?"

Peyton shook her head. She couldn't do that. It was a thought she'd had more than once since his death. It had taken a long time, but she could finally look back on that time with equanimity. "I'm ten years older and, hopefully, a little wiser. I agree with you."

She clocked Avangeline's surprise, then Jack's. They'd both expected her to disagree, and she liked seeing the dawning of respect in Avangeline's eyes. Jack's too.

She looked at Jack and lifted her eyebrows. "So, are you going to tell her, or should I?"

His face went slack with shock. "Now?"

What was the point in waiting? Nothing would change. Jack was Noah's dad, and it was time to acknowledge him as such. "Why not? We're going to have to tell her at some point, so we might as well spit it out."

Jack rubbed his jaw, his eyes darting between her and his grandmother. She couldn't help her small smile. Despite being six two and two-hundred-plus pounds of pure muscle, this grown, debonair man was still a little afraid of his grandma.

To be fair, she was still a tiny bit afraid of Avangeline too. She suspected that her tongue was sharper than a Japanese katana sword.

"Uh… Peyton and I…um…we…"

Peyton decided to help him out. "What Jack is trying to tell you, very badly, is that he and I—" how could she put this delicately, using words that wouldn't offend? "—collided two years ago."

"I presume that *collided* is a euphemism for sex?" Avangeline asked crisply. When Peyton nodded, her eyebrows shot up toward her hairline. "Is there a reason you are sharing this with me?"

Well, it wasn't because she felt the need to share the details of a hookup with an octogenarian. Peyton nodded and slid her hands under her thighs to stop them from shaking. "Yes, *obviously*. I got pregnant, and Jack is the father of my little boy, Noah. He's almost eighteen months old."

Avangeline stared at her, not looking particularly surprised. Then again, she'd seen so much, experienced so much that she was now unshockable. "I have a great-grandson?" she asked.

Jack nodded. "Yeah, you do. I found out yesterday, and I met him this morning. He's..." Jack hesitated, and Peyton saw his Adam's apple bob. "He's a cute kid. He looks like me."

Avangeline stood up and walked over to the huge glass doors and opened one, standing in the aperture to look out onto her garden. Peyton leaned back in her chair, content to give the Grantham matriarch the time to take in the news, her thoughts rolling back to the time they spent on the beach this morning.

Jack had been nervous on first meeting Noah, and she'd seen the fine tremors in his hands. Noah had wriggled to be put down on the sand so that he could chase seagulls. He'd run, plop down on his butt, then stand up and chase another one. It was, as she told Jack, his favorite thing to do.

When Noah finally sat down, Jack dropped to the sand

next to him and entertained him by drawing surprisingly good renditions of cartoon animals in the sand. When Noah got bored with that, Jack made a sandcastle with his hands, which Noah kicked down with astounding glee. Then he built another, and another.

Jack had been surprisingly patient, and Noah had instantly felt at ease in his company, something that didn't happen often. Noah liked who he liked, and not everybody made that list. Thank God he liked Jack—it would be awkward if he didn't.

Avangeline turned around to look at Peyton, her eyes gleaming with intelligence. "Is Jack named on my great-grandson's birth certificate? I want him to share custody."

Whoa, hold on. Jack only met Noah a few hours ago. Avangeline was six steps ahead of her. Peyton was still wrapping her head around Noah having a father, and she hadn't even considered any further steps. She wasn't ready to go there, and she sent Jack a what-the-hell look.

"Avangeline, *stop*," Jack said, standing up. He nailed his grandmother with a cool look. "We told you about Noah as a courtesy. You cannot come in and start barking orders. I won't stand for it and neither will Peyton."

Peyton rose to her feet. "I am Noah's mother, and I will make the decisions concerning him," she told Avangeline.

Avangeline played with her pearl necklace. "I'm not saying that to be difficult, I just want—"

"Avangeline, I'm going to—"

Peyton whirled around to see a brunette standing in the doorway, her hair pulled into a messy ponytail. She was dressed in a short summer dress and held a cardboard box in her hands. Her green eyes danced over their faces, and she pulled a face when she realized she was interrupting. "Sorry. I didn't know you had a visitor."

Avangeline's face softened and she waved the young woman in. Peyton immediately recognized her as Avangeline's houseguest, and she'd seen her in Clancy's a few times.

"Aly, come in," Avangeline told her, sounding imperious. "I want you to meet someone."

When Aly joined them by the couches, Avangeline waved a languid hand in Peyton's direction. "This is Peyton. She was Malcolm's fiancée."

Aly's eyes widened. "You're Peyton?"

Why did Aly sound so surprised? It wasn't a secret that she and Malcolm had been engaged. Aly then shocked her by walking up to her and wrapping her arms around her in a tight hug. Peyton stiffened and Aly immediately let her go.

"Sorry, sorry...you are wondering why a stranger hugged you like that."

Peyton, knowing she was missing something, looked at Jack and caught the roll of his eyes. *Right. Weird.* Peyton was pretty good at reading body language, but she couldn't tell if he didn't like Aly or whether he was wary of her. Or both.

"I've been wanting to meet you," Aly told her.

Yeah, she'd gathered that, judging by the hug she'd just received. But why? She had no connection to Aly except through the tenuous link that she was once engaged to Malcolm a hundred years ago.

"She's looking a bit lost, Aly," Avangeline said, and then glanced at the Cartier watch on her wrist. It was vintage, possibly from the art deco period, and very nice. As in exquisite.

"Jacinta should be here in a minute, and you can explain over tea and scones."

Explain what?

Aly took her seat next to Avangeline, and Peyton sat opposite them while Jack leaned his shoulder into the frame of the open door. The summer breeze ruffled his hair, and she could see gold highlights in his light brown beard. His lips, she remembered from their night together and their more recent encounter, were soft, and having been pressed up against him, she knew his lips were the only part of him that was. She'd been attracted to him two years ago—obviously, or she would never have slept with him—but now her attraction for him felt like it was on a caffeine-and-steroid high.

Was it because he was hot with a boldface capital *H*? Or because here in Hatfield, she'd managed to relax a little and let go of her stressed-out single mom persona?

Or was it just Jack and the effect he had on her?

Avangeline and Aly engaged in some casual chitchat, and Peyton realized that Aly was utterly at home in this house and in Avangeline's company. She wondered how Aly had come to land at Calcott Manor since Avangeline, as Hatfield gossips stated, had curtailed her social activities over the past few years.

Apart from her grandsons, only Jocelyn and Arthur, her oldest friends, were regular visitors to Calcott Manor. She'd never met Jocelyn, but Simon had told her about the flamboyant woman of God. She was a household name in the UK for her humorous and sincere views about her faith, and because of her late-in-life marriage to the Shakespearean actor. She was a spiritual adviser to various members of the royal family and was a guru to many celebrities.

She espoused truth and authenticity above all else, and Peyton had hoped that she'd visit Hatfield, and Clancy's, so that she could meet the lady who'd made such an impression on Simon and Keene. So far, she'd had no luck.

"Who is looking after your son, Peyton?" Avangeline demanded, breaking into her thoughts.

Peyton crossed her legs and linked her hands around her knee. "He's with my best friends, Simon and Keene. They are his godfathers, and I trust them with my life."

"Simon is a police officer, isn't he?" Aly wrinkled her nose. "Tall, dark-haired, cute and ripped?"

It was as good a description as any. "That's him. Simon is a detective in the Hatfield Police Department, and he and his husband co-own Clancy's."

Aly exaggerated her pout, and Peyton laughed, enjoying her. "You've been hanging around Calcott Manor for a couple of months," she said, darting a look at Jack. "Have none of the Grantham brothers caught your eye?"

"Fox is with Ru, Soren with Eliot, the ex-supermodel, so they are out of the running," Aly replied, sounding mournful. She darted a look at Jack, her expression amused. "Jack thinks I'm either a little touched or after Avangeline's cash, and Merrick just raises my blood pressure."

"In a good way?" Peyton asked.

"In an I-want-to-throttle-him way," Aly replied.

"I've felt that way about him a time or two," a cheerful voice said from the doorway. "I've felt like that about *all* of them at one time or another."

Peyton watched Jacinta, Calcott Manor's slim and lovely housekeeper, walk into the room, carrying a heavily laden tray. Jack immediately took the tray from her and placed it on the coffee table in front of Avangeline while Jacinta removed a bundle of letters from under her arm.

Jacinta and Peyton exchanged slightly awkward nice-to-see-you-agains—it had been a decade since they'd last met—and then Jacinta placed her hands on Jack's cheeks. Peyton held her breath, touched by the love she saw in both their faces. "So, the rumors are true then? You have a little boy?"

He rested his forehead against hers and sighed. "I do."

Jacinta hugged him tightly, and when she stepped back, she fanned her wet eyes with her hands. "I'm so happy for you," she told Jack, almost blinding Peyton with her smile. "After weeks of being battered by bad news, that is fantastic to hear. Isn't it, Avangeline?"

Avangeline nodded and looked down as if trying to hide her wet eyes. Right. Under that haughty exterior was someone who could be emotional. That was hugely reassuring.

"When can I meet him? I'm available to babysit. I can pull down the crib from the attic and put it in my spare bedroom—"

Jack held up his hands and laughed. "Jace, slow down."

She danced on the spot. "I'm just so excited! We finally have a baby in the house!"

Peyton doubted she'd be so enthusiastic when she realized how *spirited* Noah could be. Then again, she had raised four boys; she had to know that they operated at warp speed. Noah was just starting younger than most.

"Um… I need to tell you that I'm only going to be in town for another month or so," Peyton said. Nobody looked particularly fazed by her comment, and Peyton remembered that they had private planes that made crossing the country, and the world, easy. Peyton watched as Jack took the mail from Jacinta's hands and gestured for her to take a seat. As Avangeline lifted an expensive silver teapot, Jack flicked through the pile of mail. Peyton was about to tear her eyes off him—she had to stop looking at the man like he was a warm fudgy brownie she couldn't wait to eat—when he stiffened, every muscle in his body tensing.

Jack didn't lift his head, but his eyes flew to his grandmother, to Jacinta and then to Aly. Seeing that no one was paying him any attention, and with a quick sleight of hand, Jack removed what looked to be a postcard from the pile of mail and slipped it into the right-hand pocket of his shorts. What was it that he didn't want his family to see? What was he hiding?

Jack placed the pile next to the tray in front of Avangeline and sat down next to Peyton, his long thigh connecting with hers. Avangeline looked at the mail as if it were a cottonmouth about to strike.

"Anything interesting?" she asked Jack, and Peyton wondered whether she was imagining the fear she heard in her voice.

Jack sent her a bland look. "Not today, Avangeline," he told her without hesitation or missing a beat.

He'd just lied to his grandmother, and Peyton wondered why.

Five

After bombarding Peyton with questions about Noah—how big was he when he was born? When did he first walk? Is he talking?—Jace finally ran out of steam and leaned back in her chair with a cat-who-ate-the-cream look on her lovely face. She finally had the grandchild she'd been nagging her sons for, and he needed to tell his brothers that they owed him. Big time.

But maybe he should tell them they had a nephew first. "Jack?"

Jack turned to look at Aly, and she nodded at the cardboard box she'd placed at her feet. "Avangeline asked me to try and sort out the attic, and I found some things belonging to your father."

Jack eyed the box, his heart thumping. As long as nothing in the box originated from The Basement, he could deal. He did not want to open the box and see handcuffs, whips or hoods.

"It's mostly papers to do with your dad's planes," Aly told him, "and your father's flight logs."

Relieved, Jack released a very long sigh.

"I wondered if you and your brothers wanted to look at them," Aly said.

Not particularly, Jack thought. When he didn't reply, she pushed on. "I know you and your brothers think that there was a fault with the plane, but I looked at its maintenance schedule. It had a detailed overhaul and service the week before the accident."

Meaning that the cause of the crash was pilot error. Jack shook his head. "My father didn't make mistakes. He was a perfectionist."

Just like Jack was, or tried to be. He'd always tried to emulate the high standards his dad, Jesse, had set. Except that now he knew Jesse's moral code, the one he had supposedly lived and died by, had been flexible. Where did that leave him? He didn't know, and he was too tired to work it out.

"Alyson," Avangeline said, breaking into their conversation, "tell Peyton about your transplant and everything else."

Jack rolled his eyes as Aly, yet again, explained how she'd inherited some of Malcolm's traits, quirks and food cravings along with his liver. Peyton looked deeply skeptical, and Jack understood how she felt—it was a crazy-ass theory. One that Avangeline and Jace staunchly believed in, Soren and Fox kinda sorta believed in and one that he and Merrick called complete bullshit.

"It's called cellular memory theory," Aly explained after taking a big bite of a scone laden with strawberry jam and thick whipped cream. "The basic idea is that memories, quirks and personality traits can be stored in other places and organs apart from the brain."

"So let me make sure I've got this right," Peyton said, leaning forward. "Before your transplant, you hated sugar, but now you crave sweets, just like Malcolm did. You were scared of speed and cars, and now you're a—what did you call it? A gearhead? You were tidy, but now you are messy."

Aly's smile was quick. "I know, it sounds bizarre, right? I've also inherited some of his memories. I remembered a ring belonging to Jack, Malcolm and Fox's mom that no one ever saw, except Fox and Malcolm. I understood the meaning behind a sign that Soren used before every swimming race, a gesture that only had relevance to him and Malcolm."

Jack couldn't think of anything specific he and Malcolm shared, nothing that Aly could grab on to in order to prove she was channeling his dead brother. In fairness, though, she'd never confessed to doing that. She only said that she knew some things about his brother that weren't common or public knowledge, and to be honest, he still couldn't explain how she came by the information about the engagement ring Fox gave Ru.

But, more important than understanding the gobbledygook of cellular memory theory, he wanted to know why she was still hanging around at Calcott Manor. She seemed nice enough, but Alyson Garwood was up to something, she wanted something, and he was going to discover what that was.

While he didn't believe she had anything to do with the blackmailer, he'd had the private investigator they hired look into that. He wouldn't stop digging until he unearthed her secrets.

Between discovering Alyson's intentions, getting to know Noah and unmasking Avangeline's blackmailer, could he have another ten hours in the day?

Jack took a sip of his coffee and looked out on the rose garden, thinking of the postcard he'd slipped into his pocket. Like the others Avangeline had received, it was written in code and in the blackmailer's blocky hand.

His grandmother had been utterly tight-lipped on the subject of her lover—still was—and none of them could understand why. She'd had one of the most acrimonious and scrutinized divorces in living history, she'd lived through the death of her twin sons and their wives in a plane crash, and she'd given up her empire to raise them. She'd been talked about, gossiped about, had salacious and untrue stories written about her—even had salacious but true stories reported on—so why did she care whether the world found out about her longtime lover?

Surely, at eighty-plus, you stopped caring about stuff like that.

Avangeline had taken the news about Noah very well, he thought, far better than he had expected her to. A part of him wondered at her lack of surprise, her muted response to what should've been bombshell news: he'd fathered a child with his brother's ex-fiancée. But Avangeline seemed to shrug it off.

Why did he think there was so much more going on here than he knew about?

Blackmail, Noah, Alyson…

Wanting Peyton in his bed.

His hands itched to touch Peyton's stunning body. He desperately needed to feast on her mouth again and slide inside her wet warmth and hear her turned-on gasps in his ear. He couldn't believe he'd had the willpower to call a halt to their lovemaking the other night, and the lower portions of his body were still sulking. He'd wanted her, craved her, but it had been, as he'd said, a hell of a day.

And getting involved with Peyton—the mother of his child—with everything else going on, was a recipe for disaster. They'd have a quick fling, it would be wonderful—perhaps even perfect for a while—and then, within a few weeks, things would start turning sour. The sex wouldn't be as great, and the glow of their connection would disappear fast. He'd start thinking that their chemistry wasn't working, that it wasn't as good as had been or could be, and he'd want out. He'd played this movie over and over again in his mind.

But because they had a child, he wouldn't be able to walk away without a backward glance and not give her another thought, as was his normal modus operandi. She could never be simply another woman he encountered, temporarily found fascinating and then grew bored of, forgetting her when the next woman came around.

Though, to be honest, he'd never quite managed to forget the night he and Peyton shared. When making love to other women, he'd even pretended, just for a minute, that he was making love to her, that she was in his arms. Then the woman would speak, move or groan, and the spell would be broken.

The fact that Peyton was lodged in his brain was beside the point. Peyton was different from any other woman in that, because of Noah, she was going to be *in* his life for a long time. They would have to communicate, to learn to deal with each other as they co-raised their son. Jack playing an active role in his son's life was not something he had to think about. First, he didn't walk away from his responsibilities, and second, the moment he saw Noah last night, he fell utterly, irretrievably, head-beneath-the-waves in love.

Noah was his son...*his*. From this point on, it would take a meteor strike and the destruction of the world to separate him from his boy.

And he had no intention of only seeing him on alternate weekends, now and again. He'd spent last night running options though his mind, thinking about how he could persuade Peyton to relocate to Manhattan. Maybe they could convert another of the Forrester-Grantham suites into a smaller two-bedroom apartment for Peyton and Noah. If Fox balked—and he would, as they'd be removing a revenue-generating suite from their hotel offerings—he'd buy an apartment as close to the hotel as possible for her and Noah to live in.

But he suspected Peyton wouldn't move to Manhattan without a job, so, in a week or two, he'd tap Avangeline to work her contacts in the art world. If Avangeline, one of the most successful collectors in the world, put the word out, Peyton would have the directors of many art galleries and institutes falling over themselves to do her a personal favor.

Sure, Peyton wouldn't like landing a job through her connection to Avangeline, but it was an elegant solution to their two-cities-half-a-continent-apart problem. What were the alternatives? He couldn't pick up his job and move to Chicago. He ran an international empire, and New York was where the company headquarters were.

No, it was easier for Peyton and Noah to move to Manhattan than for him to move anywhere else. She was a smart, practical woman, and she'd understand that when he explained it to her.

Besides, who wouldn't want to live and work in New York City?

Peyton and Jack walked back to her car, his hand on her lower back. She liked it there and felt as if it belonged there. *Silly girl.* She wasn't a teenager anymore, and she shouldn't be reading into polite gestures. Jack was a courteous guy, and his light touch didn't mean anything.

Standing on the wide driveway in the bright sunshine, Peyton thought back to the eventful hours she'd spent inside the Grantham estate. She had so many questions rattling around her brain. She tipped her head up to look at him. "What do you think of Aly's idea that memories can be stored outside the brain?"

Jack placed his hand on the roof of her small hatchback and considered her question. "Since hearing about it weeks ago, I've done some research. Scientists consider it impossible, say that it's a load of BS."

"So no scientific basis to it at all?"

"Nothing," Jack confirmed. "A lot of doctors blame the stress of having a transplant and the drugs for the odd flash of insight."

"So you think she's talking nonsense?"

Jack rocked his hand from side to side. "Intellectually, I do. But she's come up with stuff that would be, if not impossible, exceedingly difficult to know. The ring story is hard to explain."

Jack detailed how Aly had described an exceptional opal ring once owned by Jack's mom, Heather. Only he and Malcolm had ever laid eyes on the ring. Heather had neither worn it nor seen it, as it was still wrapped up in glittering paper in the safe-deposit box, waiting to be revealed on her next birthday—the birthday that never came. "I never saw the opal ring and it was never described to me. Aly also said that you returned Malcolm's engagement ring a few weeks after the funeral."

"Wouldn't most women return a family heirloom to the family?" she asked.

"Actually, no, a lot of women would've kept it."

Peyton shrugged, remembering the fat emerald Malcolm had presented to her with his on-one-knee proposal. At nineteen, she'd adored that ring—it had been big and blingy and not something she'd choose to wear now—but she'd been right to return it. Harry had pitched a fit when he'd heard she'd given it back. Apparently, he'd had it appraised and told her she could have gotten close to a hundred grand for the rare, old Colombian stone.

Selling it had never occurred to her because it hadn't been hers. But Harry always looked at everything in dollar terms. Even she, his only child, was a commodity, and since her breakup with Malcolm, she'd lost value and was no longer worthy of his interest.

Her father would never win a father-of-the-year award.

Peyton pulled her attention back to the present. "I don't know what to think about the traits she says she's inherited from Malcolm. If it's true, I wish she'd tell me what went wrong between him and my dad."

Jack tensed and frowned. "They were going into business together. Malcolm put up a hundred grand to pay for market and feasibility studies. Harry misappropriated the funds."

Her mouth fell open, and she shook her head. "No, he didn't. There was no business, and Malcolm didn't give him any money."

"He told us he did," Jack insisted.

They had to have misunderstood, Peyton thought. "Malcolm told me that my dad wanted to do business with him and was becoming annoyingly persistent about them setting up a company. Malcolm refused because he didn't believe in mixing business with family. He said that if it went wrong, then it would affect his and my relationship.

"According to Malcolm, Harry started harassing him for the money. They had so many arguments behind closed doors, and Mal told me that he couldn't take it anymore, that I had to choose between him and my dad," Peyton said.

Jack folded his arms and rocked on his heels. "But I distinctly remember him telling us—the entire family was around the table—that Harry had misused funds earmarked for a hotel development they were looking to establish and that he couldn't have someone in his life who'd cheated him. Mal was very black-and-white that way."

Peyton felt as if she'd been tossed into an industrial washing machine. "Why would Malcolm tell me one thing and you another?"

Jack shrugged his big shoulders. "I have no idea. What explanation did Harry give you?" he asked, rubbing his chin.

Peyton held back her snort of disbelief. "You are mistaking Harry for someone who shared stuff like that with me. I asked him what happened between them, and all he'd say was that they'd had a disagreement but that Malcolm would come around eventually. There was no mention about business, and, trust me, if Harry thought he had even a chance of going into business with Malcolm, he would've told everyone and anyone who would listen."

Jack stared at her as he rubbed the back of his neck. "That is so weird."

That was life with Harry. You never knew where the truth started or ended. Not wanting to waste another breath on her father, she returned to the subject of Avangeline's houseguest. "How much longer will Aly be staying at the manor?"

"I have no idea. Just like I have no idea what she wants with Avangeline. And she has a weird interest in the plane crash that killed our parents."

Peyton leaned her hip against her car door. "What do you mean?"

"She thinks she's being subtle, but we've all been questioned about the plane crash. What we remember, whether my father was a decent pilot, whether he had any health issues."

Why would a stranger be interested in a tragic accident that happened over twenty-five years ago? "That *is* strange," she said. "Maybe she's just one of those people who are fascinated by tragedy."

"Could be," Jack agreed. "Or there could be something that she's not telling us."

Peyton tipped her head to one side. "For a white knight, you're pretty cynical," she told him.

"Or maybe it's just that I have to completely understand a situation to feel comfortable with it. To make it better."

"Not everything has to be made better, Jack. Some things just are."

Jack didn't look convinced. "If we stop striving to understand, then we start accepting mediocrity."

Oh God, he was a perfectionist. Well, being a dad would soon knock that out of him. Being a parent had taught her which battles to fight and which hill she was prepared to die on. When you had little people in your life, you quickly had to accept that control was an illusion and that if a toddler could upset your carefully constructed plans, he would.

Jack liked having all his ducks in a row. She didn't know where her ducks were, but they were probably all in a club getting wasted or sitting in the back of a police cruiser.

Unlocking her car, Peyton yanked open the driver's door and slid behind the wheel. She switched the ignition on and hit the button to pull down the window. She turned her head and looked at Jack's stomach area, where she saw the unmistakable outline of a postcard in his pocket. "Question?"

"Mm-hmm?"

"Why are you stealing your grandmother's mail?"

He ducked down to look at her. "What are you talking about?" he asked, puzzled.

Peyton arched an eyebrow. "You slipped a postcard from Avangeline's pile of letters into your pocket."

He narrowed his eyes at her. "How do you know it wasn't for me?"

She snorted in disbelief. "When was the last time anyone

of our generation received a letter, let alone a postcard? We communicate via email and text messages, not by ink and paper. And this is your grandmother's house, not yours."

Jack cursed softly. "Busted."

Well, at least he wasn't going to insult her intelligence by trying to deny it. "It's complicated," he told her.

And that was code for "mind your own business." She might be the mother of the first of the next generation of Granthams, but she was still an outsider. She'd lost her chance to be part of the inner circle at Calcott Manor when she and Malcolm split, and she'd never have that chance again.

She knew that. She accepted that. So why did it still hurt? Why did her heart still long for something she couldn't have?

Was it because, to her, the Granthams embodied family loyalty and shared a bond she'd never come across before? Avangeline sacrificed a glittering career and her empire to raise her grandsons, showing the world what love looked like in action. The cousin/brothers and Merrick, who was raised with them, were and had always been a tightly knit group.

They'd go to war for the people they loved and were the family she'd always wanted to be a part of. And, sure, maybe that had played a part in why she'd said yes when Malcolm proposed. He'd had a big family and she'd so tired of living life on her own.

Sure, she'd had Harry, but he never gave a damn for anyone but himself and the size of his bank balance. To Harry, Peyton was a nuisance, a drain on his resources, a pain in his butt. The only time she'd felt loved and noticed was when she met and then became engaged to Malcolm. For six months, she basked in his approval and his affection. Back then, not only had her relationship with Malcolm given her the Granthams, but it had given her what she'd always craved from Harry, a loving father-daughter relationship.

Malcolm and her father would mend their fences, she'd thought, and she'd been angry and amazed that Malcolm had the temerity to ask her to walk away from her dad—the only family member she had—because of a stupid argument over the business. It had been such an out-of-the-blue, crazy request that she'd thought that when he calmed down, he'd realize how unreasonable he was being.

But Malcolm had never wavered and, uncharacteristically, neither had she. Over the weeks they were apart, she'd started to wonder whether she loved him, whether she was ready for marriage, whether she was ready to commit.

Hours later, she had heard that he was dead...

Jack tapped the hood of her car. "Peyton?"

She blinked and met his concerned eyes. "Yes?"

He stroked her cheek with his thumb. "Are you okay?"

She nodded briskly, hoping he didn't pry. "It's been a strange morning. There's been a lot to take in."

His expression was gentler than ever she imagined it could be. He pulled his hand away and sighed. Was that reluctance to leave her that she saw in his eyes? Maybe.

"That's an understatement. Look, I've got some stuff to do. I'll see you later, okay?" He straightened and walked away and Peyton started her car.

See you later. It was such a nebulous concept. When was later? In a few hours? Tonight? Tomorrow? Later in the week?

Arrgh, she thought, driving away. The distance between her teenage and adult self was, sometimes, indiscernible.

Later that day, Peyton put Noah into his stroller and walked down to the harbor, thinking that she could pick up ice cream to counter the effects of a long, hot and stressful day. After surviving her meeting with Avangeline, she figured she deserved something sweet, chocolatey and laden with calories.

As she approached the food truck serving gelato, she saw a man approaching her out of the corner of her eye, and icy prickles covered her skin. She immediately went into protective mommy mode, moving to stand between him and Noah. Harry wore a fedora and sunglasses, but she'd recognize him anywhere. They'd managed to successfully avoid each other for two months, but just a few hours after meeting Avangeline, he'd sought her out.

Was his timing suspicious or what? Was his being here just a coincidence, or did Harry keep closer tabs on her than she thought? And wasn't that a creepy idea?

"Peyton."

"Hello, Harry," Peyton replied, keeping her voice cool. She hadn't thought of him as her dad in ten years and never would again. "What do you want?"

He ignored her brusque question and gestured to the food truck. "Can I buy you something?"

"No," Peyton snapped. Hurt, hot and bitter, rolled through her, and she remembered begging him in the days and weeks after the funeral to engage with her, to tell her what she'd done wrong and why he'd distanced himself from her. She'd needed to know why he'd gone from loving her to ignoring her and what had happened to the man who'd told her he was proud of her and that he loved her. Was it any wonder that she found the concept of love difficult and trust impossible? Her only parent had played her like a fiddle...

The bastard.

Harry gestured to the stone wall that separated the beach from the pedestrian path. "Can we talk?"

They were already garnering attention, and Peyton didn't

want to cause more gossip by storming away from him. She pushed Noah's stroller to the wall and angled it away from her father, who foiled her by walking around to stand in front of the stroller, his hands on his hips as he stared down at Noah. "So this is my grandson, huh?"

"No. This is *my* son. You will have nothing to do with him, ever," Peyton told him, sounding fierce even to her own ears. "I will never give you the chance to play the same mind games with him that you did with me."

"Still pissed about that, huh?"

"I refuse to waste that much energy on you, Harry," Peyton snapped back.

He grinned, but the gesture was void of kindness—and humanity. "Rumor has it that he's Jack's son. Keeping it in the family, right?"

She desperately wanted to smack the smirk off his face. There was no way she was going to confirm or deny Noah's paternity to her waste-of-oxygen father. "I'm going to give you one more chance to tell me what you want, and then I'm going to walk away," Peyton said, warning him.

Harry pulled his gaze off Noah and smiled again. He used his charming smile this time, the one pulled out when he wanted to butter someone up. "I thought that we should try and be a family again, that we should reestablish our relationship."

Was he high? "We never had a relationship, Harry. I was never anything more than a commodity to you."

"You are my daughter, and I love you!"

Oh God, what bullshit. He looked sincere, but Peyton knew he was looking for an angle, that he was working a scheme. She thought about asking him for an explanation for his and Malcolm's falling out—maybe he'd tell her the truth, maybe he wouldn't—but she didn't want to spend any more time in his company. As it was, she already felt the need to take a long shower.

"Go peddle your crap somewhere else, Harry. I'm not buying."

Harry laid his hand on his heart, looking shocked. "How can you say that?"

She was done with him, done with this conversation. "I'm not a naive kid anymore, Harry, and I'm not stupid. You've heard that Jack might be Noah's father, so you want to re-establish a relationship with me because, like before, you think I can give you access to that rich world."

Greed whipped across his face before he wrangled it back. "You are so cynical!"

It was an accusation she'd leveled at Jack earlier, but in Harry's case, cynicism was well deserved. "I'm going to say this once, Harry, just once. Stay away from me. I'm not interested in anything you say or do."

"Peyton—"

Peyton grabbed the handle of the stroller and power walked away from her father, cursing him and cursing the tears that burned in her eyes. The last thing she had expected today was an encounter with Harry, and it had rocked her more than she liked. He shouldn't affect her, but he did. He was still her father, the only blood relative she had. He was Noah's grandfather. As both her parents were only children, she had no aunts or uncles and no cousins. Harry and Noah were the only branches on her family tree.

He didn't matter; only Noah was important. But, damn it, why, despite knowing he was a horrible human, did a small part of her still long for his love and approval?

Six

Peyton's father and her father-of-her-child troubles were put on the back burner when she returned to her apartment after her walk and found water pouring down her outside stairs. Pulling Noah out of his stroller, she perched him on her hip and hurried into the kitchen, then into the bar. Simon, who stood behind the bar, took one look at her face and launched himself over the counter in an impressive move that had her gasping. His hands came to rest on her biceps.

"What's the matter? Is it Noah?"

Noah sent him a gummy smile. "He's fine, as you can see," Peyton told her friend. "If I didn't know you were gay, I'd do you for that James Bond move, Simon."

"Ha ha. What happened?" Simon demanded, looking thoroughly impatient.

"There's water running down the stairs," she told him. "I think a pipe has burst in my apartment."

Simon cursed, grimaced and then nodded. "Water we can deal with." He placed a hand on his heart and briefly closed his eyes. "I thought something momentous happened today."

Well, Noah had gained a father, grandmother and great-grandmother, and Peyton had had a run-in with Harry, but her news could wait. Right now, they had to stop the flood and see how badly her apartment was damaged.

"I need to close the valve that sends water upstairs," Simon told her. He looked at his watch, scanned the room and instructed one of the waiters to take over behind the bar. Peyton wrinkled her nose. He was a new hire and would soon become overwhelmed. She would work the bar herself, but she had Noah to look after.

"What's wrong?"

Peyton whirled around to see Jack walking toward her, concern on his face. She looked past him and through the bar's windows to see his expensive car parked a few spaces from the front door. And, yay, he could take Noah while she manned the bar.

"Can you look after Noah for ten or fifteen minutes?" she asked as Noah waved his pudgy hands in the air and leaned toward Jack. Jack didn't ask why but took Noah, wrapping his arm around his chest and holding him between his legs so that Noah could look out at the world.

"What's going on?" Jack asked, following her to the crowded long wooden bar. She opened the flap, took an order and some money from a customer, and told the waiter to go back to his duties.

"I came home to find water streaming down the stairs from my apartment. Simon has gone to shut off the main valve. I must have a burst pipe or something," she told Jack.

Jack grimaced and looked around. "This is an old building, and plumbing doesn't last forever."

"The boys redid the plumbing and electrics downstairs when they bought the place but figured they'd save some money by leaving the renovation of the upstairs area for later," Peyton told him, popping the lids off two beers. She buzzed around behind the bar, and after ten minutes, she looked past Jack to see Simon and Keene approaching her, annoyance on their faces. Simon joined her behind the bar, and Keene stood next to Jack.

Peyton introduced Jack to her friends, and Keene and Jack chatted amiably as Peyton continued to help Simon serve. Then the bartenders due to start the evening shift walked through the swinging doors leading from the kitchen and took over the bar.

The four of them, with Jack still carrying Noah, walked down past the restrooms, stepped through the door marked Private and stopped at the base of the inside set of stairs leading up to her apartment. The carpet covering the stairs was soaked, and Peyton knew that the rest of her apartment would be too.

They carefully climbed the stairs, and when Peyton opened her front door, a stream of water gushed over her flip-flops. Simon and Keene cursed, and Peyton noticed that the water had soaked the hems of their jeans as well as their trendy sneakers. Jack, closest to the wall, had managed to avoid the deluge.

"We're going to have to go home and change," Simon told Keene.

Keene nodded and looked at Jack, then Peyton. "We'll be back in five. Pack up some stuff and you can move in with us until we get this sorted. Depending on where the leak is, it might take a few days to sort this place out, possibly a week."

Oh, that wasn't going to work. Simon and Keene were renovating their house, and they were only using a few rooms to live in. Adding another adult and a baby meant that they would be falling over each other.

"No way am I moving in with you," Peyton told them. "I'll book a motel for a week."

That would take a bite out of her savings, but what else could she do?

"That would be a solution," Keene agreed, "but it's the height of summer, and everything is booked. There's no room at any of the inns, Peyton."

There had to be. If not, what the hell was she going to do?

"Just move in with us," Simon said, placing his hand on her shoulder. "We survived camping in Yosemite in that tiny tent, so we can survive a few days in a two-roomed house."

"Yeah, but I didn't have Noah then," Peyton argued.

"I have a solution," Jack said, his deep voice breaking into their bickering.

She looked at him—so at ease holding Noah, whose head now rested on Jack's chest. Their eyes were the same brilliant blue, and they looked so alike that her breath caught in her throat.

"We're open to suggestions," Simon told him, lifting his foot to shake off the excess water. But when he put it down again, his sneaker squished and he grimaced.

"There's an unused apartment over the garage at Calcott Manor. It has a solid Perspex railing on the balcony, so Noah will be safe. It has two bedrooms, is fully furnished, and all you need is Noah's cot and your clothes."

Peyton bit the inside of her lip. She couldn't stay here, moving in with the boys would be problematic, but she wasn't sure if relocating to Calcott Manor was the answer. By doing so, she might as well take out an ad in the local newspaper telling the good residents of Hatfield that Jack was Noah's father.

But what did it matter if they knew, if *anyone* knew? How did Noah's paternity affect anyone besides the three of them? She wasn't going to put down roots in Hatfield, and who cared if she had a baby outside of marriage? This wasn't the 1950s, for goodness' sake!

"That sounds like a perfect solution," Keene told Jack.

It did. But it didn't. It would put her and Noah close to Jack, and she didn't know if she was ready for that. "I don't know…"

Simon nudged Keene. "Let's leave them to figure it out," he told his husband. "We need to go home, change and get back before the place starts heaving."

Simon kissed her cheek, gave her a quick hug and placed his lips near her ear. "It'll be okay, Pey."

Peyton didn't know if he was talking about the flood, about her moving in with Jack or about life in general. She smiled at him, and when he and Keene walked down the stairs, she looked at Jack. "Before I say yes, let's look at what I'm dealing with. Maybe it's not that bad."

Jack kicked off his flip-flops and left them outside her door. "I suspect that a tidal wave behind a door is never good news," he told her, following her into the lounge.

Damn. Her entire living area was one big puddle. She sloshed through the water to walk down the hallway and peeked into Noah's room, then hers. The floor was an inch deep under water in both. Jack appeared behind her, Noah fast asleep on his chest. "It's been pumping water for hours," he said, grimacing.

"Luckily, our clothes are in a chest of drawers with feet off the ground," she said. "God, it's going to be a nightmare getting this cleaned up."

"There are specialty companies that will bring in pumps and industrial blowers, but the carpet will have to be ripped up and replaced. The decorative stuff can only take place after they find the leak, and that could take some time."

Peyton grimaced and rocked on her heels. "Would Avangeline be okay with me using the apartment temporarily?"

"I'm sure she would be fine with it," Jack replied. "Besides, she owes you for being such a monster to you after Mal's death."

Peyton waved that away. Avangeline had been grieving, and grief could turn nice to nasty in a heartbeat. The thing was, she could spend the next hour phoning around, but she knew Keene was right. Hatfield was heaving with tourists and she wouldn't be able to find a room at the height of the season. She didn't want Noah to live, however temporarily, within a construction site, so Jack's offer was the most sensible. What other choice did she have?

"Thank you," she told him, sighing. "I'd appreciate it. Hopefully, I'll be back here in a week.'

"I think you are being optimistic, but we'll see," Jack replied. "Why don't you grab a bag and pack it with what you need for tonight? We can come back for the rest of your stuff tomorrow."

That sounded like a solid plan. She gestured to Noah. "Are you happy to hold him?"

"Always," Jack replied and Peyton cursed herself for wishing he felt the same way about holding her. Whoo boy. This situation was rapidly becoming more complicated.

Jacinta walked down the road toward the entrance to Hatfield, little Noah toddling beside her, his hand wrapped around her finger. He was such a happy little guy, and he looked so much like Jack. He was his daddy's boy, of that there was no doubt.

Had circumstances been different and had Malcolm and Peyton married, their children would be a lot older than Noah was now. Malcolm had wanted children with a passion bordering on obsession, something that had worried Jace. She, like Avangeline, had never believed Peyton was the right girl for Malcolm, as she was nothing like the sophisticated and sharp girlfriends he'd usually brought home.

But she and Avangeline had made a huge mistake when they'd expressed their doubts about their relationship lasting, and Malcolm, being stubborn, had dug his heels in, determined to prove that he could make a commitment and stick to it. Had his relationship with Peyton been more about having a baby, his own family and proving them wrong than him being in love with her? It was highly possible.

Malcolm had been the most complicated of the boys, the one who'd been the most wounded by the horrific events of their childhood. His attraction to Peyton—younger, unsophisticated—still made no sense to her.

And what was going on with her and Jack? Yes, they had a baby together, but she saw the looks they exchanged and could taste the electricity in the air whenever they were together. Their attraction crackled, and they couldn't keep their eyes off each other. God, she hoped they didn't end up burning out or, worse yet, scalding each other. Peyton had experienced enough hurt at the hands of the Granthams, and Jack was, despite his urbane and charming exterior, a hard nut to crack. Would Peyton be another of his short-term flings, or could she, maybe, turn out to be his happily-ever-after? She hoped for the latter but had no expectations. She liked Peyton, she always had, but love couldn't be forced. Sometimes circumstances conspired against you.

Noah said something incomprehensible, and Jace smiled, joy in her heart. She had a grandchild, finally. Oh, not legally, not by blood, but the lack of both didn't concern her in the least. Noah was Jack's boy, and that meant Jacinta was his grandma. What would he call her? Nan? Grandma? Simply Jace?

Labels didn't matter—only love did.

Jace dropped to her haunches to see what had caught Noah's attention. He'd picked up a stone and started to put it in his mouth. Jace gently removed the stone from his hand, distracting him by pointing out a bird when he looked as though he was about to protest. And that was how Pasco found her, balancing on her tiptoes, talking to the latest love of her life.

"Hey, babe," Pasco said, stopping next to them, his bare chest wet with perspiration from his midmorning run. He wore athletic shorts and sneakers, and she blushed as she recalled exercising her tongue down his happy trail earlier.

"Hey," Jace replied, standing up. He moved in to kiss her and she backed away, lifting her hand to ward him off. "Uh, no. You're sweaty."

"Eight miles, brisk pace," Pasco told her, his eyes moving from her to land on Noah, who was looking up at him with wide eyes. "Who is this?"

"Noah," Jace said. "He's Jack's child."

Pasco frowned and put his hands on his hips. "I didn't know any of your sons had kids."

"He didn't either," Jace wryly told him. "He only found out about Noah a day or two ago. Do you remember me telling you about the rumor I heard about Jack fathering a child? Well, it turned out to be true."

"And he's already got you babysitting for him?"

Jace heard a note in his voice she wasn't sure of and didn't like. "What do you mean by that?"

Pasco shrugged, his eyes not leaving hers. "You're the housekeeper, not the babysitter. Make sure they don't take advantage of you, babe."

She was far too old to be called babe, as she'd told him many times before. And how dare he think that she was weak enough not to be able to say no when she needed to? She'd been on her own for a long time and had survived, *flourished*, without his input. And she and Jack might not share a surname, but she was his *mom*. In every way that counted.

"Peyton's flat flooded, and Jack has gone to help her pack up her things. They asked if I would look after Noah for a few hours, and I said yes. Nobody is taking advantage of me, Pasco."

He nodded, unfazed by the bite in her voice. He was so damn sure of himself, sure of her and their relationship. He didn't see any pitfalls ahead, and whenever she raised the subject of how they'd continue to see each other when he returned to the city, he either ignored her, distracted her or told her they'd work it out and she shouldn't worry.

She liked making plans, knowing where she was going and how she was going to get there, and she couldn't see the way forward. All she could do was count the reasons why they couldn't work, why they wouldn't work. He was in his early forties, and she was fifty-two. He was still young enough to have kids of his own, whereas she was starting to go through menopause—and all the delightful experiences that brought! She was, as of two days ago, a grandmother for God's sake, while he was a hot still-young guy.

She was a square peg in a round hole, and the only place they worked was here at Calcott Manor as temporary lovers.

"If there was an Olympic medal for overanalyzing and overthinking, you'd win it," he told her, and she heard the irritation in his voice.

And if there was one for putting his head in the sand,

he'd win that. She opened her mouth to speak and he held up his hand.

"Do not tell me that you think I should be thinking of having kids of my own, that we're too different, you're too old—blah, blah, blah. I don't want to hear it."

He might not want to hear it, but it didn't make her words less true. And if she told him that she didn't think she was enough for him, that she'd hold him back and be a millstone around his neck, he'd be even angrier.

But she wasn't right for him, not long-term. How could she be? She belonged here with Avangeline, taking care of the only family that'd given her and her boy more than she'd ever imagined.

At one point in her life, their survival had been questionable. That they'd thrived was due to Avangeline and the life she'd created at Calcott Manor.

"How's your maquette coming along?" she asked, changing the subject. He'd been asked to submit a maquette—a small version of the full-scale piece—to a Japanese bank president who wanted a sculpture for his boardroom.

"Badly," he muttered. "I've done about five, and I hate them all. I've run out of inspiration."

Jace winced. Maybe that was because Pasco belonged in the city being courted and feted by collectors and connoisseurs, using Brooklyn and the Bronx as inspiration for his incredible sculptures. He thrived there, he once told her. He needed the city's energy as food for his creativity. She wanted to be with him desperately, but she'd wither away without fresh air and space. He was one of the best sculptors of the past quarter of a century, and if being in the city was where he needed to be, then he should go.

As the mother of four boys, she'd learned how to push her wants and needs aside, to give the men she loved what was best for them. As a fling, they were magic, but for anything long-term, she was not good for Pasco.

"You said that you needed to step away from the oversize sculpture for a while, so why don't you go back to your studio in the city and work from there?" she suggested, swinging Noah up onto her hip.

"Are you trying to get rid of me?" he asked, narrowing his eyes. His dark eyes flashed with hurt, and his lips thinned. Jace closed her eyes, wishing she could tell him that she was hurting too. But they had to get used to not being in each other's lives, and maybe now was a good time to start, as she'd told him.

"And you just decided this all on your own?" Pasco asked her, his expression tight and his words tinged with ice.

He didn't give her a chance to respond. "I am not one of your sons, Jacinta, and I sure as hell don't want or need you making decisions for me. And if you want out, just say so. You can break it off at any time you like, Jace. I'm a big boy, I can handle it."

"I don't know what I want!"

Jace glanced down at Noah, who was looking at them with big eyes. She didn't want to fight with him in front of Noah; she didn't believe in exposing kids to adult drama.

"Look, I'm sorry. There's just a lot going on."

"There is," Pasco told her, "but you're looking for a reason to push me away, an off-ramp. You need to make up your mind, Jacinta. You're either with me or not."

Hearing the warning in his voice, she cocked her head. "What are you trying to say?"

"I'm not trying to say anything, I'm *telling* you. Decide what you want, and when you do, come and tell me. And if you want me, us, then be prepared to be flexible, and to introduce me as your lover to your sons, and to Avangeline. I'm sick of being a secret. I want to stop hiding what we have."

They were being discreet, not flaunting their affair. There was a difference between that and hiding. "We are not hiding," Jace protested and knew that her protest was weak.

"Yeah, we are. But what pisses me off the most is that you are hiding from yourself."

Jack tossed a pizza box on the island counter, placed a bottle of white wine in the fridge and followed the sounds of a childish belly laugh. He stopped in the doorway of the bathroom and looked inside. Noah sat in the tub, enjoying a bubble bath, and Peyton, on her knees, was watching Noah attempt to bat a bubble around. They were both laughing like loons.

They made such a lovely picture, a son—his son—and his mom. Peyton had a smudge of soap on her cheek, and Noah's smile was wide. The room reverberated with the sound of their laughter, Noah's surprisingly deep and rich for a baby and Peyton's melodic.

This was what perfect looked like…if the word needed an ad campaign, Noah and Peyton were it. But perfect, like those bubbles, never lasted. And, as he knew, chasing it was an exercise in futility, but he couldn't stop. He had to be the best he could be, for himself and for the legacy his parents had left behind.

But their legacy of perfection—a wonderful life, business success, an amazing marriage—had been blown to smithereens with Fox's revelations.

Jack placed his fist on his heart and gently banged it against his ribs, frustrated. He couldn't reconcile the last memory of his laughing blue-eyed mother and his debonair dark-haired, green-eyed father as they walked from Calcott Manor's front door to the car that would take them to the local airport.

Fox said that they'd hated each other, that they'd been screaming at each other and talking about divorce just a short while before they'd left. He didn't remember them fighting, not ever. How could he have read them so wrong?

But maybe he was just remembering what he wanted to remember, not the truth. If he pushed himself, he did remember dinners when his parents barely spoke, nights when his father didn't come home. He recalled watching his mom as she stared out of windows, remembered photographs and papers being hastily shoved into desk drawers or under couch cushions.

Yeah, if he looked past the surface and dug a little, he remembered interactions that made him pause, things that didn't make sense.

But Fox still should've told him. He'd had no right to keep this information to himself. Jack knew his just-older brother was trying to protect him—and he hadn't wanted to destroy the happy memories he had of his childhood—but he far preferred being hurt by the truth than comforted by a lie.

He thought back to the message he received from Fox just before he walked over from the main house to the garage:

I hear that you've moved Peyton into the apartment above the garage. Just a reminder that both Soren and I fell in love with the women occupying the apartment. It's a dangerous place, bro. Wink, wink, nudge, nudge.

When he didn't reply, Fox sent another message:

Okay, I get that you're mad, but you're going to have to talk to me at some point. Just get over yourself, already. Or do I need to come back to Hatfield and kick your ass?

Maybe they should rumble, maybe that would be a good way to purge his anger, to release some frustration. He and Fox would each land some hard blows—as kids, Jace had insisted their punches be below the neck, and they'd stick to that rule—and they'd each end up with a couple of bruises on their ribs and grazed knuckles. But they'd walk away as friends.

Maybe.

As for this idea that he'd fall in love with Peyton, just because she'd moved into this apartment and just because Fox and Soren fell in love with their future fiancées here, well, that was pure bullshit. Seriously, sometimes he wondered who Fox was and what he'd done with the grumpy bastard he'd grown up with. He wasn't going to fall in love with anyone; he didn't even believe in love. It was too hard to nail down, too nebulous, like trying to capture mist just before the sun came out. It wasn't something that could be drilled into, exposed and understood. Jack didn't engage in what he didn't understand.

Besides, what was love? Avangeline had had an acrimonious divorce, and his parents had kept up the so-in-love facade but were deeply unhappy beneath their gilded-couple image.

Love was a gamble, and he only bet on sure things.

But lust, attraction, he understood. Just standing here, eyeing the curve of Peyton's ass, the fall of her hair, the smoothness of her long neck, he felt the urge to take her to bed, to see that long, slim, surprisingly strong body naked again. He wanted to hear her gasp his name as she came, taste her between her legs, drive into her until they both saw stars.

Love? Love had nothing to do with it.

He must've moved, made a noise, because Peyton whirled

around and sat back on her heels, her eyebrows raised. "I didn't hear you knock," she said, her tone a little pointed.

Right, he hadn't. He should've, he silently admitted.

"Sorry," he said on a small shrug. He resisted the urge to tell her he felt so at home in her company that the thought of knocking hadn't crossed his mind. He felt as if he belonged in any room that had her in it.

Goddamn it, where did these thoughts come from? Why did they storm in out of the blue to ambush him?

"And why are you standing at my bathroom door?" Peyton asked him.

Right; he had an answer to that question. "Well, I thought that it might be a good idea to learn Noah's routine and how to look after him. I feel like I am playing catch-up."

"You are playing catch-up," Peyton told him before gesturing to the bath, "but bathing a toddler isn't hard. You run a bath, dump him in it, soap him down, rinse him off." He saw the humor in her eyes and knew she was teasing him.

"Smart-ass," Jack grumbled. Noah shot him a gummy grin and beat the surface of the water with his flat hands, splattering water onto Peyton's face and chest.

"Atta boy," Jack murmured.

Peyton whipped her head around to frown at him. "What did you say?" she demanded, but Jack caught the amusement in her tone.

He lifted his hands and winked at Noah. "Nothing, I said nothing."

"Hmm." Peyton stood up, grabbed a towel from the railing, tucked it under her arm and lifted Noah from the bath. He wiggled as she tried to dry him off, and she got in three swipes of the towel before he took off down the hallway buck naked.

Peyton tipped her face to the ceiling and sighed. "He hates wearing clothes and will take any chance to be nude."

Jack jammed his hands into his pockets and grinned at her. "Don't we all?"

"Ha ha," Peyton replied and shoved the towel at him. "You can grab him, dry him and dress him. Everything, including the diaper, is on the bed in the second room."

Jack looked at the towel and back at her. "But I don't know how to put on a diaper!"

Peyton sent him a breezy smile and patted his chest as she walked past him. "You're a smart guy, you'll figure it out. I did."

Seven

Between Avangeline and Harry and the flooding of her apartment, it had been a long, strange day.

"Go and sit on the balcony," Jack told her, placing his hand on Noah's back. He'd just put him in his crib, and his eyes were already closing. He'd be asleep in a minute. "I'll make sure he's asleep, and then I'll warm the pizza and open a bottle of wine."

Wine and pizza? Heaven.

"I can do it," she told him from the doorway of Noah's room.

"I know you can, Pey, but let me," Jack said, gently patting Noah's little bottom with his big hand. "I might live in a hotel, but I can throw a pizza in a microwave and pull a cork."

If he was offering, she wasn't going to say no. She was soul-deep exhausted, and just a little thing like someone bringing her wine and pizza on a plate was enough for her to feel looked after and special. When had that happened last? She couldn't remember, ten or more years ago? Back when her father pretended to love her? When Nate, Mal's best friend and roommate, used to throw together amazing meals for them—Harry included—to share?

Yeah, probably then. That was a long time to feel alone, to do everything yourself all the time. She was allowed to feel grateful for the little things.

What happened to Nate? Peyton wondered. *Where is he now?* Like so much else in her life, he'd faded away after Malcolm's death, and they'd never spoken again. How had everyone dismissed her so easily from their lives—why did they forget about her so quickly? Had she been that unsubstantial, that unremarkable?

Peyton stood by the railing and looked out onto the purple-blue sea and the wide, private beach, watching the waves gently roll up to the shore. She could see the lights of a small vessel, and one or two stars had pierced the sky. The night was warm, fragrant and quiet. She'd become used to the sounds of cars and city noise, of inebriated and happy revelers in the bar downstairs, and she'd forgotten what true quiet sounded like.

It washed over her and settled somewhere near her soul. She needed quiet, but it wasn't enough to stop her washing-machine mind.

And after nearly two months of having Simon and Keene's company, and their help with Noah, how was she going to cope with being on her own in a strange city, starting a new job? She didn't know, but she was going to have to learn to cope. And quickly. She would deal with anything that came her way. She'd left Hatfield, survived LA, gotten her degree and birthed a child. She could do anything and handle anything life threw at her.

Peyton turned at the sound of Jack stepping onto the balcony, and she watched as he placed their plates, paper napkins and the pizza box on the table and handed her a glass of wine. He picked up his beer and twisted the cap off, then took a long drink from the bottle before resting it on his forehead.

"Hell of a day," he said.

"Hell of a day," she echoed, sighing when the tart wine slid down her throat. "Thanks for arranging for us to stay here. It's a lovely spot." The apartment was exquisitely decorated, had every appliance she could want or need, and one of the best views she'd ever seen. *Lovely* was an inadequate word.

"It's not terrible," Jack said in his self-deprecating way, his words accompanied by a wry smile.

They sat down at the outdoor dining table and tucked into the pizza, content to sit in silence. After they'd eaten, Peyton leaned back in her chair and looked out to sea. "Jacinta gave me a message from Avangeline...your grandmother is offering me a guided tour of her art and sculpture collection."

Jack's eyebrows shot up. "Really? You're honored. She doesn't do that often."

So she'd heard. "Maybe it's because I have a degree in art history, or maybe she's still feeling guilty at how she treated me."

Jack grimaced. "Once Avangeline apologizes, she's done. The offer of a tour wouldn't be made out of guilt."

Good to know.

"Tell me about Simon and Keene," he said, running his finger up and down his beer bottle.

"Simon and I grew up together. He's been my best friend for all of my life."

"I don't remember him from when you were with Malcolm."

"That's because he was away at college and there wasn't

money for him to come home often. He's always felt so guilty for not being there for me when Malcolm died."

Simon still didn't know how much she'd needed him there, how alone she'd felt. Nate sat with the Granthams at the funeral, and Harry didn't attend. It had been the loneliest and hardest day of her life.

"I was thinking about Nate earlier," she told Jack. "Do you remember him?"

"Yes, of course I do. He and Mal were close," Jack answered.

"How is he? Where is he?" Peyton asked.

Jack frowned, then shrugged. "I have no idea. The last time I saw him was when we cleared Mal's stuff out of the apartment they shared in Tribeca. Coming back to your friends…" Right, they'd been talking about Simon and Keene. "Was their wedding the first time you returned to Hatfield?"

Peyton nodded. "I was their maid of honor. It was such a beautiful ceremony."

"You looked stunning that night."

Sweet of him to say, but she doubted that he remembered what she wore. Men weren't *that* observant. Jack's eyes met hers; they were an intense blue that took her breath away. "You don't believe me…"

"I believe you found me attractive," she said, choosing her words carefully.

"You wore a tight-fitting mint green dress, strapless, and beige-colored shoes with very high heels. Your hair was in a loose braid pinned up with tiny white roses."

Wow. He did remember. "I'd forgotten about the roses, and those shoes were hell to wear."

"I haven't forgotten anything about that night," Jack said, his voice turning growly as fire began to burn in his eyes.

"Not the way you smelled, not the way you kissed me, not the sound you made when you came."

Peyton swallowed and felt a warm buzz between her legs, and her nipples tightened against her T-shirt. He wanted her, and she wanted him too. She wanted to lose herself in his touch, bury her face in his neck and run her hands down his thighs as she took him in her mouth.

She wanted to be his lover, his muse, the entire focus of his world. Just for an hour, maybe two. She wanted to step outside her role of mommy and just feel, just *be*. To take pleasure and give it.

"How can I still want you so much?" she quietly asked him, holding her wineglass in a tight grip. "I see you and I *want*. It's…it's madness."

"You're not alone. I come within thirty feet of you, and all I can think about is backing you up to the nearest wall, stripping you down, hooking your legs over my hips and driving into you. I like control, but you make me lose it."

A taut, tense silence filled the space between them as they stared at each other, each wondering who would make the first move. They both knew where they were going and understood how this night would pan out. But as they allowed desire and lust, want and need the space to grow and expand, the anticipation was lovely.

"Are you coming to me or am I coming to you?" he asked after a lengthy silence.

"I think we should both just go to bed," Peyton told him, astounded by her forthrightness. She wasn't someone who stated what she wanted so openly and honestly, but she didn't want to play games with him. She was past that.

She didn't need anything but sex from him tonight. Tomorrow, the next day, a week from now, they could discuss Noah, child support and all the details about custody and parenting. Tonight she needed a lover. She needed someone to make her feel like a woman.

And nobody did that better than Jack. She needed *him*.

He stood up and held out his hand to her. She lifted her eyebrows and slid her hand into his, and he tugged her to her feet. He led her into the apartment and down the hallway, his hand wrapped firmly around hers, as if to keep her from bolting. There was no chance of that; she wasn't going anywhere.

In the lovely cream-and-duck-blue bedroom, complete with a king-size bed, Jack closed the door and turned to face her. In the light from the moon, coming in through the wide, open windows, she saw the concern on his face, in his eyes.

"Sleeping together is going to make our lives more complicated. Are you sure you want to do this?"

"Do you?" she challenged. What if he got cold feet? How would she be able to let him walk away?

He took her hand and placed it, palm down, on his long steel-hard erection. She sucked in a breath and her eyes flew to his face. He looked as if he was in pain, as if he had to restrain himself from bursting out of his skin. "Does that answer your question?"

Oh, yeah.

"You didn't answer mine," Jack told her, keeping her hand pressed against his cock. She slid her thumb over its tip and relished his harsh gasp.

"More than I want to keep breathing," Peyton told him. *Too much? Why can't I just say yes like a normal person?*

He moved in a blur of power, yanking her to him and covering her mouth with his. His tongue slid past her teeth, and Peyton could taste his need and want there as he twisted it around hers. He yanked her T-shirt up and covered her back with his hands, palming her butt and pulling her into him so that her stomach pushed into his erection. Then he boosted her up, and her legs encircled his hips. She slammed her core against his length, rocking herself against him, loving the feeling of the fabric of her panties against her wetness as he pushed into her.

It had been so long, and she didn't know if she could hold on. She was going to come just like this. Right damn now.

"Oh, no you don't," Jack growled, as he walked her over to the bed and lowered her down to the mattress. "I want you naked when you come for me again."

She watched as he stripped down, yanking his shirt up and over his head and pushing his shorts and underwear down. A light layer of hair covered his chest and arrowed down his ridged stomach into his groin. His shaft looked hard and thick and bigger than she remembered.

All the moisture in her mouth disappeared. They were doing this...

Peyton sat on her knees and stroked her hands over his chest, down his stomach, encircling his hardness with her hands, her thumb rubbing his tip. Jack closed his eyes, and she heard his raspy breathing as she stroked him, her touches becoming firmer. He bucked into her hands, his movements coming faster with each stroke, and she watched, fascinated, as his eyes turned from ink to cobalt blue, lightened by the heat of desire.

There was such power here, and making a man like him—strong, powerful, utterly masculine—pant with need was an amazing feeling. She'd never felt as feminine as she did now; it was as if she held the combined power and knowledge of generations of muses, witches and wisewomen.

Jack released a huge sigh and bent down, forcing her to release him. She narrowed her eyes in displeasure, as she was enjoying touching him, but her annoyance soon

faded when he placed his mouth on hers and fed her a su-
percharged kiss. He broke away from her mouth so that he
could pull her shirt over her head, and returned to feeding
her drugging kisses as he pulled her pants down her legs.
Needing to be completely naked, she fumbled with the clasp
of her bra. Jack batted her hands away and twisted it open
with one hand. He pulled the lacy fabric away and immediately dropped his mouth to her breast, pulling her nipple
deep into his mouth. She held the back of his head as rib-
bons of concentrated pleasure rocketed through her, heating
the space between her legs, drenching her with moisture.

As if reading her thoughts, Jack's hand delved between
her legs, and his eyes flew up to meet hers, wonder in his
gaze. "You're soaking."

There wasn't any point in pretending. "I want you. I want
you *now*."

She just needed him inside her, and she knew she'd come.

Jack released a deep groan, placed his hands on either
side of her head and nudged her legs open with his knee.
He lowered himself and positioned his cock at her entrance.
"It's not going to be pretty," he said, warning Peyton.

She didn't want pretty, she wanted him. Now. Unable to
wait, she launched her hips, and he slid inside her in a long,
hard stroke, burying himself inside her as deep as he could
go. Peyton saw stars and they both froze, as if unable to believe that being joined could feel this good. It was a cliché,
but having him inside her made her feel complete, as if he
were the puzzle piece she'd been missing. Her body recognized his and seemed to sigh and say, "Welcome home."

But behind recognition, need rolled in, hot and desperate. "Jack, *now*."

He didn't hesitate and plunged into her, correctly assuming that she was there with him, reading her body in the way

only he could. He slid his hand under her butt and tipped her up, changing the angle, and then he was deeper inside her, if that was at all possible. Then he hit her sweet spot, the one that had her head thrashing on the pillow and her body weeping with joy.

Peyton felt outside of herself, carried away on a band of pure pleasure, as if she were operating at a higher, deeper, darker frequency. Her body was his, and for now, he could do what he liked with it. As long as he…

Kept.

Doing.

That.

Light pulsed behind her eyes. She stiffened and dug her nails into the skin of his butt so hard that she knew she'd leave half-moon marks. She didn't care. She needed to…

Needed to…

She released a keening sound as her body splintered into shards of pure sensation and rainbow-colored crystals. Waves of intense pleasure rolled through her, higher and higher, until they body-slammed her, shattering her again. She heard Jack's groan, then he stiffened, and she felt him pulse inside her.

After a few minutes—or a week or possibly a millennium; time had lost all meaning—Peyton started to gather her pieces and stitch herself back together. She could only take shallow breaths because Jack's weight pushed her into the mattress. With his face buried in her neck, and his hand still beneath her butt, their bodies felt welded together.

In the distance, she heard waves crashing against the beach. The tide had turned and was rolling in.

Jack pushed himself up and looked down at her, his eyes a little foggy and quite bemused. "Holy shit," he whispered. "What was that?"

She lifted a heavy hand and pulled a strand of hair off her cheek. "I have no idea."

He rolled off her, sat on the side of the bed and looked down. Peyton was about to touch his back, when he stiffened. She pulled back her hand and sat up. Something was wrong. They'd just had earth-rocking sex. What had happened between then and now?

He looked back at her and pulled a face. "Crap, Pey."

She jerked upright. Was he having regrets? So soon? Jeez, not even five minutes had passed. He could, at the very least, enjoy the afterglow. "Are you having second thoughts already?"

"I don't regret making love to you, Peyton. It was fantastic. I thought the sex we shared two years ago was unbelievable, but that, whatever that was, blew it out of the water."

Then why did he look as if she'd just kicked a kitten? "Then what's the problem?"

"We failed to use protection."

Oh...damn.

Peyton lay on Jack's chest and yawned, enjoying the sensation of his fingertips massaging her scalp. They'd cleaned up, and after ascertaining that neither of them had any condoms, had indulged in highly erotic oral sex, making each other orgasm using their hands and mouths. Feeling hot and sticky, they'd jumped into the shower, and after Peyton had checked on Noah, she'd climbed back into bed with him and rested her head against his chest.

"Is there any chance of you getting pregnant again?" Jack asked.

She wrinkled her nose and counted days in her head. "It's very unlikely," she told him. "But if you are worried, I can pick up a Plan B in the morning."

He shook his head. "Not if you don't think it's necessary. But will you tell me this time if you are?"

She looked up at him and nodded. "Of course I will," she assured him. "I know what it's like to raise one baby alone, there's no way I'd cope with two."

His arm tightened as he pulled her closer to him. "Looking after him on your own must've been so hard, Pey."

So hard, but she'd managed. She was stronger than she knew, as she now realized. Aside from losing Noah, she didn't think there was much life could throw at her that she couldn't work through. "I managed. We all do, I guess."

She pulled her attention back to their all-consuming desire, which had clearly bypassed their brains. She looked up at him and frowned. "How can we, two responsible adults, forget to use contraception, Jack? That's insane."

He stroked his hand down her naked butt. "I have no damn idea. All I know is that once I kiss you, all rational thought goes out the window."

That happened to her too, but they couldn't keep taking chances. "If we can't remember to use condoms, then we need to make another plan." She grimaced. She assumed he wanted to keep sleeping with her. Maybe he didn't. "Is sleeping with me something you want to do again?"

He looked at her as if she'd just fallen out of a mango tree. "Uh...*yeah.*"

Yay! Then they needed to get smart about protection. She'd been meaning to get an IUD fitted, and maybe this was the time. Did protection start immediately? She'd have to research that. But if it didn't, then they'd simply have to remember to use a condom.

"Maybe this is a good time to discuss expectations," Jack said, his voice low and slow.

Ugh. She didn't want to.

Peyton pulled herself off his chest and sat up, reaching for her tank top, which still lay on the bottom of the bed. There was no way she could have this conversation naked. She'd met him again two days ago. She didn't know how she felt about him or the future or anything else. She just wanted to sleep with him again.

Was that too much to ask?

Jack placed his hand on her knee. "Sex with you is astoundingly good, Peyton, but right now, that's all it is."

Well, yes. *Obviously.*

"We have a lot to work through with Noah, we have a future to plan, but that future doesn't include rings and pre-nup agreements."

She jerked back, unable to believe that he assumed she wanted something permanent. After just a couple of hours in bed? God, could he be more arrogant if he tried?

"Do all of your lovers demand a wedding ring or some level of permanence after one sexual encounter?" she demanded, irked.

He winced. "One or two have," he said.

"Jeez." Peyton pushed her hands into her hair and raked it back. "Relax, Jack. I know the difference between love and sexual attraction, and I won't be asking you for anything more than this. I don't believe in love anyway."

"You don't?" he asked, surprised. "Why not?"

She shook her head and shrugged. When she started to get up, he pressed down on her knee, silently asking her to stay. "You and Malcolm loved each other."

"I was nineteen, Jack, far too young to know what love was. And he didn't love me."

Jack frowned at her. "Why do you think that?"

"Because he didn't *know* me, Jack! He didn't know anything about me! I was so desperate to please him, and please my father, that I was their echo chamber. I thought that by agreeing with them, they'd love me more. I parroted their views, their opinions, their tastes. It was only after I left Hatfield that I started forming my own opinions, my loves and hates, and goals and plans."

Jack rubbed his jaw. "I never knew that."

She shrugged. "Avangeline was right the other day, Jack. I still don't know what he saw in me. I was so much younger and so damn naive. I don't understand what we had, what it was."

Jack rubbed the back of his neck. "I wish I could help you out, but Malcolm and I weren't that close. He was my older brother, and I suppose, like the others, I worshipped him because he was so big and bold and intense. I loved him, but I don't know that I knew him. I don't know if anyone did."

"He didn't let anyone in. You could dig, but then you hit this solidly hard barrier, and that was it, you couldn't go any further. And if you pushed, he punished you by ignoring you," Peyton mused.

"He was a complicated guy," Jack said.

"And I was too young and too naive to do complicated," Peyton told him. "Anyway, we were talking about you and me, not Malcolm. So, yes, I know that this is just a sexual attraction. You can relax."

"Relaxed is the last thing I feel around you," Jack told her as he placed his hands on her hips and easily lifted her so that she straddled his thighs. Her core hit his erection, and he immediately hardened. Peyton moved up and down him, closing her eyes as pleasure skittered over her skin.

She wondered what the chances were of Jack doing a condom run...

Eight

Jack's feet pounded the hard sand of the beach and his heartbeat inched up, his lungs screaming for more air. His thigh muscles burned, and perspiration ran down his bare chest as he dodged an incoming wave. Running along the beach was damn hard work, but it was an excellent workout, and he needed the exercise to blow the cobwebs from his mind.

He glanced at his state-of-the-art watch, thinking that he could run for another fifteen minutes, but then he needed to hit his desk. He needed to focus on exposing Avangeline's blackmailer and he had a pile of work to catch up on, work that he'd been neglecting over the past ten days because he'd spent the majority of his time with Peyton and Noah, getting to know his son.

And his son's mommy.

Over the last week and a bit, he and Peyton had settled into this weird friends-by-day, lovers-by-night dynamic. When the sun was out and they were around others, she treated him like a platonic friend. At night, she turned voracious, unable to get enough of him and their lovemaking. They made love often, sometimes two or three times a night, and he was, frankly, exhausted.

He didn't know if he could keep up at this pace. No, he knew he couldn't. But he couldn't stay away from Peyton's bed either. And every night after he helped Peyton feed, bathe and put Noah to bed—he'd started reading to his son as well—they usually ate together, meals she made or he ordered in, before retreating to the bedroom.

Sometimes, they didn't even make it that far and they used whatever flat—or vertical—surface they found. It was madness, complete insanity, but the intensity of their passion seemed to be deepening.

He'd be dead by the end of the month.

And man, if his brothers heard him complaining about his fantastically hot and inventive sex life, they'd kick his ass. He was having stunning, frequent, no-complications sex with a gorgeous woman. What was there to complain about?

Well, and yes, he was nitpicking, but he didn't like the fact that Peyton could draw the line so very easily between sex and their friendship. He did that, was good at it—he knew he was being outrageously hypocritical—but he didn't like that she could switch off her emotions with such skill. Jack scowled at a seagull sitting on a log that he was passing and wondered if he was, actually, starting to lose his mind.

He didn't want anything more from Peyton; what they had right now was perfect. She wasn't demanding commitment from him, wasn't talking about the future in anything but in the most general terms. And he had yet to broach the subject of her and Noah moving to New York City. He'd been putting that off because he hadn't wanted to do or say anything that would impact their fun-filled days and hot nights.

Right now, his life was perfect.

But perfect never lasted, and soon enough, real life would intrude, and things would start to sour. And when they did, he'd find himself getting itchy and antsy, and the need to free himself of a relationship would rise. It would start with vague comments from a tiny voice that would grow in intensity, becoming louder every damn day, telling him that he needed to get out, that he needed to look somewhere else for the perfect life and relationship. The voice would say that there was someone better out there, someone who could give him more. Someone perfect.

That Peyton wasn't what he needed long-term.

And he was adult enough, rational enough, to know that nobody was. He was looking for something unattainable, something indescribable, something unreal, because his father said that was what he should do. After all, he had never felt good enough for the Grantham family. Malcolm had been charismatic and bold, Fox was intellectually brilliant and he was...*there*. Jack was smart enough, athletic enough, charming enough, but not quite as brilliant as his brothers.

He'd had to carve out a role for himself, and he became the driven businessman, the family troubleshooter. He was the one who dived in and made things right, who tried to perfect everything imperfect.

But chasing perfect was so damn lonely. He hadn't known how lonely he was until his little boy fell asleep with his head on his chest or until he woke up to Peyton cheerfully telling Noah how loved he was and how he was the best little boy in the world. Sometimes he could hear her words, and sometimes just the tone of her voice conveyed how in love she was with her—*their*—son.

He wanted to be loved like that, wanted it beyond description, but he was too much of a coward to try to find it, to risk his heart.

Frustrated with himself and his wayward thoughts, Jack kept pounding the sand, focused on Avangeline and her blackmailer, thinking that he'd neglected his grandmother's problem and the reason he'd relocated to Hatfield. But, frankly, he didn't know where to start. There was no way to trace the postcards, and the emails Avangeline first received had come from a fake email address. Ru, Fox's fiancée, who had some hacking skills, had traced the IP addresses to internet cafés—two in Pakistan, three in Cyprus, one in Kansas City—which were a dead end because they couldn't isolate an address. The blackmailer's demands hadn't wavered.

She had to keep making regular purchases of cryptocurrency, and on her death, he was demanding that she leave a substantial sum to a Cayman Islands–based company, owner unknown. If she didn't acquiesce, the identity of her longtime lover and the facts surrounding his parents' ownership of a sex club would be revealed.

He couldn't allow that to happen.

But he didn't know where to start to track down Avangeline's extortionist. Who could've stumbled across such highly confidential and intimate knowledge about his grandmother and his parents? Who had been around back then? Who could've accessed that knowledge?

He dialed Fox using his Bluetooth earbuds. He didn't have the time or energy to fight with his brother and, after telling him he'd castrate him if he kept anything from him again, tossed those questions at him.

Fox didn't answer immediately, and Jack had to listen to the sound of his coffee maker dispensing espresso. He slowed down to a walk, giving his heart time to slow down. He could murder a cup of coffee.

"I've been thinking the same thing," Fox replied. "Who are our possible suspects? Tommy firstly."

Tommy, whom Fox had met, had been the manager of the sex club and the face of the business. But there was no way Tommy could know about Avangeline's lover and the postcards. Not only did he live in the Bronx, but there was no way the former addict would have crossed paths with the superrich Avangeline, who kept her social circle small.

"Our grandfather?" Jack mused.

Their paternal grandfather was a viable suspect, but the man was wealthy beyond belief—thanks to a massive divorce settlement Avangeline paid him thirty years ago—and had enough to last for several lifetimes. And while he hated Avangeline with a passion, he'd adored Jesse, their father, and worshipped his memory. Even if he knew about The Basement, Fox thought there was no way he'd leak that information to the press.

"What about Avangeline's butler, the guy who Jace replaced?" Jack snapped his fingers, trying to remember his name.

"Larchmont? I checked. He died about seven years ago. He had dementia."

Jack released a frustrated growl. "Damn it. Did he have any kids?"

"Ru is trying to track them down," Fox replied. "Talking about kids, when am I going to meet my nephew?"

On hearing about Noah, and unable to keep the news to himself, he'd placed a video call to his brothers and told them that they were uncles, worried about how they'd take the news that he'd slept with their brother's ex-fiancée. They'd been thrilled to hear about Noah, and no one had mentioned Peyton's relationship with Mal. Or their one-night stand. He wondered why. His brothers were never shy about voicing their opinions.

"Do you think it's weird that I hooked up with Peyton?"

he asked Fox, whom he could rely on to tell him the unfiltered truth.

Fox didn't reply, and Jack heard him shuffling papers on his desk. "Fox?"

"You know what, I *don't* think it is weird. Is it weird that I don't think it's weird?"

Jack took a moment to untangle his words.

"Peyton and Malcolm seem like a dream, like something that didn't happen," Fox continued.

But it did. They'd been engaged. "What are you trying to say, Fox?"

Fox released a deep sigh. "I was talking to Ru about this the other night. Damn, I wish she was here so that she could explain what I mean. She'd say it so much better than me."

"Well, she's not—she's in Australia," Jack snapped. "Just spit it out, Fox."

"The more I think about and remember that time, the more I remember that their dynamic was weird. Malcolm was over-the-top crazy about her. It was like he was trying to convince us how perfect they were together, how much he loved her. He never spoke about any of his girlfriends like that. I sometimes wonder if he was trying to convince himself."

"Funny, Peyton said the same thing the other night. That she thought he loved the idea of her more than the reality. Or something like that."

"Of all of us, Malcolm was the one who liked to look at life through rose-colored glasses. He wasn't a fan of reality, and he lost it when I told him about our parents and The Basement."

Jack braked, every muscle in his body tensing. "Malcolm knew about The Basement?" he asked, shocked.

"Yes, I told you that I told him."

"No, you damn well did not," Jack retorted.

"Didn't I? I thought I did," Fox said.

"When did you tell him?" Jack gripped the bridge of his nose and squeezed.

"Probably only a week or two after he and Harry had their dustup," Fox replied.

Jack explained that he wasn't sure there had been a dustup and that Malcolm had told them and Peyton two different stories about his and Harry's fight.

"Huh," Fox said. "He was as mad as a snake when I told him about our parents, and I had to force him to take the folder containing the copies of the documents I'd gathered on them. He took it, but assured me that he wouldn't open it."

"There are documents? Like, solid proof?" Jack asked.

"Sure. Copies of ownership of the building and the company's founding documents. The terms and conditions of the sex-play in The Basement, emails and text messages between our parents, and copies of the newsletters they sent out to the club's members. They had a newsletter, for God's sake! It was solid proof."

"Where are those documents now, Fox?" Jack asked, his words machine-gun fast.

Fox took a long time to answer him. "Well, the originals are locked away in my safe. Mal's copies? That's a helluva good question, Jack. I don't know."

"Then I suggest we find out," Jack replied grimly.

I think we should try and reset our relationship. Can we meet?

Peyton looked down at her phone and frowned at the message. This was the third one she'd received from Harry this week—she wanted to murder the person who gave him her number!—and just another one she'd ignore.

Sitting on the lounger next to the outdoor pool, she watched as Jack skimmed Noah across the surface of the pool, both their faces wreathed in smiles. Noah adored water, and if she could stay in Hatfield, she knew she'd have to get him water safe as soon as possible. Well, she'd do that no matter where they ended up. She added swimming lessons to her mental to-do list. Where she'd find the time to do that in Chicago, though, God only knew.

Her heart sank to her toes every time she thought about their fast-approaching move. She'd secured an apartment and a day care for Noah—both of which she'd confirm when she arrived in the city—but she was dreading leaving Simon and Keene and Calcott Manor. Avangeline adored Noah, but from a distance. She had no idea how to relate to babies. Jacinta, on the other hand, had slid into her role as Noah's grandmother as a baby duck took to water. She was now one of Noah's favorite people, and Peyton trusted her implicitly. Partly because, alongside Avangeline, she'd raised four boys and because, despite liking Jace ten years ago, she now felt a deep and instant connection to the woman Jack considered his mother.

Jack's brothers had also met Noah, and he now had three extra bodyguards, not that he needed any with his doting dad in his life.

She couldn't keep dancing around what she didn't want to consider. She didn't want to go to Chicago, because she was going to miss Jack. Horribly. She'd been acting her ass off these past couple of weeks, knowing she couldn't allow him to suspect that she was head-over-heels crazy for him. She knew that if she gave him the slightest hint that her emotions had come out to play, he'd bolt. The only way they could work was if they kept the lines between them carefully delineated, so she played it cool...

All.

The.

Damn.

Time.

Acting was exhausting, and Peyton was quite sure she'd earned herself a couple of Emmys and an Oscar nomination. She didn't know if she was in love with Jack, but she was certain she wanted him in Noah's life and wanted him in hers. For the longest possible time.

Simply…forever.

Noah let out a little squeal of delight, and Peyton turned around to see what had caught his attention. She smiled when she saw Jace walking toward them, carrying a pitcher of lemonade and two glasses. Noah shouted at Jack to let him go, and Jack walked through the shallow end to put him on his feet. Their little boy hurtled toward Jace, wrapping his arms around her thighs and plastering his wet body against her legs.

Peyton got up and rescued the pitcher and glasses, and Jace, unfazed by the wet bundle, swung Noah up into her arms. He rested his head on her chest, his eyes drooping a little.

"I can take him up to the house and give him some lunch," Jace suggested. "Then I'll put him down for a nap."

Peyton looked at Jace and bit her bottom lip. "That's kind of you, Jace, but you've had him a lot lately, and I don't want you to feel like I'm taking advantage of you."

Jace smiled and shook her head. Peyton noticed the blue smudges under her eyes, and that her eyes held a fair dose of unhappiness. She placed her hand on Jace's arm. "Are you okay?" she asked, keeping her voice low.

Jace nodded and smiled, but Peyton noticed that her wattage had dimmed. "I'm fine. I'm enjoying this little guy, and

I want to get as much time with him before you move to Chicago." She kissed Noah's head and pulled a face.

"Why are you moving to Chicago again?" she asked.

"It's a little thing called a job," Peyton replied dryly.

"I keep offering to pay her enough support so that she could stick around, but she won't consider it," Jack said, looking straight at her. His forearms rested on the side of the pool, and he'd slicked his hair back. His beard glinted with gold in the sunlight, and his eyes were a brilliant blue.

How was she supposed to walk away when he looked at her like that?

"Every girl needs a measure of independence, Jack," Jace told him.

"I just wish she didn't have to be independent in Chicago," Jack muttered.

She'd applied for jobs in New York, but none of the institutions had invited her for an interview. "You find me a job in New York, and I'll take it," she told Jack.

He nodded. "Will do."

He turned and swam to the other end of the pool, and as Jacinta walked away with Noah, she wondered whether he'd taken her words seriously. Would he use his power and influence to find her a job? And if he did, how would she feel about that? Could she take it, knowing that it was nepotism, knowing that she hadn't interviewed for the position and hadn't jumped through enough hoops? She wanted to say that she'd categorically refuse such an offer, that she was better than that, but she didn't want to leave the East Coast. She hated the idea of Jack being half in and half out of Noah's life.

Her life.

Her phone beeped again with another message from her

dad—Well, what do you say?—and Peyton frowned. Why was Harry pushing this? Why now?

"Everything okay?" Jack asked, pulling a towel off the back of the lounger and wrapping it around his hips. He reached for the jug of lemonade and filled two glasses with the icy liquid, then passed one to Peyton.

Peyton wrinkled her nose and crossed one leg over the other. "My father is pressuring me to reset our relationship."

"What does that mean?" Jack asked, sitting down on the lounger next to her.

"To be honest, I have no idea," Peyton replied. "I haven't had any contact with him since Malcolm died, and within a couple of days of hearing that you are Noah's dad—it's all over Hatfield by the way—"

Jack shrugged, unconcerned, and Peyton continued. "—he's pushing to reconnect with me. And Noah."

"And you are skeptical about his motives?"

"Wouldn't you be?" Peyton replied. "In ten years, he's never reached out to me once, but as soon as I realign myself with the Grantham family, he wants back in my life."

Jack placed his hands behind him on the lounger and leaned back. To anyone else, he looked like a surfer boy taking a break, but Peyton saw the intelligence flickering in his eyes, and she knew he was turning her words over and looking for an answer.

"Why didn't he attend Mal's funeral?" Jack asked.

Peyton shrugged. "He'd moved on," she replied. "From Mal and from me."

"Can you explain that?"

"Harry was never interested in me, and my mom's death was terribly inconvenient. He was left with a kid to raise, and he hated being responsible for me. But from the moment I started dating Malcolm, his attitude toward me changed.

He became this doting, interested, wonderful human being who loved and adored me. I'd never had that amount of love and attention from him before, and I relished it. It was completely wonderful. And Malcolm treated me like this princess, like I was made of spun sugar, and placed me on this pedestal. I rather liked being adored."

"Don't we all?" Jack murmured.

"But then it came crashing down. Malcolm and Harry had their falling-out, and Mal told me that I had to choose. He wanted me to divorce myself from my father. Believing that my loyalty should be to him, Harry demanded that I support him. I asked Malcolm for some time, and he took that to mean that I was breaking up with him. I never said or meant that. I just wanted some time."

Now that she was this far in, she may as well tell him the rest. "After the funeral, Harry's attitude toward me did a three-sixty. He went back to being cold and unemotional and uninterested. I wasn't going to be part of the Grantham family, so I was no use to him anymore. I felt…" She gulped, remembering feeling as if she'd been eviscerated with a teaspoon. "I felt lost and confused and so damn alone. All I ever wanted was for him to notice and love me, to be a dad, you know?"

Jack placed his hand on the center of her back, and Peyton blinked back tears.

"I still don't understand how everything went so badly so quickly. I still feel like something was happening offstage, that there was some subtext that no one explained to me."

Jack narrowed his eyes. "Maybe there was, Peyton. Maybe there's something you're missing, something we're both missing about what happened back then."

She looked at him, puzzled. "What are you trying to say, Jack?"

He swiped a hand over his beard. "As you said, his timing is suspect. You've been back in town for weeks before I arrived, so why didn't Harry contact you then to make amends? Why does he want to reengage only after he's heard that I'm Noah's dad? If this isn't about you, and sorry, sweetheart, but it's not about you—" Yeah, she understood that, and it hurt like hell. Harry was her father, but she wasn't naive enough to believe that he had changed his spots. "—why does he want a connection to the Granthams? What will he gain?"

She shrugged. "I don't know."

Jack put his arm around her shoulders and gave her a quick squeeze. "Maybe it's time we had a chat with Harry, Pey. Maybe it's time to get some answers."

He was right. She wanted to be able to look at the past clearly and then put it behind her. She was so sick of feeling as if she had a part in the play, but that her script was in Ancient Greek.

She refused to be a passive player in her life.

Jack furrowed his brow. He was holding back about something.

"What's going on, Jack? What aren't you telling me?"

His eyes met hers, and she saw chagrin and determination and a hint of fear. "Quite a bit, Pey." His broad bare chest rose and fell before he stood up and held out his hand to her. "Can you give me some time to think, to sort some things out in my head before I explain? There's some family stuff going on, and I need to work out what I can tell you and what I can't."

His words were a sharp reminder that, despite being the mother of his child, she wasn't a Grantham or a part of their inner circle. She couldn't be fully trusted. Peyton faced him, thinking that this was the way it would always be; she'd always have one foot inside the circle.

Good enough for some things, not good enough for others.

"I'm raising your kid, Jack, and if you trust me to do that, then you should be able to trust me with *everything*, because he should be your most important priority. If you decide to talk to me, then you either trust me with everything or nothing at all. I'm not nineteen anymore, and I won't be kept in the dark."

Nine

He'd hurt her, something he'd never intended to do. *But how can I just blurt out my family secrets?* Jack asked himself as he walked across the green lawn that separated Calcott Manor's main house from the garage apartment. His parents had the reputation of being one of America's perfect couples, as golden as the sun, beautiful and brilliant and besotted. And only he and his brothers—and his grandmother's blackmailer—knew about the dark undercurrents that had swirled through their world.

How did he tell her that his family had been anything but perfect, that what the world thought of them was a million miles away from what they were? Would she understand? Could he trust her? Did he have a choice?

Somehow, he didn't know how, but Harry was connected to whatever was going on now. It was too much of a coincidence that as soon as he returned to Hatfield and showed his face, rumors started to swirl that he was Noah's father. And shortly after that, Harry wanted to revive his relationship with Peyton. Something was very out of whack, and he suspected that Harry, Malcolm and the past had a bearing on what was happening now. Could Harry be Avangeline's blackmailer? He was narcissistic enough and didn't have a moral compass, so it was possible.

Anything was possible.

But, damn it, he couldn't connect Harry to the postcards; there was no way he could know about them.

Jack raked his hand through his hair, frustrated. Was he trying to make connections that weren't there? Was he conflating two different issues because he was furious at Harry for being such a terrible father, for hurting Peyton so deeply? He'd heard the devastation in her voice. It had been covered by a layer of bravado, but he'd caught it. All she'd wanted was to be loved, to feel loved…

Didn't they all? Didn't everyone want someplace to put their emotions, someone who they could trust with all the ugly bits of themselves? He had that, to an extent, with his brothers. Soren, Merrick and Fox knew him inside out. They knew when to call him out for his mistakes and, in hard times, when to bolster him up with encouragement. He trusted them implicitly to have his back, and he knew he would never have to go through life or take on the world on his own.

It seemed as if Peyton had done that all her life. Well, she wasn't alone anymore—she had him, and through him, the backing of his family. But if she was part of the family, then she needed to know the whole truth, not just bits of it.

He hauled in a breath. He needed to tell her about the blackmail attempt on Avangeline, about his parents' past, about the postcards. He had no choice. On a practical level, he needed to talk to Harry, and he couldn't do that without involving Peyton. Harry held a piece of this puzzle. He just knew it.

But he also wanted to tell her because, yes, he heard what she'd said this afternoon. She was raising his son, a baby boy who was infinitely precious to him. If he could trust her with Noah's well-being—emotional, physical and spiritual—then he should be able to trust her with everything else.

He wanted to open up, he *needed* to. Having his brothers' support was great, but having Peyton's would be...

Amazing. Life-affirming. Goddamn wonderful.

Jack jogged up the outside steps of the apartment and, after briefly knocking on the door, stepped into the living area. It was uncharacteristically silent, and Jack looked at his watch. She normally bathed Noah around this time, and then she read to him, and both were tasks he'd started sharing with her. But only silence greeted him.

His heart climbed up his throat, threatening to choke him. Had she left? Was she that annoyed with him that she'd returned to Hatfield and taken their son with her? No, she wouldn't do that, she wouldn't leave without telling him where she was going.

Taking a deep breath and pushing back his panic, Jack walked down the hallway and pushed open the door to Noah's room, frowning when he saw his freshly made bed. Turning, he noticed that the door to the master bedroom had been left half-ajar. He pushed it open, and there they were, both fast asleep, an open book lying on the bed beside them. Noah's cheek rested on Peyton's chest, and her temple was on his head, her long eyelashes golden against her slightly freckled cheeks.

So beautiful, he thought as he leaned his shoulder into the doorframe of the bedroom, content to just look at them. They simply made sense. They looked right.

And they would look better in his life permanently, on

a wake-up-and-see-you and hold-you-at-night basis. He couldn't let them relocate to Chicago—they belonged with him.

Was this love? He didn't need to answer the question about Noah; of course it was. It couldn't be anything else. But did he love Peyton? Maybe, possibly…

But he'd loved other women before, perhaps not as quickly or as deeply, and they'd never worked out. Something always came up because he was constantly looking for mistakes, looking for an out, looking for a reason why the relationship—or the woman—wasn't perfect. He used his search for perfection as a barrier to getting hurt. Whenever he felt too much, he looked for faults and errors to justify pushing women away so they couldn't hurt him.

Maybe it was time he stopped doing that, stopped chasing perfect. Maybe he should let people be as they were. Maybe he should plant his feet and take a chance. He could have a family with Peyton, something he desperately wanted. He'd done the man-about-town, sleep-his-way-through-the-city thing, and now he wanted more. Peyton was special, always had been, and he was halfway to being in love with her.

Stick. Stay. Try to make this work, and for God's sake, don't run.

Panic and fear welled up inside him. What if he handed over his heart and she cheated on him, decided he wasn't what she wanted? Took Noah and bolted?

Yeah, but what if she didn't? What if they made a life together, had a few more kids and raised an amazing family? What if *that* happened?

His stomach released one of its knots, then another. He wasn't going to let her go, not without a fight. He'd be fighting himself, fighting long-ingrained habits, but he was up to the challenge. Peyton, the possibility of what they could have—could be—was worth it.

He straightened and walked over to the bed and skimmed his mouth across Peyton's forehead. She stirred as he lifted Noah from her arms and blinked once, then again, looking like a lovely, bemused owl.

"Hey," she murmured.

He adjusted his grip on Noah and looked down to see that his son hadn't stirred. "Let me put him in his bed," he whispered.

"I fed him and he's had his bath," Peyton murmured, her eyes closing again.

"I've got him, sweetheart. Go back to sleep."

"'Kay," Peyton said and rolled over onto her side, her eyes closing. Jack smiled, and his eyes moved from her to Noah and back again. She wouldn't be able to fall asleep like that if she didn't trust him with her most precious treasure: her son.

Maybe it was time he reciprocated her trust.

Peyton woke up around nine, and after washing her face and checking on Noah, who was fast asleep in his bed, she walked through the dimly lit apartment. She stopped in the living room, wondering if Jack was still around, or whether he'd gone back to Calcott Manor. She noticed the open doors to the balcony and walked onto the deck, sighing as the warm night enveloped her. Jack sat at the wooden dining table, his laptop in front of him and wire-rimmed glasses perched on his nose. A glass of white wine sat next to his elbow.

"Jack," she said, her voice still raspy with sleep.

He looked up and smiled. It warmed her from the inside out, making her feel both sexy and safe. In Jack's presence, she felt wanted. His was the smile, the face, she wanted to look at for the rest of her life.

"Did you have a good nap?" Jack asked as he stood up. He pulled off his glasses and dropped them onto the table.

"Mmm," Peyton replied as he walked over to her. She sighed happily when he dragged his mouth across hers. "I don't know why I'm so tired."

"It could be that we only got a few hours of sleep last night before our monster woke us up at six," he told her, pulling her into his body. She felt his semihard erection, and it stiffened further with the pressure of her stomach. It didn't matter that they'd spent half of last night making love and the nights before that doing the same, she wanted him now, *immediately.*

Peyton hooked her arm around his neck and stood up on her tiptoes, then she placed her lips on his, her tongue coming out to swipe the seam of his mouth. He groaned and opened his mouth, his tongue winding around hers. Heat and need flashed through her, and she dropped her hands to undo the buttons of his shirt. Pushing aside the fabric, she dragged her fingers across his chest, over his nipples, and pushed them between the band of his shorts and his skin.

Jack sucked in a breath as she touched the tip of his length. Frustrated by the barrier of his clothes and blown away by the need to touch him and taste him, she sat down on the nearest chair and pulled him so that he faced her, her eyes aligned with his lower abdomen. She looked up at him as she pulled his belt buckle apart.

"Is this okay with you?" she asked him.

"Very okay." His words were accompanied by a low, slow groan. Slowly—far more slowly than she needed to— she pulled down his zipper and pushed his shorts down his hips. His erection strained the fabric of his Calvin Kleins.

She nuzzled his shaft with her nose, caught up in the scent of fresh laundry and hot man.

"Peyton…"

Jack pushed his underwear down his hips, and his erection sprang free. But instead of taking him in his mouth as she knew he wanted her to, she dropped tiny kisses up and down him, sucking and nibbling at his skin, ignoring his tip. She felt his fingertips digging into her hair and heard his groans, but she didn't want to stop exploring him, taking her time, because she was enjoying getting to know him in such an intimate way. She cupped his scrotum, felt him tense and heard his plea to take him into her mouth.

Smiling at the desperate note she heard in his voice, she folded her lips around his tip, sucking gently.

"Take me deeper," Jack told her, and Peyton allowed him to slide over her tongue, sucking him as hard as she could. She couldn't believe that giving pleasure, hearing him pant and moan, could be such a turn-on. Without pulling her mouth away, she pushed her shorts down her thighs, needing to touch herself. She slid her fingers under the band of her panties and found her clit, closing her eyes as pleasure speared through her.

He was close and she was too. A few more slides of her fingers, a couple more sucks, and he'd…

In one fluid movement, he pulled out of her mouth, pushed her back on the lounger and swatted her hand away. He pulled her panties to one side, and, lowering himself down, he slid into her fluidly, filling her, pushing inside her as far as he could go.

He maneuvered his fingers between their bodies, stroked her clitoris, and she launched her hips up, slamming into him as she came, colors dropping like a glitter ball in her mind.

Jack placed both hands on the lounger next to her head

and pumped his hips, long fluid strokes that didn't match his tortured groans. He made it to two, maybe three—who cared?—and he tensed, releasing a low roar in her ear as he pumped his seed against her cervix. She thought she was done, but his undoing, his lack of control, had her spiraling up again. She ground herself against him, and he drove into her with renewed intensity, dragging another orgasm from her, not as bright or as bountiful as the first, but still amazing. And unexpected.

Multiple orgasms? Yes, please.

After taking a quick shower, Peyton pulled on boy-cut pajama shorts and a tank top and returned to the balcony to find a plate of chicken salad and an icy glass of white wine on a place setting at the table.

After thanking Jack, she popped a baby tomato in her mouth. "Are you not eating?"

"I ate earlier," he told her, sitting down opposite her. He yawned and grinned. "Holy hell, woman, you exhaust me."

"That was rather intense," she admitted.

"You nearly blew my head off," Jack said after taking a large sip of his wine. "Both of them."

She grinned, pleased with herself. Would sex between them always be this good? Or would they, in a week, or a month, or a year, stop thinking that the world would come to a screeching stop if they didn't take each other *right now*? Did other people have this crazy need, this ability to look at each other and only see want? She didn't know, and she was too scared to ask. Were they special or normal? And why was he the only man who could set her alight with a look?

She speared a piece of chicken and lifted it to her mouth with some lettuce, forcing herself to eat, and to think. Right now, all they had was Noah and good sex. They might have a crazy need for each other, but that was just their libidos going haywire. It didn't mean anything, could never mean anything, if he didn't trust her, if he couldn't share the ins and outs, the triumphs and the disasters, of his life. Without trust and talking, they were just fuck buddies.

It was amazing how much that hurt.

Peyton sipped her wine, suddenly not that hungry. She wanted more from Jack—hell, she wanted everything he could give her. She wanted hot sex, slow sex and tender sex. She wanted the forehead kisses and the gentle hugs and the long conversations. But most of all, she wanted to know him, inside out. She wanted to know what drove him, what made him scared, what made him mad. What he dreamed of, what gave him nightmares.

She wanted. God, she wanted.

"Avangeline is being blackmailed."

Peyton stared at him, unsure that she'd heard him correctly. *"Sorry?"*

"A few months back, we realized she didn't have a current will. My brothers and I started asking her to update it, to write a new one—hers was outdated and wouldn't hold up in court—and we couldn't understand why she wouldn't. We discovered that she hasn't done that because she is being blackmailed and has bought and sent millions in Bitcoin to the blackmailer. He also wants her to bequeath an enormous sum to a foreign entity on her death. That's when most of her assets—life insurance policies, investments and long-term fixed deposits—will be liquidated."

"How much are we talking about?" Peyton asked.

"Avangeline is a billionaire, and on her death, she'll have cash assets in the hundreds of millions."

Peyton's eyes widened. That much money was hard to imagine.

"That day you and I reconnected again, she informed me that she has until the end of the month to draw up a new will, have it filed and notarized, and get a copy to the blackmailer. She's refusing to do that."

Peyton leaned back in her chair. She lifted her heels to rest on the edge of her chair and picked up her wineglass, balancing it on her knee. Part of her was amazed that Jack was confiding in her, and the other part of her was trying to make sense of his words. His grandmother and blackmail? She couldn't imagine it.

"Can you tell me what dirt he has on her, or would you rather not?" Peyton asked him.

Jack rested his forearms on the table, a frown pulling his eyebrows together. "Essentially, there are two things—one she knows about, one she doesn't."

"Right, well, that makes no sense at all."

Jack went on to tell her that Avangeline was receiving postcards from a secret lover, someone whose identity she wouldn't reveal. "The blackmailer is threatening to tell the world who that person is."

Skeptical, Peyton twisted her lips. "Jack, she's eighty-something years old. She's divorced and has more money than God. Who would care whether she has a lover or not? Why would that cause such a stir? I'm not meaning to make light of this, but it's not that big a deal."

He surprised her by nodding his agreement. "We know, Pey, and that's what we don't understand. Who can it be, and why can't she say, 'Hey, this is the person I love?' I mean, even if he's married and they are having an affair, why not just admit it? It's not ideal, but infidelity is not the scandal it once was. And because she's, mostly, out of the public eye, who would care?"

Peyton thought about his words. "Maybe it's not about her

but him. Maybe he's the one who can't afford to be outed, the one who will be affected if this all comes out. Maybe he doesn't want the world to know they are having an affair. She might be protecting him."

Jack stared at her. "I can't believe none of us thought of that," he replied. "We thought she was the one whose image would be tarnished."

"And why wouldn't you?" Peyton asked. "She's your grandmother. But maybe she loves someone so much she's not prepared to have him hurt by this coming out."

"She's putting a hell of a lot at risk."

"Maybe he's worth it," she suggested. "Maybe she loves him that much."

"Maybe," Jack said, running his finger up the stem of his wineglass and looking contemplative.

"You said there are two things," Peyton said, reminding him. "Can you tell me what the second issue is?"

Jack immediately tensed up, and she knew whatever came next would rock her, because it clearly had rocked him. To his core. She saw it in his eyes, in the way his shoulders crept up to sit just under his ears, in his hunched back and in his pronounced swallows. She leaned forward and stroked her fingers over the back of his hand. "If it's too hard, you don't have to tell me, Jack. I'll respect your privacy." She wouldn't like it, but she'd respect it.

"Nah, just give me a second."

She waited, curiosity bubbling within her, and after a few minutes, Jack started to speak. She listened as he explained about his parents and their less-than-vanilla sex lives, and that the blackmailer knew about the underground S and M club they owned. *Wow! Okay then.*

Jack looked at her with trepidation, obviously worried about her reaction.

"Look, it's shocking because it's so out of whack with the image we know of them," Peyton slowly stated, keeping her voice nonjudgmental. "People are allowed to like what they like. It's not my cup of tea, but they were consenting adults…" She shrugged.

Jack blew out a breath. "Thanks for not being shocked. I hear you and I agree. Unfortunately, some of the things they did were borderline illegal and definitely immoral. They hired sex workers, male and female, who were in their late teens and vulnerable. That's not acceptable."

No, it wasn't.

"And—" Jack swallowed "—my mom was flirting with some deep and dangerous stuff. She was part of a dark-web chatroom where sexual fantasies went beyond harmless."

Peyton crunched her eyes shut. "Crap, Jack."

Jack closed his eyes and nodded. "Yeah. Hard to reconcile that with America's sweetheart, right?"

She heard the pain in his voice, and her heart ached for him. "And you knew nothing about this?"

He shook his head. "Not until Fox told me about it a few weeks ago. I thought he was kidding, and then I got mad at him because he wasn't. Then I was furious because he was trying to protect me."

"And maybe you were mad at him because you couldn't be mad at your parents."

He stared at her, his eyes wide with shock, and he finally nodded. "Probably, possibly. I thought they were perfect, you know?"

"And perfect is important to you?" Peyton asked.

He looked away from her, but not before she saw that he wanted to agree. "It has been," he finally said. "I'm trying to get out of the habit of chasing perfection. I know it doesn't exist."

Was he winning that battle? She didn't know. But those were his demons to fight. She had her own. She pulled their conversation back to the subject they'd been discussing. "You said that Avangeline doesn't know about your parents and the club?"

"No, she's totally in the dark about that."

Peyton whistled softly, trying to get her thoughts in order. "Look, I'm not a PR person—I don't understand how these things work—but I imagine that such a bombshell revelation would make headlines around the world."

"It would," Jack admitted. "She adored my parents, worshipped the ground my father and his twin, walked on. Obviously, it would be a horror show if a paparazzo, or any journalist, got hold of this information."

That was obvious. There was nothing the press loved more than seeing a golden couple—whether they were dead or not—have feet of clay. "So what are you going to do about it?" she asked. "Is your grandmother going to go to the police?"

"She's not prepared to risk somebody leaking that she is being blackmailed to the media." Jack shook his head. "Fox and I have contracted one of the best private investigative agencies in the world to look into her connections, old and new."

"And?"

"They haven't dug up anything we don't already know." He peeled the label off his bottle of beer, his thoughts far away.

"Look, it's not inconceivable that people outside the family knew about The Basement. A friend of theirs could've spilled the beans, had photos and kept notes. But the blackmailer knows about the club *and* the postcards. Only people very close to the family would know about the postcards, and it took Pasco to notice that the postcards were written by two different hands."

"The sculptor renting Avangeline's guesthouse?" When Jack nodded, she asked whether he could be the blackmailer.

Jack shook his head. "We considered that. He's not that much older than us, and he only came to the States fifteen years ago, when he was twenty-five. He's the son of Australian farmers, and they have no connection to Avangeline."

Fair enough.

"It's not Pasco. But it is someone who has had access to the family, who knows the history. Jace, Soren, Merrick and I didn't know about The Basement until Fox told us about it. Avangeline still doesn't know about it. Who else might know about the postcards and The Basement?"

His stare was intense, as if he were waiting for her to connect the dots. It took her a while to get there, but she did eventually. "Malcolm," she stated.

She didn't want to point out the obvious, that there was a great big hole in his plot, but it needed to be said. "Malcolm's dead, Jack."

"Mm-hmm. But he knew about the Basement—Fox told him a decade ago—and he could've known about the postcards. Maybe he confided in someone."

"But who?" Peyton demanded. "I was the person closest to him. He told me everything." On hearing those words, she shook her head. "No, that's wrong. I don't think he did tell me anything of importance."

Jack leaned forward, his face sympathetic but resolute. "As you said, maybe he loved the idea of the two of you more than he loved you."

She pushed away the hurt. "It's hard to hear, but you're right. I couldn't get him to tell me where we'd live after we married, whether I'd move to the city with him. I wanted to go to school, but every time I raised the subject, he brushed it off, telling me we could decide later, that it wasn't important."

"But it was important to you," Jack murmured.

"Very. But Malcolm never understood that."

"My brother could be a self-involved ass," Jack said, frowning. "He was a lovely guy, but he was spoiled. Life was all about him all the time. But, even for him, his treatment of you was out of the norm."

"What do you mean?" Peyton asked.

Jack drew patterns on the wooden table with the edge of his thumbnail, his expression miserable. He looked away from her and frowned. It was obvious that he didn't want to hurt her but knew that continuing this conversation would. But it was necessary, and maybe, when they were done, it would be cathartic.

"Just speak, Jack. I can handle it."

"I don't want to hurt you, Peyton."

He sighed and finally spoke. "I think Malcolm might've been using you and the wedding as a front, as a way to divert the press from something else he didn't want them to see."

Peyton pushed her hands into her hair, trying to untangle the meaning behind his words. "Are you suggesting that he knew of a breaking scandal, and he was trying to get ahead of it by manipulating the press with an old-fashioned love story?"

"A small-town girl finding a rich prince is good copy, Peyton."

And the hits just kept coming. But unfortunately, she couldn't deny that his theory made sense.

"I think he might've been trying to manipulate the media, Peyton. He was good at that. What do you think?" Jack asked her, looking intense. "Is it possible?"

Anything was possible. Even a decoy love story.

"When I look at our relationship from that angle, it makes sense," she told him reluctantly. "Yeah, it makes a lot of sense.

"I don't know how you are going to find out what Malcolm knew back then and why he was hiding it and what, if anything, any of this has to do with Avangeline and her blackmailer." She had no idea where Jack was going with any of this.

Intelligence radiated from his eyes and face. "Who, besides Fox, Merrick and I, was in constant contact with Malcolm at that time?"

Peyton thought back. "Nate Watkins. He, Malcolm and I spent a lot of time together."

"Malcolm's college buddy. Who else?" Jack asked.

He was going to make her say it, and she didn't want to. If she said his name out loud, then she'd have to deal with him, and she didn't want to do that either.

Jack reached across the table and stroked the inside of her wrist with his fingers. "Harry was the other person who was around back then. I know he hurt you, Peyton, and what he did to you was inexcusable."

She placed her tongue on her top lip and blinked her tears away. "The breakup with Malcolm hurt. His death was a knife through my heart—"

"But your father reverting to the coldhearted person hurt the most."

She nodded, ashamed. He'd lost his brother, but here she was, whining about her cold father.

"It was a bastard move, Pey, and I could punch him for being so cruel," Jack told her. "But I need to talk to him."

"Why?"

He looked past her, his fingers tapping his thigh. "I'm not sure, but my gut is screaming that he knows something."

"So go see him. You know where he lives," Peyton told him, trying to hide her churning emotions behind flippancy.

"I could. But you need to be there, Pey. Not because I need you to hold my hand but because you need closure."

Peyton bit her bottom lip and shook her head. "I promised myself I'd never go back, that we were done. That I'd never ask him for anything ever again, that I would never allow him back into my life."

"I'll be with you, Pey," Jack said, pushing her.

"Jack…"

Peyton shot to her feet. "So, I'm a pawn, yet again? The means to you getting information?"

"I'm just trying to help, Peyton."

No, he was suggesting that she visit a man who had ripped out her soul. But, yeah, what did it matter if her soul got kicked around a little more? She stared at him, feeling sick and sore and off-balance.

"I need to stop whoever is blackmailing your son's great-grandmother so that Jace and my brothers do not have to live through the hell of seeing my parents' sex lives become headline news. That's what I'm trying to do, Peyton!"

What about what she needed? When was anyone going to consider that?

Never was the answer to that question. Jack and his family had priorities, and she didn't make the cut. *Got it. Message received, loud and clear.*

What did she need? Really?

Well, she kept saying that she wanted the truth, but when she was provided with a means to get it, she'd balked. She couldn't keep hoping and not doing. If she wanted to stop standing on the outside looking in, if she was sick of receiving information in drips and drabs, then she had to confront her father.

Jack, damn it, was right about that.

She swallowed past the sick feeling that had lodged itself in her throat. "I'll do it."

"Okay," Jack told her. "But before we meet him, I think we need to talk to my family about what's going on and get their take on this."

Peyton nodded, then gestured to the dark apartment behind her. "I'm going to go to bed. I think I need some time alone, Jack."

She caught the shock on his face, then a flash of anger. Well, tough. She was angry, hurt and discombobulated. She needed some time alone, time to think and process her feelings. She'd worked her ass off to become financially independent and had worked even harder to become emotionally independent. She felt as if she were teetering on the edge of an abyss, about to fall into a cold, dark chasm, and she was worried that if she tumbled into it, she'd never find her way back.

She was so very tired of fighting, of clawing her way back up. She didn't know if she could see her father and cope with all the old hurts and negative feelings a visit with him would yank to the surface. How was she going to push them away and forget about them again?

She also didn't know how she was going to recover from loving Jack when he didn't love her back.

Dealing with both at the same time was ridiculously unfair.

Ten

Jack had arranged to meet his family at Clancy's, and Peyton had asked Keene to reserve the semiprivate area in the back, where two leather sofas and a wingback chair sat in front of an ornate, empty fireplace. Keene was on Noah-sitting duty, and Peyton sat on the smaller couch, grateful to have Jack's hand on her knee, his shoulder pressing into hers and his thigh lying against hers. She'd never admit it out loud, but she felt nervous as hell.

Soren, Fox and Merrick sat opposite her on the bigger couch, three big guys who sat shoulder to shoulder, all looking equally powerful and equally serious. Jacinta sat in the wingback chair, and tension hung like a static-filled blanket between them.

They were here to discuss Avangeline's blackmailer, who he was and where to find him.

Jack had this idea that Harry was the culprit. She wasn't completely convinced—Jack had no evidence—but she knew her father was completely capable of that and more.

Harry had never found a get-rich-quick scheme, illegal or not, that he didn't like.

Would they hate her when they found out he suspected Harry? Would the sins of the father be passed on to her—and then to Noah? Would the Granthams be that petty? She hoped not. Not only for Noah but for her.

She wanted more than anything to be part of this family, to be able to return to Calcott Manor over weekends and vacations. She wanted Noah to visit here and play with his cousins, climb the big trees of the estate, fish in its pond and use the private beach as his sandpit. She wanted to be able to share Jack's suite upstairs, to spend hours looking at the art in the house, to be at Jack's side when his brothers got married, when they welcomed the arrival of their babies and when they said a final goodbye to Avangeline.

She was supposed to be part of this family, but not when she was nineteen. Now. She belonged with Jack—they belonged together. But would he realize that? Or, when their passion cooled and life returned to normal, would he return to chasing perfection? Looking for something that wasn't attainable?

And if he did that, if what she could give him wasn't enough, how was she going to handle being rejected again? Would she cope?

A voice deep inside reminded her that she had a child to raise, to guide and to love. She would do whatever she needed to be a good mom to Noah, but God, it would be hell seeing Jack, knowing that their son wasn't enough for him.

Just like she'd never been enough for her father.

Jacinta cleared her throat and looked at Jack. "You called this meeting, Jack. Why?" she asked in a cool, no-nonsense voice. But Peyton saw the fear in her eyes and noticed the fine tremor affecting her fingers. "And why isn't Avangeline here?"

"We needed to be able to speak freely, Jace," Fox told her. He frowned. "I thought you would've invited Pasco."

Jace glared at him. "And why would I do that?" she asked, her eyes flashing with annoyance.

"Why would she invite Avangeline's tenant?" Merrick demanded, confused. "He's not family."

Jack winced and looked at Fox, then Soren, and Peyton knew he was silently asking them to help him out. Merrick hadn't spent much time at Calcott Manor lately, and Peyton doubted he knew about Jace and Pasco's relationship.

Jacinta bit her bottom lip and sent Merrick an uncertain look. "Pasco and I...we were together, briefly."

All the brothers pulled in a deep breath, and Peyton's eyes bounced between them and Jacinta. "You and Pasco?" Merrick clarified.

"Yes." Jacinta nodded, blushing. "But it's over."

Merrick did not look impressed. "Is he the reason you have stripes under your eyes and you look washed out and worn out? What did he do? And where is he?"

Jack had told her about Merrick's protective streak, and she now understood how deep it ran. Merrick looked as though he was about to go to war. Jacinta leaned forward and put her hand on his arm, waiting for him to meet her eyes. "I called it off, Merrick. I promise you, I *promise* you, he didn't hurt me."

It took a few beats before the tension left Merrick's body. He pointed a finger at his mother. "We will be discussing this again, Mom." He turned his attention to Jack. "Right. Jack, get on with it."

The Grantham men relaxed, and Jack placed his hand on Peyton's thigh and squeezed. Instead of feeling reassured, she felt as if her and Jack's feet were glued to the railroad tracks and they could see the train's rapidly approaching lights.

"We think that Peyton's father, Harry, might be, somehow, involved in the blackmail attempt," Jack said, his voice calm and so very controlled. This is how he'd sound in the boardroom, Peyton realized. Direct, cool, powerful. "Or if not involved, then he has some knowledge of what's going on."

Fox looked at her and then returned his gaze to Jack's face. "Why?" he demanded.

Jack pulled a face. "To be honest, it's more of a gut instinct than anything else."

"Based on what?" Fox demanded.

Jack leaned forward and rested his forearms on his thighs. "I need to go back, so bear with me. Firstly, there was no deal between Harry and Malcolm—no money was exchanged. There was no feud."

Various frowns accompanied Jack's statement. "Harry's misused funds were earmarked for hotel development. That's what Mal told us," Fox stated.

"I checked, and I spoke to people who would've known about any proposed developments Malcolm and Harry were looking at back then. There wasn't a hint of a business deal happening between them. And Malcolm gave Peyton and us differing explanations of the source of their feud. He told Peyton that Harry harassed him to go into business and that he wouldn't stop pushing for a deal."

"What did Harry tell you?" Merrick asked Peyton.

"Nothing. Harry wasn't the type to bother with explanations." Peyton brushed her fingers across her aching forehead.

Jack looked at his brothers, then Jace. "I think that maybe

Harry knew something about Malcolm that he didn't want to come to light."

A swell of objections greeted Jack's words, and Peyton held up her hand, asking for quiet. "Before you brush Jack's words away, there was this weird dynamic between him and Harry. I'd catch them exchanging looks and then Harry would smirk. I didn't remember that until Jack and I started discussing the situation."

"Mal was a helluva guy, but he loved playing mind games, and he could be ruthless," Fox added.

"How dare you speak about your brother that way!" Jace shouted at Fox, her voice shaky with anger.

It was Merrick who caught his mother's eyes, who made her look up. "Mom, we loved Malcolm, you know we did. But we've all been looking at that time, at him, through a lens of grief. He was a great guy, but he wasn't perfect, far from it. He was difficult and moody and impulsive and tempestuous, especially toward the end of his life."

Jace looked as if she wanted to argue, but Merrick shook his head. "If we are going to get to the bottom of this, we need to be honest, Mom. It's going to be hard but it's the only way to get to the truth."

Jace nodded, brushed away a tear, and looked down at the floor. When nobody spoke, Peyton broke the heavy silence. "Is there any way Harry could've found out about The Basement? Could he have been blackmailing Malcolm about that?" Peyton gently asked, raising the subject none of them wanted to talk about.

Fox spread his hands out and shook his head. "I spent weeks tracking down that information, and I gave Malcolm copies of my research about two weeks after you broke up, Peyton, and after he'd severed his relationship with Harry.

How would Harry have found out? And, crucially, why did he sit on such salacious information for ten years?"

Jack rubbed his face and groaned.

"None of this adds up," Merrick said. "There's so much that doesn't make sense, and I'm not sure what to focus on."

"Harry is the key. I know it," Jack insisted.

Soren leaned forward, his wide shoulders taut with tension. "Be careful that you are not looking to make him the bad guy because you are angry at how he treated Peyton, Jack. Yes, he was a terrible dad, but that doesn't make him a blackmailer."

Fair point, Peyton thought. Could that be true? Were they just making Harry the scapegoat because he'd been an utter bastard to her?

Soren placed his ankle up on his knee and played with the laces of his shoes. "And don't forget that the blackmailer knows about the postcards. There is no conceivable way Harry could know about Avangeline's lover."

Jack threw his hands up in the air, frustrated. "Shit!"

"Maybe Harry does know about the postcards," Jace said, her voice quiet.

"But he doesn't, Mom," Merrick told her. "He can't."

Jacinta's blue eyes looked troubled. "About a year ago, maybe a little more, my car broke down in Hatfield. I arranged to have it towed to a garage. Harry offered me a lift home. I'd just been to the post office. I had to collect a parcel, and I picked up the mail at the same time."

They all sat up straighter, waiting for her to finish her explanation. Tension snapped and crackled, and Peyton felt as if they were sitting on the edge of a swinging rope, about to fall. "I accepted Harry's offer, but I asked him to stop at the store so I could pick up...something. I don't remember what. I left the mail on the front seat. He could've gone through it, and if there was a postcard in the pile…"

"Was there?" Fox demanded.

Jacinta shrugged. "I don't know. They came quite often, so it's possible. All I know for sure is that I left a pile of mail on Harry's passenger seat, and I was gone for ten, fifteen minutes."

Peyton bit the inside of her cheek. "Harry would've gone through it in a heartbeat. He has no concept of privacy. I can see him being intrigued by seeing code on the postcard, taking a photo of it, and then trying to work out what it said."

"It's so Harry," she added. "He loves having dirt on people. It's so his thing."

Fox's eyes met hers, and she saw the pain there. "So you think it's feasible that he could've had dirt on Malcolm?"

She nodded. "Absolutely. Maybe he tried to blackmail him."

"And maybe Mal started dating you as an insurance policy," Fox mused. "Maybe he promised Harry something in exchange for not revealing the dirt. And he used you to keep an eye on Harry, Peyton."

And Harry needed to stay close to Malcolm, so he pretended to be a doting dad. They'd both used her, Peyton realized. And then the circumstances changed, and Malcolm told Harry to take a hike. Why? She needed to know.

"But what would Harry have on Malcolm?" Soren demanded. "There's nothing about his life that we don't know."

There was a lot we didn't know, Peyton thought. Time and distance had made her realize that Malcolm had been adept at playing roles and that he'd showed people the Malcolm they wanted to see. She had no doubt that he'd been more troubled and far more ruthless than his family wanted to believe—and a great deal unhappier than they'd ever imagined.

Jack linked his fingers with hers. "We need to talk to Harry," he told his family. "And Peyton is coming with me."

"Want some company?" Fox asked, looking tough.

Jack looked at her and Peyton smiled. No, she didn't need Fox to play the heavy. Hell, she didn't even need Jack to be there, but she'd take him along to get the answers she was seeking. Harry couldn't hurt her anymore—she was done giving him any energy.

"I'm good, thanks," Peyton said, her voice strong.

Fox grinned at her. "Yep, I think you are. Go kick ass, Peyton."

She intended to.

After hugging her and wishing her luck, Jace and the Grantham brothers left the room. Peyton tapped a message to her father, asking if she could come over to his house. His answer—Give me thirty minutes—came back almost immediately. Peyton dropped back down to the couch and let out a long breath.

Jack sat beside her and placed his hand on her thigh. "Are you okay?"

"I'm exhausted, and I haven't even spoken to Harry yet," Peyton admitted, resting her temple on Jack's shoulder.

"I won't let him hurt you," Jack told her, lifting his hand to stroke the side of her face.

Oh, she wasn't worried about Harry; he had no power over her anymore. The only reason she was going to see him was to get some answers about the past, to help Jack and his family and Avangeline. While she was an outsider, Noah was a Grantham, and she wanted to protect her son's new family as much as she could.

She loved them. She loved Jack.

And she would do anything to protect him.

Oh, how she wished they could be a family, wished with all her heart that they could raise Noah together. Her doubts had vanished; she knew she loved him. She'd probably loved him ever since their eyes had met in the lobby of the country club two years ago, and that was the reason she'd gone to bed with him just hours after meeting him again. He was why she hadn't dated anyone in two years, why no other man interested her.

Despite having had no contact with him, it had been all about Jack. Only about Jack.

"I can hear your thoughts," Jack said. "A penny for them?"

She wanted to ask him where they went from here, whether he thought they had a future. Were they simply going to carry on sleeping together without a plan, giving no thought to a relationship? Taking life as it came? Could she cope with that? Could she live with knowing that Jack would, one day, probably sometime soon, decide they were done, that he wanted or needed someone else, someone different? That she and the family she wanted to create with him weren't what he had envisioned?

Should she tell him how she felt and take it from there? Or would that scare him off? Peyton didn't know what to do, and she hated it. Talk and risk everything? Or stay silent and wait for the hammer to fall?

Jack sat up and half turned to look at her, excitement on his face. "God, I forgot to tell you!"

"Tell me what?" Peyton asked, linking her hands around her knees.

Jack grinned. "I asked Avangeline to work her art world contacts, and she has an offer for you. It's a New York–based job as an art adviser, working with clients on purchases and sales, liaising with museums to organize exhibitions and attending auctions. There will be some travel involved."

Her rocketing excitement took a nosedive. "I can't spend a lot of time away from Noah, Jack," she told him.

"Of course you can't," Jack told her, "and your new employer—potential new employer—knows that."

He looked like a little boy who'd received everything he wished for on Christmas day and a great deal more. "God, this is so fantastic. You can move to New York, and life can carry on as normal," he told her, looking very pleased with himself.

She was about to ask who'd offered her a job and what she was supposed to do about the Chicago opportunity when his words sank in. She stared at him, and her heart plummeted to her toes. Suddenly, the new offer wasn't that important.

"Carry on *as normal*?" she quietly asked, praying that he'd give her a completely different answer to the one she could see hovering on his lips.

"I'll find you an apartment close to mine so that I can spend lots of time with Noah, and so that the commute from my place to yours won't be a hassle."

Right. Unlike her, he wasn't thinking of moving in, of taking this to the next level. "We'll have to find Noah a nanny, but that shouldn't be a problem. Your job will be flexible, but I'll need some help when you go away. I'll have to get a bed for Noah for my apartment for when he stays over."

When *he* stays over, not when *you* stay over. It was such a little thing, two words, but they held a wealth of meaning. Noah was moving into his life, but she would be staying on the periphery. She was going to remain on the outside of the Grantham circle.

He had it all worked out. Nothing much would change from the arrangement they had here at Calcott Manor. He'd come over when it suited him, stay over when it suited him, and his life would carry on as per usual. While she didn't object to a New York City–based job, she did object to the fact that he was making plans without any input from her, assuming that she'd fall into line.

And all without a hint of commitment from him.

How was this fair?

"You haven't asked me who your employer will be, what you'll be doing," Jack stated, a tiny frown pulling his eyebrows together. "And why don't you look excited?"

Because she wasn't. She didn't want the life he was offering. But she couldn't tell him that, not as they were about to confront Harry. Her father was wily and conniving, and Jack, even though he was super smart, needed to be on his game if he wanted to win the battle of wills with her father.

Now wasn't the time to discuss her job, the move he was proposing and their relationship. She couldn't even begin to process it all. "We'll discuss this later," Peyton told him. She glanced at her watch and stood up. "We should get going," she told Jack, who still looked confused.

"Why do I think that I'm missing something here?" Jack asked as he followed her to the door.

Because he was. He didn't realize that she loved him, would always love him and that she needed more from him than to be his bed partner and coparent to their son.

She needed to be the reason his sun rose and the wind blew. The reason his heart beat and his lungs drew air. She needed him to be her home, the one person she felt completely safe with.

How could he be that, how could she feel that, when he still had one foot out the door?

* * *

In his car, Jack sent Peyton a glance and sighed at her cold expression. Somehow, in the past twenty minutes, they'd gotten badly off track, and he didn't know what he'd said, how they'd gone from laughter and intimacy to having a steel barrier between them.

And why hadn't she seemed more excited about her New York City job offer? Why hadn't she asked him who her new employer was, the terms of her job? Instead of peppering him with questions, she'd just stared at him, her eyes hot with excitement, then cold with disappointment. Did she not want to move to Manhattan? Did she think that having two hours of flight time between them was the best way to raise Noah?

He thought back over their conversation and couldn't figure out where he'd gone wrong, what he'd said to upset her.

This is why he avoided relationships; he never seemed to get it right. Just when he thought he'd navigated all the treacherous mountainous curves and steep valleys, the train always got pushed off the tracks. It was a complicated journey, and it was so easy to go off the rails.

He didn't like getting it wrong.

Did she not want to be with him? Was spending every night with him too much? Was she feeling crowded? Annoyed by his constant presence? Jack swallowed his snort. That was the way he usually felt. He was the one who felt tied down and constricted, the one who went looking for the exit sign.

He conceded that they barely knew each other, hadn't spent that much time together, and then they'd been tossed into a coparenting situation while succumbing to an intense physical relationship. Their physical connection scared him—he'd never had it so good with anyone else—and if it made *him* stop and think "What the hell?" then it probably felt overwhelming to Peyton, who didn't have the experience he did.

Maybe he should back away and give her some time and space. Maybe she was feeling crowded; maybe she needed to find her feet and get used to him. If his ex-girlfriends had just given him some room to move, he might've stuck around more often. Or maybe not.

He and Peyton had gone from lovers to practically living together, and it was a lot to take in. And he was also very aware that she'd been burned by a Grantham before, and she needed time to trust him, to understand that he wasn't stringing her along, that he wasn't Malcolm, the sequel.

That he wasn't anything like Malcolm.

He was cautious and thoughtful, and he considered every action twice, especially personal choices. He didn't make rash decisions. He wanted her and Noah in his life. He hadn't worked out the details yet, but he and Peyton needed to ease into this, to take things slowly, to give them time to trust each other.

He saw the driveway to Harry's place coming up on the right. Activating his turn signal, he pulled in a deep breath. This wasn't going to be a fun meeting, but he'd put himself between Harry and Peyton. He wouldn't let him hurt her again. And if Harry tried anything, if he started talking shit, he'd remove Peyton from his presence and track him down later…

And the gloves would come off.

Jack pulled up in front of Harry's house—Peyton's childhood home—and switched off the engine to his Mercedes. Trying to take Peyton's hand, he frowned when she pulled her fingers away and lunged for the doorjamb.

"Let's get this done, okay?" She tossed the words over her shoulder, as brittle as dried-out leaves at the end of autumn.

Shaking his head, Jack watched as Peyton stomped across the lawn to the front door, her arms crossed over her slim chest and her head bowed.

Yeah, he was definitely missing something.

Thirty minutes later, in the living room of Harry's apartment, Peyton wished she could teleport herself somewhere else. Anywhere else but here.

So far, their conversation had been perfectly civil. Jack had led Harry along, pretending theirs was a social call, with Jack subtly implying that he was encouraging Peyton to mend fences with him. But Harry wasn't interested in her or Noah. Oh, he'd asked the right questions—what degree did she get? How long was she going to stay in Hatfield? How old was Noah, and did he look like him at all?—but his eyes had glazed over when she'd given him detailed answers.

He definitely didn't want a relationship with her, and as soon as he could, he flipped the subject to Avangeline. Was she in good health? Was anything affecting her? "She's getting on, right? She isn't displaying any signs of dementia, is she?"

In other words, how was she holding up under the strain of being blackmailed?

Peyton's eyes drifted over the photographs on the mantelpiece. They were all of Harry: Harry on a yacht, Harry playing golf. There wasn't one of her, nor was there one of her mom. And wasn't a picture, or a lack of one, worth a thousand words?

Jack, standing by the mantelpiece, took a sip of the coffee Harry served and lifted one eyebrow. "Avangeline is perfectly rational and as sharp as a tack," Jack said in a very normal, nonconfrontational tone. "And she won't be paying you another cent."

Harry's expression slackened, and all the blood drained away from his face. He swallowed audibly, and Peyton could read the truth in his eyes, in the way he wriggled in his chair, in his unsuccessful attempt to regain his sangfroid.

"I have no idea what you are talking about," Harry spluttered. Peyton saw his eyes go to a whiskey bottle on a corner table and knew he was desperate for a drink.

"You know exactly what I am talking about, Harry," Jack told him, his voice dropping way below the freezing point. "You've been blackmailing my grandmother, and I'm trying to restrain myself from walking over to you and beating you senseless."

Peyton didn't think it was possible, but Harry went from looking pale to being practically translucent. "You can't prove a thing," he blustered, his voice rising.

Jack reached behind a framed photograph and pulled out a stack of generic postcards, idly flipping through them. From where she sat, Peyton couldn't tell whether there was writing on them or not. "They're blank!" Harry yelled. "You can't connect them to the ones that were sent to Avangeline."

Jack's head snapped up, and Peyton saw triumph blazing from his eyes. "I said that Avangeline was being blackmailed, not *how* she was being blackmailed. I didn't mention the postcards. You did."

Harry stared at him, and when he closed his eyes in defeat, Peyton knew that they had him. Her father was behind the blackmailing attempt. She'd so wanted to be proved wrong.

Jack threw the postcards in Harry's direction, and they

fluttered to the floor. "Start from the beginning, Caron. Don't leave anything out."

Harry leaned forward and clasped his hands together, his eyes on his shoes. "Malcolm was addicted to opioids," Harry said, his voice reed thin. At that moment, he looked every one of his sixty years.

"How did you discover that?" Jack asked, shock in his eyes.

Harry lifted a scrawny shoulder. "I was too. His dealer was mine, and he boasted about selling a megarich boy oxy. I was curious, so I followed my dealer, saw him with Malcolm, recognized him."

"And decided to blackmail him," Jack muttered.

Harry nodded. "I accosted him outside his gym, told him to pay up or I'd leak the story to the press. He paid up, and I thought I'd gotten away with it. It was a one-and-done deal.

"But I didn't expect him to turn the tables on me, to find out who I was," Harry continued. "The next time I met him was when Peyton introduced him as her new boyfriend. He told me that we were going to play one big happy family, but there was a new deal on the table..."

Peyton held her breath for the next shoe to drop, but it was Jack who answered. "You became his supplier and dealer."

Harry nodded. "Your brother was as sly as a fox and as cool as a cucumber. Just like you are."

Harry was right: Jack did look like he was negotiating a not-so-important business deal, not digging into his brother's murky past. "What changed?" Jack asked.

"He did. He wanted to get clean and knew he needed rehab. Not wanting to lose my source of income, I kept throwing pills at him. He knew he had to get away from me if he wanted to get clean. That's when he told Peyton she had to choose between him or me."

Harry's faded eyes met hers. "He loved you, in his way. He wanted to protect you from me."

"He was right," Jack growled. "So why didn't you go to the press then? Tell them about his drug abuse?"

"He had the goods on me, and I would've gone to jail for dealing. He didn't want the world to know he was an addict, so we walked away." He sent Peyton a confused look. "I still don't know why you chose me, girl."

"You gave me what I desperately wanted, a father who loved me. But it was an act, wasn't it?"

To his credit, Harry didn't hedge. "Yeah, it was. I've never loved anyone but myself."

It was the most truthful statement she'd ever heard him utter. And it annihilated the last bonds of affection she felt for him. Peyton knew from this day onward that she no longer had a father. If she'd ever had one.

Harry moved his gaze onto Jack, and Peyton saw the malice in his eyes. "Malcolm liked being high. He liked the wild side, just like your parents did."

Jack sat down on the arm of her chair, entirely focused on Harry. "And that brings us to you blackmailing Avangeline. How did that start?"

Harry leaned back, now enjoying the attention of his captive audience. He explained how he'd seen the postcards when Jace had left them in his car. He'd seen the code and, as she'd thought, had taken a photo of it. He'd broken the cipher and took a chance on seeing if he could get money out of the old lady. "I was shocked when she paid me. I didn't think she would, and then I knew I was onto a good thing."

"Hold on," Jack held up a hand. "Are you telling us that you don't know who her lover is?"

"Haven't got a clue. But I kept saying I did, and she kept paying."

Speaking of... Peyton narrowed her eyes. "So where's the money, Harry? You haven't spent it on making this place look better."

Harry winced. "I gambled it away."

"Millions?" Peyton asked, incredulous.

"It's not that hard to do," Harry replied, sounding sulky. "When you are making quarter-million-dollar bets at the poker table, it doesn't go far."

Peyton sighed. Harry was never one to do things by halves.

"And how did you stumble across the information about The Basement?" Jack asked.

"When Peyton came back to Hatfield, it stirred up the past. I remember that Nate dropped off a box of Peyton's stuff from Malcolm's apartment, but I forgot to give it to her. I dug it out, and mixed up with her stuff was a folder with copies of business licenses and the sex club's newsletters. It wasn't hard to figure out your parents' involvement. Not so clean-cut, eh?"

Peyton put her hand on Jack's leg and squeezed, silently telling him not to let Harry get to him. Jack hauled in a deep breath, then continued. "Did you demand a lump sum on Avangeline's death because you were worried that your cash cow would dry up when she died?"

"Wouldn't you?" Harry asked. "It just makes sense, doesn't it?"

"In your world," Peyton snapped.

She needed to get out of there. She couldn't breathe. She needed a shower, to wash her hair, to rid herself of the stain Harry's company engendered. She was so, so glad that Noah would never know him, that Harry would never pollute his life.

Peyton stood up and folded her arms across her chest. "I

can't look at you any longer—I can't be in the same room as you. You are a vile, horrible man, and I pray that any genes Noah or I inherited from you will burn themselves out as quickly as possible. You are dead to me, finally and forever," Peyton stated, her voice strong and clear. She would not cower, she would not let him see her as anything other than the strong, independent woman she'd become.

She turned to Jack. "I'll wait for you outside. Don't hurt him too badly. Not because I care about him, I don't, but because I don't think he's worth the assault charges."

Peyton walked out of the room, her head held high, and when she heard the crack of a fist against a jaw, the muted whimper from somewhere behind her, she smiled. And wished she could've punched the man herself.

Eleven

Peyton looked around and saw that Jack had pulled into a lookout off the main road and cut the engine of his powerful car. In front of them was an empty beach and the green and the glittering Atlantic Ocean. Jack rolled down the windows and rested his elbow on the sill of the driver's side door, his eyes on the wide expanse of sand and the endless sea.

"Do you believe him?" Jack quietly asked her, flexing his hand. She saw the bruise blooming on his knuckles and didn't say anything. His eyes met hers. "I didn't do any lasting harm, Peyton. He was cursing me when I left."

Honestly, she thought Harry got off lightly. "I know that, Jack. And, yes, I do," she said, answering his question. "He told us his version of the truth. But we didn't ask if he spread the rumor about you being Jack's dad," she said, frowning.

"I asked him after you left. He admitted it, told me that he wanted to distract me from looking for Avangeline's blackmailer."

Peyton took a deep breath. She didn't want to ask the next question but knew she had to. She needed to know whether

Malcolm's secret was something that would stay between them. "Are you going to tell your family about Malcolm's opioid addiction?"

Jack pushed his hands through his hair. "Yes. I hated it when Fox kept secrets from me, so I'm not going to do that to them. I think it helps to know that he wanted to get clean and that was why he had the falling-out with Harry."

"Are you going to pursue charges?"

"If we do, it'll hit the press," Jack replied.

"If you don't, he might sell the story anyway."

Jack tapped the face of his cell phone. "I don't think so. As soon as we get back to Calcott Manor, I'll send him the video clip of our interaction." He touched the pocket of his shirt. "I put my cell in my pocket, video camera facing out. He knows I have him on video admitting to blackmail. He doesn't want me going to the police, so he won't talk."

Clever man.

Jack released a long sigh, his eyes dropping to his phone as it beeped as message after message landed. He picked it up and turned it to show Peyton, and she read the many messages coming in from Jacinta and Jack's brothers. They were all desperate to know the outcome.

It's all sorted, Jack typed. I will explain the ins and outs later. Calcott Manor. 6:00 p.m.?

Another flurry of questions came through, and Jack switched off his phone. He rested his wrist on the steering wheel and looked at his watch. "What time do you have to pick Noah up?"

There it was again, the *you* instead of a *we.* "Fourish. Why?"

He sent her a low, heated smile. "Then let's go back to Calcott Manor. I know a way we can sneak into the apartment without anyone in the house seeing us, and we can spend the next ninety minutes or so in bed."

Peyton stared at him, trying to make sense of the thoughts tumbling around in her washing-machine brain. Was that all she was? A quick bang whenever he had time? A way to relieve stress? A way to celebrate? She didn't mind being any of those, provided she had his love and the security that went along with having a long-term relationship. And no, she didn't care that he was as rich as Croesus, she just wanted to know that she could rely on him, that he wouldn't decide one day soon that he was done with her and dial back their relationship to being coparents.

He had never promised her anything. She had no right to ask him to love her, to be her person, to make her the center of his world. _

Peyton got out of the car and walked around to the hood, leaning back against its sleekness. The wind whipped her hair across her face and into her eyes, and Peyton peeled away a strand that had molded itself to her lips. She'd been so desperate for Harry to love her, to notice her, to give her love and attention that she'd twisted herself in knots trying to give him what he thought he wanted, to make herself into the person she thought he could love. And with Malcolm, she'd been prepared to accept whatever she could get, because being with him made Harry notice her.

But she wasn't nineteen anymore, and she didn't need her father's love or a man to make her feel complete. She'd left Hatfield, lived on her own, gotten her degree, given birth and looked after a baby by herself. She hadn't needed Jack's help to secure her job in Chicago. He couldn't love her the way he needed her to, and she wasn't going to settle for less.

Out of the corner of her eye, Peyton saw Jack walking around the car toward her, but she kept her eyes on the horizon, knowing that if she didn't walk away now, she never would.

"Who offered me a job, Jack?" she asked, although she had a fairly good idea.

"Avangeline."

That was a surprise. *Not.*

"She has art ferreted away in warehouses, on yachts and in her homes dotted all over the world, and she wants you to be her adviser. She needs to do a proper inventory before she, as she says, 'pops her clogs.'"

"You don't look surprised," Jack continued, and she felt rather than saw his frown. "It's not a small job, Peyton."

"But she only offered me the job because you asked her to," Peyton replied, folding her arms. "Avangeline doesn't need me to advise her, Jack. And I bet she knows exactly what she owns."

He didn't disagree with her. "She would also like you to curate specific shows when she loans her art out to museums and galleries. She's even talking about maybe having a moving exhibition of her best works in some of the major cities in the world. She believes art should be shared."

"And she wants me to be in charge of that?" Peyton asked.

"Why? Aren't you up to it?" Jack asked blandly.

How dare he ask that! "Of course I am!" she retorted, her tone hot.

"So then, what's the problem?"

She turned to face him, her hand holding back her hair. "The problem is that she wouldn't be doing this if you hadn't asked her, if you didn't want me to move to New York so that you can be closer to Noah!"

"And to you," Jack quietly added.

"The job is a convenient solution to keeping me in New York, a way to solve a problem."

"You are not a problem to be solved, Peyton!" Jack told her. "Why would you say something like that?"

"Because that's the way I've always felt! Harry never loved me, and when he acted as if he did, it was a lie. To Malcolm, I was a means to keep Harry quiet. So, what am I to you, Jack?"

He hesitated a beat and her heart plummeted to the floor. "It's too early for both of us to tell, Peyton."

"Don't you dare tell me what to think, how to feel!" she yelled.

Jack looked at her as if she were an unpinned hand grenade about to explode. He wasn't in love with her, not even close. "So, am I supposed to carry on being your bed buddy? Be there whenever you feel like a screw?"

His eyes flashed with anger. "That's not fair. I have never treated you like that!"

No, he hadn't. Peyton rubbed her hands over her eyes. "No. But you haven't told me where you think this is going, where it *can* go, either. Tell me now, Jack."

Oh, Jesus.

Jack thought that he could handle this talk, that he was ready, but he wasn't, not by a long shot. Earlier, he'd thought he'd known where they were going, what he wanted. He'd thought they just needed time to cement their relationship, but...

He'd been wrong. He needed time. Space.

He was scared down to his size thirteens. Scared that if they jumped, the parachute wouldn't open, that they'd—*he'd*—be a splattered puddle on the sidewalk. Peyton would stand up and dust herself off; she was far stronger than him. But he'd be a mess for God knew how long.

This was why he never allowed relationships to progress this far. Oh, he could bullshit himself by saying that he was chasing perfection, that he was looking for something else, something better, but it was all unadulterated crap.

He was terrified of the reach-the-sky high and the devastating fall that would follow.

It was far easier to walk away, to find an excuse and to keep himself emotionally uninvolved.

"I can see you looking for the exit ramp," Peyton muttered.

Not an exit ramp but the slow lane, a place where they could be sensible and thoughtful, where he could regain control of his emotions and the situation. He wasn't a fan of mental skydives.

"We need time to make sure we're not making a mistake," he said.

"And by we, I presume you mean you?" Peyton shot back. Tears, hot and furious, threatened to spill from her eyes. "I am so tired of allowing people to dictate how I should feel, how I should be loved and to what degree."

He didn't know how to respond to that. Peyton lifted her chin, her eyes now filled with determination. "That's the difference between us, Jack. I knew it two years ago! I saw you and thought, 'Yeah, there he is.'"

He wanted to pull his eyes off hers, but he couldn't, and he couldn't get his mouth to work. Not that he knew what he'd say.

"I want you, Jack. I want us. I want to be the one thing, above everything else, that you can't bear to lose. I want to mean enough to you for you to take a chance on me, to think, 'Hey, she's worth the risk,' and that having me in your life is worth any heartbreak."

He felt the sour taste of panic and a hand squeezed his heart in a cold grip. He was losing her, but he didn't know what to do or say.

"But I'm not, am I? I'm not perfect, and I don't measure up to that idealized person you have in your head." Tears rolled down Peyton's cheeks, but they were quickly dried by the wind. "Newsflash: I'm not a stepping stone to this magical person you are looking for, because she doesn't exist, Jack!"

"I know that!" Jack shouted. She was all he wanted, all he could dream of, but he couldn't say the words.

"Do you?" Peyton demanded. "Then why are you emotionally backing away? Why aren't you telling me that you love me as much as I love you, that you'll give us a shot?"

Because he was goddamn petrified. Soul-deep scared.

She threw her hands up in the air and turned away from him, disdain on her face. Seeing her look at him like that made him pull the plug on the dam wall holding his emotions back. "I can tell myself that we need time, that we need to be sensible, but to be honest—"

"That would be a first," Peyton interjected, looking scornful.

She wanted honesty? Okay, then.

"This isn't real, Peyton. It can't be!"

She frowned at him, confused. "I don't understand."

Neither did he, not really, but he'd try to explain. "Of all the women I've dated, you're the only one who makes me feel like I can conquer the world, like I can move mountains with my bare hands. You make me think we can have today, tomorrow and forever, but that's even more of a lie than anything I've heard before."

"You're still not making sense, Jack."

"The sex, the companionship, the completeness I feel with you is a *mirage*, even more of an illusion than I ever imagined. I've spent my life chasing perfect, and now that I've found it, I know it's life messing with me." Because nothing was perfect, not his parents, their marriage or his life. But Peyton? She came pretty damn close.

She snorted in disbelief. "You are a piece of work, Jack! Nothing is good enough for you, is it? And nothing will ever make you happy, because you won't let it." She jammed the tip of her finger into his chest. "You are looking for excuses to keep yourself apart and safe, to not engage. And you'll grab on to any safety rope your big brain hands you."

She closed her eyes, frustrated. "I am not perfect. You are not perfect. *This* isn't perfect. No relationship ever is. Or ever will be." Peyton's bold eyes slammed into his. "But the thing that makes a relationship and two people click is understanding that and choosing to love anyway. It's about connecting with someone in a wonderful way, accepting their strengths and loving them despite their flaws. Being brave and taking a chance—that's what matters."

He wasn't brave, not when it came to love. He never had been. And up until this point, it had never mattered. He stared at her, wishing he had a fraction of her courage. But it was too risky. Love was the flip side of pain. Of disappointment.

Peyton looked away from him and pulled her bottom lip between her teeth. "I'm done. I'm not going to beg you to love me, Jack." She gestured to the car. "I need to collect my son, Jack."

Heat and fear rolled through him and tightened his face. *Her* son? Where did that leave him? Was there still a place for him? And why did he feel like anything less than everything was no longer acceptable?

I know they want to know who has been sending me postcards and are frustrated at my lack of an explanation. But releasing his name would not only hurt people I love, but it would diminish what we have. Sharing him would make us less...

And I can't bare that...

Peyton heard the soft sound of a throat being cleared and turned around to see Aly in the doorway to her bedroom in the garage apartment. She'd been packing her belongings in a daze. Her fingers gripped a pile of her underwear, and she looked down, unable to cope with the sympathy she saw in her visitor's eyes.

"I knocked, but you didn't hear me," Aly said softly. "Can I come in?"

Peyton nodded, not surprised she hadn't heard Aly's knock. Since Jack dropped her off at the bar yesterday, she hadn't heard much, eaten nothing and hadn't been able to focus. Thank God Keene and Simon had been available to babysit Noah last night. At the moment, her little guy was being spoiled rotten by Jace.

"Where's Noah?" Aly asked, coming to sit on the bed between two piles of clothing she'd yanked from the chest of drawers. Peyton was clearing out the apartment because she needed to leave Hatfield as soon as she could.

"Jace has him," Peyton told Aly.

Aly pulled her knees up to sit cross-legged on the bed. "So, the blackmailer is your father?"

Peyton sank to the floor, her eyes brimming anew with tears. She couldn't believe she had any left to cry. "Does Avangeline hate me?" she whispered.

"No, but she's seriously pissed that you aren't taking her art adviser job," Aly told her. "I wasn't there but Jace told me some of what Jack explained to the family last night. They also asked where you were, how you were doing. They are worried about you. Jack most of all."

Maybe. But there was nothing she could do about that. "How did they take hearing that Malcolm was…um…" Had they told Aly everything? Or was she giving away family secrets?

"About his addiction?" Aly asked, frowning. "Yeah, they did. They felt they had to because I received an organ from him."

"Did his being addicted to opioids affect your liver?" Peyton asked. She liked Aly, and she couldn't bear for anything to go wrong for her after she'd gone through so much.

Aly managed a small smile. "No, I'm fine. After all, I've had Mal's liver for ten years already and have been problem free. It isn't ideal, but studies have shown that donated organs from addicts are mostly safe. Weird, huh?"

It was, but Peyton was glad that Malcolm's liver had helped Aly have a second chance at life. Over the past few weeks they'd become friends, and she'd miss her when she left Calcott Manor. She'd miss everyone. From crabby Avangeline to lovely Jace to Jack...

No, she wasn't going to think about Jack. If she did, she'd start to cry again, and she needed to pack. Stupid man for not giving them a chance, for being scared to love her and have a wonderful life together. Stupid, stubborn, annoying...

"So, I don't suppose that Avangeline has told anyone who her lover is?" Peyton asked.

Aly rolled her eyes. "Have you *met* Avangeline? No, of course not. But I have to say, apart from being very cross with you—*Granthams don't run*—" Aly mimicked Avangeline's very blue-blooded English accent.

"I'm not a Grantham," Peyton muttered, wishing she was.

"—she's in remarkably good spirits," Aly continued. "Having her blackmail issue resolved is a weight off her shoulders."

Her father had put Avangeline through hell—no. She didn't have a father, not anymore. And she wasn't responsible for Harry's actions.

Peyton forced herself to think of something else. "Have

you heard anything about Jace and Pasco?" Peyton asked, swallowing her tears. "Have they kissed and made up?"

Aly winced. "Nope. Word is that he's gone back to Australia."

Peyton's heart dropped. "Oh no! Permanently?"

Aly shook her head. "No, I don't think so. He has an upcoming exhibition in Manhattan in a few weeks. Anyway, Jace is still looking like a ghost and only smiles when she's with Noah. Your little boy can make hearts melt, Pey."

He really could. As a mom, there was nothing better than receiving a compliment about your kid. Peyton closed her eyes as guilt swamped her. She was taking him away from his family, from his grandmother and great-grandmother, his uncles and his dad. But she couldn't stay. Not when she knew that Jack couldn't love her or give her what she needed. Maybe in six months, when she was stronger and her heart had started to mend, she could consider a move back to the East Coast. She'd contact Avangeline, and if she hadn't offered the job to anyone else, she'd ask her for a second chance. But she couldn't stay, not now.

Now, like ten years ago, she needed distance. It was the one thing that she knew helped mend a broken heart.

Stroking Peyton's hand, Aly pulled her bottom lip between her teeth. "I get the sense that Malcolm wanted to protect you from your dad, Pey, and that's why he asked you to choose."

Peyton scrunched a T-shirt in her hands. She shrugged. "Maybe. But he, like Harry, used me. I loved them both, but they didn't love me."

"I think he did love you, in his way," Aly said, her voice low and slow.

Peyton tried to smile. Despite her so-called connection

with Malcolm, Aly couldn't know that. Not for sure. Aly was just trying to make her feel better.

"He's been watching over you," Aly insisted. "I've known it from the moment I met you. Of everybody, he's been most worried about you. That's why I felt compelled to hug you the first time I saw you at Avangeline's."

Oh God, now things were just getting weird. Peyton threw her hands up in the air. "Look, Aly, I know that you are trying to make me feel better but—"

Aly wrinkled her nose. "But you don't believe me."

Peyton winced. "Sorry," she said. She didn't want to hurt her feelings. There were too many hurt feelings at Calcott Manor already, and she didn't want to alienate one of her few female friends.

"He's so sorry. He wants you to be happy, and he thinks your happiness lies with Jack."

Okay, this was getting to be a bit more than she could handle. Peyton was about to speak when Aly jumped up and took her hands, squeezing her fingers.

"This isn't fun for me either, Pey, but I've never felt him as strongly as I do right now. Not with Soren or Fox." Aly squeezed her hands again and sighed. "Look, I can see that you are getting annoyed, and I don't blame you, but can I ask you to do one more thing? When you get settled, check the rose-patterned box that holds the stuff of his you kept. You know, the one with the photographs, that pressed rose Malcolm gave you, the notes he sent you?"

It took Peyton a minute to make sense of her words, and when they did, Peyton turned cold, then hot, then cold again. How did she know about the box?

"There's a photo in it, the one of the Grantham family, taken at your engagement party. He wants you to look at it, really look at it," Aly insisted.

Peyton blinked. "Okay. Why?"

Aly shrugged and dropped her hands. "I have no idea."

"Well, I have a copy of that photo on my cloud. I scanned and saved it. I can download it."

Curious, Peyton picked up her phone, located the photo, and when it appeared on her screen, she and Aly sat down on the bed and peered at it together. Avangeline and Jacinta sat on a couch, and Peyton, the Grantham men and Merrick stood behind them. She looked so young and a little scared standing between Malcolm and Jack.

"It's a standard family photo," Aly said, disappointed.

Except that it wasn't. While Malcolm rested his hands on the sofa behind Avangeline's head, it looked as if Jack's hand was on her lower back—she didn't remember him touching her at the time—and she was leaning sideways, toward him and away from Malcolm.

"If you didn't know the family, you'd think that you and Jack are together, not you and Malcolm," Aly said, putting her thoughts into words. "And I think he's very okay with that."

Peyton felt a surge of hope, then squashed it. "I think we are reading far too much into a photograph."

But she couldn't help but wonder how Aly knew about the box, the faded roses, the photograph. And, yes, it was comforting on some level to hear that Malcolm was sorry. That, despite everything, he'd cared for her, had worried about her. That he thought she and Jack were a good idea.

But here on Earth, where it *mattered*, Jack didn't. So there was that.

Peyton swallowed, conscious of her dry mouth. "Is there anything else?"

"From Malcolm? For you?" Aly asked. Peyton closed her eyes, unable to believe she'd asked that question. But what the hell? It had been a strange few days.

Aly shook her head. "Nope. But, respectfully, that's not the message he most wants to deliver."

There was a message? Peyton frowned at her, confused. "What's the message?"

Aly twisted her lips and shrugged. "The hell if I know. Why do you think I'm still here?"

Right, okay. At least Aly had a reason to stay, woo-woo or not. She didn't.

Except that this was her son's family, his father was here, and she loved Jack with every breath she took.

Except for that.

The day Peyton was due to start her road trip to Chicago, she arranged to meet Jack at Calcott Manor so that he could say goodbye to Noah.

She looked up at the facade of the ivy-covered house and clenched her fingers around the steering wheel. She could do this, she *could*. She'd left Hatfield at nineteen with barely any money, and she'd survived LA living on ramen noodles and fresh air for the first few years. She'd dealt with an unexpected pregnancy alone, had given birth alone...

She could be alone.

But she wouldn't be. She had Noah. She turned around to look at Noah in his car seat. He was waving his hands in the air and had a huge grin on his face.

Peyton saw Jack walking down the steps, the wind picking up his light button-down shirt just enough to give her a glimpse of his tan ridged stomach. He wore brown shorts and flip-flops. He hadn't shaved, and he looked a little disputable. And very hot.

Her hands clenched the steering wheel tighter as their eyes met through the windshield, and she noticed that his were a muted blue. His mouth was pulled down into a tight, thin line.

Yeah, he wasn't happy about this, but then again, neither was she.

Jack reached the car, walked around to Noah's seat and opened the car door. Her son—their son, because he was Jack's as much as hers—chortled in delight.

"Hey, bud. How's my boy?" Jack crooned, dropping a kiss on his head before reaching for the clasps keeping him in his seat. He swung Jack into his arms and cuddled him for a minute before whipping around and walking back to the house.

Where...what? What was he doing? Kidnapping her son? Peyton tried to pull her hands off the wheel but couldn't. All she could do was watch her son and the other love of her life walk away. Then the front door opened and Jack handed Noah over to Jace, who put him on her hip and gave Jack a quick smile.

Jace and Noah disappeared, and Jack walked back to her, this time coming to stand by her door. He pulled open her door and bent down to look at her. "Let's go, Pey."

"Go? Where?" Her voice sounded rusty, as if she'd been crying for days. Maybe because she had been.

"We need to talk," Jack told her brusquely. "Are you getting out?"

She glanced at her hands and tried to move her fingers, but they felt stuck. She raised her eyes to his. "I can't lift my hands off the wheel."

His hard blue eyes warmed as he moved to stand between the door and her, bending down so that their eyes were level. "Just let go, sweetheart. I've got you."

Peyton shook her head, feeling as if there wasn't enough

oxygen in the air. "I think...maybe...feels like...panic attack."

The words were barely spoken when Jack dropped his mouth on hers, warm and lovely. Heat spread through her as he cradled her face gently with his hands. His mouth moved across hers, feeding her kisses. She felt her fingers uncurl one by one, and she lifted her hands to rest her fingers on the edge of his jaw.

"That's it, baby. Keep kissing me," Jack murmured against her mouth. His tongue traced the seam of her lips, and she sighed, allowing his tongue to slip inside. An injection of heat shot through her, and every cell in her body started vibrating at a higher frequency.

Everything suddenly made sense: if Jack was kissing her, all was right with the world. She needed him any way she could get him. If that meant for three months, three years or thirteen, then she'd take it. She couldn't leave Hatfield.

Jack pulled away, but his eyes were fixed on hers. He took one of her hands in his own, gently swiping the top of it with the pad of his thumb. "Better?" he asked.

Peyton nodded. Everything was better when they were together; it was just a fact of life. Like gravity and the restorative power of a gooey chocolate brownie.

Jack unclipped her seat belt and tugged the hand he still held. "Come with me, Peyton."

It wasn't an order but a strong suggestion. And, yes, what else could she do but put her hands in his and allow him to take her where he wanted to go? Keeping his hand wrapped around hers, he led her away from the house, past the garage, to the beach.

At the edge of a dune, he tugged her over to a wrought iron bench. "Sit down, Peyton."

She shook her head. If she sat down, her butt might weld itself to the seat, and she might never move again.

"It's okay," she said, gesturing in the vague direction of the car. "I should get going."

She didn't want to. God, she *really* didn't want to.

"Stay."

Peyton resisted the urge to bang her hand against her ear, not sure if she'd heard him correctly.

Jack slid his hands into the pockets of his shorts and stared down at his feet. "Please stay, Peyton. Please don't leave me."

Peyton's butt hit the bench seat with an audible plop. She put her face in her hands and shook her head. She knew she should be strong enough to tell him that she couldn't be with him without a commitment, without love, but she wasn't. She'd take whatever she could get.

Jack sat down beside her, thigh to thigh, and half twisted to rest his forehead on her shoulder. "My life means nothing without my family," he murmured. She heard the pain in his voice, the longing, and her heart flipped over. Jack had been the Grantham family troubleshooter for so long, the person they relied on to pick up the pieces, but he needed someone to do that for him. He needed his own family.

Did she love him enough to give him that? Love him enough that she could give and give without getting what she needed back—love and the security of a long-term commitment? She pushed her palms into her eye sockets. Leaving him would be easier than staying and living without love. But, on the other hand, she loved him too much to go.

She dropped her hands. Turning to look at him, she lifted her shoulders in a small shrug. "Okay, I'll stay. I'll take the job with Avangeline, and I'll look for an apartment close to yours."

Jack sat up and narrowed his eyes at her, looking confused. "Uh…no. That's not how this is going to work."

Peyton threw her hands up, utterly confused. "I don't know what you want, Jack!"

He traced her cheekbone with the pads of his fingers, his eyes soft. "You, Peyton. I want you—in my bed, in my house, in my life—to be the center of my world. None of it makes sense without you."

A ball of emotion lodged itself in Peyton's throat, and she swallowed once, then again. But she couldn't pull her eyes off Jack, terrified that this dream would evaporate if she moved a muscle.

Jack's mouth tipped up at the corners. He tapped his fingers against her cheek. "Peyton? Are you in there? Are you going to say something?"

She cleared her throat. "You and I, together?" she clarified.

"You, me and Noah."

She had to ask the question, as hard as it was. "For…for how long?"

He pretended to think. "Hmm, how long is forever?" Jack looked down at the ground, winced and shook his head. "Okay, let's do this."

Do what? Yet again, she was playing catch-up.

Jack dropped to one knee in front of her and winced again. "Thank God I'm only ever going to do this once… Peyton, will you marry me?"

Joy, bright and bold and oh so wonderful, flooded her system, and she leaned forward to pepper kisses on his mouth, cheek and chin. She had found her happily-ever-after. She and Noah were going to be Granthams—no Chicago, no living apart, no damn child support…

"Peyton?"

She pulled back to see his wry expression. "Yes?" she asked, feeling a little—okay, very—breathless.

"Do you think you could give me an answer so that I can get up?"

Peyton looked down at his knee pressing into the dirt and grinned. "Maybe. But I think you've left something out. It's a tiny little thing, but I think—no, I *know*—that I need to hear it."

Emotion softened his masculine face, and Peyton watched as he stood up and leaned down, one hand on the arm of the bench, the other on the seat next to her hip. He traced her features with love-filled eyes. "I've never loved someone the way I love you, Peyton. I never will. You are my world, the arrow that goes straight through me, everything that makes sense. Be mine?"

Tears rolled down her face, and Jack lifted his thumb to brush them away.

She leaned her face into his hand. "I love you, Jack. There's nothing I want more than to be your wife."

As his mouth settled on hers, her arms encircled his neck and her soul sighed. It was time to stop running and to start loving. And living…

They'd found their perfect, and it was deliciously imperfect.

* * * * *

KEEP YOUR
ENEMIES CLOSE...

One

I know that I'm not long for this world, but I've lived a long life. I'm not going to be trite by saying it was a happy life. How could it be when I have endured so much tragedy? First the death of my twins and their wives, then Malcolm, my oldest grandson... So bold, so brilliant. So scarred. The best that could be said is that I, Lady Avangeline Forrester-Grantham, did the best I could and put my family first.

Three months ago

For a one-night stand, the first of Aly Garwood's life, he'd been remarkably affectionate, and incredibly thoughtful. Not only had Merrick asked her whether she was okay with him kissing her here, or there—newsflash, she'd been okay with him kissing her *everywhere*—he'd treated her as a lover and not as a way for him to get his rocks off.

He'd explored her body but hadn't commented on her scar; his lips had simply roamed over its edges and then moved on to nibble her hip. He'd loved her thoroughly, taken her to heights of pleasure she'd never reached before and, through it all, kept her smiling and feeling safe.

Best. Sex. Ever.

Sitting down on her side of the bed, Merrick lifted his big hand, pushing a strand of hair behind her ear, his blue eyes locked on hers.

"This isn't something I normally do but…can I have your number? I'd like to see you again."

Aly looked away, taking her time to answer him. She hadn't expected them to connect so quickly, or to laugh so easily together. They'd met the night before in Clancy's, Hatfield's popular Irish bar, when he'd casually offered to buy her a drink. At last call, four hours later, she'd invited him back to her room, and allowed him to undress her and make love to her.

She'd loved every moment with him, but despite his request to see her again, she was sure that he didn't want anything more than a repeat of the hot sex they just shared. And while the sex had been amazing, a no-strings fling wasn't what she was looking for right now. She'd tried no-strings before but, somehow, she always got more invested than she should. Aly knew it'd end badly, for her at least.

People always left—sometimes by choice, sometimes not—it was an unassailable fact of her life. It was always better to walk away first, to pull back before becoming emotionally attached. Merrick, with his great body and masculine face, had it all. He was considerate, had superior mattress skills, and was the type of man women brought home to Mom. That is, if she had a mom and if that was something her family did.

She didn't and it wasn't.

The point was, he was the type of guy she could fall for,

not that he would appreciate her doing that. But he wouldn't want her to fall for him. And she didn't need any love in-duced complications right now.

Or ever.

Aly wanted to say no, suggest they call it done but couldn't form the words. For some insane reason she thought that if she let him go, she'd regret it for the rest of her life. She was a lawyer, practical and unimaginative, so her dreamy, romantic thoughts—after just one night!—were both out of character and immature. But, despite her best efforts to keep it tethered to reality, her cynical heart soared. The rest of her day was going to be stressful, and knowing she'd be seeing Merrick again later was a bright spot she could hold on to. She was in Hatfield, Connecticut, to introduce herself to her donor's family, to thank them for her second chance at life and to tell them she was crazy grateful.

Whether she told them the rest was a decision she'd yet to make. She'd see how the meeting with Avangeline For-rester-Grantham went. Either way, she was sure she'd be stressed out and emotionally drained by the end of it, and the company of a funny, smart, sexy guy would smooth her ragged edges.

"Sure, call me later," Aly said, draping her arms over his shoulders. She placed an open-mouthed kiss on his lips, the bedcovers dropping to reveal her bare chest. His big hand cupped her breast, and his thumb caressed her nipple. Aly immediately deepened the kiss, dropping her hand to his shaft, hot and hard and ready.

He pulled back and laughed. "I can't, I've got to get going. I have a meeting in thirty minutes."

She grinned and slung her thigh over his, settling her core onto his hard, gorgeous cock. "This is worth being late for."

He looked at her with those eyes the color of old-fashioned ink and grinned. "It really is," he told her, laughing as he rolled her onto the bed, reaching for a condom before sliding inside her in one smooth move. She'd expected hot and fast but yet again, she got slow and sexy...

And Merrick was an hour late for his meeting.

Sitting in the exquisitely decorated salon at Calcott Manor, Aly looked out onto an impressive rose garden, filled with what she recognized to be rare Heritage roses. Avangeline Forrester-Grantham's house, or the little bit she'd seen, was filled with art and fine furniture, but Aly was drawn to the rose garden and the wild English country garden beyond it. Her mom would've adored it, Aly decided. They'd lived in tiny, awful apartments all her life, but Martine grew African violets, herbs and various indoor plants, and they'd brought a cheeriness to what was otherwise a soulless set of rooms.

After her sister Avery's death and Aly's diagnosis, Martine neglected her plants, and her health, until both withered away.

Avangeline, the epitome of elegance, leaned forward and patted her hand. Aly hadn't known what to expect on meeting the grandmother of her organ donor, but both the billionairess herself and Avangeline's housekeeper, Jacinta Knowles, the two women who'd helped raise Malcolm after his parents' death, welcomed her with open arms and even a few tears.

Well, she and Jacinta cried a little, but Avangeline remained stoic despite meeting the woman who housed her beloved grandson's liver.

"Tell us about yourself," Avangeline demanded.

Aly told them a little about her life: that she was a lawyer specializing in social media publishing and litigation, and that she was an orphan who lived in Jersey City. She explained that she'd contracted hepatitis C and that the disease decimated her liver, requiring a transplant.

She decided not to explain that, every now and then, for the last few months she'd had a recurring, blisteringly fast vision of a plane slamming into a mountain.

Avangeline's bright blue eyes drilled into her. "What aren't you telling us?" she demanded.

Aly dropped her eyes. "Why would you think I'm keeping something from you?"

"My dear," Avangeline replied in her aristocratic English accent, "I ran an international empire for thirty years, I *was* the woman who shattered glass ceilings. I know when people are withholding information."

It seemed that Avangeline hadn't lost any of her sharpness.

"Okay, there is something else, and I need you to keep an open mind."

Avangeline and Jacinta exchanged puzzled glances, and Aly wondered how to explain something she didn't fully comprehend either. She believed in facts, rules and laws; she believed in science. But what she was feeling and experiencing was considered fringe science, at best. Bullshit, at worst.

She looked at her hands. "I know that Malcolm, my donor, liked machines, especially cars and motorbikes."

"He loved speed," Jacinta agreed.

Aly hauled in a deep breath. "I never learned to drive, and I didn't have much interest in learning. I was terrified of going anywhere fast. Public transport suited me just fine. But shortly after the operation, I asked a nurse for the latest edition of *Popular Cars*, and I devoured it. Up until that point, I couldn't tell an SUV from a hatchback. I now understand torque and horsepower and engine capacity. I have my driver's license, and I dream of someday buying a fast car and, maybe, a motorbike."

Avangeline's forehead creased in a frown. "I presume you have a point?"

Yep. Aly plowed on. "Before my operation, I never ate sugar, I hated anything sweet. I now take sugar in my coffee, have a candy addiction and I cannot go to bed without eating salted caramel ice cream."

Jacinta placed her hand above her heart and her eyes turned misty. "Salted caramel was Mal's favorite flavor, and I used to nag him about how much sugar he consumed."

Exactly. Aly rested her forearms on her thighs and linked her fingers together. "There's a theory out there called cellular memory. It's hypothesized that personality traits and memories can be stored in cells and organs other than the brain. I have to tell you that there is no accredited scientific evidence for this idea. I don't want to believe in it, I'm far too rational and pragmatic—"

"But?" Avangeline demanded.

"I can't explain my love of speed and machines, my sugar addiction. Still, if that was all it was, I would never have mentioned this to you."

Avangeline nailed her with a hard look. "What else is there?"

Oh God. Oh well, if Avangeline kicked her out after this then she'd have, at least, met and thanked her. She'd just have to hope that the flashes of the plane crash eventually went away.

"I feel like there's something else, something flitting around on the edge of my consciousness. Unfinished business, if you will." Essentially, she needed to know why that plane crashed but she'd keep that to herself for now. "I feel like I need to be here, in Hatfield, close to you and your family, to figure it out. That's why I took a sabbatical—and once it's over, I'll be working remotely for the rest of the summer, with my boss's permission. I just…can't go back to my regularly scheduled life until I've worked through this."

In the ensuing silence, Aly closed her eyes, listening to the sound of the sea and inhaling the gorgeous smell of the roses wafting in on the early-summer breeze. Calcott Manor was a private estate on the Connecticut coast, just forty-five minutes from New York City, but Aly felt like she was sitting in a house in the English countryside. It would be incredibly relaxing if she wasn't waiting for the proverbial axe to fall.

"Would you like to visit with me for a while?" Avangeline asked.

Aly jerked her head up and opened her eyes, shocked. "I'm sorry?"

When Avangeline just smiled at her, Aly spread her hands in a gesture of confusion. "Did you understand what I said about cellular memory theory? Do you understand that I am having weird, unexplainable thoughts about Malcolm?"

"I'm not an idiot, my girl. Now, are you staying or are you going?"

Right. Um. Aly looked at Jacinta, but she just nodded as if this was perfectly normal. "Uh… I can spend the rest of the day, and tomorrow, with you," she answered. She wanted to keep her evening free in case Merrick contacted her. "Or I could come back tomorrow?"

Avangeline shook her head. "I was thinking that you could stay here for the summer. We'd like to get to know you better."

"You'd want to do that?" Aly asked, doubtfully. Avangeline was American royalty, and Aly was…*not*. She was a child of borderline poverty, someone who had had to fight against impossible odds just to have the solidly middle-class life she now enjoyed. Avangeline had hosted royalty at her home in the past. Aly had never even *seen* royalty before.

"There's a beach at the bottom of my garden, horses to ride, woods to explore. I have a private gym—my grandsons insisted on it—two swimming pools and a massive library that is the envy of bibliophiles everywhere," Avangeline told her.

A compelling argument, to be sure, but a better one was that here, at Calcott Manor—Malcolm's home—she might finally figure out why she was compelled to dig into the plane crash that killed his parents and his aunt and uncle.

But the lawyer in her needed the terms of their agreement to be stated up front. "I'm not asking for anything, I don't *want* anything from you. I don't need money or your influence or anything else but a little time with you. I'd like to make that very clear."

She'd looked after herself, and her younger sister, for most of her life—she'd had to as her mom worked three jobs to keep a roof over their heads, food in the fridge and clothes on their backs. She didn't need anything from anybody.

Avangeline waved her words away. "I know that, Alyson. I would not have allowed you onto my property without having you thoroughly vetted. I like to know with whom I am meeting."

Okay, then. Aly released a breath. "Thank you. Spending some time with you here would be lovely."

"Excellent," Avangeline stated.

While Avangeline and Jacinta discussed lunch—fresh salmon steaks and a garden salad sounded amazing—Aly checked her phone. Her heart did a backflip when she saw she'd received a message from Merrick. Silly thing, it had never behaved so badly before.

She opened up the message and read it once, then again.

Hey, any chance you are free for a late lunch? I can meet you in an hour or so, I've just arrived at Calcott Manor and just have to chase off some charlatan trying to con my grandmother. I can be back in town in an hour, and would love to find you in bed, naked, waiting for me.

Aly's blood ran hot, then cold. The words of his message were still settling on her skin, sliding into her brain when her lover from last night stepped into the room, a scowl on his handsome face.

His eyes landed on hers at the same time his hands landed on his hips. Disdain, disappointment and shock chased each other through his eyes and over his features as he realized *she* was the charlatan he'd come to oust.

"Shit," he muttered.

Shit, indeed.

Present day

Merrick Knowles stood in Avangeline's favorite salon at Calcott Manor and scowled at the swathe of rosebushes outside. There wasn't a breath of wind, the sky was a bright blue and it was a perfect late-summer day.

Merrick wanted to punch his fist through one of the cottage panes that made up the eight-foot-high sliding door. Resting his palms on the door, he dropped his forehead to rest it on the cool glass and slowly inhaled. Then exhaled. Did it again. Nope. He was still pissed off.

He shouldn't be. Avangeline's blackmailer—the one she'd tried to keep hidden from the family, and the reason why she'd been dragging her feet on updating her will—had been exposed at last. Avangeline had summoned her longtime, long-suffering lawyer to Calcott Manor to draft an updated will. One of the two major issues that had been weighing on Merrick and his brothers had been resolved.

It all started in the spring, when they—he, Soren, Jack and Fox—realized Avangeline's will was out of date. Because Avangeline was both a shareholder and lender in their businesses, he and his brothers had been worried about their operations being caught up in red tape should their favorite octogenarian pass on. Their grandmother's balking at what should be a sensible action raised their suspicions, causing them to do some digging to figure out why.

They'd eventually learned about the blackmailer—and so much more, including family secrets like Jack and Fox's parents' unconventional side line. They'd also discovered that Avangeline had a longtime lover, whose identity was still unknown.

On the plus side, they'd unmasked Avangeline's blackmailer, who also happened to be the father of Peyton, Malcolm's old, and Jack's new, fiancée.

On the downside, the *other* issue they'd faced at the start of the summer—detaching Avangeline from Alyson Garwood—hadn't gone nearly so well. And now she actually had his brothers believing her story about carrying Malcolm's memories.

Merrick sighed. Explaining this to anybody would be a nightmare.

He heard a door behind him open and turned to see his mom walk into the drawing room, carrying a silver tray on which stood a coffee carafe and mugs. Sometimes Jace didn't look any older than the young woman she had been when they'd arrived here for her to start work as Avangeline's housekeeper when he was eight. On other days, she looked like the fifty-something woman she was. Still slim, still lovely but wiser, her face a little more lived-in.

And, right now, sad. Merrick gritted his teeth. If he could find Pasco Kildare, he'd shove one of his own sculptures up his ass for hurting his mom. He wished he could go back in time and prevent a romance from ever starting between his mom and the famous former artist-in-residence. Or better yet, he'd have kept Avangeline from inviting the man in the first place. Nobody was allowed to hurt anyone he loved, *ever*.

And there, *that*, was the source of his intense rage. He was the Grantham family protector, the one who looked after the Grantham boys—his brothers in everything but blood—along with Jacinta, and, when she'd let him, Avangeline. He was the one who'd joined the military and who had specialized skills, the one who could get things done.

But what had he contributed to discovering the black-mailer? Sweet f-all.

"You're going to have to stop glowering one of these days," Jace told him, shoving the tray into his hands. He took it and she turned away to open one of the two huge doors. She stepped out onto the patio area and walked over to a wrought iron table. Merrick placed the tray on the table, poured himself a cup of black coffee and sat down, stretching out his long legs.

"It's very quiet now that everyone has left," Jace commented.

His brothers and their women had all left that morning. To him, it felt like Calcott Manor, the ivy-covered, gray stone mansion behind him, had closed her eyes and settled back to have a little snooze.

"We had a lot to discuss," Merrick said, crossing his ankles.

"I feel so sorry for Peyton. She's such a lovely girl and knowing her father was blackmailing Avangeline was, *is*, horrible for her."

"She has Jack and Noah to concentrate on," Merrick stated. Noah was her and Jack's baby, the result of a one-night stand two years ago. Theirs was an ONS stand that worked out well—eventually. By contrast, his and Aly's turned out to be a train wreck.

"And we're not the type of family who blames the kids for the father's sins," Jace stated.

He felt Jace's eyes on his face and, behind his sunglasses, he closed his eyes. No, they weren't. People made their choices and they lived with the consequences.

"They've been through a lot," Merrick agreed, "especially lately. It's been a hell of a roller-coaster ride."

Merrick was extremely grateful that Harry—Peyton's father, and Avangeline's cryptocurrency-demanding black-mailer—couldn't name Avangeline's lover; he'd only known she had one. Harry, not wanting to go to jail, had also agreed to keep quiet about The Basement, the hardcore BDSM club with some questionable legal practices that was secretly owned by Fox and Jack's parents before their deaths. His brothers were convinced Avangeline didn't know about The Basement, but Merrick had his doubts.

Avangeline always knew about everything.

In her time, she'd built a massive hotelier and restau-rant empire, and had been regarded as one of the best en-trepreneurs—male or female—of her generation. She was incredibly smart and super connected. He suspected she knew about the sex club and her oldest son and his wife's involvement in it but he wasn't brave enough to raise the subject with her. He'd face down armed insurgents any day, but Avangeline Grantham in a towering temper? No, thanks.

"She's pretty amazing, isn't she?" Jace quietly asked. "She's my hero."

"She's mine too," Merrick quietly told her. "As are you, Mom."

Jace waved his words away, but he sat up straight, pulled off his glasses and gripped her hand. "*Mom*. She did incredible things but don't forget what you did."

"I should never have married him, Mer."

"You were seventeen years old, how were you supposed to know that a monster lurked beneath his charming exterior?"

Merrick's face tightened, remembering his mother begging his father for food, clothes, cleaning materials and getting a backhand for her trouble. He remembered how the man wore handcrafted leather boots and expensive cologne while his wife and child wondered when they would eat again. The bruises on his mom's face and body, that slap of a leather belt on his buttocks, his back.

"He was an abusive bastard, but you got away from him and for two years, you kept up safe, kept us fed all on your own. You had no education, but you had determination in spades. If we stayed, I had no doubt he would've killed us."

"I know." Jace looked around and softly smiled. "Thank God we landed here, Merrick. With Avangeline."

Merrick nodded. Jace's job at Calcott Manor had been a lifeline. Of course, they hadn't known they'd arrive just a few days before Avangeline's twin sons and their wives were killed in a light plane crash. His mom helped organize the funeral, sorted out rooms for the four boys and hugged them when they cried. He kept a low profile, knowing that he had to keep his head down, and be invisible. He didn't want to do or say anything that would cause the family, or his mom, additional stress.

Then, about six weeks after the funeral, after hearing that Avangeline wanted to formalize Jace's employment, his heart had dropped to the floor. At eight, he didn't know how the system worked, just that they needed to stay out of it so his father couldn't find them.

He'd never told Jace, and never would, that he'd slipped into Avangeline's study to plead their case. Avangeline had lifted an eyebrow and asked him what he thought he was doing barging in on her.

He'd lifted his shirt and shown her the still pink scars from where he'd been whipped. He pointed to a scar on his chin, another below his eye. "If my father finds us, he will kill us," he told Avangeline. "But I'll make a deal with you..."

She'd tipped her head to the side. "I'm listening."

"You protect my mom and I'll protect your grandsons."

"You're eight," Avangeline had pointed out. "What can you do?"

"Send me to the same school and I will protect Malcolm, Fox, Jack and Soren."

Avangeline held out her hand, he shook it and when he enrolled at school later that month, he became Merrick Knowles instead of Merrick Cantor. When he was fifteen, Avangeline sat him and his mother down and told them his father was dead, and that they could stop looking over their shoulder. She offered to pay for them to resume their former name, but they decided they wanted nothing to do with their past.

Avangeline did far more than was required in their original agreement: she'd paid for his schooling, then college, treating him like another grandson. She'd supported him when he decided to join the military after college. Whatever her grandsons got, he did too, a situation he still wasn't comfortable with. And when he returned from the military with the vague idea to run a food truck selling healthy meals, she'd helped him put together a business plan and had given him the start-up capital to craft his vague dreams into a multimillion-dollar, multistate and international franchise. She was his grandmother, in every way but blood, and he'd do anything for her.

But he'd done absolutely nothing to help track down the blackmailer.

"Why are you looking like a thundercloud, Merrick?" Jace looked around, craning her head. "I don't see Aly in the vicinity."

He pulled a face. "Ha ha, funny."

He and Aly had shared one night of mind-blowing sex followed by three months of verbal slaps and bites. Possibly because he hadn't been polite about telling her, just moments after they crossed paths on her first visit to Calcott Manor and eight hours after he rocked them to an intense orgasm, that he thought she was a con and bullshit artist and that he intended to expose her for the charlatan she was.

Her words still rang in his ears. *Lucky for you that you got me into bed before I knew how much of a prick you really are. I'd rather pull out my toenails with pliers than repeat that night of sheer stupidity.*

The thing was, it hadn't been stupid. It had been amazing...

That night he spent with Aly had been one of the best sexual experiences of his life—and he'd had a lot, probably more than he should.

He and Aly had hot sex, then tender sex, sex in the shower and morning sex, which caused him to be late for an appointment for the very first time in his life. He hadn't been able to get enough of her and he'd even asked to see her again, something he never did. He wasn't a fan of commitment, of being tied down; his memories of how his father treated his mother had soured him on the concept of love and forever. He knew he would never treat a woman the way his father treated his mom, but believing in love and a happy-ever-after was a step too far.

Yet he still couldn't dislodge Aly, with her reddish-brown hair and amazing eyes, a strange mixture of gold and brown and green, from his mind. He wanted her but he didn't understand her; he definitely couldn't trust her. Her motives for being at Calcott Manor remained a mystery to him, but he was still convinced she *had* to want something, from Avangeline, or the family. No way could her cellular memory story be her real, genuine motivation. But he was no closer to figuring her, or her motives, out than he was three months ago.

He hadn't been able to do a damn thing with the blackmailer situation, but the Aly situation was one he was *going* to fix—one way or another.

Two

On the other side of the French doors, Aly Garwood watched Merrick chat with his mom, sadness flowing over her like an icy river. The Grantham family, headed by Avangeline, was one bound by love more than blood. Fox and Jack—and the long-dead Malcolm—were brothers, Soren was their cousin, and Merrick had been raised as one of them. The boys all considered Jace to be their mom, Avangeline to be their grandmother, and DNA and blood types weren't a significant factor.

She wondered if they knew how lucky they were. Some people, like her, didn't have anyone. Yes, they'd faced tragedy in the loss of their parents, but they were still so lucky to have a support system, a soft place to fall, and people who would always be in their corner.

Her youngest sister died from a drug overdose, and eighteen months after Aly's liver transplant, her mom passed away. Ever since then, Aly had been completely and irrecoverably on her own. The grief of losing Avery, then pouring all her energy into raising the funds to pay the medical costs of the transplant—Martine had run GoFundMe campaigns, appealed to charities and foundations and taken out two mortgages on their apartment—had taken everything out of her mom, and she simply faded away.

It was cancer, the doctors told her. Terminal, they stated. To this day, Aly was convinced stress and grief had kickstarted her cancer. Martine's body simply hadn't been able to keep up with working long hours, looking after a sick daughter, grieving her other daughter and raising funds for the transplant. There was only so much a person could take and when Aly was well on the way to recovery, her mom's body decided that it had had enough.

Aly pushed her hands into her hair and pulled the heavy strands off her face. Nine years had passed, and she still missed her mom, possibly even more than she did back then. Why was that? Wasn't grief supposed to lighten as the years passed?

She just felt so damn alone.

But she still had Malcolm. He wasn't going anywhere. Not yet. Not until she figured out why his father's plane crashed.

Aly sighed at her unlawyerly and unscientific thoughts. She didn't believe in ghosts; she didn't even know if she believed in an afterlife or God. She didn't believe that Malcolm was directing her thoughts, but she accepted that she was compelled to dig into the past because she *was, somehow,* connected to Malcolm.

In the beginning, for the first few years after her transplant, and after she'd discovered her love of machines and candy, she'd tried to shrug off the idea. She also ignored the odd feeling, the occasional out-of-nowhere thought.

But the closer she came to the tenth anniversary of her transplant, the stronger her connection to Malcolm became.

Then the short flashes of a plane crashing arrived, ambushing her when she least expected them. With every unwelcome vision, the urge to meet with the family, to visit Calcott Manor, became a compulsion.

She'd been staying at Avangeline's house for more than three months now and she hadn't found out anything more about the crash than what was in press reports, which was basically nothing. Jesse—Malcolm's father—was the pilot, and they crashed into a mountain in bad weather. The general feeling was that it was a pilot error. Aly knew it wasn't, but she couldn't, with a gun to her head, explain *how* she knew.

That was why she was still working out of the smallest of the sitting rooms in the west wing. She'd never break her connection to Malcolm unless she got answers about the plane crash, and this felt like the right place to find them.

Aly stared at Merrick's broad back, her eyes dancing over his impressive physique. He was the tallest of the brothers, possibly the strongest, his long body built for power and speed. His face reflected some First Nation heritage: he had a perfectly straight nose, high cheekbones, and jet-black hair cut short. But his eyes were Jace's, a brilliant blue found in Arab mosques and Moroccan villas. He was a striking man, stunningly attractive and whenever he walked into the room she felt like she'd been plugged into a lightning bolt. Her womb tumbled over and the space between her legs heated.

Despite his distrust and dislike of her, she was still madly attracted to him. And because she knew how good they could be together, she wanted more of him. Whenever their eyes met, she knew he was remembering the way he put his hand under her butt to lift her, sliding into her, strong and smooth. In his blue eyes, she could see their naked bodies rolling over and over the bed, straining to get closer...

But those memories, his and hers, were obliterated by whoever spoke first. One of them would make a sarcastic, or scathing, comment, and their defenses would shoot up. He thought she was a con artist, out to get something from Avangeline. She thought he had a stick shoved up his ass.

Aly rubbed her hands over her face. She needed to get away from Calcott Manor, and the constant stress of not getting anywhere with her investigation—if you could even call it that. Despite trawling through books written on Avangeline and Grantham history, she had no leads. She needed a break from repeatedly going nowhere.

Since she'd sublet her apartment in Jersey City, she'd ask Avangeline if she could use her Fifth Avenue apartment again. It stood empty, as did most of Avangeline's properties around the world. Avangeline had told her to use it whenever she liked, but asking permission was still the right, and polite, thing to do.

When she was in New York, she would also take a trip to Jersey City and visit her law firm. Her approved period of working remotely was coming to an end and it was time to have a conversation with the managing partner about her career. She was one of the few lawyers specializing in social media law and knew she was up for promotion. Was that what she wanted? Or did she want to move on to a bigger or more prestigious firm? Maybe.

A couple of days in Manhattan would make her feel calmer and would take her away from Merrick, who always seemed to be at Calcott Manor lately. She knew he didn't have a permanent office, and that he worked online, but wasn't there a food truck or diner that needed him somewhere?

Well, if he wouldn't go away, she would.

Maybe it was time for her to permanently leave Calcott

Manor—and leave behind the investigation too. Resign herself to not having answers to those questions. Could she do that?

She was beginning to think that she'd have to.

Aly felt a piercing pain under her ribs and put her hand on her heart. Damn, there was another bout of indigestion, something she'd been experiencing a lot lately. If this carried on for much longer, she would have to go to a doctor—something she hated to do. She'd spent more time in doctors' rooms and hospitals than one person should ever have to.

But as an organ recipient, she couldn't afford to take chances. She figured that pain in her chest region wasn't likely to have anything to do with her liver, but she couldn't know that for sure. She could only hope that it would prove to be nothing more than indigestion, brought on by prolonged bouts of Merrick's not-so-merry company.

After a few days away, she'd feel better.

And if she didn't…she'd deal with making a doctor's appointment then.

Merrick exited the taxi, handed over some cash and looked up the prestigious building. Avangeline bought this apartment building over thirty years ago, at the height of her success, and she'd handed each of her grandsons, along with a sizable trust fund, an apartment in the building. To his surprise and shock, on his twenty-first birthday, he'd received the same. He'd tried to persuade Avangeline to change her mind, insisted she'd done enough by paying for his education.

He remembered her words as if she'd uttered them five minutes before. *You have lived in my house as my grandson, eaten at my table as my grandson and been subjected to the same rules and expectations as my grandsons. You* are *my grandson. Now do go away, as I am finding this conversation excessively tedious.*

He'd taken his trust fund, invested it and rented out his apartment those years he was in the military. When he returned, he bought a food truck, then another, and dotted them around the city. He took his brand to Miami, then LA, and these days, his food trucks and fast-food diners were synonymous with healthy eating. A vegetarian since he was twelve, he'd found it difficult to find decent and fast vegetarian food, and on seeing a gap in the market, aimed to fill it.

His business suited him. He worked wherever he felt comfortable: sometimes that was an unused conference room at Fox and Jack's headquarters, sometimes here at his apartment and frequently at an airport, as he was often on the road. His accountants and marketing people, his publicity crew all worked online too. It was the modern way...sometimes a little lonely but streamlined.

Merrick greeted the doorman, and headed for the elevator bank. He punched his floor number, and the doors started to slide closed until, at the last minute, a feminine hand slid between the frame and the door, stopping its progress. He lifted his head and jerked it back when his eyes connected with Aly's golden-green gaze. Her mouth dropped open and they stared at each for a couple of seconds before she stepped into the elevator.

"I presume you are staying in Avangeline's apartment?" he asked, his voice ice cold.

She rubbed the area over her chest, and he couldn't help taking in her yellow-and-white crossover dress, skimming her slim body and ending midthigh. She wore trendy white sneakers on her feet and the strap of her bag crossed over her chest to rest between her breasts. Breasts that he'd worshipped, suckled, with pretty pink nipples he'd laved with his tongue.

Merrick felt his pants tighten and silently cursed. She was the last lover he'd had and, judging by the way his body went into hyperawareness mode whenever she was near, he suspected he'd gone too long without. But whenever he thought of going to a bar to find a hookup or calling up an old friend who knew the score—a fun night, no commitment—he found something else to do.

He didn't want any woman; he wanted Aly. The one woman he couldn't stand. Who hated him in return. Aly placed her fist just below her sternum and wrinkled her nose. "Can we not argue today, Knowles? Just for a change?"

He noticed her paler-than-normal face and frowned. "Are you okay?"

She shrugged. "I've just got stupid heartburn. I've had it, on and off, for a couple of weeks, and it seems to be getting worse."

"Have you seen a doctor?" he demanded, going into fix-it mode.

Aly responded by rolling her eyes. "I've seen many doctors, Knowles. It tends to happen when you've had an organ transplant."

His heart swooped at the thought of her being in a hospital, fighting for her life. Thin, pale, eyes dull with pain. It made him feel a little sick, and a lot sad. He cleared his throat and forced himself to narrow his eyes. "I meant recently, smart-ass."

She looked away. "No. I suppose I should, but I'd rather have my toenails pulled."

"Not a fan, huh?"

Her arched eyebrows raised. "Would you be?"

Fair point. He noticed that the elevator doors were still

open and he plugged in the code that would take the elevator directly to the penthouse apartment. Avangeline handed over the code years ago because she frequently used them as couriers to ferry pieces of expensive art between her apartment and Calcott Manor.

As she informed them, there was a reasonable chance of her not killing them if a piece was damaged in transit. She couldn't guarantee that with anyone else.

Avangeline loved her art.

"Do you often come to the city and take advantage of Avangeline by staying in her apartment?" Merrick demanded as the elevator doors opened up directly into her exquisitely decorated open-plan living area.

"You like to think badly of me, don't you?" Aly quietly asked as she walked into the sitting room and pulled off her bag. She dropped it onto a rare African throne chair and ambled over to the floor-to-ceiling windows, looking down at the tiny trees and minuscule humans in Central Park. "Do you do it so that you can push the memories of that night we spent together away?"

No! Yes. Maybe.

That and because he couldn't wrap his head around her inheriting Malcolm's traits, memories and thoughts. He believed in what he could feel, see, hear and smell. And he also believed that this life was all someone got. If you screwed up here, you didn't get to live on in someone else and use them as a vehicle to make it right.

"I don't believe in your connection to Malcolm," Merrick admitted. He walked over to where she stood and leaned his shoulder into the glass, looking down into her lovely face. "I'm looking for an alternate explanation."

She surprised him by nodding. "I spent years doing that. Like you, I believe in what can be measured and evaluated.

Some people find comfort in thoughts of the afterlife, and in connecting with people who have passed on, but I'm not one of them. I would never consult a psychic or a medium. I've tried to rationalize it away, but I can't help what I'm feeling!"

He stared at her, not allowing his eyes to drop. "You can be as *connected* to Malcolm as you like, but all I care about is that you aren't taking advantage of Avangeline and my mother."

She shoved her hands into her hair and gripped the long strands, looking intensely frustrated. "Have I asked them for money?"

"No," he admitted.

"Has anything gone missing from the house?"

"No."

"Have I broken anything, dropped Avangeline's name, spoken to the press about her? Have I done anything but sort out some photographs for her, spend some time with her and look into the Grantham family history?"

She hadn't. In fact, she'd been the perfect guest. Interested, helpful, undemanding. Avangeline approved of her and Merrick's own mother adored her. "No. But the question remains…why are you still at Calcott Manor?"

"Not that you'll believe me, but I'm looking for some answers and I can't walk away until I find them."

Merrick rubbed the back of his neck, taken aback by the frustration in her eyes, the anxiety that he caught the occasional flash of.

"Answers to what, Alyson?"

She hesitated, the shrugged. "I'm drawn to the plane crash that killed the Grantham twins and their wives—Jack, Fox, and Soren's parents. Why did it crash? Was it a pilot error or something else? I think—oh, this is ridiculous!—but I think—"

"What do you think, Aly?" he prompted her.

She shook her head and knew she wouldn't give him a direct answer to his question. "In my spare time, I've researched the history of the house, and read up on the family. But I'm drawn specifically to the crash. I've studied the NTSB report and dug up every article I could find on it, but they all say the same thing. I haven't been able to get anything that isn't on public record. Avangeline hasn't given me permission to dig any further. But maybe that's where the answers to my questions are. Maybe that's where I'll find out why that plane went down."

Merrick considered her words. She'd been asking questions about the Grantham twins since she arrived at Calcott Manor, so her statement didn't surprise him. But it was her frustration and annoyance with the situation that made his suspicious nature recede, just a little.

And maybe, instead of fighting with her, poking at her and trying to chase her off, something he hadn't had much success with, he should try understanding her a little better. If he did that then, maybe they could find the answers she needed so she could leave his life all the sooner.

It sounded as good a plan as any other.

"Go away, Merrick. I don't have the energy to fight with you today," Aly told him.

Merrick pushed his hands through his hair before looking more closely at her. Over the past few months, he tended to look past her, not liking the fact that her green-gold eyes could make his heart jump, resisting the urge to stroke his hand over her thick hair.

She looked thinner than when he first met her; some of her luscious curves had narrowed and her heart-shaped face seemed a little more gaunt. Her pale skin was more white than creamy and there were dark stripes under her almond-shaped eyes. She looked like she hadn't been sleeping and his surge of protectiveness irritated him. He wanted to see her as the woman who was taking advantage of Avangeline, but he was having a hard time doing that.

He needed her to leave so they could all go back to normal. But what would normal look like, especially since the Granthams knew Aly carried a piece of Malcolm? All the rest of them liked her, and she'd reconnected all three of his brothers—through a couple of wild guesses that somehow hit the mark—with Malcolm, the man who'd made such a huge impact on their lives.

He had to look at things clearly, because everyone else sure as hell wouldn't. Couldn't.

When she had more information on the plane crash and some of the answers she needed—if it was even possible to get to the truth after such a long time, with no survivors to provide a firsthand account—she'd stop hanging around Calcott Manor and would go back to her life. In time her connection to the Granthams would fade, as most connections did. He needed her back in Jersey City, out of sight, out of mind. Then he could start to breathe again. Date. Sleep with a random woman without imagining her lithe, lovely body under his, the taste of her spicy mouth, the gorgeous womanly scent he inhaled when he kissed her between her legs.

He could go back to normal. Merrick *really* wanted to go back to normal.

"I'll help you."

Her head snapped up at his abrupt words. "What?"

He lifted his hands and let them fall. "I'll help you try

and work out why the plane crashed. Maybe then you'll have some peace."

Aly tipped her head to the side, and he couldn't miss the scorn in her eyes. "You mean *you'll* get some peace and I'll be out of your hair."

He held her gaze and tried not to flinch. She was so damn smart. Brains and beauty were such a killer combination. "It annoys you that you don't like me and definitely don't trust me, but that you still want me. Doesn't it?"

How was he supposed to answer that question without putting himself in an untenable position? Yeah, he hadn't been able to switch off his feelings, to dismiss her from his thoughts. And she was wrong in one regard; he *did* like her. From the moment they first started speaking in Clancy's, he'd liked her fast wit, her self-deprecating comments and her insightful observations. He liked her a little too much, and that was a huge problem.

Sex he could dismiss. Liking someone, not so much.

"So, are you going to let me help you?" he asked, ignoring her question. "My brothers trust me implicitly, so if you say yes, I might be able to get better access to their parents' private documents."

He mentally winced. Yeah, he wasn't sure if Jack and Fox would be happy about Aly knowing about the hard-core sex club Jesse and Heather Grantham owned and operated and their parents' dangerous, and borderline illegal actions connected to that club. If they didn't want her to have that knowledge, then he could steer her away from anything that might hint at it. He could hand her information on a very need-to-know basis, and only if it pertained to the air crash.

He could be the buffer between her and his brothers, protecting his guys as he'd promised Avangeline he would over twenty-five years ago.

"What else would you bring to the party?" Aly asked him, sounding skeptical.

"Knowledge of the aviation industry."

"You fly?"

He did. He'd flown helicopters in the military and after leaving the military, he'd continued to pursue his passion as a hobby. He now knew how to fly most planes ranging from Cessnas to small jets. Besides his business, aviation was his true love and Merrick felt sad it wasn't something he could share with his brothers. They flew for convenience, while he flew because he loved being thousands of feet above the ground. Whether he was just cruising along, far above the world and its troubles, or doing a stall turn in an Edge-540 or a barrel roll in an Extra 330SC, everything about flying was incredible. Nothing compared—except for maybe sex with Aly.

"Yeah, I fly."

Aly, because she was Aly, lifted her eyebrows at his brief response. She bit the corner of her lip and tapped her finger against the glass pane, the tips of her nails unvarnished. He badly wanted to drop his mouth to where her shoulder met her neck, to taste her sweet-smelling skin. Her head spun around to look at him again and their eyes collided. Within hers, he saw want and need, and more than a hint of desperation.

"I hate that I can't stop thinking about you, that I desperately want a repeat of that night."

"Me too." It was a small admission but one he wanted. No, needed.

He wasn't sure who moved first, him or her, but just seconds later, his fingers were tunneled in her hair, his palms held her face and his mouth was on hers, desperately exploring. She sucked in air, and he slid his tongue past her teeth, taking the opportunity to rediscover her sensual mouth. Her lips were softer than he remembered, and she was even more delicious than he recalled. Lust and need and want combined to form a fireball that ran down his spine and lodged in his balls. His cock jumped to attention, and he pushed it into her stomach, loving the fact that she pushed back.

In fact, her hands were streaking over his shoulders, tugging up his shirt to find his bare skin, betraying her eagerness. He felt her fingers dance up and down his spine and he covered her breast with his hand, quickly finding her nipple and teasing it to a hard point. Using his other hand, he tugged the fabric of her dress up her thigh and curled his hand over her butt, warm beneath the thin fabric of her panties. He slipped his fingers under the seam and moved his fingers down, stroking her from behind. Her legs fell open and he sighed at the wet warmth of her entrance— proof that she was turned on, that she wanted him. She might not like how strongly she responded to him, but her instinctive, breathy reaction to him was proof their blazing attraction was as scorching hot as ever.

Aly practically climbed up his body and he boosted her up, holding her with one forearm under her butt as she wrapped her legs around his hips, rocking against his cock, her head tipped back, and her throat exposed. Merrick dragged his tongue over her exposed collarbone, down her chest, and pulled her nipple into his mouth, fabric and all.

"God, I've wanted you," he muttered, "wanted this."

"I don't like you, but I like what you do to me," Aly whipped back, her words punchy with lust.

Merrick lifted his head, caught by her bold green eyes. She didn't like him, but she liked what he did to her. Her words pierced through his tough exoskeleton, and for a moment, he wondered what it would be like to have this woman actually *like* him, love him even. What would it feel like to have like and love, need and want and lust combined as he lowered her to the floor, or took her up against the wall?

What would that look like? How would it feel?

He didn't know and he was appalled that, just for a nanosecond, he desperately wanted to find out. Shock rushed over him like cold water, cooling his ardor.

Merrick loosened his arm. Her legs dropped down, and when her feet hit the floor, he stepped away. He couldn't do this—he *shouldn't*. Aly affected him too much; she was too potent and too wrapped up in his family for him to play with. Sex between them would make a complicated situation worse, and he didn't need the additional hassle of juggling a lover who loved his body but didn't like him.

And could he blame her for that? They'd had one blazing night together, but from the moment they'd reconnected in Avangeline's study, he'd given her nothing but grief. He'd openly dismissed her and baited her. He hadn't been at his best…and he felt ashamed of himself,

Merrick walked over to the kitchen area of the apartment, which was a massive open-plan room, found two glasses and shoved them under the fridge's water dispenser. He half-filled both glasses and walked back over to Aly, who'd yet to move from her position half slumped against the wall, her expression miserable.

He shoved a glass into her hand and she drank deeply.

Would she let him help her with her investigation? His stomach clenched at the thought that she might say no, knowing he'd be deeply disappointed if she refused his offer. Crap, she tied him up in knots. Because he didn't like feeling that way, his words came out harsher than he wanted them to. "Do you want my help or not? It's the last time I'm offering."

Three

Did she? Want his help?

Aly turned away from him and flicked her thumbnail against her front teeth.

She'd initially thought that her curiosity about the plane crash was just that, inquisitiveness, but that explanation always left her unsatisfied and uncomfortable. But when the five-second clip of the plane smashing into a mountain started recurring more frequently in her mind, she knew why she needed to be at Calcott Manor. It was unexplainable, irrational but she knew this was something she had to do.

The question now was…did she want Merrick's help in trying to track down what caused the plane to slam into a mountain? She could do with his aviation expertise, given that what she knew about airplanes could be written on the back of a postage stamp. And yes, maybe the Granthams would feel more comfortable and would be more forthcoming, with their memories and the twins' personal papers, if they knew Merrick was helping her. They trusted him implicitly.

On the other hand, accepting Merrick's help would mean working closely with him and being in his company. When he dropped by to see his mom and Avangeline at Calcott House, she'd mostly managed to avoid him. It was a big place, and she knew he evaded her too, which made it easy to keep from crossing paths. When they had to be together, on the odd occasion when she was invited to a family dinner or lunch, she sat at the opposite end of the table from him or kept to the other side of the room. Despite it being months since they slept together, it still hurt her when he looked at her with mistrust and suspicion in his eyes. Aly knew that he thought that she'd set him up, that she'd used sex as a way to gain better access to his family.

If she'd even thought that far, Merrick was the last Grantham family member she would've chosen to try to manipulate. Within two minutes of meeting him, she knew he was a guy who would never be forced into doing anything he didn't want to do.

And yes, she could use his help, but she didn't want to spend the next couple of weeks sniping and fighting with him. It was exhausting.

But she wanted her life back. Wanted to walk into the new phase of her life unencumbered by whispers of Malcolm. To do that, she needed to follow her gut instinct and investigate, as much as she possibly could, the plane crash—no matter who she had to work with to get it done.

"I didn't know who you were when I met you in Clancy's," she told Merrick, needing to explain. "I didn't know of your connection to Avangeline. I knew about her grandsons, but not about you."

He didn't look convinced.

She didn't like having her word doubted but she carried on. "As for the whole cellular memory thing, I know how weird it all sounds, Merrick." She tucked her hands under her armpits. He knew that she'd confronted Fox about a ring owned by his mom, Heather, that no one knew about; he also knew that she'd understood the secret sign Soren and Malcolm used to use before each of Soren's races. She didn't know if Peyton told anyone of how she had correctly recalled a box containing a long-ago photograph of Peyton and Jack, but that was Peyton's story to tell, not hers.

She knew things she shouldn't—things only Malcolm had known—but Merrick refused to acknowledge that fact.

"I'm going to say this once more, and never again... I don't have some kind of hidden end game," she told him. "I don't know why I need to find out about the crash, just that I have to. That's it. That's why I'm still here."

He stared at her, his face blank. God, she hated the lack of emotion on his face. She far preferred him to be angry than impossible to reach. "If you can't trust me, or accept my explanation, I can't accept your help. I don't want to spend the next couple of weeks trading barbs with you, arguing with you and constantly trying to convince you I'm not out to hurt your family.

"And if I agree to your help, then I'd like you to be pleasant. Or, at the very least, polite," she added.

Merrick rubbed the back of his neck and then jammed his hand into the pocket of his pants. "Are you asking for us to be friends?"

That would be pushing it, Aly conceded. "I'm asking for us to *not* be enemies. Acquaintances, perhaps? Colleagues?"

He considered her words. "Okay."

Um...what exactly was he agreeing to? "We're going to

be friends?" she asked, annoyed at the hint of hope she heard in her voice.

A touch of humor danced through his eyes. "Let's aim for not being enemies and work our way up." He glanced at his watch. "I have an online meeting in ten minutes. So, are we doing this or what?"

It was do-or-die time. "Yes."

"Good." Merrick nodded once, spun on his heel and strode toward the hall. A few seconds later, Aly heard the private lift open and close. Right. Okay then.

Bye.

A few seconds later her phone dinged with a message.

Come up to my place after seven. Bring a vegetarian pizza. We'll go from there.

Aly fought the urge to salute, both irritated and, ridiculously, a little turned on at his commanding attitude.

Merrick opened the door to his apartment and Aly sucked in her breath and told her suddenly weak knees to behave themselves. His dark hair was mussed from running his hands through it, his eyes were a little unfocused behind black-rimmed glasses—so hot—and his feet were bare. Nice feet. *Big* feet...

He glanced down at the enormous pizza box in her hand and she heard the rumble of his hungry stomach. She'd guess that meant he hadn't stopped for food since he'd left her earlier that morning.

"I'm starving," he said, stepping aside and gesturing for her to enter.

"I heard," Aly answered, handing over the flat box. She shoved her hands into the back pockets of her best jeans,

the ones that made her legs look longer and her butt shape-
lier, and feeling his eyes on her, tried to focus on taking in
his apartment.

It was smaller, a lot smaller than Avangeline's penthouse
monstrosity, but was also open plan. But Merrick had gone
for the industrial aesthetic, leaving steel beams exposed, a
rough concrete wall and masculine furniture. A dramatic,
stormy seascape dominated one wall.

She slowly turned, taking in the wide desk against the opposite wall, the bank of computers. "No separate offices?"
she asked.

"You're confusing me with my grandmother," he told her,
walking behind the kitchen island and dropping the pizza
box on its clean surface. "Her apartment is ten times bigger than this one."

He turned around and reached for a bottle of red wine
from a built-in wine rack and briefly inspected the bottle
before nodding. He took two huge wineglasses out of a cup-
board and asked if he could pour her a glass.

Was that a trick question? She nodded.

"The place has three bedrooms, but I use one of them as
a gym," he told her. "I like the view from this room best,
so I work here."

"Do you miss not having a permanent office?" she asked,
sitting down on the edge of the leather couch and crossing
her legs. She played with the cuffs of her striped, men's-
style button-down shirt. Apart from the night they first met,
this was the first time they'd spoken without sniping at each
other and she felt nervous. How silly.

She accepted the glass he handed her and took a grateful sip. Rich, mellow, fruity liquid slid down her throat and
she knew it was an outstanding wine. When she returned
to her real life, drinking cheap wine again was going to be

hard. Unfortunately, she wouldn't be able to afford the excellent wines Avangeline and her family took for granted.

"I've never had an office, so I don't miss it," he explained, sitting down next to her and stretching out his long legs. "I sometimes work out of the boardroom of Fox and Jack's headquarters, partly to bug them, partly to keep an eye on them."

"Why would you need to keep an eye on them?" she asked, placing her glass on the wood-and-glass coffee table in front of her.

"Well, Fox has a temper and gets irritable quite quickly and Jack overworks himself. I can usually get Fox to see sense and I can always distract Jack, so I tend to head there whenever I'm in town. Unfortunately, I'm not in town as much as I'd like."

"So you're your brothers' keeper?"

He laughed, but it was a touch forced and he failed to meet her eyes. "I think their partners have them firmly in hand these days."

"Do you like them?" Aly asked. She'd connected with all three women in different ways and liked them all.

Merrick smiled, and for once, it was snark-free. "I do. They are funny and smart and strong enough to keep my bossy brothers from trampling all over them."

She liked that Merrick didn't refer to their looks, especially Eliot, who'd recently retired as a supermodel. It seemed that he rated intelligence and strength over hair and perfect features. She picked up her wine and stood up to look at his collection of vintage records. She flipped through his vinyls, which included everything from opera to hard rock and punk. It was a reminder that Merrick Knowles couldn't be put into a box. "You call them your brothers, yet you were never legally adopted into the Grantham clan, were you?"

After telling her to choose some music and set up the player, Merrick answered her question. "I've lived with them since I was eight," he told her. "I was never treated like the housekeeper's son and I never felt out of the circle."

"Never?"

He shook his head. "A few weeks after the others arrived, Malcolm asked Avangeline if we could all move into one bedroom. After losing their parents, it was natural that they all wanted to be together. Avangeline agreed and converted one of the attics for them. I had my own bedroom in the housekeeper's apartment, but Avangeline put four bunk beds in the attic bedroom—enough for all five of us and friends—and I spent more time up there than I did in my room."

A smile touched his sexy mouth, and she saw the memories rolling through his eyes. How lucky he was to grow up within such a large family, whether he was a legal son or not.

"Very quickly, it became obvious that we were a gang of five and Avangeline treated me exactly the same as she did the others. She also paid for my schooling and gave me a trust fund when I turned twenty-one. She gifted me with this apartment, too—not to mention the start-up money for my company."

The mellow sound of a blues track filled the room, but Aly caught a note of hesitation in his voice. "You don't feel comfortable with all that she's given you," she stated, sinking to sit cross-legged on the floor in front of the record player and his collection, glass in her hand.

"I'm so appreciative of her generosity but I'm not her blood relative," he said, his eyes sliding away from hers.

"So, you can act as her grandson, be protective of her like a grandson, treat your brothers as your own, but you can't take her money?"

"Uh…"

"You can't pick and choose, Merrick," Aly gently told him. "Avangeline is an all-or-nothing type of woman. You're either all in or all out. You can't cherry-pick which elements of the relationship you feel comfortable with."

He sucked in a small breath, and Aly felt like her words hit a target she hadn't known was there. She mentally shrugged, refusing to take back her words. She hadn't said anything that wasn't true. Avangeline didn't care about DNA or blood; Merrick was her grandson, end of story. It just was the way it was, and she would act in accordance with that belief.

Merrick sat up, leaned forward and put his glass on the coffee table. "Would you like to eat here or at the dining table, or the breakfast bar in the kitchen?"

Right, conversation closed.

Aly looked around. The dining table looked a little too fancy, the stools at the bar appeared uncomfortable and she was perfectly happy where she was. "Here is good."

Besides, she wasn't a fancy girl. She knew enough not to embarrass herself at an upmarket restaurant but when it came to a relaxed meal like pizza, she liked to keep it casual.

Merrick returned with plates, paper napkins and the large pizza box. Aly flipped it open and inhaled the smell of tomato and basil. "I went for a margherita. I hope that's okay."

"It's always okay," Merrick told her, sitting down on the floor opposite her.

"No meat, though," Aly commented, reaching for a slice. "Have you always been a vegetarian?"

Something deep and dark flashed in his eyes and he stared down at his slice of pizza. "Pretty much."

She wanted to push but then she pulled back, remembering that she hated answering personal questions. She usually kept her distance from people, always terrified of becoming emotionally attached because people made a habit of abandoning her. When she got sick, she'd lost the few friends she had—it was pretty hard to keep up friendships when you were either in the hospital or too sick to move. Her family had been all she'd had left, until her sister and mother had left her in the most final way.

What made it worse in Avery's case was that she'd *chosen* the path that led to her death. That was what Aly had trouble wrapping her head around. She'd told her sister, time and time again, that she was flirting with danger, that she had to get clean and that if she didn't, she was going to die. But Avery just sank deeper and deeper into that world until Aly's worse fears came true.

You've got pretty close to Avangeline and Jacinta, an annoying voice piped up from a corner of her heart. *You've bonded with Peyton and Ru, and Eliot. Despite your vow to keep yourself apart, it's the first time in years you've made genuine connections.*

Somehow, without knowing how, she'd found a confidante in Jace—she genuinely adored Merrick's mother. She also enjoyed Avangeline's wisdom and straight talking. Calcott Manor was the closest thing to a home she'd had in years.

She bit down on her slice of pizza, chewed and reminded herself that when she left Calcott Manor, those connections would probably fade, then evaporate. She'd like to keep those women in her life, but the truth was that she'd probably go back to working insane hours and wouldn't be able to spare the time relationships required. Everything would go back to normal.

And she would go back to being alone. And lonely.

She gave herself a mental shake. Her visit to Calcott

Manor was a step out of time; it wasn't real life. Living in a mansion, having access to a private beach, being among priceless art and enjoying the company of amazingly bright and interesting people wasn't an anomaly: that was Malcolm's life.

It wasn't hers.

"Tell me again why you are determined to get to the bottom of the plane crash," Merrick asked her, after wolfing down another slice of pizza. He wiped his fingers on a napkin and placed his elbows on the coffee table.

She didn't want to, because prior experience had taught her that discussing Malcolm meant fighting with him.

"We've managed forty-five minutes without biting each other's head off," Aly pointed out. "And if I tell you, you're going to roll your eyes and say something insulting and I'm going to snap back and probably storm out." She sighed. "I don't want to do that, not tonight."

His blue eyes connected with hers and her heart flopped against her rib cage. He really was the most gorgeous man. "Fair enough," he replied. "But if we don't talk about something else, I'm not going to be able to resist the urge to lean across the table and take your mouth. And then you."

She wanted that—she did. But it was precisely because she wanted it so much, craved him so much, she knew she couldn't let things go that far. Merrick wasn't a guy she could easily forget, and she didn't need to make things more complicated when she left Calcott Manor soon.

"My feelings about Malcolm, and the weirdness and the memories, weren't so strong right after my surgery," she told him, pushing away her plate on which lay her half-eaten slice of pizza. "I initially thought the fact that I liked candy and cars suddenly was a little funny, maybe charming. It was fine, something I could easily live with if it meant a second shot at life."

He didn't say anything but rested his forearms on his bent knees, his focus entirely on her. "The urge to meet Malcolm's family grew stronger and I reached out and asked to meet. As soon as I drove through the gates of Avangeline's house, I felt different. And no, before you ask—I wasn't bombarded with Malcolm's memories. I just felt like I'd come home."

She was also, pretty much immediately, aware of whispers of guilt even though she was unable to pinpoint its source.

"Mal loved Calcott Manor," Merrick said, surprising her. "He, being the eldest, had an attachment to the property. He researched its history and had plans for the garden. He wanted to restore the orangery and folly that had been there when the property was first built."

Aly linked her arms around her bent knees and, because Merrick hadn't shut her down, proceeded with her explanation. "Before I met them, I researched the family, just like Avangeline did me. I read about the plane crash, and that night, I had this…"

She bit her lip, not sure whether to continue. This was going to lead to an argument; she just *knew* it.

"You had what, Aly?"

"A vision." She hauled in a breath and sat up and lifted her chin. "Look, I don't get flashes of Malcolm's life or anything like that but…*but* I saw a plane crash into a mountain."

He winced but didn't say anything, for which she was grateful. "After meeting Avangeline, the image morphed into a five-second clip. And it just keeps playing, over and over again. All the time. That's why I'm doing this—I just want it to go away."

* * *

Merrick rotated his glass so that his wine swished from side to side. "These visions you have—" his tone was so bland it caused her hackles to rise "—are they graphic?"

She shook her head and shrugged. "No, not really. A plane hits a mountain and then explodes. I don't mean to make light of what happened, but..." She shrugged.

He looked at her, his expression inscrutable and, once again, she couldn't read him. What was he thinking? Was he silently mocking her, rolling his eyes? So far, they'd managed to avoid an argument and Aly thought it was an excellent time to go. "I think it's time for me to leave."

"Why? I didn't say anything," Merrick protested.

"But you want to," Aly muttered, standing up. He didn't deny her statement and she sighed. One step forward, a hundred back.

"We're not going to get anywhere if you keep walking away, Alyson," Merrick said, getting to his feet. "Sure, I don't understand any of this, and not understanding makes me irritable, but walking away doesn't help."

He was right: it didn't. But, after a lifetime of living with two highly strung and volatile women, walking away was how she dealt with conflict. After all, someone couldn't yell at you if you weren't there, right?

But being with Merrick—this man who made her blood heat, the man she wanted to see naked again—made her feel vulnerable. Being with him felt very personal indeed.

But he was right, walking away wouldn't solve anything.

Aly dropped down to sit on the edge of the chair and stared down at his rather fine Persian carpet in shades of maroon and royal blue. Maybe they could talk about the plane crash without arguing. Hopefully.

"Please don't give me grief about the vision, Merrick. It's

hard enough for me to wrap my head around it, let alone let anyone else know about it."

"You haven't told anyone else about what you've been seeing?" he asked as he sat down next to her. He placed his hand in the center of her back and Aly leaned her shoulder into his, enjoying his warmth and steadiness.

"No."

He was so solid, like a tall and thick tree that barely registered a raging storm, standing strong and providing shelter. She wanted to curl up in his arms and have him be the barrier between her and the world, the barrier between her and Malcolm's memories. She just wanted to rest, just for a minute.

It was pretty damn exhausting always being on your own, all the time.

"How can I help you, Alyson?"

She didn't hesitate. "You could ask Jack and Fox whether there's any chance of me being allowed to look through the twins' papers, particularly Jesse's, to see if I can discover anything relevant. Despite the vision and knowing some things I shouldn't, I have an analytical mind and I'm good at picking up things others have missed."

"I can ask them. I'm certain they'd like some closure about the crash, so I can't see them objecting."

Aly looked up at him, taken aback at his easy agreement. "Thank you."

"But the chances of getting an answer after so long are not good. You do realize that, don't you?"

She nodded. It was her biggest fear. What if she went on this journey, found nothing and left Calcott Manor and the family behind with a dozen questions still unanswered? Would she live with the guilt of failure, for not doing more for the rest of her life, or would it fade?

She didn't know but that was a question for later. For now, she had to give everything she had to this search and hope that she'd be able to start the next chapter of her life guilt and question free.

She'd also be Merrick free.

That thought made her heart hurt.

"Thank you," she told Merrick, briefly resting a hand on his muscled thigh. She felt him tense and when she looked at him, found him staring at her mouth. It took all her will-power not to lift her chin and press her mouth on his. But if she did that, all her clothes would come off…

Would that be such a bad thing? A part of her, a big part of her, thought not.

Merrick obliterated the moment by standing up and reaching for the wine bottle. He held it up to the light and Aly saw that it was empty. "I'll get another bottle."

Ah, *no*. Alcohol and lust were never a good combination. She rose to her feet and crossed her arms and looked toward the door. "I think I should go," she told him.

"Why?"

"Because if I don't, I'll ask you to take me to bed and I'm not sure if that's a good idea."

"It's a terrible idea," Merrick replied, sounding a bit ragged. "Let's do it anyway."

She managed a smile. "That's your small brain talking, Knowles." She wanted to kiss his cheek but settled for patting his arm. "Talk to your brothers, see what they say and come back to me. You have my number."

Merrick nodded. "I do." He gestured to the half-eaten box of pizza. "Are you sure you've had enough? You didn't eat very much."

Aly knew that he'd noticed that her clothes were a little

baggy and that her face was a little thinner. Food hadn't been sitting well with her lately. "I'm fine, thanks."

She walked to the door, Merrick on her heels.

At the door, she stopped and turned. "So, you'll call me and tell me what they say?"

He reached past her to open the door and she inhaled his citrus-and-sandalwood cologne. So sexy. "Yeah, but I'll have to get them all together and that might take some time."

She was going back to Jersey City in two weeks. "Sooner rather than later, yeah?"

He nodded and dropped a light kiss on her temple. "Want me to walk you up?" he asked.

Aly didn't know if he was being serious or not. She looked down the hallway to where the elevators were. "I'm going to the penthouse in the same building, Knowles. I think I'll be okay."

He gripped the frame of the door above his head, his muscles bunching. "There might be monsters in the elevator." Right, he was definitely teasing now.

But he didn't know that she wasn't afraid of monsters. It was the twin dragons of guilt and not-knowing that terrified her.

Four

Jacinta stood in the bigger of Calcott Manor's two greenhouses and looked around, unsure what she should do. There were basil seedlings to transplant, tomato vines that needed tying and weeds to pull. She didn't have the energy to do anything.

She sat on a stool and stared down at her too-clean hands. Apparently, endorphins were released when you scrabbled about in the dirt, tending to plants, but Jace thought there weren't enough endorphins in the world to make her feel better at the moment.

She missed Pasco. Missed him with every fiber of her being.

She glanced toward the door of the greenhouse and, on the big screen of her mind, saw him standing there. He'd often tracked her down here, knowing that it was her favorite place on the estate. He'd find her, filthy from gardening, and pull her dirty and hot body into his. He'd lay his mouth, warm, wonderful and wicked, on hers. He'd even taken her, one Wednesday morning, as she stood leaning against that bench.

Hot sex in the greenhouse; it sounded like a scene out of a raunchy erotic novel.

Jace stood up and picked up a tray of seedlings, the pad of her finger drifting over a tiny leaf. Calcott Manor didn't feel the same without Pasco around. It felt empty, like some of its energy had dissipated.

It didn't feel like home anymore.

And that was a huge problem. For around half her life, Calcott Manor had been her home and her refuge, her favorite place in the world, and now it felt like a too-tight blanket.

Twenty-five years ago, she'd wandered into Hatfield holding a little boy's hand, with twenty dollars in her pocket and zero options. Then she met Avangeline, was offered a job and she hadn't left the place since. She could've, but she'd never wanted to. Everything she wanted—the house and the grounds, the boys she thought of as her own, and her favorite person and savior, Avangeline—was here.

And then Pasco arrived to rent Avangeline's guest house and turned her life inside out and upside down.

She broke their affair off on the excuse that she was too old for him—there was a twelve-year age gap between them—but the truth was that it wasn't so much the age gap but the experience gap between them that bothered her. She might be older, but Pasco was far more courageous and knowledgeable about life. Pasco was able to meet the world as it was, not how he wanted it to be.

Because, to Jace, Calcott Manor was how she wanted the world to be. She was sheltered and protected there—Avangeline's wealth and power ensured that.

But instead of feeling comfortable and at ease, she now felt restricted and tangled up. She usually loved the peace and the tranquillity of the setting, but she was craving light and sensation, the sound of crowds, the smell of car exhausts and the mournful wail of emergency vehicles.

She was craving the city because Pasco was there.

Because wherever he was, was where she wanted to be.

Jace dashed away a tear, telling herself not to be stupid. Calcott Manor was her home. She loved managing the estate, working in her greenhouses, liaising with the farm's employees and acting as Avangeline's representative. She yanked a tiny basil plant out of its container and rammed it into a bed of too-dry soil.

This was where she belonged.

Wasn't it?

Merrick felt unaccountably nervous—which was ridiculous. He was meeting his brothers, the men who'd been at his side for the past quarter century. They were the people who knew him best, who knew his faults and foibles. He trusted them and they trusted him back.

He buttoned his jacket and then unbuttoned it and caught saw his tense face reflected at him in the closed doors leading to Avangeline's, Jack and Fox's multi-award-winning restaurant in their iconic Manhattan hotel, The Forrester-Grantham.

They'd agreed to meet here just before the lunch service began. Merrick didn't think he'd be able to eat, not with how nervous he felt.

After all the brothers had been through lately, especially Fox and Jack, asking them to dive back into their parent's past was going to take some finesse.

Not something Merrick had an abundance of.

He opened the door to the restaurant, walked in and saw Jack, Soren and Fox sitting at the table kept open for VIPs.

They all looked relaxed, at ease in their skins and their lives. They also all looked like they were getting regular, hot sex. Lucky bastards.

He hadn't gotten laid since he hooked up with Aly three months ago. Hooked up? That sounded too tawdry to describe the amazing night they spent together. He'd wanted to see her again, couldn't actually wait—something that was highly unusual for him—and then he'd walked into Avangeline's sitting room to see her sitting on the couch, laughing. Within a few seconds Merrick knew exactly who she was—the recipient of Mal's liver. In a few seconds, he noticed that she'd charmed Avangeline and his mom and he'd immediately decided that her presence at Calcott Manor would upend all their lives. He'd also concluded that she had been using him the previous night.

He now knew that she'd been oblivious about his connection to Avangeline but his irritation at not being able to stop craving her remained.

"Jeez, duck for cover," Fox said as he approached the table.

Merrick frowned at him. "Why?" he asked, sliding into his seat.

"You look like the human equivalent of a thunderstorm," Fox told him. Fox was normally taciturn and snappy, so his teasing was a bit of a shock.

"I preferred you when you were silent," Merrick told him, before greeting the waiter and asking for a glass of club soda with lime.

"What's wrong with you?" Jack asked him, reaching for a slice of sourdough from the basket on the table. He placed it on his side plate, tossed some Irish salt over it and dipped the edge into a small bowl of olive oil. Jack bit down and closed his eyes in delight. "So good."

"How's my nephew?" Merrick asked him to dodge the question. Jack was always more than happy to let any conversation turn to his son. Noah, at eighteen months old, was immensely skilled in wrapping the adults in his world around his overdeveloped baby finger.

Jack grinned, delight in his eyes and on his face. "Fast, demanding, and he exhausts me," he admitted. "But he's amazing and I can't wait to have more kids."

Two kids or twelve, his previously perfectionistic brother was embracing the chaos of fatherhood. Merrick turned his attention to his Olympic-medal-winning brother, Soren, and told him that it was good to see him. They hadn't touched base for a couple of weeks.

"I've been so busy trying to get our foundation up and running that I haven't looked up for a while," Soren admitted. "How's Jace, Merrick?"

He rested his arms on the table and winced. "Flat. Unengaged, unless she's with Noah." He didn't know how to explain it, but he felt like there was, for the first time he could remember, a barrier between him and his mom. They'd always been super close but her affair with Pasco Kildare had changed something between them and Merrick hated him for that. And for leaving her so sad. "I could punch Kildare. In fact, every day I have to talk myself out of going to his studio and having it out with him."

"What did the guy do?" Fox asked.

Merrick looked at him, astounded. What the hell kind of question was that?

Fox leaned forward, frowning. "No, that's a serious question. What, *exactly*, did he do?"

"He had an affair with my mother," Merrick replied, through gritted teeth.

Soren grimaced. "Look, Mer, none of us feel comfortable

thinking of Jace in those terms. Frankly, it hurts my brain.
But, as much as I hate to admit that Fox is right—because
we know that being told that he's right goes to his head—"
Soren rolled his eyes at Fox's smirk "—Kildare didn't do
anything wrong. Jace broke it off, he didn't."

"But…" Merrick said, then stopped.

"She thinks she's too old for him, not sophisticated
enough, that she doesn't fit into his world," Fox explained,
and Merrick glared at him.

"What are you talking about? He'd be lucky to have her
in his life!"

"Well, *we* know that, and I'm pretty sure Kildare knows
it too—but that's not the way Jace thinks, according to
the collective intelligence of our lovely women," Fox said.
"They talk to Jace, and she's let a few things slip."

Merrick tipped his head back to look at the ceiling, trying
to process this new intel. Much as he hated to admit it, he
could see how it fit with his mother's world view. In some
ways, she was still the scared, frightened woman she was
when she arrived in Hatfield twenty-five years ago. She was
supremely confident in her role as caretaker, housekeeper,
friend, mother and now grandmother, but stepping out of
those roles required a certain level of courage she hadn't
yet mastered.

Walking into Kildare's world would be, to her, like stepping into another universe.

"We were thinking we should invite her here, to spend
some time with us. Maybe take her to a show, out to dinner, to some social events. She's always resisted in the past
but if we are around to buffet her, to give her some support, maybe she'll get the confidence she needs to feel like
she could, occasionally, dip her toe into Kildare's world,"
Soren continued.

He appreciated their thoughtfulness—though he had no doubt it was one of their women who had thought up this idea—and he was grateful for their concern. There was just one problem with that scenario... "Are you seriously telling me you all think that they should be together? Are you nuts?"

Kildare was too alpha, too take-no-bullshit, just too *much*, for his gentle mother. No, Jace needed someone kind and low-key, a gentle rainfall rather than a hurricane.

"Did you see how happy she looked when she was with him?" Soren asked. "She glowed."

Ack. That wasn't what he wanted to hear. Thinking about his mom and Kildare made his stomach cramp.

"I agree with your suggestion about bringing her here. Maybe we should invite Avangeline too. After everything that's happened, they could both do with getting away from Calcott Manor for a change of scene," Jack said.

His brothers agreed and Merrick told them that Jocelyn and her husband, Arthur, Avangeline's oldest friends, were coming over from the UK next week. "Maybe we could entertain them all in the city for a week."

"I'll get Ru working on an itinerary," Fox said. Ru was his fiancée and a world traveler, and for a change, she was actually around. Merrick admired their commitment to making their relationship work, despite frequently being on different continents.

He couldn't do that. He'd never fall in love with or commit to a woman—he'd seen how destructive love could be—but if he did, he'd want his wife with him, every day and in every way. Otherwise, what was the point?

Jack gently slapped the table. "That sounds like a plan," he said. "I'm starving but before we order, tell us why *you* wanted to meet, Mer."

Right, there was no getting out of this now. Merrick looked down, searching for the best way to broach the subject. "The blackmail attempt is behind us, thank God, and Avangeline has updated her will, but there's still something that hasn't been resolved."

All three of them looked confused. *Oh, come on!* "Alyson Garwood," he explained, feeling the muscles in his face tighten.

"What's there to be resolved?" Jack asked.

Since Aly hadn't given him permission to explain about her plane crash vision, he kept his explanation simple. "Look, she feels...*compelled*...to figure out what happened to your parents, guys. She wants to investigate the crash, see if she can get some answers."

Their heads snapped up at his emphasis on the word *compelled.* They exchanged glances and Fox picked up the gauntlet. "Does this mean that you are starting to believe her?" he asked, a little warily.

He believed that *she* believed she'd seen an image of a plane crash, and he believed that she believed she was carrying Malcolm's memories—but that was as far as he would go. He wasn't buying what she was selling. The only reason he was doing this was so that she could go back to Jersey City, and they could all go back to normal. Merrick liked normal; he liked stable. Having spent his first few years in a house where the mood could go from laughter to anger with the flick of a switch, he liked things to remain calm, to chug along.

Aly was a catalyst for change, but he couldn't allow himself to be sucked into the whirlpool she created. And the best way to keep her from messing up his life would be to help her so she could leave all the sooner. Besides, if he helped her, then he could prepare his family for any surprises she found. He'd have advance warning if anything they discovered had the potential to blow up in their faces.

He genuinely didn't believe they'd find anything of significance—too much time had passed and had there been anything suspicious, an intrepid journalist would've dug up the truth decades ago. But, because he believed in hedging his bets, he'd go along for the ride. He was protecting his family; it was what he did. What he'd promised Avangeline he'd always do.

He dodged Fox's question by asking whether they felt comfortable with Aly looking at some of their parents' more private papers. Fox looked at Soren, then Jack, and nodded. "We've destroyed all the documentation related to The Basement, so we know she won't find out that our mom and dad ran a hard-core sex club. What could be worse than that?"

"Finding out that my parents were involved in it too," Soren stated.

Merrick's eyes widened. "Do you think they were?"

Soren shrugged. "The twins were close, two sides of the same coin. If Jesse was into that, there's nothing to say that my dad wasn't, too."

"There's also nothing to say that he was," Fox pointed out. "And your folks traveled extensively before the crash, Soren. We hardly saw you. It's not like they would have been around to go to the club much."

"They do have sex clubs overseas," Soren replied.

Jack shook his head. "There's nothing to suggest their involvement, Soren. Don't go looking for trouble, bro."

Soren nodded and Merrick saw his shoulders drop in relief. Wanting to move on, he looked at his other two brothers. "About Aly?"

"If Aly did find out about The Basement, I don't think I'd have a problem with her knowing," Fox mused.

Merrick frowned at him. "You wouldn't?"

"She feels like part of the family, like a younger, slightly kooky sister. I like her and I am inclined to trust her."

Now that was a hell of a statement coming from Fox. His brother only trusted a handful of people. It was a shock to learn that Aly was on the list. He turned his gaze on Jack, then Soren, and saw them nodding. "Seriously?" he demanded. "You all trust her?"

"Shocking, isn't it?" Soren said, smiling. "But Eliot trusts her, and I trust Eliot's judgment."

"At any time during the past few weeks, she could've contacted the press and told them about the blackmail attempt on Avangeline," Jack pointed out. "It wasn't hidden from her. She could've sold the story for a lot of money and generated a lot of publicity for herself. But she kept her mouth shut. As far as I'm concerned, she's proved her loyalty." He lifted his glass and tipped it in Merrick's direction. "Why are so determined *not* to trust her? To get rid of her?"

Merrick knew he was about to squirm, and forced his muscles to stay still. He knew the answer to Jack's question—it was because he'd never reacted so strongly to a woman before, and she could upend his world. He didn't want his world upended; he liked it the way it was—but he had no intention of telling his brother that. Instead, he picked up the menu and looked down at it, scanning the vegetarian options.

"I'm starving, let's eat," he said, his tone making it clear the subject was closed.

His brothers' laughter sounded like nails on a chalkboard.

Aly wiped down the long marble counter in Avangeline's spacious kitchen, nodding when she was satisfied that the surface was free of dust. She was leaving the apartment in a couple of hours and was determined, as she always was, to leave the apartment in tip-top condition.

She looked around and decided she preferred Merrick's apartment to this white-and-pale-blue expanse. Avangeline's apartment, unlike Calcott Manor, didn't reflect her personality. Admittedly, gorgeous twentieth-century art hung on the walls—Aly recognized a Nicholson and Dali, and there was a Picasso sketch in her bedroom—but the apartment wasn't warm or lived-in. Maybe that was because it wasn't where Avangeline spent much time.

Aly walked into the living room and sat down on the white couch and put her head in her hands. She was waiting for Merrick, who'd told her that he'd give her a lift to Calcott Manor after he'd had lunch with his brothers. She knew he'd be telling them about her request to access their parents' private papers. Anxiety coursed through her, and her stomach was a mess of knots.

And indigestion was kicking her butt today.

Aly heard the sound of footsteps crossing the apartment and looked up to see Merrick standing across the room from her, looking tall and solid and so very sexy.

"Hey, are you okay?" he asked.

She swallowed and nodded. "Mmm, fine." Well, she was, mostly.

"You're looking pale again," he commented, sliding his hands into the pockets of his smart gray pants.

He sat down on the backless couch opposite her and nodded at her packed bag next to the couch. "Are you ready to go?"

She nodded. Being driven to Hatfield, sitting alongside Merrick, was going to be a far more pleasant trip than taking the train. She rubbed her damp hands on her thighs and sent him a shaky smile. "Are you going to tell me what your brothers said?"

"They are happy for you to dig into the plane crash. Obviously, they've always had questions and would like answers. However, like me, they don't believe we'll find anything."

That was what she was scared of. But if they found nothing, at least she could say she tried. That had to count for something, surely? She stood up and gestured to the door. "That's great news. Shall we go?"

"No, we're not going anywhere until you tell me what's going on."

She frowned at him and tried to act blasé. "What are you talking about?"

He narrowed his eyes at her. "That's the second or third time I've seen you rubbing your chest. Are you in pain? Do you need to see a doctor?"

No! Yes? She didn't know. Aly wrinkled her nose and crossed her arms, rocking on her heels. Damn Merrick for being so very observant. She'd had her annual checkup not too long ago. Her endocrinologist was very happy with her, and her tests had flagged no problems. Surely this was nothing serious. "I've just got indigestion, that's all," she told him.

"Sit down, Aly, and breathe."

She didn't like taking orders but when she saw the implacable expression on Merrick's face, she knew that he wouldn't be budging until he was ready. She sat down, crossed one leg over the other and looked out the window, idly noticing that it was a beautiful late-summer's day. Soon the autumn weather would start moving in, the trees would start to turn and the wind would turn cold. Where would she be at Halloween? Sitting in her rented apartment, ignoring the ringing of her doorbell? Or still at her office, working?

Whether at work or home, she'd go back to living a life devoid of personal interactions. Leaving Calcott Manor and the Granthams was going to be so much harder than she'd ever expected it to be.

Maybe she should never have accepted Avangeline's offer to stay. Maybe the compulsion to find answers would've died with some distance. This wasn't even *her* story...

But it *was*, sort of, because she carried a piece of Malcolm inside her. She felt she owed it to him, to thank him for her second chance at life, to solve this puzzle.

"I have never heard anyone think as hard as you do," Merrick told her, leaning back to put his ankle on his opposite knee. "Tell me why you needed a liver transplant, Alyson."

She loved the way he drawled her full name, making it sound so much sexier than it actually was. Her stomach flipped over and then his question slammed into her. Despite being at Calcott Manor for nearly three months, she'd never told anyone why she needed the transplant.

Her story wasn't a pretty one, and it was far from anything she'd imagine the Granthams had ever experienced. She shook her head and wrinkled her nose. "It's an ugly story, Merrick."

"I'd still like to hear it," he said, his eyes steady on her face. Aly sighed. Maybe telling him would create a barrier between them, something she desperately needed. He was the first guy ever who made her act first, think later, who could have her libido humming just by walking into a room, and who could, with one kiss, make the world fade away. She couldn't fall for him; that would be stupid in the extreme. Maybe telling him about her past would let her get over him when she saw that he was put off by it. Leaving her heart behind with him, at Calcott Manor, would be more than she could bear.

She pulled a strand of hair off her cheek and tucked it behind her ear. "I grew up on the fringes of the projects, one step away from being a true inner-city child. My mom was a single parent, and she worked two, sometimes three jobs, to keep it together. My sister and I spent a lot of time on our own."

He didn't react, in any way, and his lack of emotion allowed her to continue. "I was a bit of a nerd and lost myself in books. Avery, my sister, was far more social, and, by the time she was twelve, she was running with the wrong crowd. By fourteen, she was hanging with a gang. By fifteen she was addicted to pot and tablets."

Aly touched her top lip with her tongue, unable to look at him. Out of the corner of her eye, she saw him shift and rest his forearms on his knees, his hands dangling between his thighs. "Did she manage to kick her addiction?"

"No. And by the time my mom finally accepted that she had a problem—Avery herself was never willing to admit that—she was on the hard stuff. Heroin, mostly."

"Ah, baby," he murmured. God, she hoped he wouldn't move over to her and try to comfort her. If he did that, she might just shatter. No, it was better to keep herself rigid and get through it. Memories rolled through her, and she continued to talk.

She could still smell the combination of cabbage and cigarettes, the scent of desperation as she walked up the dark stairs to their apartment, constantly alert to danger. She held her breath, as she always did, as she slid her key into the lock, praying the apartment would be empty, and that Avery hadn't brought anyone home.

As soon as she stepped into the apartment, she sensed something was wrong. The place was a mess, but then it always was when Avery was in residence. She quietly closed the door and flicked on a switch and immediately saw a stranger passed out on their ratty couch, his stringy long hair touching the floor. Avery lay on the floor next to him, looking way too still—with blood dripping from her lips. Aly rushed over to her, frantically reaching for a pulse. She yanked a needle out of her arm and yelped when her foot crunched onto another needle buried in the carpet, cursing when the point jabbed her. Ignoring the pain, she wiped the blood away from Avery's lips and blew air into her mouth, pounding on her chest to get it to restart.

"When the EMTs arrived, they said she'd been dead for a while. By the time I got there, there was nothing anyone could do. She and her friend died from heroin that was laced with fentanyl. I was sixteen—she'd just had her seventeenth birthday."

Merrick winced. "I'm so sorry, Aly."

Yeah, so was she. "A few months later I started feeling awful, desperately tired and I had no energy. I was fading away. My mom took some time off work and took me to a clinic. They did a hundred million tests and diagnosed me with hepatitis C, the bad kind. My liver was shot."

"From the needle you stepped on?" Merrick asked.

She nodded, surprised he knew that contact with infected blood was the likeliest way to contract the disease. "Most likely yes, though we'll never know for sure. I could've got it when I wiped away the blood off Avery's face. Either or."

Merrick's attention didn't waver from her. "So you got sick… How did you raise the funds for the transplant? It's not cheap."

"Tell me about it," Avery muttered. "My mom decided she wasn't going to lose another daughter and she swung into action. She took out mortgage number three on the apartment, started a GoFundMe campaign and in between working all hours she could, she bombarded charities and foundations with requests for money to save my life. She sold everything that wasn't nailed down, and every spare cent was put into my transplant fund. I had to pass on two livers and we nearly passed on Malcolm's liver too because we didn't have nearly enough to cover the medical bills. Then, miraculously, an anonymous donor agreed to make up the shortfall."

Merrick's eyebrows shot up. "Avangeline?"

Aly lifted a shoulder. "I suspect so. I think someone told her about me. But she denied it when I asked her."

"She would," Merrick stated.

Merrick stood up and paced the area in front of the large window. "And after the operation? What then?"

The months after her operation were harder than any others in her life. "I recovered but it took a while. After that, I went back to school and graduated. Because my mom had made a million contacts with charities and foundations, I managed to get a scholarship to college. I suspect Avangeline had a hand in that too. I think she tracked me for years before I rocked up at her door a few months back. I'd expected it to be a lot harder to get an appointment with her."

"That wouldn't surprise me," Merrick replied. "She might know your story, but I don't. Carry on."

"Well, with every forward step I took, my mom seemed to take one back."

Merrick's sharp gaze pinned her to her seat. "What do you mean by that?"

"The stronger I got, the weaker she became. It was almost as if her fight to get me well took everything out of her. She'd lost one daughter, saved another and she was done. She started to fade away. Then she was diagnosed with stage-four pancreatic cancer. There was nothing to do but manage her pain."

"That must've been hard watching her slip away," Merrick commented, his voice laced with sympathy.

She tried to smile but knew it came out as more of a grimace than a grin. "I wouldn't know. She refused to let me come home from college and see her. She said that I had my own life to lead, exams to pass and a degree to get. I was out of the apartment, and she didn't want me to come back." She swallowed, ducking her head so that he wouldn't see her tears. "We said goodbye via a phone call. A week later she was gone. There was nothing I could do but buckle down, and graduate. Then I did my post-grad in law, I got another out-of-the-blue scholarship—"

"Color me shocked," Merrick said.

"As I said, it's an ugly story, but at least it has a happy ending—mostly," Aly said. She sent a longing look to the door, wishing they were on their way. Or, at, least, not talking about her past anymore. She wasn't ashamed of where she came from—plenty of people started in poverty, and had awful stories about drugs. She was damn proud of her mom, proud that she'd inherited her work ethic from her. But the story was still ugly, and she didn't like to talk about it.

Nobody liked to revisit a painful past.

Then Merrick surprised her by walking over to her, pulling her to her feet and gathering her into his chest. One hand covered the back of her head and her nose pushed into his collarbone. Aly closed her eyes, enjoying his heat and solidity. His other hand wrapped around her back, and she felt secure and safe. And seen.

Dear Lord, he gave the best hugs. Tight but not constricting, warm but not overpowering. She could stay like this forever, with him as a barrier to the world. She wouldn't—

not for long, anyway. She was an independent woman who created her shields, built her own barriers and did her own thing.

But just for a minute or two, it felt fabulous to rely on someone else.

"Thank you for telling me about your transplant and your past, Aly," he murmured, his deep voice washing over her. "You've had a rough ride and you should be proud of what you've achieved."

She was but she sometimes felt that other people paid a higher price. Avery, her mom, Malcolm. She was here because of them, and the guilt threatened to consume her.

But she couldn't change any of it, couldn't rewrite the past. She hadn't been able to stop Avery from taking drugs or her mom from killing herself with overwork and she'd had no impact on Malcolm's decisions at all. All she could do was honor their lives as best she could.

She'd got her degree as her mom wanted, had a lovely apartment and was upwardly mobile. And all that was left for her to do, before ending this chapter of her life, was to slot this Malcolm-shaped puzzle piece into place.

And in the meantime, she also had to do her very best not to fall for Merrick.

Five

Holding her like this, and knowing he couldn't take it any further, was torture. Merrick felt his cock filling and thickening. This wasn't the time to make its presence felt but it wasn't getting the damn message. He pulled back but Aly followed his movement, and he knew the moment she felt his erection, noted the tension that skittered through her body.

He wouldn't apologize for his body's natural reaction, but he wouldn't push for more. This wasn't the time or place. She'd just recounted an emotional story—he'd heard the pain in her voice, saw it in her eyes—and making a move on her would be taking advantage of her.

He wasn't the type to use a woman's emotions against her.

He was about to step away when Aly lifted her head and her eyes slammed into his, deep, dark green and gold flames. He was an experienced guy, and he knew when a woman wanted him, could tell with a quick scan of her face and body. Her skin was flushed with a pale pink and the pulse point on the side of her neck fluttered. Her nipples poked through the fabric of her expensive white T-shirt and her legs were a little open. It would be so easy to sweep his hand up and under her skirt, to slide his fingers under her panty line and find that special place between her legs. She'd be wet and warm for him...

Merrick stepped toward her and yanked her to him, plundering her mouth with his own. There was no room for finesse, for thought. He just kissed her mouth like he was starving for her touch.

And God, he had been.

His hands streaked over her body, squeezing one firm butt cheek, then the other. He bent his knees and dragged her nipple into his mouth, tonguing her through the fabric. For a moment, just a few seconds, she was stunned by his actions but when she realized that he wasn't holding back, she tangled her tongue with his, her low groans telling her that she thoroughly approved of his lack of finesse. Merrick pulled her T-shirt up and over her head, and looked down, his eyes nearly rolling back in his head as he took in her lovely breasts. They would be even lovelier if they weren't covered in pretty lace. Using one hand, he twisted the clasp open and pulled the frothy garment from her body, allowing it to drop to the hardwood floor. Aly looked up at him and grinned, and his heart flipped over. She was so strong, so smart and so gorgeous, refusing to accept anything less than everything. From the urgency of her touch, he could tell that she wanted hot and raw, fast and furious, and while he wanted to give that to her, he also wanted her to scream his name, for this encounter to be burned into her brain.

He wanted her to blush every time she walked into this room or every time she had a memory of staying in this apartment. If she thought about Manhattan, he wanted her to think of him. Of this.

Looking around, he saw the window and grinned. Oh, yeah, that would work.

Pushing her skirt to the floor, he pulled her into him and walked her backward to the massive glass pane. When her back rested against the cool glass, he helped her pull his shirt up and over his head and felt her mouth on his nipple. Nice but not what he most wanted to do. Forcing himself to focus, he pulled his wallet out of the back pocket of his pants and, tossing cards and receipts onto the floor, dug out a condom. God knew how old it was, but it would have to do. He felt Aly's hand on his belt buckle, heard the sound of his zipper, and sucked in an enormous breath when her hand burrowed under his briefs to wrap her fingers around him. He was so hard that he was certain he could be used as an oil drill.

He pushed into her fist, dimly aware of his clothes hitting the floor. Yeah, that was okay; he needed to get naked at some point.

That said, if she didn't stop stroking him, he was going to come way too soon and then he wouldn't be able to give her the sexy experience he was thinking of. He stepped back, sat down on the hardwood floor and rested his back against the glass. Reaching for her, he pulled her into position and caught her wide eyes.

Excited eyes, she wanted this.

"In front of the window, Merrick?" she asked, her voice tight with eagerness.

She knew that nobody could see in; they were too high, and the glass didn't allow people to see in anyway. But the thought was intoxicating, and he liked the idea of her being turned on by something new.

Aly, needing no further encouragement, placed her feet on each side of his thighs and bent her knees just a little, and widened her legs. She was so very pretty. He couldn't wait to taste her, to feel her come on his tongue. He lifted his hands, opened her folds and licked her, closing his eyes at her sexy woman smell, loving the way she rocked against his tongue. He opened his eyes and looked up and saw that her palms were flat against the glass pane. She was watching what he was doing to her, enjoying the erotic show. He lifted one hand, rolled her nipple between his fingers and pulled her clit between his lips, feeling her swell. Her groans filled the air between them and as she heated up, her woman smell became stronger. His balls tightened and his cock thickened. He desperately fought the urge to pull her down so that she straddled his legs, filling her to the max. But she was enjoying this too much, loved being the star of her private sex show, and he couldn't help wanting to give her more.

Merrick pushed his tongue into her, pulled away to suck her and repeated the action. He heard her yell his name, then groan it. She was close. So was he. Despite not being touched, he knew that if he got inside her, he'd blow.

And blow ferociously.

Aly surprised him by jerking away from his mouth and sinking down onto him, dragging her wet channel up and down his shaft. He patted the floor for the condom, ripped it open with his teeth and pushed it into her hand, and ordered her to get it on. "I don't care how but do it."

Aly placed the condom on his tip and then, in a move that surprised him—this woman kept doing that—used her lips to roll it down, until most of his shaft was in her mouth. Merrick tensed every muscle in his body to force himself to hold still. If he pumped once, he'd lose it and he wanted to come inside her.

Needed to come inside her.

Using his strength, he lifted her off him, told her to strad-
dle him and when her opening met his tip, he slid up and
into her…

This was home; this was where he most wanted to be.
This hot, tight place was what he'd been craving, needing
and dreaming of…

Aly ground down on him and arched her back, offering
her breasts for him to suck. He covered a nipple with his
lips, pulling her flat against the roof of his mouth, enjoying
the way her hand held his head in place. Then she started to
ride him, setting the pace, sliding up, and slamming down.

He loved that she was taking control and was happy to let
her have her fun, knowing that if he started to pump, this
would end way too soon. He watched her as she flew, her
head thrashing from side to side, her body flushing a deeper
pink and her mouth falling open as her orgasm rushed over
her. Then her eyes flew open, and he saw the waves of pleasure in them and felt her clench around her.

Later, he'd wonder why he didn't come. Maybe he'd been
too enthralled by her to remember his own needs. She cli-
maxed in a scorching rush and then slumped against him,
her breath hot against his neck. He was still embedded in
her, but he was happy to take the moment, to prolong his
pleasure to enjoy the way she melted into him, her body
completely relaxed.

It took thirty seconds, maybe a minute of waiting but
then she blinked and stretched, her eyes sleepily connecting with his. She wiggled, and awareness jolted into her
and she tensed.

"Want to come again?" he casually asked.

She grinned. "Always."

He flipped her over, making sure that her head and back
didn't connect with the hard floor, and pulled her legs up,

as high as they could go. He felt her clench around her and then she lifted her hips, and he knew that her pleasure was starting to build again. He slid his hand under her butt, lifted her and, by some miracle, sank further into her, hitting something deep inside her that turned her movements furious, then frantic.

She was so responsive, so incredibly sensual and he loved sharing sex with her, with someone who could keep up...

Frail his ass.

Merrick, leaving everything on the table, gave her every inch of himself, a part of him shocked that someone so small could take all of him. But she did. Pleasure built in his balls, and he knew that he couldn't hold back any longer. Maneuvering his hand between them, he dragged his thumb over her clit and Aly reacted the way he expected her to, slamming her hips up and flying over the edge.

Heat and light and intense pleasure spun through him as a rainbow-colored tornado danced up and down his spine. He came, hard and fast, with an intensity that fried a good portion of his mind. Feeling her aftershocks, he kept pumping and, shockingly, felt her reach another, tiny orgasm. Now, that was a first.

Holy shit.

Aly lay underneath him, her legs wrapped around his hips, and he rolled her over, allowing her to use him as a mattress, her stomach on his, her face tucked into his neck, her legs on either side of his.

He patted the floor, idly wondering if they'd affected the structural integrity of the building. He'd never had such intense sex, and never felt so shattered afterward.

"I'm dead."

He stroked his hand over her soft hair, turning to place

a kiss on the top of her head. "There's a reason why the French call it a minideath."

"There is nothing mini about you. Or that," Aly told him, and he grinned. He stared up at the ceiling, wondering when she'd move, happy to lie in the late-afternoon sunshine on this hard-as-hell floor and wait for her to move.

Or die here. Either was optional. Because how the hell could that be topped?

The next day, at Calcott Manor, Aly heard Merrick's size thirteens on the steps leading up to the attic and lifted her head from the sheaf of papers in her hand. Merrick's dark head appeared in the doorway and then the rest of his amazing body appeared, tall and broad and looking all too edible in his loose cotton half-sleeve shirt and deep brown cargo shorts.

"You're late," she told him, making a show of looking at her watch.

"Yeah, sorry about that but a conference call ran over," Merrick said, walking over to her and dropping a kiss on her temple. Aly was glad he didn't kiss her mouth because if he did, then these papers definitely wouldn't get sorted. She'd been late to another online meeting this morning because they'd started kissing...

Do not look at his mouth, Garwood. Or his body.

Aly looked around, taking in the many dormer windows and the light flooding into the room. This was like no attic she'd ever seen before, light, clean and ruthlessly organized. It had been easy to find the boxes relating to Jesse and his wife, Heather, mostly because everything in the attic was stored according to date, and clearly labeled with the name of the person the contents related to.

Merrick walked over to the long trestle table and leaned

his hip against the table, his eyes flying over the piles of paper. "You've done a lot in a short time," he commented.

Aly pointed to the walls of boxes. "The boxes themselves are beautifully labeled but less care was taken with the contents. Business papers are mixed in with medical records and personal papers."

Merrick picked up a sheaf of papers and flipped through them. "I see what you mean," he said, wincing. He nodded at the piles of paper on the table. "What's your system?

Aly nodded. "Moving from right to left...medical records, business records, correspondence, hobbies and anything relating to their sons." She pointed to an open space on the table. "That space is for anything to do with Jesse's flying."

"You seem very organized," Merrick said.

He sounded surprised. Everyone at Calcott Manor seemed to forget that she was a lawyer and that being tidy and detail-orientated was an essential part of her job. "I hate mess and I hate wasting time looking for anything. Things must be filed in an orderly and logical manner."

Merrick grinned. "I bet the paralegals and interns hate you."

Aly grinned. "They do." She handed Merrick a pile of papers. "You can start with this pile."

After ten minutes of working in silence, Merrick spoke again. "You are placing two papers on a pile for every one of mine."

Oh, so he was competitive? Shocker.

Aly looked up to see him frowning at the paper in his hand. She walked around the table to stand next to him, enjoying the hit of his cologne, and looked down at the paper in his hand. It was an invoice for lawyers' fees.

"Ginley and Hubert," she murmured. "I've never heard of them."

Interesting. Aly plucked her phone out of her pocket and pulled up the firm's website. She hit the 'about' tab and after skimming through the blurb, turned the phone so that Merrick could read the paragraph.

"They specialize in high-income divorces," he said, and his eyes met Aly's as he flicked his finger against the paper. "So Fox was right, his parents were talking divorce."

"Or at least, Jesse was," Aly stated, pointing to the line item. "This says that the consultation was with Mr. J. Grantham, not Mr. and Mrs. Grantham."

Sure, it was interesting, but they were here to find out information about the plane crash, not the state of the couple's marriage. Aly returned to her box and lifted a file from the depths of the box. She flipped the cover and released a soft whoop.

Merrick looked over at her. "What is it?" he asked her.

"This file contains all his flight records, invoices from his flight instructors and logbooks."

Merrick looked over her shoulder. "Okay, this could be helpful. If we can track down his flight instructor, then we can find out what type of pilot he was. Fox and Jack are steadfast in their belief that he wasn't a maverick, but they could be believing what they want to believe. They were kids at the time and all boys idolize their fathers. His flight instructor will know whether he really was a good pilot or not."

That made sense. Merrick pulled the file toward him and started flipping through the colored tabs. "Hey, here's the maintenance history for the plane that crashed. We can talk to the mechanic who did the service...*wow*...the week before the plane crashed."

All good news, Aly thought as she went back into the box. She lifted a cardboard box and took off its lid. Inside was a cell phone, with an invoice wrapped around it. Aly removed the elastic band holding the two together and opened the invoice. Her heart picked up as she stared at the date on the invoice. "Hey, Merrick?"

"Yeah?" Merrick asked without looking up at her.

"This phone here was sent in for repairs a few weeks before the crash."

Merrick caught something in her voice and cocked his head to the side. "Okay...? What are you thinking, Aly?"

"If a phone stopped working, what would you expect a wealthy Grantham to do?" she asked.

"Send a minion to buy another one."

"Exactly! So why would Jesse pay to get his phone fixed?"

Merrick rubbed his jaw. "That's a good question. It's not like he would have photos on there—phones didn't have that capacity back then. Nor email."

Aly rubbed the back of her neck. "Text messages? Would he want a record of the messages he sent?"

Merrick frowned. "I think texting was only available around 2000, wasn't it? That's after they died."

Aly picked up her phone and consulted the internet again. "So, in 1999, the first text messages between different carriers were sent. But people on the same carrier could send text messages in 1995 already."

Merrick sent her a slow smile that made her stomach roll over. "That's smart thinking, Aly."

His approval warmed her in places she didn't know existed. It had been so long since anyone cared what she thought or how her brain worked.

Merrick surprised her by wrapping his hand around her neck and placing an open-mouthed kiss on her forehead. "Good work, Garwood. And stop looking all flushed and sexy— we've still got hours to go and many boxes to get through."

That was true. And ugh.

* * *

Merrick walked over to the glass doors, sliding them open. He pulled in a deep breath of sea air and gripped the railing, his eyes tracking the line where the sea met the sky.

He couldn't hear anything but the whish of the waves as they washed up the beach, the sound of a ride-on lawn-mower and, in the distance, the rumble of a tractor. He definitely couldn't hear the constant chatter of three octogenarians, whose upper-crust English accents seemed to reach every corner of Calcott Manor's ridiculously big house.

Arthur and Jocelyn Jones-Carr had arrived the day before. It had been a long time since he'd seen Avangeline that animated. Their joie de vivre seemed to lift his mom out of her funk as well. Merrick had met the couple many times over the years, and he prayed he'd have half their energy when he hit his eighties. Jocelyn still worked as a minister and was a well-known television personality. Arthur was quietly charismatic, as only a Shakespearean actor of world renown could be. They were still a power couple and when you added Avangeline to the mix, they were sometimes more than he could handle.

Mostly because they. Didn't. Ever. Stop. Talking.

Merrick felt his phone buzz and pulled it out of his pocket, smiling when he saw Jack's incoming video call. Jack's new responsibilities left little time for him, and Merrick missed their after-work drinks and dinner and their runs around Central Park. He missed his best friend.

It made him a little sad to realize that everyone else was moving on, but his life was the same. But at the same time, that was the way it had to be. He liked stability and things staying the same; change normally brought circumstances that were hard to handle. He was glad to see his brothers doing so well with their new loves, and new lives, but that wasn't for him.

He and Jack exchanged greetings and then Jack narrowed his eyes. "Why are you standing on the balcony of the above-the-garage-apartment? Why aren't you staying in your suite in the main house?"

Merrick rubbed the area above his eyebrows. "Jocelyn and Arthur arrived yesterday. It's been gin and tonics, croquet matches and poker nonstop ever since. They keep dragging me into their arguments to play referee."

Jack grinned. "And they never shut up, right?"

"I even put a Do Not Disturb sign on the study so I could get some work done but Arthur wandered in. He spent the next fifteen minutes trying to persuade me to join him for a round of golf while regaling me about stories about how he and his mates played St. Andrews drunk—"

"And got their best score ever," Jack finished for him.

"It's like when they are on holiday, everyone else must be too," Merrick grumbled.

Merrick sat down on the edge of the wide lounger and stretched out his long legs. He'd love to be on holiday, so would Aly but they both had work to do, and a certain number of hours to put in. They still had more boxes to get through before they headed back to the city with the three octogenarians. He knew Aly was looking forward to the city-based activities, but he wanted the two of them to stay here at Calcott Manor and have the estate to themselves. They could see how many rooms they could make love in...

When Jack cleared his throat, Merrick looked down at his screen and frowned when he saw that Fox had been patched into their video call. A second later Soren's face filled another corner of the screen. He lifted his eyebrows and wondered what was so important that they needed a four-way chat. Maybe they wanted an update on whether he and Aly had discovered anything new about the plane crash. They hadn't. He and Aly planned to trawl through more boxes tomorrow.

"So, he's in the garage apartment," Fox stated, amusement flashing in his eyes. He looked over his shoulder and spoke again. "Babe, Merrick has moved into the apartment at Calcott Manor."

Ru's lovely face appeared over Fox's shoulder, and she blew him a kiss. Her smile was as wide as the sun. "Oh, you're toast."

Her words were followed by a rumble of laughter from his brothers. Merrick lifted his hand, confused. What was Ru on about? And what was so funny?

"How long do we give him?" Soren asked, grinning.

"A few weeks at the most," Fox replied.

"Two," Ru's voice floated into their conversation. "They are on a time crunch."

Who? What were they talking about? Merrick glared into the screen. "Does someone want to fill me in on the joke?"

Fox wiped his streaming eyes, and Merrick saw him at eleven, rolling around their attic bedroom, clutching his stomach and roaring with laughter. "You do realize that we all started our relationships with our women in that apartment, right?" Fox asked, between bursts of laughter.

Well, yes, Merrick knew that. But was Fox's point? "So?"

Fox called Ru and she wound her arms around Fox's neck to look into his camera "Tell Merrick what you told us about the apartment the other night," Fox said.

Ru's smile held sympathy but also a healthy dose of amusement. "Well, we believe someone's cast a magical have-great-sex-then-fall-in-love spell on the place."

He stared at her before shaking his head in disbelief. "You're not being serious, are you?"

Ru shrugged. "It happened to all of us. Once is an anomaly, twice is a coincidence, but three times?" she told him. She pulled back, kissed Fox's temple and told them that she had to go.

Merrick thought about telling them he and Aly started their affair in his apartment in Manhattan but pulled the words at the last minute. They'd had *sex*; they hadn't started *anything*. She wasn't interested in a relationship, and neither was he. And if the two of them wanted to indulge in some blow-your-socks-off sex as single, consenting adults, then they could. He didn't need his siblings, and their women, going all hearts and flowers on him, coming up with some nonsense about spells.

"What happened to my smart and sensible siblings?" he grumbled. "Seriously, since finding Eliot, Peyton and Ru, your brains have turned to mush. You all now believe in Aly's connection to Malcolm—"

"Don't you?" Fox demanded.

He considered his answer. He didn't believe that she was channeling Malcolm's thoughts and feelings, but *something* was going on with her. He just didn't know how to explain it. "I believe that she believes it," he carefully replied.

Soren rolled his eyes at his reply. "Sometimes when it quacks like a duck and walks like a duck, it is a duck."

He wouldn't go that far. Not yet, anyway. Merrick pushed his hand through his hair. "I've agreed to help her with this search so that she can move on from whatever is tying her to Calcott Manor."

"But in the meantime, you're going to have a very adult, sex-based, not-gonna-get-involved-with-her fling, right?" Jack asked.

Yes, *that*. Jack was the one who knew him best and frequently got his point of view before the others did. "Exactly," Merrick replied, relieved that he wouldn't have to defend his corner anymore.

"Right," Jack said, dragging out the word. Mischief appeared in his eyes and Merrick felt a frisson of *oh shit* run up and down his spine. His corner was still under attack and Jack's next words confirmed it. "You don't get it, do you, Mer? We *all* started our relationships as flings, every one of us. None of us intended to fall in love."

"It was the magical fairy spell," Fox said, trying and failing to sound serious.

"That apartment definitely has magical properties," Soren agreed.

Merrick knew they were winding him up and lifted his middle finger before breaking the connection to their howls of laughter.

They'd definitely lost a whole heap of IQ points when they fell in love. That would never happen to him.

He was immune.

Six

Merrick was still in a bad mood when he stomped down to the beach later that afternoon. After his too-stupid-to-think-about conversation with his brothers, he'd buckled down to get some work done and, miracle of miracles, wasn't disturbed for the rest of the afternoon. As a result, he'd made great progress and would only need to do a few hours of work later to finish catching up.

Merrick saw a swimmer bobbing behind the ocean's backline and, squinting, realized it was Aly, her hair slicked back from her face. He smiled when she flipped onto her back and floated, looking completely relaxed.

At the edge of the water, Merrick discarded his T-shirt and after balling it up and throwing it onto the dry sand, walked into the sea, noticing that it was a degree or two colder than it had been the last time he'd waded in. In another few weeks, the temperature would drop exponentially, and the inhabitants of Calcott Manor would do all of their swimming in the heated Olympic-sized pool.

Merrick ducked under an incoming wave and swam to

where Aly was, needing just a few seconds to cover the short distance. He grabbed her ankle and grinned when she let out a shriek and thrashed against the surface of the water.

When her eyes focused on his face, she skimmed her hand across the water to launch a wave of it into his face. "You jerk! I thought you were a shark!"

"A shark with fingers that grab your ankle?" he asked, grinning at her.

She obviously didn't appreciate his logic and her glare intensified. "Jerk," she repeated, as she trod water.

Merrick was tall enough to stand so he pushed his feet into the sand and pulled her into his body. There was no point in her expending energy when she could hold on to him. It had nothing to do with the fact that he'd missed her all day and wanted her in his arms. Aly, so much smaller than him, wound her arms around his neck and her legs around his waist and leaned back to look in his face.

"You look frustrated," she told him, a little frown pulling her finely arched eyebrows together. "Are you okay?"

"Apart from having a stupid conversation with my brothers, being constantly disrupted by the old people and having to move from my very luxurious room into the guest apartment to get some peace, I'm fine," Merrick muttered.

"Avangeline's above-the-garage apartment is very nice, so stop being a snob," Aly crisply told him. "And Arthur and Jocelyn just want to spend time with you—they haven't seen you for ages."

Well, that told him. He grimaced, feeling a little embarrassed at her take-no-shit approach to his complaints.

"How did your brothers irritate you?" she asked, her thumb drawing circles on the back of his neck.

His immediate thought was that he couldn't tell her that they thought he was in danger of following in their footsteps and falling in love. But then again, he reasoned, why not? Maybe talking about it would be a way for them to both make sure they were on the same page.

"They think the apartment has magical powers and that we are in danger of falling in love," he told her, inserting as much derision into his voice as he could.

Instead of looking horrified, she just laughed. "I know, Ru and Peyton and Eliot have teased me about it too. They spent five minutes discussing it with our group. I saw the messages just a short while ago."

His blood cooled. "You have a *group*?"

"Mmm-hmm."

"You are in a group with my brothers' women?" he clarified. While he didn't have vast experience of being in an actual relationship—as opposed to just sex—he knew that having four smart women on one messaging group could be dangerous. For all they knew, the quartet could be planning world domination.

Aly nodded. "It's so much fun and I enjoy them so much. It's nice having friends." Her cheeks pinked up. "I tend to keep my distance from people. I have this idea that it's easier, and less hassle, to be alone. I haven't been able to do that here. Between them and Jace, it feels like they decided I was going to be their friend and that I didn't have much say in the matter."

From the softness in her eyes, he could tell she loved being part of their girl-gang. "But you're not complaining?"

"No, it's been amazing. I'm just surprised and grateful they accepted me so easily."

"Why wouldn't they?" he demanded.

She shrugged. "Eliot was a supermodel, and Peyton is a supermom who's so knowledgeable about art and history.

Ru is the bravest woman I've ever met—she'd spent years traveling on her own."

"Yeah, and you haven't really done anything, right?" Merrick said sarcastically, annoyed she couldn't see herself as he did, how incredible she was. "You were raised in borderline poverty, and you found your sister shortly after she overdosed. Instead of following the path of drugs and despair, you studied and worked. Then you pushed through a life-threatening illness and then went to school and qualified as a lawyer. If anything, I'd bet that Eliot and Ru, and Peyton, are in awe of you."

She buried her face in his neck and when she spoke, he barely heard her words. "I haven't told them."

He stroked her back, covered by a one-piece swimsuit. "Told them what, Al?"

"Everything, *anything*. They don't know about my sister, how I got sick, my mom dying, any of it. You're the only person I've ever told about my past. You know more than anyone."

He didn't know how to process that information. It didn't make sense. *He* was the person whom she trusted the most? That both scared and thrilled him. He held her close and hugged her tight. When his ego subsided a little—*She'd told him! Only him!*—he realized how dangerous she was, how out of control whatever this was could get.

"I'm glad we are friends, Alyson, I'm glad that you trust me, but…"

She lifted her head and her eyes clashed with his. "But?"

He sighed. "This isn't going anywhere, remember? You, us…we're not going to have a happy ending. Sleeping together and moving into the apartment might have done something for those other couples, but it won't for us. That shit isn't going to happen."

Aly lifted her hand and dragged her thumb up his stub-bled jawline. "After losing the two people I loved the most, I didn't think there was anyone more terrified of commit-ment than me. But you are even more scared than I am."

Scared was a strong word. He'd describe himself as cau-tious, maybe. Sensible. Not one to jump before he knew he'd land safely.

Or jump at all.

Merrick couldn't think of anything to say so he opted not to say anything at all. After a moment of tense silence, Aly released a long sigh. "Stop worrying, Merrick. We'll enjoy each other in bed, and when we are done—which has to be in a couple of weeks, come hell or high water—we'll go our separate ways."

He put his back to a stronger wave and looked down at her, frowning. "That's very definite. What's the rush?"

"My bosses only agreed to have me work remotely for the summer," Aly told him. "I need to get back to work. As in, going to the office every day. If I don't, I can kiss goodbye any chance of a promotion or a partnership."

He heard the doubt in her voice. "Is that what you want?"

She took a little time to answer him. "If you asked me that before I came to Calcott Manor, I would've told you yes, and explained why, very emphatically."

"But not now?"

"I'm second-guessing everything. There are great things about my job, but there have been some issues too. There are cases I want to take, but the partners are risk averse. They want to win, and this is still a new area of the law so things can go awry no matter how good a case I present. They have me playing it safe by doing a lot of intellectual property cases and I'm bored with those," she told him.

Merrick linked his arms around her lower back. "If you

want to pick and choose the cases you take, why don't you set up a law practice and hire your own people?"

Her eyes widened and she bit her bottom lip. Then she grimaced. "That's a huge decision, and one I'm not ready to make."

He could see her working like he did, online and remotely on a permanent basis. She had a skill set that was obviously in demand—she shouldn't have to compromise when it came to focusing on the work she enjoyed. "You should think about it," he told her. "There's a demand for what you do."

She stared at him and he knew her mind was working a mile a minute. He'd planted the seed; he wondered if it would take root. He hoped it did, because for some reason he didn't like the idea of Aly doing the daily, grinding commute, working at something she wasn't enthusiastic about and having to deal with endless corporate BS. She was worth more than that.

He felt her shiver and realized that they'd been in the water for far longer than he'd intended. He grimaced when he noticed Aly's lips were tinged with blue. "Let's go in, you're freezing."

"Right, and we have that video call soon with Jesse's flight instructor," she agreed, dropping her legs and swimming alongside him. "I think this might be my last swim of the year. I'm going to miss this when I leave."

"I'm pretty sure you'll be welcome back at any time," Merrick told her as they hit the shallows. He stood up, helped her to her feet and when he looked up, he saw the Terrible Trio, his mom trailing behind them, walking onto the beach. Jocelyn carried beach blankets, Arthur a flask, and his grandmother, strangely, was leaning on a walking stick. That was new; she'd never used one on the beach before. Was she ill? Or were the years just catching up with her?

Merrick jogged up to Jocelyn, took a towel and ran back to Aly, flinging it around her shoulders and rubbing it against her shoulders, back and arms, trying to get her warm. The wind had also turned, and goose bumps dotted his skin. He cursed himself for staying in the sea for too long.

What had he been thinking? He was big and fit, so he could take the cold, but she was slender and delicate—she couldn't. He'd allowed his mind to wander and his focus to shift. Stupid.

Aly looked up at him and her fingers on his chin stilled his frantic movements. "What are you doing, Knowles?"

What did it look like? "Trying to get you warm. I kept you in the sea for too long and you now look like a bubble-gum Popsicle."

Her grip on his chin tightened and Merrick couldn't wrench his eyes from her lovely face. "Merrick, *stop*. I am an adult, fully capable of making my own decisions. If I'd wanted to come in, I could have. I told you, I am not fragile, and I don't need you to protect me."

"But—"

"No, that's not your job. I've been looking after myself for a long, long time and I don't need to be pulled under your wing, or for you to treat me like I'm a helpless chick. I am anything *but* helpless."

He didn't think she was, but...

She patted his cheek. "I'm not your responsibility. It's just sex, Knowles, remember? Now, turn around and smile because the Terrible Trio is about to descend on us. And do not let them distract us for too long—we have to get back to the house to talk to Devlin Kane about Jesse."

* * *

Back in the study Aly used as her office at Calcott Manor, Merrick smiled at the elderly man on his screen, who had an awesome background image of Mt. Denali. He got a kick out of old people who could handle technology.

Even though they'd had a name to work with, it had taken some time to track down the current location of Jesse's flight instructor. Eventually he found Devlin in Alaska, where he'd moved to be closer to his grandchildren. Merrick thought that people moved from cold climates to warm ones, not the other way around.

Devlin's brown eyes crinkled when Merrick told him that. He looked like an older version of Morgan Freeman, his face well-worn but utterly dignified.

Merrick heard Aly's low laughter. He couldn't help being conscious of her bare thigh lying against his. In a snug T-shirt, shorts and her hair in a ponytail, she didn't look like the sharp-eyed, fast-thinking lawyer he knew her to be. To his eyes, she looked utterly tempting.

"How can I help you?" Devlin asked.

Merrick explained what they were doing, and the merriment in Devlin's eyes died as he recalled the crash. "I remember that day well. I was still flying out of Hatfield airfield, and we were all in a state of shock for days. It was a horrible, horrible thing."

Merrick nodded. Sometimes, twenty-five years ago felt like yesterday.

"Do you remember teaching Jesse to fly, Mr. Kane?" Aly asked, placing her chin in the palm of her hand.

Devlin nodded. "Very well. Being a Grantham, I expected him to be full of himself, but he was very nice, very polite and very respectful. A hard worker and a good student."

Merrick asked the next question. "What type of pilot

was he? His sons seem to think that he was a brilliant one, but I'd like an outside opinion. And since you trained him, you'd know."

Devlin took some time to reply. "I wouldn't say that he was an instinctual pilot, but because he loved to fly, he worked hard at being the best pilot he could be. And that meant being pedantic, meticulous and following the rules to the letter."

Merrick knew what Devlin was alluding to. He was a natural pilot, though he was better at helicopters than with planes. Flying was just another sense to him, like touch and smell. But he knew many good pilots who weren't naturals. "Natural pilots tend to crash more often because they get a little too comfortable, a little too confident," he commented.

Devlin nodded. "Exactly. Jesse wasn't someone who made mistakes or took risks. He was meticulous to the point of being anal."

Right, so the chances of pilot error were low. Fox and Jack's impressions of their father were on the money.

"I saw him that day," Devlin stated, and Aly's focus sharpened, as did his.

"You did?" Aly asked.

"He came into the clubhouse, and I chatted with him a little."

"Do you remember what you spoke about?" Aly asked, and Merrick felt the tension in her body. "I know it was a long time ago."

"Because he died so shortly afterward, it's burned into my memory," Devlin replied. "He told me his arm was sore, he thought he'd pulled a muscle. We spoke a little about the weather. It wasn't a concern—he'd flown in worse, and he was instrument rated. He spoke about his boys and said that he'd prefer to be with them rather than heading to Martha's

Vineyard. I got the impression that he was tired, maybe a little sad."

Merrick found it so touching that Jesse's last expressed desire was to be with his boys. He couldn't wait to tell Fox and Jack; they'd be glad to hear it. He couldn't remember his father ever wanting to spend time with him. His only value to his father was as a weapon to be used against his mother.

Merrick pushed his dark thoughts away and returned his attention to the screen. Aly asked a few more probing, smart questions but Devlin had no more information to give.

Merrick sighed, frustrated. Having learned barely anything new, they seemed to be treading water. They were no closer to a definite conclusion as to what caused the crash.

He'd never had great hopes for their investigation, but he was genuinely starting to believe that this was a needle that wasn't going to be moved.

The next morning Aly watched the sunrise through the drape-free window, loving the way it dropped little beads of pink light onto Merrick's olive-skinned, wide back. She wanted to run her hand over his shoulder but knew that if she did, he'd wake up—he was a superlight sleeper—and he looked properly asleep, completely relaxed.

She dropped her hand. Merrick always seemed to be in a state of tension, always ready to spring into action. He constantly scanned his environment, looking for trouble, and trying to anticipate problems before they happened.

Being constantly super aware had to be exhausting. For now, Aly was happy to let him sleep.

Sitting up slowly, she lifted her knees and wound her arms around them, resting her cheek on her knee as she watched the sun grow brighter and stronger. Merrick had suggested they take a walk after dinner last night as an excuse for them to come here and be together. She'd gone along with it, but she didn't think they were fooling any of the Terrible Trio, nor Jacinta. Not that she minded them knowing. Being with Merrick, even for just a short while, was certainly nothing to be ashamed of. Last night had been another revelation, hours of laughter and passion. Merrick was an incredibly talented lover, someone who knew how to pull every ounce of pleasure from her. From his partners, she corrected; she could not start thinking she was something special.

They were bed buddies, they were teaming up to find out some answers about the death of the Grantham brothers and that was it. They weren't embarking on a love affair.

They couldn't. Neither of them wanted a relationship, and she was convinced that a temporary relationship wasn't worth the risk of the hurt that came after. The people she loved tended to leave her one way or another. And being left behind hurt.

But why was Merrick so scared of relationships? Why did he run away from any hint of commitment? Aly grimaced and wiggled her bare butt against the sheet. He knew so much about her, but she knew very little about him. He'd come to live at Calcott Manor when he was eight, he was super protective of his brothers and he'd served in the military. Aside from that, he was a closed book. She had no idea how he and Jace landed up here, what branch of the military he served in or why he lived his life in a state of readiness.

He was, apart from being intensely sexy and panty-droppingly hot, still an enigma. Unfortunately, she loved puzzles.

But, as she'd said to him, it was just sex, nothing more.

Aly turned her thoughts to the other bombshell Merrick oh-so-casually dropped yesterday, the idea that she should set up her practice instead of returning to work in her old position. It was a tempting thought, one she hadn't seriously considered. There was a lot of comfort in working for a company. Aly liked receiving a consistent paycheck, knowing exactly how many hours she'd worked and the exact amount that would hit her bank account at the end of every month. She liked the stability, and the prospect of being short on cash terrified her; it took her straight back to her childhood and memories of bare cupboards and an empty fridge.

But the idea of making her own schedule, of taking cases she wouldn't usually see or be assigned to was very tempting.

But the risk was too great... Wasn't it?

She could think about that in two weeks, after she'd solved the puzzle of the plane crash. *If* she solved the puzzle, which was looking increasingly unlikely. Aly dropped her legs and slipped out of bed, reaching for the T-shirt Merrick dropped last night. She pulled it over her head as she tiptoed across the room, lifting her panties and shorts off the floor by the door. She pulled them on and walked down the short hallway into the open-plan living area, heading straight for the coffee machine. When her hands were wrapped around a mug filled to the brim with steaming coffee, she walked onto the balcony and rested her arms on the railing, loving the view of the sleepy sea being woken up by the sun's morning rays. She loved Calcott Manor with an intensity that surprised her. Leaving here would be incredibly hard.

She loved the buildings, the gardens and the peace of the place. She loved the family most of all...

"Did you have a good night, dear?"

Jocelyn's strong voice caused her cup to rock, and she yelped as hot coffee hit her skin. Sucking her hand, she leaned out and saw Jocelyn and Jacinta at the edge of the garden, about to step onto the path leading to the beach. Jocelyn looked amused and Jace uncomfortable.

Aly felt like she wanted the earth to open up and swallow her whole. She was sleeping with this woman's son and she'd been royally busted.

"Um...um..."

Jocelyn grinned. "Is Merrick still asleep?"

Aly tossed a wild look over her shoulder. "Uh..." Okay, any moment now she'd start to be able to form words and make complete sentences. But what did one say at times like this?

"We're going for a walk on the beach," Jocelyn told her, pushing her hand into the crook of Jace's elbow. "Would you like to join us?"

Sure, just about as much as she would love to swallow a red-hot poker. She shook her head, knowing her face was on fire. With shaky hands she lifted her mug of coffee to her lips and took a huge sip, yelping when the too-hot liquid hit her lips and tongue. She waved her hand in front of her mouth.

Even though she was ten feet up, she heard Jocelyn's amused chuckle. "That's what happens when you play with hot things, Aly dear. There's always a risk of being burned."

And Aly knew she wasn't only talking about the coffee.

Judging from the glances Merrick and Aly exchanged last night over drinks and dinner, Jace had already realized that their adversarial relationship had turned a corner, but she hadn't suspected they were sleeping together. When and where had that happened?

She glanced back over her shoulder and saw Aly still standing on the balcony, staring down at her toes, looking uncomfortable. She liked Aly—adored her, actually—and that was why she hoped that Aly wouldn't expect more from Merrick than he could give her. She'd hate to see her hurt.

"Well, that was a fun way to start the morning," Jocelyn said, her brown eyes alight with laughter. She wore a baseball cap over her braids, and no makeup on her light brown skin but, as always, her lips were covered in bright red lipstick. Jace was quite certain that no matter what happened—a hurricane, an earthquake, the end of the world—Jocelyn would reach for her lipstick, paint her lips and then square her shoulders, ready to face whatever was coming.

She was an impressive woman.

Jace released a little shudder. "It wasn't fun for me, or her."

Jocelyn waved her words away. "You can't possibly think that Merrick doesn't have sex, Jace!"

Of course, she didn't. If anything, she was well aware that he had far too much of it, flitting from one woman to another, never sticking. "Of course not! I just didn't think it would happen with Aly, that's all."

"Why not?" Jocelyn asked, curious. "She's lovely and any fool can see the sparks whenever they are together."

"They didn't seem to like each other much until recently," Jace replied. "They sniped and swiped at each other constantly."

Jocelyn laughed. "Isn't that the grown-up version of pulling a girl's pigtails?" They hit the beach and Jocelyn kicked off her sandals and buried her scarlet-tipped toes in the cool sand. "Ah, lovely. What a glorious day to be alive."

Right. It certainly seemed to be for Jocelyn. But for Jace…she didn't feel that way. She still missed Pasco, more now than ever. It was supposed to get better the longer she spent apart from him, but she simply felt worse. She was convinced that he was fine without her. She had no doubt she was simply another blip on his radar, the older woman he'd had a fling with while he rented Avangeline's guest house. But to her, his presence in her life had been life changing.

Jocelyn cleared her throat and when Jace dragged her eyes off the sea and onto her lined face, she sighed at the light of determination in her friend's brown eyes. Maybe a sunrise walk with the very nosy and bossy Jocelyn wasn't one of her brightest ideas. But when Jocelyn suggested it last night, she thought it a decent alternative to lying awake waiting for the day to start. Trying to find the courage to face another day that was Pasco free.

"Right, young lady, spill it!"

Young lady? Hardly! "I'm fifty-two years old, Jocelyn, there's nothing young about me. And there's nothing to spill!"

Jocelyn started to walk down the beach and Jace had no choice but to follow. When Jocelyn didn't speak again, Jace, wanting to fill the silence, remarked on the nip in the air, then asked about Jocelyn's always busy life back in London. When Jocelyn refused to engage on these topics, Jace threw her hands up in the air. "You can't force me to talk, you know!"

She winced at the petulant note she heard in her voice.

"Of course, I can't, but neither am I going to let you change the subject," Jocelyn replied in her oh-so-steady voice.

She wasn't going to say anything, Jace decided. There was no point; it was over. She lasted another minute before she started to tell Jocelyn about Pasco—how he made her feel, how caught up she got in the age difference, and how scared she was of stepping out of her life at Calcott Manor and into his. "I pushed him away," she admitted.

"Okay," Jocelyn replied. "And how's that working for you?"

Horribly, she admitted to herself. She missed him every

day and in every way. Jace stopped and pointed up at Calcott Manor, the stone building just visible through the trees. "That's my home! That's where I'm most at ease, completely comfortable."

"Completely *safe*."

Jace stiffened at her words, feeling like she'd been slapped. "I don't know what you mean," she stated.

Jocelyn tugged her arm, silently suggesting they keep walking. After a moment's rebellion, Jace followed her lead. "I met you in those dark days after the plane crash, Jace. I knew from the start that you were fighting bigger demons than the ones you found at Calcott Manor. You reminded me of a skittish doe who'd had a close call with a hunter."

So accurate.

"You were running from someone, and you landed at Calcott Manor. Avangeline and this place gave you sanctuary. You felt safe here and even when the threat passed—" Jocelyn stopped and sent her a look that lasered through her. "The threat did pass, right?"

She gulped and nodded. "Over seventeen years ago. He died when Merrick was fifteen."

Jocelyn's head bobbed up and down in a sharp nod. "As I was saying, this place is your safety net. There's nothing wrong with that. We all like having a safety net. Not only did you feel safe here, but you liked the work, you liked Avangeline."

"I *love* Avangeline," Jace corrected.

"And until Pasco, nobody tempted you enough to leave."

Oh, God, that was so piercingly accurate.

Jocelyn threaded her arm through hers and squeezed. "You were scared for your physical safety—now you're scared for your emotional safety."

Jace felt a tear roll down her cheek and because Jocelyn ignored it, she did too. "I don't know if he loves me, Jocelyn."

Jocelyn shrugged. "Do you love him?"

For the first time in her life, she *did* love a man, in the truest sense of the word. She nodded.

"Does he know?"

She shook her head. "I didn't tell him." She regretted that now. "But he didn't tell me that he loved me either."

"Maybe he didn't feel like he could compete with Calcott House or overcome your fear. Did you tell him about your past, Jace?"

Jace looked away, her attention caught by a piece of driftwood on the sand. She crouched down and dragged her finger across the smooth wood, thinking that Pasco would love its curves.

"For goodness sake!" Jocelyn snapped. "How does it help to keep your love to yourself? Who does that serve?"

Nobody. "If he feels the same way about me as I do him, loving Pasco would require me to leave Calcott Manor and Avangeline."

"Avangeline would be perfectly fine, as well you know," Jocelyn shot back. "Have you ever thought that she hasn't wanted to leave Calcott Manor because she doesn't want to leave you?"

Jace gasped, horrified at the thought. "No, of course not!"

"She loves you, in her irascible way, as much as you love her. She wasn't close to her son's wives so you're the daughter she never had." Jocelyn pulled her to her feet and held her hands, waiting for Jace's eyes to meet hers. "But that's beside the point. You can leave Calcott Manor, Jace. You are brave enough."

"How do you know that?" Jace cried, wiping away tears.

"Because you are the same woman who went on the run

with a little boy and no money, determined to do whatever it took to keep both of you safe. If you can do that, you can do anything, my dear."

Jace stared at her, her tears drying up instantly. She'd never looked at it that way before, never thought back to how much courage it took her twenty-two-year-old self to go on the run. She was older, wiser, and better now. Nothing—not even hearing that Pasco didn't love her the way she needed him to, that he didn't see a life with her—would ever be as hard as those years she'd struggled to look after herself and Merrick, to keep them safe.

She would be fine. She'd survived that; she could survive Pasco's rejection.

Jace leaned forward and placed her arms around Jocelyn, hugging her tight. "Thank you. You've made me see sense."

Jocelyn gave her a quick squeeze and tried to wriggle out of the hug, but Jace wouldn't let her go. She just held her tighter.

Jocelyn tapped her back. "Right, that's enough now. I'm English, darling, excessive affection gives me hives."

Jace laughed, kissed her cheek and let her go.

Seven

An hour later, Merrick and Aly started their run together. Within five minutes Aly knew there was no chance of keeping up with Merrick and quickly waved him on, immediately slowing down to get her breath back.

When she was sure she wasn't dying, she carried on with her normal, plod-plod three-mile route, stopping to look at the view whenever she felt a little out of breath. She exercised because she knew she should, not because she enjoyed it, as Merrick seemed to do.

Despite knowing that he'd intended to do a much longer run than her, Merrick was waiting for her when she emerged from the trail that led into the woods around Avangeline's estate. While her hair was falling out of her tail and she was glowing with perspiration, he barely looked like he'd done any exercise at all.

"What?" Merrick asked when he saw her frown.

She dragged her finger through the air, gesturing to his whole body from his feet to his head. "At least have the dignity to sweat a little, Knowles."

"I'd need to go a lot harder and longer than that." He rubbed the back of his neck, the muscles in his bicep contracting and sending a spike of lust down her spine. Man, he was hot. She could think of nothing she'd rather do than take him back to bed.

They'd been awake until late, had made love twice, and fooled around some more after that, but she still felt like she was standing on the edge of a bridge, waiting to bungee jump. Craving the rush. Unbelievably excited at the thought of being with him. How long would this feeling last? Two weeks, ten months, ten years? It didn't matter, she reminded herself. It all would be over soon, and they'd soon go their separate ways.

She couldn't afford to be anything but clear-eyed about where they were and weren't going. They were having a *fling*; she knew this, so why did she keep going off on a tangent?

It was most annoying.

Merrick nodded at the house. "Shall we pop in on Mom, and have a cup of coffee?"

Aly knew what he was really after and it wasn't coffee. Or not only coffee. "You know that Jace only makes croissants when there are visitors, and you are hoping to snag one."

"Or three or four," Merrick agreed, placing his hand on her lower back. She liked feeling it there, warm and steady.

"I could eat a croissant," Aly agreed. Or two.

"So, I spoke to the mechanic who worked on Jesse's plane," Merrick told her, after a few minutes of comfortable silence.

"Derek Fields?"

"That's him."

"He was interviewed by journalists at the time of the crash. I picked up his name from the articles. I tried to call him, but he wouldn't talk to me." Aly pulled a face.

"He put the phone down on me as well but I found out where he works. I think we should go to the airfield and see what he has to say."

Aly stopped and laid a hand on his arm. "Do you think he'll remember Jesse and the plane?"

Merrick nodded. "Aviation guys remember planes well. And don't forget, Jesse was already famous. Even *more* famous after the crash. Like Devlin, I bet he does remember. We can head there later this morning if it suits you."

She had some work to do for a new client, but it wasn't due for a day or two, so she could take the morning, or even the day, off. "That sounds good."

She felt a spurt of excitement and hoped the mechanic would be able to give them something, anything, that would help them understand that fateful day when the lives of the Granthams changed forever.

They skirted the greenhouse, walked through the small orchard and stepped into the rose garden, taking the long route to the kitchen so that they could cool down after their run. Well, so that *she* could cool down. Merrick was perfectly fine.

Aly saw movement within the gazebo at the opposite end of the garden and grabbed the hem of Merrick's T-shirt, forcing him to stop. He looked down at her and was about to speak but she reached up and slapped her hand across his mouth. Merrick's eyes widened, and his eyebrows lifted but he didn't say anything.

When she lowered her hand, she pulled him back, behind a bush and stood up on her tiptoes to speak in his ear. "Avangeline and Arthur are in the gazebo."

He lifted his hands, confused. "So? And why are we whispering?"

Aly peeked around the bush and saw the elderly couple

sitting on the bench in the gazebo, their expressions full of love and affection. Aly watched as Avangeline rested her head on Arthur's shoulder, and they both looked down at their joined hands. Then Arthur kissed her head, keeping his lips against her white hair for a long beat. Aly swallowed, caught up in the tenderness of the moment.

That they loved each other was obvious. But love was too small a description to describe what she was seeing; trust and tenderness, acceptance and friendship, reduced to its essence. On the surface they were simply two elderly people sitting in the dappled sunlight of the gazebo, every experience of their lives written in the wrinkles on their faces, proudly declaring they'd lived. And loved.

Loved hard. And loved often.

Aly widened her eyes at Merrick, and he looked as surprised as she did. He bent his head to speak in her ear. "Do you think Arthur is Avangeline's secret lover? The one who's been sending her postcards for…well, forever?"

Aly nodded, slowly. "Um…it sure looks like it, doesn't it?" she whispered.

Avangeline's voice drifted over to them. "How many years has it been now, sixty-eight?"

"And I feel the same way as I did back then," Arthur replied, his voice as smooth as aged whiskey. Aly placed her hand on her heart and closed her eyes, unsettled by the emotion in his voice.

"I have loved you every day since we met," Avangeline replied. "You've been my best and only love, my closest confidant."

Aly risked another peek and saw Arthur lift Avangeline's hand to kiss her knuckles. "If we'd made different choices—"

"We agreed we'd never play the what-if game, Arthur,"

Avangeline told him, her voice stronger now. "It was never the right time, I got married and then you fell for Jocelyn, and I understand why. We've always loved her too much to hurt her… Besides, we've had interesting, lovely, fulfilling lives."

Aly felt Merrick wrap his arm around her waist and she fell in step with him as he led her away. When they were out of sight, and hearing, of the elderly couple, he let her go and stepped back, raking his hand through his hair.

"We had no right to listen in," he told her as she looked back, frustrated. "It's not our business."

"I know, I know," Aly replied as they retraced their steps away from the rose garden. "But do you think he's her secret lover?"

It was a silly question. She knew he was. But…she wanted to hear Merrick say it. "I think the chances are high," he told her.

Aly skipped along beside him. "They've known each other sixty-eight years. I wonder how they met, they would've been so young. Why didn't they get together, why did they marry other people? Do you think Jocelyn knows about them?"

"Again, none of our business," Merrick stated, empathetically. He stopped abruptly and turned to face her, his hands on his hips. "Seriously, Alyson, we never saw that, we never heard any of what they said. It's got nothing to do with us."

Aly wrinkled her nose, knowing he was right. While it was always a thrill to discover something secret, she had no right to the information—and certainly no right to share it with anyone. Avangeline and Arthur's connection was profound and exceptionally personal. If Avangeline ever suspected they knew, it would taint their relationship and, possibly, dim the intensity of their connection. They'd kept their love a secret for nearly seventy years, exchanging coded postcards to keep their connection alive.

She didn't know if their relationship had ever been sexual. She suspected not, and, frankly, she didn't care. The bonds between Avangeline and Jocelyn seemed Teflon strong, they adored each other. She had no idea if Jocelyn knew and, again, it was none of her business. They'd managed to carve out successful, wonderful lives and deep, precious friendships for the best part of a century. They didn't need her or Merrick sticking their noses in.

This wasn't anyone's—not Jace's, or Avangeline's grandsons', or her or Merrick's—business. And she would not be the one to spill their secret.

Aly nodded and looked up into Merrick's questioning eyes. "I didn't see anyone sitting in the gazebo. Did you?"

He released a sigh and the tension eased from his shoulders. "No, I didn't see anyone."

Then Merrick took her hand, kissed the side of her mouth and led her to the kitchen door. "Let's go eat croissants and drink great coffee. Then we'll try to shed some light on a secret we've got permission to unravel."

Aly briefly rested her head on his shoulder. "Sounds good to me," she told him.

Later that morning, in a quaint seafood restaurant two towns north of Hatfield, Aly slapped her menu onto the surface of the table she shared with Merrick and released a soft curse. Merrick lowered his glass of beer and sent her a sympathetic smile.

"Frustrated?" he asked.

"That would be one word for it," she replied, resting her chin in the palm of her hand.

"I did tell you not to get your hopes up," he reminded her.

She was trying. She'd heard Merrick when he warned her it would be hard, but she had never thought they'd hit so many dead ends. Their meeting with the mechanic was another. He remembered Jesse Grantham and remembered his plane even better. The mechanic kept immaculate records and, after digging out the file, told them that the plane had been in near-perfect condition with no mechanical or electrical issues. Whatever happened, he insisted, the crash had nothing to do with the plane.

"I think we've got to start assuming that, even though it might not have been in character, there was pilot error involved," Merrick said. "Jesse was a good pilot, but he was only human and everyone has bad days. Sometimes, it only takes one small mistake."

Aly felt the burn of indigestion and sighed. She pushed her fist into her sternum and ignored the narrowing of Merrick's eyes.

She spoke before he could start nagging her again to see a doctor. "Even the mechanic said Jesse was an awesome pilot, that he doubted it was his fault."

Aly's finger drifted up and down her glass. "It could be that he lost concentration. Fox did say that he and his wife had an earth-shaking argument that morning. Maybe the argument continued in the plane."

"Argument or not, someone would've noticed that there was a damn big mountain in front of them," Merrick countered.

Aly shook her head. "It was cloudy and overcast. I checked into that."

Merrick straightened, his attention sharpening. "What? Are you telling me he was flying by IFR rules? Why didn't I know that?"

"I don't know what that means," Aly said, lifting her

shoulders. "I'm telling you that it was cloudy that day—low cloud. That there's a chance he didn't see the mountain in front of him."

"IFR stands for instrument flight rules. It means he was flying using his instruments instead of looking out of the window to see where he was going." Merrick looked past her, and Aly knew he was sifting through this new information, figuring out how it fit into the overall puzzle.

"As for the argument, I have a problem believing Jesse, or any pilot, would continue fighting when he needed to concentrate on his instruments. You don't scream and shout at someone while you are flying through mist and rain. In fact, any good pilot would shut down the drama."

Aly lifted her hands in the air, frustrated. "Something happened in the cockpit, that's the only explanation. But what?"

Merrick rested his forearms on the table. "I don't know if this will help, but I can ask a couple of my pilot friends, all incredibly experienced, to chat with us, to run through scenarios of what might've happened. Maybe, just maybe, one of them will have an idea that'll spark something."

Aly was grateful for the suggestion because she genuinely didn't know where else to look or what else to do. And she couldn't contemplate returning to Jersey City with this hanging over her.

"Thank you," she told him, sounding grateful. She covered his hand with hers and squeezed. "What do you fly?" she asked, changing the subject.

Merrick smiled. "Anything and everything. I flew helicopters in the military and when I got out, I started flying small planes, gradually working my way up to bigger craft. I'm rated to fly twin-engine turbines now."

"I have no idea what that means," she told him, before smiling. "But I am pretty sure I'm impressed."

Merrick grinned back before wryly shaking his head. "And here I thought you'd become a gearhead postsurgery," he teased her.

"Cars, not planes. But, and it's funny, my interest in cars seems to have faded since my arrival at Calcott Manor," she told him, frowning.

Avangeline had an impressive collection of cars and while she'd spent some time looking at them, it wasn't with the same passion she'd felt before. And, she noticed, she also wasn't eating as much candy and didn't crave a sugar hit as much as she did months ago. Come to think of it, she hadn't seen the plane crash vision lately either. Was Malcolm's influence on her fading away? If it was, why was she still so driven to find answers to the plane crash? Her desire to discover what happened had only intensified.

But she felt that if—when—she found the answers she was seeking, her connection to Malcolm might fade away for good.

A waiter approached the table. Aly asked for a chicken salad, while Merrick asked for a fully loaded burger. She took another sip of her soda before leaning back in her chair to look at her temporary lover. "You don't talk about flying much. I've never heard it discussed during a family conversation."

Merrick twisted his lips. "It's not something I talk about in front of them. After the cousins lost their parents, they all, including Avangeline, developed something of a phobia about flying. Malcolm loved anything with an engine, but he focused on cars and motorbikes. He never managed to fly in a small plane again. The rest of them got past that phobia, but flying is still not their favorite mode of transport."

After such a loss, it was understandable. "I have been besotted with aircraft from the moment I knew what one was," he said, his voice soft. "I quickly learned to keep my passion under wraps around my brothers."

"But surely they knew you flew helicopters when you went into the army?" Aly asked, fascinated. This man did anything and everything he could to make his brothers' lives easier, including hiding or downplaying something he so obviously loved.

Merrick nodded. "I didn't want them worrying about my safety, so I didn't make a big deal about it."

He made it easy for his brothers, but Aly didn't think that was fair to him.

"You said that you were besotted by planes from an early age," she pressed, wanting to give him a chance to finally open up about this. "Why? Did you grow up near an airfield or something?"

Merrick's hand clenched around his glass. "No, my uncle, my father's brother, gave me a toy airplane when I was three or four. I didn't go anywhere without it. My father and his brothers were into planes and flying."

Aly sensed that she was walking into deeper, darker waters. It had something to do with his suddenly stormy eyes, and the way his jaw clenched. He didn't want her pursuing this conversational thread and she debated whether to give him the space he seemed to want or to stomp on in. Her natural curiosity wanted to know more; her empathy told her to leave him alone.

"Do you not like to discuss your father's family?" she asked, keeping her voice low.

"I don't mind discussing them, but I won't discuss *him*.

It's difficult to discuss them without discussing him, so..."
He spread his hands out in a what-can-you-do gesture.

Aly ran her fingers over the back of her hand. "Talking about him to someone might help, Merrick. You know, open the wound so that you can get all the gunk out."

His stare turned hard. "No. That's not going to happen," he told her, his expression implacable. "My father died when I was fifteen and it was the best day of my life. And that's all I'm going to say."

Aly sat back, her mouth falling open. Wow. That was a helluva statement. It told her that there wasn't a smidgeon of love or affection between him and his dad. And, judging by how protective he was of his family, she suspected that his dad did something unforgivable, probably to Jace.

Aly wanted to push, to dig deeper, but a thick shield dropped into Merrick's eyes. She knew she would get nothing from him, not now. Probably not ever. Some wounds, she knew, were too deep and too dark to discuss.

Besides, it was none of her business. She was sleeping with the guy—she was not about to live with him or marry him. But another part of her wished that he had someone to talk to. Merrick was the one who willingly, and often, carried his loved ones' heavy loads, trying to do anything he could to ease their burden. But who helped him? She was sure his brothers wanted to be there for him, but she doubted Merrick allowed them the opportunity to help him shoulder his fears and pain. He'd set himself up to be their rock and protector, and he seemed to think that that meant he was the person they leaned on, not the other way around.

Those patterns had been set in childhood and that made them incredibly difficult to change.

Merrick smiled at the waiter carrying their food and leaned back to make space for him to put down his plate piled high with fries and an enormous burger. Her chicken salad was smaller but still much more than she could eat.

Merrick thanked the server and looked at her, his eyes a little lighter than they were before. "This looks amazing."

"Are you going to eat all that?" she demanded. There was *no* way. Okay, sure, he was a big guy, one who didn't have an ounce of flesh on him, but even he couldn't eat that much.

Merrick had a great time proving her wrong.

Eight

Two days later, on the outskirts of Hatfield, Merrick pulled off his headset and pushed a hand through his hair. He looked over to where Aly sat, sending her a lazy grin as she removed her much cheaper headset. He caught the joy in her eyes before she leaned across the seat and dragged her mouth across his. He knew it was her way of saying thank you for a truly amazing flip in his helicopter around Hatfield. If her big smile and her shining eyes hadn't told him how much she enjoyed it, then her constant chatter through the headset would've cleared that right up. He'd never heard so many "oohs" and "wows" in his life. He loved that she loved flying and was thrilled by her enthusiasm and her instinctive trust that he'd keep her safe up in the air.

Merrick left the cockpit and walked around the front of the helicopter to open her door. Aly unclipped her safety straps and all but tumbled into his arms. He loved the way she felt, a bundle of sweet-smelling femininity, against his bigger, harder body. She linked her arms around his neck and sighed when his mouth slanted over hers, his tongue sliding between her teeth. His body immediately went on high alert, and she pushed her breasts into his chest and her stomach against his hard erection, wishing that they could head back to Calcott Manor and tumble into bed.

You only want her like this because you know you have minimal time together and you don't want to waste a minute of it.

Or it could be because nothing was more important than having her in his arms. The thought of her leaving Calcott Manor was becoming harder and harder to contemplate. Whenever he thought of returning to "normality," a boulder formed in his stomach, and his chest started to ache.

He was falling for her...something he didn't want to do. Something he *couldn't* do.

Merrick leaned back and pushed a strand of hair off her face.

"I've never seen you more relaxed than you were just now, at ease but completely in control. Your confidence is such a turn-on."

He grinned, pleased at the compliment. "So you enjoyed that?" he asked, smiling as he kept his hand on her face.

"So much," Aly admitted. "I can see you did too."

Merrick's thumb brushed over her cheekbone. "It's my happy place," he confessed, looking up. "Up there, I feel free."

She nodded, stood on her tiptoes and brushed her lips against his. "I can tell," she murmured. Emotion clogged his throat. He wanted her to look like this all the time, young and joyful. It was an exceptionally good look on her.

Aly's expression turned mischievous. "Of course, you look exceptionally sexy with your aviator sunglasses and your headset."

He laughed but before he could reply, she spoke again. "The joystick between your legs was also hot."

"Mine or the helicopter's?" he asked, squeezing her butt.

Merrick swallowed at the heat he saw in her eyes. If they were even somewhere remotely private, he'd be stripping her down and plunging inside her without another moment's delay. It amazed him how they could flick the switch from fun to fierce, how quickly their desire could take over.

Aly placed a hand on his chest and rested her forehead on his collarbone. "Oh, God, don't look at me like that, Knowles," she muttered.

"How am I looking at you? Like I want to take you up against the fuselage in the late-afternoon sun?"

She moaned and scrunched his shirt in her hand. "Arrgh, now I'm going to have that image in my mind for the rest of the day."

He kissed her head before stepping back, and subtly adjusting his pants. "I'm going to have that image for the rest of my life," he ruefully admitted.

He shoved his hands into his hair, raked it back and pulled his sunglasses from where he'd hooked them into the V just above the first button of his shirt. He glanced at his watch and turned at the sight of a low, sleek plane coming into land. The plane touched down smoothly, slowed and then started to taxi down to where they stood. Merrick lifted his hand in acknowledgment and nodded toward a low-slung, glass-fronted building. "There's the bar where we are meeting my aviation friends. They should all be there by now."

He took Aly's hand and turned to walk toward the small terminal, turning back when Aly softly called his name.

"Yeah?"

"I need to show you something."

Merrick heard the hesitation in Aly's voice, and he frowned. "What?"

Aly pulled a folded-up piece of paper from her bag. "I

printed this out just as we were leaving to come here. I thought I'd wait until after the flip to show you."

Merrick took the paper and clocked the sadness in her lovely eyes. "What is this?"

"It took me a while to find a guy who could pull the text messages off that cell phone—the one we found in the attic, remember?"

Jesse's cell, the one that had been sent in for repairs. He nodded.

"My tech guy needed time to find a charger and then he needed to retrieve the text messages."

Merrick's heart thumped a one-two beat. "And?"

She nodded at the piece of paper. "That's only a sample of what he pulled off the phone. There were many more. Most of them were from Heather to Jesse—it looks like she embraced the idea of texting far more than he did."

Merrick flipped the paper open and looked down. He needed a moment to wrap his head around the fact that his brothers' mother—someone who had been viewed as America's Sweetheart—had written the vulgar and, frankly, abusive text messages. Her language was more than colorful; it was coarse and vulgar.

"Wow," he said, not knowing what else to say.

Aly slowly nodded. "She hated him, with everything she had, and made sure he knew it. She didn't hold back. I understand why he wanted a divorce."

"These are mostly Heather's text messages," Merrick said, flipping over the page to see that it was filled with even more vulgarity. If he had to judge from these communications, their marriage was steeped in toxicity.

"Jesse's texts were short, direct and they weren't personal," Aly told him. "He never once insulted her. He ignored most of her rantings. And it seems like ignoring her just made her angrier."

Merrick looked down, thinking that this was simply another example of how dysfunctional and dangerous marriages and relationships could be. These people had loved each other once. They'd made children together—a home together, a *life* together. How did they go from the happy couple he'd seen in wedding photographs in Jack's and Fox's apartments, on Avangeline's piano, to a woman who wished her husband were dead, who called him vile names, and a husband who wanted a divorce?

How did his dad go from marrying his mom in front of God and their families to sending her to the hospital after breaking her jaw? How could two people who once loved each other go from love to hate, from elation to misery?

There had been love, between the Granthams and between his parents, at one point. There had to have been because only great love could create great hate. ·

He'd always believed it was better to keep his emotions in check, to keep his love life simple. And seeing these text messages from a quarter century ago just reinforced that belief.

In the airport bar, Aly took the glass of white wine Merrick handed her and crossed her legs. She sat on a bar stool at the corner of the bar, made out of some sort of brushed steel. Then she looked closely and noticed that it had once been the tail of a plane. She nodded—it was so in keeping with the rest of the aviation-themed bar. Photographs of famous pilots dotted the wall, and pieces of aircraft memorabilia were placed on shelves around the room.

A group of men, varying in ages from their midthirties to a man who looked to be in his midseventies, clustered around her. Merrick stood behind her, his hand on her lower back. Clearing his throat, he waited for his friend's conversation to die down before speaking.

She and Merrick were introduced to the older pilot, who'd been brought along by one of Merrick's friends as someone who'd "done and seen" everything in aviation. She didn't mind; they could use any help they could get.

"Thanks so much for joining us. As I explained, Aly and I are trying to get some answers into the crash that killed the Grantham twins a quarter of a century ago."

Merrick explained his connection to the Granthams and when he was done, the pilots all looked skeptical. Aly grimaced. It was clear they didn't think she had any hope of finding out anything new.

"We spoke to Derek Fields, and he serviced the plane the week before the crash. He maintains that the plane was in excellent condition, that it had no issues," Merrick continued.

"If Derek said that, then you can take it to the bank," the oldest pilot stated, and the rest nodded their heads in agreement.

"We accept that," Merrick replied, his tone easy. "We were hoping you could give us some scenarios of what might've happened in the cockpit."

"That would call for speculation on our part."

"I'm not asking you to make a sworn statement, I just need to hear your theories." Aly slid off her seat so that she could see Merrick's face. He nodded, his expression somber. "We're looking for any ideas as to what could've happened. Look, I fly but I don't have the hours you do, not in a plane anyway."

The pilots exchanged some meaningful glances and the old-timer spoke again. "I was around when Jesse Grantham was flying. I didn't know him, but he had a good reputation. He wasn't a cowboy."

"So we've heard," Merrick answered. "So, what we know for sure is this... Firstly, he and his wife had a bad argument a couple of hours before they took off."

"We're trained to put that aside and concentrate on flying," one of the younger pilots commented.

"That's what Merrick told me," Aly said, crossing her arms. "Merrick doesn't think that Jesse would've allowed the argument to continue in the plane or to distract him once he was flying. Besides, they had company, and who wants to argue in front of other people, even if it's your twin and his wife?"

"Did his brother know how to fly? Any of the other passengers?"

Aly shook her head at the question. "I've heard nothing suggesting that any of them knew how to fly." Aly picked up her wineglass, took a sip and rested it back on the bar.

"The second thing we know is that they flew into clouds and mist," Merrick stated.

"Could something have gone wrong with the instrument panel?" Aly asked.

Everyone looked doubtful. "If it had a full service, those instruments would've been calibrated and tested."

Merrick had told her the same thing.

David, the oldest pilot, tapped his finger against his thigh. "There can be only three reasons for the crash. One, there was an issue with the plane. Two, Jesse Grantham made a mistake or, three, he became incapacitated. The plane was mechanically sound, and at the time he was flying, he was deemed to be an excellent pilot. The scenario that makes the most sense is that something happened after they took off that left him unable to fly, and the other passengers didn't know how to handle the situation."

Aly stared at David, her brain whirring. "What are you suggesting? That he passed out?"

David shrugged. "It would explain why an experienced pilot flew into a mountain. The passengers could've been trying to revive him when they realized there was a mountain in front of them."

"Or maybe, because they were flying in cloud, they didn't realize anything at all," someone else suggested. "The passengers could've been sleeping, reading, doing their own thing."

Aly held up her hand. "Are you suggesting he lost consciousness?"

"It's a possibility," David replied.

It was her turn to look, and feel, skeptical. She sent Merrick, who was looking thoughtful, a small grimace. "He was a fit guy, exceptionally healthy, according to his family. He ran marathons and went to the gym, and was very active," Aly said.

David shrugged. "You asked what could've caused the plane to crash. That's what makes the most sense to me."

Aly scratched her forehead. "Sorry, I didn't mean to dismiss your input, I just don't see it."

Merrick's blue eyes rested on hers. "I think we have to look into it, Aly."

Oh, *yay*, doctors' records—all supremely confidential. They weren't going to make any progress there. But Aly nodded, grateful these men had given up their time to talk to her about a crash that happened so long ago.

She was about to thank them when David turned to Merrick, a frown pulling his bushy eyebrows together. "Were you raised in Phoenix, son?"

Aly felt Merrick stiffen and, for some reason she started to hold her breath.

"For the first few years, yeah," Merrick replied, the icy coating on the word suggesting that it wasn't a subject he wanted to pursue.

"I think I knew your father. He was a cop, and he flew a Cessna in his spare time, right? As I recall, his brother was a pilot in the army, flying helicopters until he was killed on a training exercise."

Merrick nodded and Aly reached out to grab his hand. His fingers encircled hers, squeezing them hard. He didn't want to be rude, but she could see this was torture for him.

"I flew out of the same airfield for a while," David said. "You look just like him. How is he? What is he doing now?"

Merrick stood statue still and Aly jumped in. "Merrick's father died over eighteen years ago." David stumbled over an apology, and she sent him a gentle smile. "I can't thank you enough for your time, and your insights. We'll be sure to explore Jesse's health angle. Can I buy you all another drink to say thank you?"

On a chorus of thanks, she turned back to the bar, caught the barman's eye and ordered another round for the pilots. But when she turned around, she saw Merrick slipping out of the door.

Using the flashlight from her phone, Aly picked her way from the restaurant and walked past the air traffic control building to where Merrick's helicopter sat. His gunmetal-and-deep-green helicopter was a smudge in the dark night, but she caught movement within the cockpit and knew that Merrick was sitting in the pilot's seat.

Stepping onto a rugged skid, Aly tugged open the door and scrambled up into the seat next to him, gently closing the door behind her. She leaned back in her seat, tucked one leg under her thigh and switched off her phone's light. She looked around, taking in the now dark instrument panel, and inhaled the combination of aviation fuel, Merrick's sexy scent and leather. It was her new favorite scent.

Content to just sit here with him, she rested her head on the edge of the seat. The helicopter was a cocoon, warm and safe and wonderfully quiet.

"Are you just going to sit there?"

She lifted her eyes to look at Merrick and, in the shadows, saw his confused expression. "What do you want me to say? Or do?" she gently asked.

He dragged a hand over his face. "Aren't you going to ask why I stormed out of the bar?"

"I presume it had something to do with David mentioning your father," Aly replied, keeping her tone even. "I never knew that the aviation world was so small."

"You have no idea," Merrick muttered.

"And you didn't storm out—you slipped away," Aly corrected him. "I'm pretty sure that you will either tell me why, or not. It's not my job to force you to talk, Merrick."

His sigh filled the space between them. "And because you don't, you make me want to explain."

Aly hoped he didn't see the small smile tugging at the edges of her mouth. "You can if you want to. If you don't, that's fine too."

He poked a finger into her thigh. "Oh, that's so sneaky."

She turned sideways so that she could look at him straight on. "I can understand why you think that but, honestly, I'm not here to drag things out of you. Despite our ability to set each other on fire in bed, I do consider you to be a friend, one of the few I have. Maybe I can be a friend to you as well."

He turned his head away from her and stared out of his side window, his face hard with tension. "Only Avangeline knows the entire story."

Aly remained quiet, knowing that if Merrick shared anything with her it would be because he wanted to, not because she asked him to. Like love, trust was something that had to be given freely. If it came through badgering or nagging, it didn't mean as much.

"My earliest memories are confusing. I remember both a very happy childhood and one that was filled with violence. My memories of my father are the same. He was, at times, a brilliant dad—funny and charming, really charismatic. At other times, he was a monster."

Aly held her breath as his voice filled the cabin, strong and solid. But beneath the steady tone, she heard confusion and pain. The wounds from your childhood never quite healed, she realized. They could flare up again with the slightest bump.

"I clearly remember him beating the crap out of my mother," Merrick stated. "The year I turned five, the beatings became more frequent and more severe. I was young, but I knew that one day, he would go too far."

She touched his hand with her fingers, gently urging him to carry on. "Her family, and his, tried to intervene, but he had this larger-than-life personality, and he could twist any situation to benefit himself. Added to the fact that he was a sergeant in the Phoenix police department..." Merrick shrugged. "My mom didn't have a hope in hell of leaving or going anywhere without him finding her. He even told her she could go, but I had to stay."

"What was the catalyst to you finally leaving?" Aly asked, because she'd seen enough to know that there was always a trigger, a line that was crossed, an action someone couldn't walk back.

"He came home, and he started in on her. I'd had enough and thumped him with my baseball bat. Because I was like, five and a half, it didn't do much damage except to enrage him further. He put me in the hospital that night and told his colleagues I fell down the stairs."

"And they believed him?"

"Have you heard of the blue line, the old boys' network?" Merrick asked, raising an eyebrow. "They wanted to believe him, so they did. He behaved himself for a few months and was a brilliant dad, involved and loving and present. But neither of us was fooled." Merrick rubbed his hands up and down his shorts. "We knew it was the calm before the storm."

"You knew that? At five?" It wasn't that she didn't believe him, but it was hard to imagine that such a young child could be that aware.

"C'mon, Al, you lived in a tough place. You know what it means when the back of your neck starts to tingle," he replied. He waited for her to nod. "The tingle never stopped."

She winced, unable to imagine how terrible it must have been for him.

"We left when he least expected it," Merrick told her. "My mom walked me to school, as she always did, but instead of stopping we simply kept on walking. For weeks, she'd been stashing clothes at her best friend's place, just a few things at a time, and one day, she simply grabbed our duffel bags, put us on a bus and we left."

"Where did you go?" Aly softly asked him.

He released a half snort, half laugh. "Everywhere, nowhere. We stopped for a few weeks here, and a couple of months there. But he didn't stop looking for us, and nearly caught us once or twice. We steadily made our way across the country, and he never stopped looking." Merrick folded his arms across his chest and rested his head back, closing his eyes. "By the time we got to Hatfield, I was eight and we'd been running for a little more than two years. We'd just missed being caught by him. A family member we'd thought we could trust had let him know our location, and I could tell that my mom was at the end of her rope. She was so close to calling it quits."

"She was so brave. You both were," Aly said, a little choked up.

"I remember walking down the road into Hatfield. The sea was on the right and I just wanted to get on a boat and leave. We came across this very irate Englishwoman swearing up a storm." He opened his eyes and smiled at her. "Do you know that Avangeline can swear like a sailor?"

"I didn't."

"Trust me, she can, and I heard *all* her words that day. It was a week, maybe ten days before the plane crash and she was rushing back to Calcott when she got a flat. My mom helped her change the tire, because Jace knows her way around cars. Avangeline offered her money, but Mom told her what she really needed was a job and a place to stay. Avangeline—I can still see her in her yellow dress—looked at us, nodded and told us to get in. We arrived at Calcott Manor and never left."

She was grateful they'd found sanctuary with Avangeline but she knew that wasn't the full story. "Tell me everything, Merrick. Please."

He rested his hand on her thigh, turning his hand so it was palm up, and Aly placed her hand in his. "Her family descended on the place a few days later and suddenly there were four boys to play with. I was in my element.

They pulled me into their gang and for a couple of days we ran wild—it was amazing. Mom slid into making beds and cooking food and acting as Avangeline's housekeeper."

"Then the twins died."

"Then they died." Merrick turned to look out of the window onto the night. "A few weeks after the funeral, I caught Avangeline alone and asked if we could talk. I offered her a deal."

What sort of deal could an eight-year-old offer a billionairess? Intrigued, Aly leaned forward.

"I told her I would protect her grandsons. I was taller than even Malcolm, and bigger. I promised to keep them safe if she protected my mom. I remember her asking me about my dad, what he did, etcetera. Having left Phoenix when I was so young, I don't know how much information I gave her. But I do remember that she nodded and held out her hand to shake, which I did."

"How did she protect you?"

"In every way she could," he replied. "She arranged for me to go to school with the Granthams, and at school I became Merrick Knowles. I'm pretty sure she told the principal that if any information was released about me to any outside party, she'd yank all future donations. That was enough to scare him. She paid Jacinta in cash, and she even got a social security number and driver's license for my mom, in the name of Jacinta Knowles."

Aly's eyes widened. "Really?"

Merrick nodded. "God knows how she managed it, or through whom, but she did. And for seven, nearly eight years we lived under the radar, protected by Avangeline and her wealth. One day after school, Avangeline called us into her study and told us that my father was dead. He'd been shot while responding, ironically, to a domestic altercation. He wasn't even supposed to be on duty—he heard the call come over the radio and was close. Avangeline kept tabs on him, she knew every move he made, all the time."

"She's quite a woman," Aly commented.

"She really is," Merrick agreed.

"Have you been back to Phoenix, reconnected with your family?"

"My mom has. I've met them, but my family is here, in Hatfield. Avangeline, and my brothers—that's who I consider my family."

She could understand the subtext: Jace's family never managed to protect them back then, but Avangeline did. It was hard to measure up against the loyalty that engendered.

"I hate being associated with him. I hate the idea of his genes being part of me," Merrick quietly murmured. "That's why I walked out tonight after David brought up how much I look like him. I felt...dirty."

What could she say to that? How could she reassure him? Aly took a moment to think it through and to choose her words carefully. "I do understand how you feel, Mer. But I also know that you are so much more than his son, just like I am more than a girl from a rough background. I am more than the surroundings I grew up in—and I refuse to allow my sister's death or my organ transplant to define me too. I'm creating, or trying to create, the person I want to be, the life I want to have. And I am trying to take the positives of what my mom gave me—a solid work ethic and her fierce determination—and leaving behind the negatives, like the fact that her jobs kept her working so much that we weren't able to be as close as I wanted us to be. Maybe you can do the same for your father."

"He didn't give me anything good," Merrick scoffed. "His height and his build, I guess, but that's about it."

Aly shrugged. "He taught you, in an ass-backward way, to be protective. So take that. You learned to be brave, take that. Leave him, and everything else, behind. Otherwise, you're giving him, and his memory, too much power."

Merrick looked at her, and she could see him turning over her words, inspecting them, trying to make sense of them. She allowed him time and space to do that, and just kept her hand in his and allowed him to think.

After a few minutes, he squeezed her fingers and sent her a small smile. "I hear what you are saying."

"But you're not sure if you can get there?" she asked, giving him a small smile when he nodded. "It's not a race, Merrick. It's just an idea that needs time to settle and take root. It's not an overnight process."

He leaned forward and brushed his lips across hers, before resting his face against hers, his mouth close to her ear. "Thank you. For being here. For listening. For not judging."

She placed her hand against his cheek and rubbed her cheek against his. "We all have our baggage, Knowles. Sometimes it helps to lay it down now and again."

Merrick sat up, rubbed his face and lifted his wrist to look at his watch, a he-man Rolex with what looked to be far too many dials. "If we hurry, we can drive to the city and join everyone for dinner at Mack's."

Right, tonight was the start of the Manhattan portion of Jocelyn and Arthur's vacation. Aly wrinkled her nose. She needed to shower and change and do her makeup. Mack's was one of the best restaurants in the world and she didn't think she could rock up in skinny jeans and an off-the-shoulder sweater. "Honestly, I'd settle for a pizza and an early night."

"Me too," Merrick admitted. "We could drive down in the morning and join them for brunch."

That sounded like a much better option. Aly reached for the handle of her door and was about to push it open when Merrick's question reached her. "So, the pizza? With or without me?"

She looked over her shoulder. "What do you mean?" she asked, confused.

"We've been spending a lot of time together and we've just had another intense conversation. I was wondering if you needed some time alone."

She shook her head. "I'm good. Do you? Want to be alone, that is?"

He hesitated before shaking his head. "No."

Aly sucked in a deep breath as she stepped onto the skid and then onto the grass below. She tipped her head back to look at the star-studded sky—diamonds on a rich velvet cloth—and rocked on her heels.

Given a choice to be with or without him, she was starting to think that she'd always choose to be with him. And that was a major problem.

Nine

In the much quieter VVIP section of Glass Houses, a club housing four dance floors and many bars, Merrick sat next to Aly and nursed a glass of twelve-year-old whiskey. This was what he loved the best, spending time with his brothers and their warm, sharp-witted, funny, and lovely, women. Eliot, looking every inch the supermodel she used to be, perched on Soren's knee, her metallic minidress inching up her shapely thigh. Ru and Peyton were in deep conversation and Fox, Jack and Soren were listening to Aly recounting a tricky social media case she'd handled.

She wore long, wide-legged black pants and a sleeveless vest number with shiny lapels, a riff on a classic tuxedo. The front of the vest dipped toward her navel and made his mouth water.

With her hair falling in loose waves, and natural makeup, she looked incredible. She fit in so well with his family. If he took a deep breath and closed one eye, he could see her at family functions, laughing with his sisters-in-law, her arm around Jace's waist, leaning her head on her shoulder.

Over these past few days at Calcott Manor, he'd become aware that Aly and his mom were closer than he realized before, and he was both surprised and moved by their connection. Maybe it was because they both had hard times, got through them and recognized the strength it took to make the decisions they did.

If he and Aly got together—in this fictional, never-going-to-happen world he was visiting in his head—he could easily see his mom siding with Aly in any argument, serious or not.

He would be seriously outgunned.

The thought should scare him but, strangely, it didn't. Something had shifted in him since their conversation last night in the helicopter, and he felt more mentally and emotionally at ease with her than he ever had before. It felt right to tell her things about his past he'd never shared with anyone, not even his brothers, events he and his mom no longer discussed.

The image of Jace, still looking sad and washed-out, flashed in his mind and he felt a stab of guilt. She was unhappy over her failed romance, and he'd done nothing, *nothing*, to help her through it. He knew she needed encouragement from him to try to repair her relationship with Pasco and he felt guilty that he hadn't made the effort to talk to his mom.

Part of it was embarrassment—but he was a grown guy, he could accept that his mom had a love life—and part of it was his discomfort with change. If she and Pasco committed to being together, would that mean she'd leave Calcott Manor? If so, what would the house be without his mom? What would Avangeline do? How would she cope?

But his mom deserved to be happy, and he knew Avangeline would never stand in the way of that. So why was he? Maybe he hadn't actively stopped her but neither had he encouraged her to be with someone who made her exceptionally happy.

The thought made his stomach clench and left him feeling ashamed of himself. When Jack asked him whether he'd sucked on a lemon, he grimaced. "I was just thinking about my mom and how unhappy she is."

The rest of their group fell silent at his words, and he saw his worry in his brothers' eyes. They didn't like seeing Jace looking so diminished any more than he did. He pulled his phone out of the inside pocket of his jacket and flipped it from hand to hand.

"Do you think it would help if I gave her my permission?" he asked. "Not that she needs it, but—"

"I think it would go a long way," Jack told him. "You're her life and your approval is exceptionally important to her."

Yeah, but an *artist*? Someone who was not that much older than them? "Will he make her happy?" he asked, hearing the worry in his voice.

Aly placed her hand on his knee and squeezed. "I think so, Merrick. She's spoken to me about him, just a little. I know she misses him. When they were together, she glowed, and she couldn't stop smiling."

He trusted her opinion. He slowly nodded before tipping his head up to look at the dim lights high above his head. "How do I tell her?"

Aly pulled his phone out of his hand and started to type. When she handed the phone back, he read the message on the screen.

Mom, I've been an ass about Pasco. I hate seeing you unhappy. What can I do to help you fix whatever went wrong between you?

Not giving himself time to think, he pressed the send button and tried to shrug away the spurt of panic flying up his throat. These past few months had been full of change, and he didn't like it. But if it made his mom happy, he'd learn to deal.

He felt his phone vibrate and looked down at the screen, seeing his mom's reply.

You made me cry, darling. While I would love someone else to try and fix this for me, it's something I've got to do myself.

Being a grown-up is hell, would not recommend it, she added.

He passed Aly the phone so that she could read the message and they exchanged a small, secret smile. Placing his hand on her lower back, he found a bare strip of skin where her top rode up and caressed it with the edge of his thumb. He couldn't wait to take her back to his apartment—she was staying with him as Jocelyn, Arthur and Jace were in the other guest rooms in Avangeline's apartment. He was already imagining her in his bed. The one he'd never brought a woman to before.

"Talking of Calcott Manor residents, is Avangeline feeling okay?" Peyton asked, leaning forward and resting her folded arms on her bent knee. "Has she said anything to any of you?"

He and his brothers frowned. It was Fox who answered Peyton's question. "We saw her when we all traveled up to Calcott Manor to discuss her new will."

After all the drama regarding the blackmailer and the four of them nagging Avangeline to write down her wishes, her brand-new will had, at long last, been drawn up and notarized. It was simple enough—all their loans were forgiven, and the shares she held in their companies would revert to them. There was a bequest for Jace, and the bulk of her money would go to charity. After that, and a few items set aside for close friends, the rest of Avangeline's assets would be shared equally between her three grandsons. And him. Even after twenty-five years, he didn't understand how he'd lucked out by landing with this family.

"She seemed fine," Fox continued. "Chirpy, on the ball, incredibly focused."

Peyton looked uneasy. "She looked tired tonight, and when she stood up after the show, she wobbled, as if she were going to faint."

Fox held Ru's hand against his thigh. "Let's be honest, keeping up with Jocelyn is going to tax anyone. And it's been a long and stressful couple of months. She probably just needs time to recover. We tend to forget that she is in her eighties. Her stamina's not going to be the same as it was twenty years ago."

Peyton shook her head. "I hear you, but nothing energizes her like art and while we were going through the house—I was trying to get accurate provenances of all her works— she bailed halfway through, telling me she was tired. That's not like her."

"Feel free to suggest she should see a doctor," Soren said, smiling. "We'll enjoy seeing your head roll down Calcott Manor's drive."

They laughed and Eliot was the first to address the elephant in the room. "Do you think we'll ever find out who her long-time lover is?"

He caught Aly's eye, and she returned his look, her face not displaying any emotion. Yes, they had their suspicions but it had nothing to do with any of them. Avangeline wanted to keep her lover a secret and he owed it to her to do exactly that.

"I doubt we'll ever know," he told them.

"And isn't it better not to know?" Aly chimed in. "Once you know, you *know*. This way is so much more romantic and intriguing."

He sent her a grateful glance, silently thanking her. Aly adroitly changed the subject and soon they were discussing whether they could keep up with Jocelyn as she whipped around Manhattan on what she called an epic shopping spree scheduled for the following afternoon. She, Peyton, Eliot and Ru all agreed that they would be drooping with exhaustion by the afternoon but that Jocelyn, and possibly his mother, would still be going strong. Previous generations of women were far, they glumly admitted, tougher than they were.

He wasn't sure he agreed. Shopping stamina aside, he thought Aly was pretty damn tough, quite amazing. She'd been handed a set of circumstances that would cause most people to buckle and bend and she'd pushed back her shoulders and faced adversity head-on, her chin raised. If he ever decided to settle down—not that that was likely—he'd want to live out life with someone like her, someone who could face the fire and walk through it anyway.

"How goes the search to find answers about the plane crash?" Soren asked, his expression sober.

Merrick sipped his whiskey, then answered. "We're convinced there was nothing wrong with the plane," he replied, keeping his voice gentle.

"Jess was too good a pilot—" Fox retorted but Merrick lifted his hands to cut off his words.

"Give us a bit more time, we still have work to do," Merrick told him.

Fox looked like he was about to argue but when Ru squeezed his hand, he just nodded, albeit grudgingly. Out of the corner of his eye, Merrick saw Aly rub the area under her left breast, pain flashing in her eyes.

Avangeline wasn't the only one who needed to see a doctor but Aly, like Avangeline, wouldn't take kindly to being nagged into doing something she didn't want to do.

Jacinta had changed outfits six times, eventually settling on a pretty but stylish dress in various shades of blue, thinking that the colors made her eyes a little brighter. She'd pulled her hair into a loose knot and sprayed herself with the perfume she'd purchased yesterday, a new Jo Malone fragrance she adored.

She had never been so nervous in her life.

After a brunch with Jocelyn, Arthur and the entire Grantham family at the Forrester-Grantham hotel—their eggs Benedict were to die for—she'd excused herself from the epic shopping trip Jocelyn, Peyton, Ru and Eliot were embarking on.

Arthur was meeting an actor friend and Avangeline was heading back to her apartment to, so she said, catch up on some correspondence.

Jace was a little worried about Avangeline, her friend dominating her thoughts as she sat on a bench across the road from the fancy gallery where Pasco was staging his latest exhibition. And yes, sitting here thinking about Avangeline was an excellent way to procrastinate instead of heading inside and laying her heart on the line.

Her heart, stupid thing, was curled up in the corner, arms over its head, trying to remain invisible.

Avangeline, her oldest friend, her savior, seemed more weary than usual, as if the city, one of her favorite places in the world, was almost too much for her. Jace could understand why, after the peace and genuine quiet of Calcott Manor, she felt bombarded with noise and sensation too. Here in the city, she felt like everything was dialed up to maximum, with waves of energy smacking her in the face at regular intervals. She could understand why Pasco loved it, how inspiring he found it but, God, the New York she knew was noisy. A little dirty. A lot crazy.

But if she wanted to be part of Pasco's life—and she *so* did—then she would have to get used to it. She would have to learn to love it or, at the very least, tolerate it. She could always escape to Calcott Manor for a visit when city life got too much.

But how was she going to leave Avangeline? She didn't know...and couldn't think about that now. First, she had to find out whether she'd blown it with Pasco or if he actually wanted her in his life. If he did—and that wasn't guaranteed—then they could move forward, finding a solution together.

Either way, sitting here wasn't going to get her anywhere. With a mixture of great determination and great reluctance, she stood up and headed to the gallery's entrance. Not allowing herself to second-guess herself, she yanked open the door and told the gallery assistant she was simply browsing before she walked into the cool, light-filled rooms. She just needed a minute to catch her breath, then she would find the assistant again, ask if Pasco was around and, if not, where she could find him.

She had his phone number, but she didn't want to give him any warning that she was coming. If she caught him off guard, then she could read his eyes, see the expression on his face...and she'd know.

She'd *know* whether they had a future or not.

She walked through the gallery, populated with framed, preparatory sketches of some of his more famous works, and realized that while his sculptures had made him famous around the world, he was pretty good with a piece of paper and a pencil too. She stopped when she came to a drawing of a figure standing in the greenhouse, her hands buried in a bag of soil. It was quickly sketched, rough but powerful, and he'd caught the contentment on her face.

Gardening was her happy place and Pasco, somehow, managed to convey that on paper. Pulling her eyes off the in-profile sketch—it was so weird to see herself up on a wall—she walked into the center of the room, where a clay sculpture of a naked female figure lay on her stomach, her head on her arms. Jace lifted her hand to her mouth as she took in the familiar features, her too-wide mouth pulled up in a sexy smile, her half-closed eyes. She remembered waking up from a doze after they made love to find Pasco sitting in the armchair, a sketch pad on his lap. She'd never once suspected he'd been sketching her.

Jace tipped her head to the side and winced when she saw how accurately he'd depicted the lines around her eyes, the furrow between her eyebrows and, God, the sag under her arms. Her butt looked okay-ish—but her hips were rounded, her thighs accurately chubby, unfortunately.

Yet, it was—*she* was—still, somehow, beautiful. She looked confident, and incredibly content. Soft and lovely, a woman who'd lived and fought and worked and argued. A woman at ease in her skin. Was that the way he saw her? If yes, then this sculpture, in clay instead of his usual abstract iron pieces, was a love letter…

To her.

Or, at the very least, a "like" letter.

Jace closed her eyes and folded her arms, cursing the

lone tear that managed to escape her tightly scrunched lids. She'd been scared to reach out and take what he offered, and she'd put what they had in jeopardy. Her fear had led to weeks of heartache, lonely nights and her dragging her bottom lip across the floor. She should've been braver, tougher, less of a coward.

Jace opened her eyes, frowning when she saw the red sticker on the plinth of the sculpture. She had picked up enough from Peyton, who was Avangeline's art adviser, to know that meant the sculpture had been sold. She didn't know how she felt about her naked form being in a museum or someone else's house but there was nothing she could do about that. She had other problems anyway, the biggest of which was where to find the artist.

The easiest way would be to phone the blasted man and ask him to meet.

He answered quickly, as if he'd been waiting for her call. "Hey."

Jace swallowed. "Hi. Um…can we meet?"

"Sure."

Right, well at least he was prepared to talk to her. Jace stared down at the sleek laminated floor. "When would suit you?"

"Now."

Jace heard the call disconnect and she stared at the screen, confused. Pasco could be prickly, especially when his work was interrupted, but he was seldom outright rude. And hanging up on her was rude. Besides which, what did he mean by "now"?

"Do you like it?"

At the sound of his voice, she whirled around. For a moment, her vision tunneled in and out, not able to believe that he was standing in front of her, dressed in a pair of faded jeans and a rich red, obviously expensive, button-down shirt. Her eyes danced over him, and she took in his gaunt face, his overly long stubble and the wariness in his eyes. He'd either been working extralong hours—very possible, given what she knew of his workaholic tendencies—or he'd spent the past month lying in bed staring at the ceiling, not sleeping. Like her.

"What are you doing here?" she asked, her voice suddenly croaky.

"I'm having an exhibition here," he told her, sliding his hands into the back pockets of his jeans. She'd raised five boys and could spot an evasion from fifty paces. Pasco half smiled and shrugged. "Merrick sent me a message, and implied that you might swing by."

She always knew she liked that boy.

"I've been hanging around and annoying the staff for the past three hours," he admitted. "I was planning on running into you, pretending it was all a coincidence."

Now that was very unlike Pasco, who took the world by the horns and shook the hell out of it. Jace, caught thoroughly off guard, pushed her fingers into her hair and silently cursed when she dislodged most of it from her loose top knot. She was about to excuse herself to go untangle it when Pasco lifted his hand and pulled the pin from her bun, making it tumble to her shoulders. Well, that solved that problem.

"You didn't answer my question," he said, gesturing to the sculpture in front of them. "Do you like it?"

She heard the note of insecurity in his voice and wondered at it. Pasco was, always had been, exceptionally confident of his art, and his place in the art world. "It's been a long time since I've done a life study," he added apologetically.

"She's... *I'm* very real," Jace said, biting down on her bottom lip.

"But very beautiful. When I couldn't stop thinking about you, I started to sculpt you. It was my way of trying to expel you from my system."

Jace sucked in a harsh breath. "Did it work?"

He glared at her and pushed his hand into his hair. Jace noticed his fingers were trembling. "No, it fucking didn't. I see you everywhere, I can't sleep, it's taken every ounce of willpower I have not to call you, not to return to Calcott Manor. I've been trying to give you space."

"I don't want space, I want you."

Pasco stilled and his eyes bored through her. "What does that mean?"

Jace shrugged her shoulders. "When you left, I felt all the energy, and color, leave Calcott Manor. I've been living a half life, reassuring myself that at least I'm safe, that nothing can hurt me while I stay on the estate. But..."

"But?" Pasco demanded, his shoulders hunched.

"But I hurt anyway. Not being around you, with you, *hurts*. From my hair to my toenails, I ache."

"Then let's stop hurting, sweetheart." Pasco held out his hand and Jace slid hers into his. As easy as that, the world suddenly made sense again. Colors returned and every muscle in her body relaxed. As he pulled her into his body, she turned her head to look at the sculpture of herself again. Before they got into the details, where they would live, how she was going to leave Calcott Manor, before they went to bed and didn't emerge for a week, she wanted him to know one thing.

"I'm a little freaked out that some stranger has bought that, Kildare."

He laughed and dragged his amazing mouth across hers.

She arched her into him, wanting more, but he pulled back, his face full of joy. "Whether in sculpture form or real life, the only place you're going to be is with me. Nah, that one is just marked with a sticker so everyone knows it isn't for sale."

Oh, *thank God.* There was only one man she wanted looking at her naked form for the rest of her life, one man who hadn't looked at her naked for far too long. "I think you should take me back to your place and take me to bed."

He nodded. "Apart from coming here today, I think that's the best idea you've ever had."

A few days later—four days before Aly was due to return to Jersey City and to work—she realized her indigestion issues were happening more frequently and were also becoming a great deal more painful. She could no longer ignore the possibility of there being something wrong. In fact, she was beginning to think she had an ulcer. So, after bidding Jocelyn and Arthur a fond goodbye, she slipped out of Avangeline's apartment and called her doctor, asking for an urgent appointment.

Because of her previous medical issues, she was slotted in immediately and told to present at his practice in Jersey City as soon as she could. Walking down the stairs to Merrick's apartment, mostly to give herself some time to think, she wondered whether to tell him she was going for a check-up or not. She didn't want him to fuss. Knowing his protective instinct, he'd probably want to accompany her.

If there was something wrong, some not-so-minor problem, she wanted time to absorb it herself, to work out how she was going to deal with whatever prognosis she got, before anyone else found out. If Merrick, or anyone else came with her, she'd feel like she needed to protect them from the news, to be upbeat and buoyant for them. She, like Merrick, had her own protective streak.

No, she needed to do this by herself. Besides, it wasn't like she and Merrick were in the kind of relationship where accompanying her to medical appointments was expected. Their fling was scheduled to fizzle out soon. It was better if she simply got used to living her life solo, dealing with her stuff by herself.

Aly approached the door to Merrick's apartment and keyed in the code that allowed her access inside. She dropped her bag on the hallway table and walked into the empty room, frowning when she didn't see Merrick at his desk. Then she caught movement on his balcony. As if sensing her, he turned and lifted his hand in acknowledgment. He lifted a finger, asking her to give him a minute, and she nodded and sat down on the closest club chair, looking past him to the view of Central Park on a sunny day.

Her fairy-tale life was coming to an end and soon she'd be stuck in a standard office block, working long hours in her windowless office. Winter was on its way, and she'd leave her apartment in the dark, and return home in the dark. There would be no more walks on a deserted beach, standing on the balcony of the garage apartment to watch the ever-changing sea, taking long walks and stumbling runs around Avangeline's estate. She was going to miss Calcott Manor.

But God, she was going to miss the family more. How was she going to cope with not having a leisurely cup of coffee with Jace in the morning, talking about everything and nothing? She spent lots of time with Avangeline too, accompanying her on walks through the extensive Calcott Manor gardens, and listening to her tell stories about her life, her business and her boys.

Peyton, Ru and Eliot had made her promise to make time for them to have girly lunches and brunches, movie nights, and for her to come to dinner—but she knew that friendships faded rapidly when they no longer had regular excuses to see each other. They had busy lives, and so did she. The chances of maintaining a friendship with them were unlikely at best.

Leaving was going to hurt, far more than she'd bargained for. And it would be far more painful than the occasional flash of pain under her rib cage, burning through her stomach lining.

"Did you say your goodbyes?" Merrick asked as he stepped back into the living room from the balcony.

Aly nodded. "Jack organized for the hotel's limo to take them to the airport. It's been so much fun having Jocelyn and Arthur around and getting to know them."

"How's Avangeline?" Merrick asked and Aly heard the subtext to his question. He was really asking how his grandmother felt about Arthur leaving.

"She seemed fine, if a little pale. I think that while she loves having them, it's easier for her when they are far away. I guess that having the love of your life in front of you, while having to hide your feelings, must be hell," Aly said.

She kind of, sort of, knew how that felt. She'd reluctantly, and very stupidly allowed her feelings for Merrick to deepen. She wasn't in love with him but she was close, and keeping him from suspecting that was killing her.

Silly woman. Silly, foolish woman. But the heart wanted what it wanted, and Aly knew her heart wanted Merrick.

"Do you think Jocelyn suspects?" Merrick asked her, sprawling into a chair opposite her, his long legs crossed at the ankles.

Aly thought about that. "I think that Jocelyn is one of

the smartest women out there. If she didn't have at least an inkling, then I'd be surprised. But I think she knows they have a history she was never part of and is okay with that. Jocelyn is sensible and pragmatic and not overly dramatic. And he does love her—Jocelyn, I mean."

Merrick nodded. "While he's not demonstrative, I can see that. I can also see, looking carefully, that he loves Avangeline too. I don't know if I would've noticed it if I hadn't seen them in the gazebo."

"Me neither," Aly admitted. She saw him glance at his watch and cocked her head. "Do you need to be somewhere?"

He nodded. "I have a meeting with the bank, and because it's just around the corner from the hotel, I'm heading to the boardroom at Forrester-Grantham for a conference call with my top management. It's going to take most of the day, possibly longer. I might be home late."

"You don't need to explain your itinerary to me," Aly replied, perhaps sharper than she meant to. "We're not in a relationship or anything."

Merrick frowned at her. "I was just trying to be considerate, Alyson."

Yes, she knew that and knew she was out of line. But, because she needed to put some distance between them, in preparation for her leaving his life at the end of the week, she shrugged. "You could stay out all night, hook up with someone else, and there's not a damn thing I could say about that."

"Are you trying to pick a fight?" he asked, his voice remaining steady. "And if so, why?"

He never lost his temper, and never came across as being anything but perfectly unruffled, and calm. It was very annoying. And yes, of course she was trying to pick a fight.

She needed an excuse to create a crack between them so that when she left, she'd be better able to deal with the chasm between them.

But it wasn't his fault her feelings had changed. She was in the wrong here, not him. Standing up, she walked into the kitchen and took two bottles of water from the fridge. She handed Merrick one and he cracked the lid, handing her the open bottle before opening the other one for himself. It was a little gesture, but it said so much. Merrick thought of other people first, and went out of his way to make life, whenever he could, easier for them. It was as instinctive to him as breathing.

What would a life with him look like? It would, she realized, be filled with little moments like this, him opening bottle tops and doors. He'd be a hand on her back, a body to curl up against at night, a steady opinion and a calm reaction when she felt off balance. He was the only person who'd managed to slide behind all her barriers, someone with whom she felt completely comfortable showing her insecure, sometimes irrational, authentic self. Would she ever find someone else who could do all of that?

No, she doubted that. There was only one Merrick.

But circumstances, and his antipathy toward commitment, made a future for them impossible.

Aly felt sadness roll over her. Knowing that Merrick would see it in her eyes, she turned her back on him to look out onto leafy Central Park. In a few weeks, the leaves would start to turn, and the wind would carry a hint of ice.

"Did you manage to get Avangeline and your brothers to sign that letter for Jesse's doctor, asking them to release Jesse's health history?" Aly asked, changing the subject.

"Yes, I emailed you the copy. I don't know whether it's

going to be enough. Some doctors take that confidentiality clause very seriously."

"He's been dead for twenty-five years," Aly protested.

Merrick shrugged. "You might get something, you might not," he said. "Again, it's a long shot."

"*Me?* Aren't you coming with me?"

He grimaced. "I have to fly to Toronto to check out a new venue for one of my food trucks. My managers can't come to a consensus," Merrick told her. "I'm going to fly out there tomorrow morning."

And so it started, the beginning of the end. Merrick joined her at the window and put a hand on her lower back. "What are your plans for the day?"

She fought the urge to lean into him. "I'll see if can see Jesse's doctor today. After that, I've got some errands to take care of. I might go back to Calcott Manor with Avangeline, since your mother is loved up with Pasco."

He pulled a face. "While I'm excited for both of them, the thought of them being loved up still makes me want to stick my fingers in my ear and sing 'la-la-la.' But Mom said that they are going back to Calcott Manor as well, so Avangeline won't be alone."

"Is Pasco going to move there?" Aly asked. If he did, it would be the answer to all their worries about Avangeline living in a monstrously big house alone. While Avangeline was the first to say that Jace had to live her life, everyone— Jace included—was worried about how Avangeline would adjust to living without her. She could more than afford to hire a replacement housekeeper, but it would be difficult at her age to adjust to new staff. As they knew, Avangeline was very set in her ways.

Merrick leaned his shoulder into the glass. "I don't think

they've made any long-term plans yet—they are just enjoying being together."

It was so exciting that Jace, one of her favorite people, was getting her happy ever after.

Merrick ran his hand up her arm, down her chest, skimming over her right breast and down her stomach. "So, stay here tonight, go back to Calcott Manor in the morning. I'll try and wrap up my meeting early and we can spend the rest of the night in bed." An emotion she couldn't identify flashed in his eyes and a rueful smile lifted his lips slightly. "I want to make the most of these nights before we have to start working around our equally crowded work schedules…."

Wait! What? "So you still want to see me after I return to work?"

He nodded, squeezing her hip. "I guess." He *guessed*?

"But how that is going to work with me being in and out of the city and you working all hours because you are on track for a promotion, God only knows," Merrick added.

He made it sound like their future lack of time together was going to be her fault, like she was unfairly moving the goalposts. Aly felt a rush of irritation. "If the idea of keeping this up is too hard, then we can always end it when I leave," she told him, her voice frosty. "I don't need you doing me any favors."

He jerked back, a frown pulling his dark eyebrows together. "Wow, you are in a snit this morning." He kissed her temple instead of laying his usual open-mouthed, sexy kiss on her lips. "I've got to go. I'll see you later, okay?"

Without another word, he walked away from her, snatching up his leather laptop bag. Within seconds he was out of the door.

Right. Well.

She'd known that starting a relationship with Merrick—sleeping with him, she corrected—would complicate her life but this was ridiculous. Aly sighed, rested her forehead against the glass, and gently banged her head. She could either stay here and analyze whatever they had and whatever they were...or she could go to Jersey City and see her doctor. And make the appointment to see Jesse's doctor too.

None of the three options filled her with excitement.

Ten

Aly had planned to visit Jesse's doctor, now retired, sometime that morning but it was closer to five before she rolled
up to his Long Island home. She pulled her phone out of her
bag to call Merrick to tell him that she was going to be late
getting back to his apartment but discovered her phone had
died. She'd been so distracted by Merrick that she forgot to
plug it in to charge.

That was very unlike her. What was next? Forgetting to
brush her teeth? Aly tossed her dead phone back in her bag,
thinking about her day. Her doctor, the one who guided her
through the transplant and oversaw her postoperative care,
looked worried when she told him about her chest pains.
She tried to explain to him that she didn't think there was
anything wrong with her heart, but Dr. Cross grabbed her
shoulders, looked her in the eye and told her that he wasn't,
given her history, taking any chances.

Before she could take a breath, he marched her into the
private hospital across the street and hooked her up to several machines, running a gamut of tests. They drew blood

and put a rush on the results. Aly tried not to think of the costs as his deep frown got deeper as he failed to find a simple explanation for her symptoms.

Hours and hours later, she sat on the other side of his desk and lifted her eyebrows, feeling a bit sorry for Dr. Cross, who looked genuinely perplexed. "You are perfectly fine. There's nothing wrong with your heart, all your blood markers are perfectly normal. You're a bit skinny but as healthy as a horse. There's nothing to indicate an ulcer and I cannot find anything, medically, wrong with you. You must be suffering from indigestion, but I don't know why."

Now that all the other options were off the table, Aly had to face something she'd been avoiding. She only experienced pain when she was talking about Malcolm or discussing the plane crash. Her chest pains—indigestion—were likely psychosomatic, in her head rather than her body. And the only way to get rid of whatever was happening to her, to free herself from this connection to Malcolm, was to solve the riddle of what had caused his parents' crash.

She'd declined to share any of her insights with Dr. Cross and simply took the prescription he handed her for chronic indigestion and tossed it in the first trash can she found.

Aly looked at the pretty house in front of her before pulling the folder out of her bag and flipping it open. Inside was the letter asking Dr. Foley to give her and Merrick any information about Jesse's health he could remember. She understood that patient confidentiality was imperative, but Jesse had been dead for more than a quarter century and she had permission from his family to discuss any health concerns. Still, if the doctor refused to talk to her, she'd be toast. There were no more stones for her to turn over—nowhere else she could think of to look for answers.

Oh, well, she could only try.

Aly pushed the gate open and walked down the path bisecting a very pretty garden to the front door. She rang the doorbell and a few minutes later the door opened, revealing a fit-looking man in his midsixties, an icy glass of white wine in his hand.

Damn, she could do with one of those.

"Dr. Foley, my name is Aly Garwood."

His blue eyes, a little annoyed, met hers. "We had an appointment for this morning, Ms. Garwood."

Knowing that she was on shaky ground, she opted to give him the truth. As a medical man himself, he might understand. "I'm so sorry, my phone died, and I've been tied up with doctors all day. I went to see my doctor earlier because I've been having odd chest pains. Because I'm the recipient of a donor's liver, he insisted on running a barrage of tests and he only released me a little while ago."

Interest replaced suspicion. "And you're okay?"

"Perfectly. It's probably just indigestion." Aly smiled. She gestured to his wineglass. "I know it's not a good time, but I'd really appreciate ten minutes to talk to you."

He stepped back, allowed her to enter his house and led her down a light-filled hall to his study. Aly glanced through an open door and looked through the lounge to a patio beyond, where a younger-looking woman sat in a summer dress, her bare feet up on an ottoman.

In the study, she handed over the letter from the Grantham family. Dr. Foley picked a pair of glasses off his desk and slid them over his face. He perused the letter and tossed it on the desk. "I'm not a fan of revealing patient information to strangers, letter or no letter."

Damn. "His sons want to know whether there are any medical conditions they should be aware of, medical issues that might run in the family."

"But I *am* a fan of big donations. This letter says I can expect a substantial donation to any charitable cause I support if I release the information. There's an inner-city hospital I know of that is in desperate need of a new X-ray machine. It needs the machine more than Jesse Grantham needs his confidentiality."

Pragmatic. Dr. Foley picked up another file from his desk, one that looked depressingly slim. He gestured for her to sit down in the visitor's chair and Aly did, crossing her leg over her knee. She waited, trying to hide her impatience as Dr. Foley read through the file, then read through it again. He eventually lifted his head and shrugged. "As I told the other brother—"

Aly jerked her head up. "What brother?" she demanded. "Who did you tell?"

"The one who died ten years back. He came to see me."

Malcolm had spoken to this doctor about his father? Why did he do that?

"But, as I told him, there's not much here. Essentially, I was concerned about his elevated cholesterol levels. They were high but not excessively so. I told him he had three months to bring them down or else he had to start with a statin to lower his cholesterol."

Aly subconsciously rubbed the area above her heart. "Was he at risk for a heart attack?"

Dr. Foley shook his head. "Not as far as I could see, unless there was another issue I failed to pick up. But he was a very fit man, so I wasn't overly worried about him dropping dead from a coronary."

Aly stared at the landscape painting behind his desk, a seascape of a fishing boat caught in a wild Atlantic storm. "What would you give his chances of having a heart attack?" Aly asked him.

"Ten percent, at most. He didn't smoke, he didn't drink excessively. He exercised daily. Apart from the cholesterol, he was one of my healthiest clients."

She kept hearing how healthy Jesse was, and how he should've lived a long life. If they had a body to autopsy, they could've found an answer, but Jesse's remains were scattered across a mountain. It was both sad and deeply frustrating.

Aly nodded at the file. "Is there anything else I should know about?"

Dr. Foley grimaced before looking at her. He lifted one shoulder. "He was impotent. And had been for a while."

Her eyes widened. "Really? For how long?"

He glanced down at his notes. "For about five or six years. I treated him with everything I could, and I had some success in the early years, but nothing seemed to work in the last few months of his life." He looked embarrassed and Aly didn't blame him. She doubted it was a condition anyone would be truly comfortable discussing. "I eventually concluded that it was a mental issue rather than a physical one. Another thing... I believe that for the last two years of his life, he suffered from severe stress and, I'm convinced, depression. I recommended counseling but he wouldn't go, and neither would he consider taking an antidepressant. He said he knew the cure, he just had to find the guts to do it."

Dr. Foley rubbed his chin. "When I heard about the plane crash, I wondered if he—"

Aly knew where he was going with this. "Committed suicide?" She wrinkled her nose. "I might agree with you if he'd been flying alone, if he didn't have his twin and their wives in the plane with him. From everything I know, he wouldn't have left four little boys without a single parent if he'd had any choice in the matter."

"I take your point. But I maintain he was depressed."

Jesse's marriage had been on the rocks, and he'd been involved in The Basement. Merrick had told her about the club the other night, giving her the bare-bones facts: Heather had connected with some people on the dark web who took S&M to a new level, and they'd hired barely legal sex workers. Aly and Merrick hadn't felt the need to dig further into The Basement, but based on the texts they'd unearthed from Jesse's phone, it seemed like that had been just one of many bones of contention for the couple. Jesse wanted them to take a step back—Heather emphatically did not.

What if Jesse wanted out of the marriage and the club and his wife wouldn't let him leave? That would explain his depression. "Would stress affect his impotence?"

Dr. Foley confirmed it would.

Mmm. "Did he open up and talk to you at all?"

"Very little. He was incredibly good at hiding his feelings, and it took me a while to diagnose his depression."

Apparently, Malcolm, the oldest Grantham, had been the same. He'd been so good at showing the world he was fine that he'd managed to hide an opioid addiction from the family—and Peyton, his fiancée—for years. Hiding your feelings and pretending could be dangerous to your mental and physical health. Hiding behind a facade and suppressing your emotions could, Aly was convinced, affect your physical well-being. She genuinely believed that the mess in a person's mind was reflected in their body.

"So we have incredibly high stress, impotence and elevated cholesterol levels," Aly murmured. "Could all three of them together be a recipe for a heart attack?"

Dr. Foley shook his head. "There's not enough scientific evidence to jump to that conclusion. His cholesterol wasn't high enough to be treated with medication, and he never admitted to the depression. All I can say for certain is that he was stressed. Is it possible he had a heart attack? Sure. He could've also had a panic attack—the symptoms mimic a heart attack."

"And his impotence? What role did that play in his state of mind? Come on, Doctor, he was a guy in his late thirties. Sex would've been pretty important to him." Especially important to Jesse, who owned and used, apparently, the sex club he and Heather set up. But, hold on, did he?

Did he ever actually *use* the sex club? If he was sexually impotent for years, how would he partake? By watching? No, that didn't sound right. As she'd heard from Avangeline, who loved to talk about her twins, Jesse was a doer, a guy who got his hands dirty; he wasn't a voyeur or a spectator. So, if he didn't watch, how was he involved?

Was he involved, or had it been mostly Heather's passion project? Was it her needs that drove them to invest in the club?

"And you told Malcolm all of this? Including the information about his impotence?" Aly asked, flicking her thumbnail against her teeth.

He nodded, then shrugged. "He also paid for information on his father. His donation bought a new incubator for a rural hospital."

Aly bit down on her bottom lip. She needed to talk to Merrick. She needed his calm, no-nonsense input. She'd thought they were done with the club, but this information raised questions about Jesse's involvement in The Basement.

Because why would a man who wasn't interested in sex— who couldn't get it up—want anything to do with the all-for-one-and-one-for-all sex club?

It made no sense. And why had Malcolm taken such an interest in his father's death?

* * *

Across town, Merrick was midway through his meeting when his world fell apart. It was Jack who opened the door to the conference room, his normally tanned face white. Merrick looked past him to see Fox, who also looked like he'd been hit by a two-by-four. Merrick pushed his chair back so hard it hit the wall behind him as he surged to his feet, his meeting forgotten.

"What is it?" he demanded, "What's wrong?"

"Jace just called. Avangeline collapsed as she walked into the hall of Calcott Manor," Fox told him, his voice raspy with fear. "Pasco was there, and he picked her up, put her in the car and raced her to Hatfield Hospital."

Merrick yanked his jacket off the back of the chair, his heart pounding. "And? What are they saying?"

Jack shrugged. "She's in ICU. Apparently they've already had to resuscitate her once."

Merrick felt hot, then cold, then hot again. In the hallway, Jack ran his hands over his face and Fox leaned his shoulder against the wall, looking like he'd had all the stuffing knocked out of him. Knowing that someone needed to take charge, he steered Jack, then Fox into the empty conference room and pushed them to sit down in the chairs he pulled away from the table. Slamming the lid to his laptop closed, he swallowed down his questions, knowing neither Jack nor Fox was in a position to answer them. Their grandmother was severely ill, possibly dying. They were in a state of shock.

He couldn't think of Avangeline in a hospital bed, her tiny body being shocked back to life, her haughty, aristocratic face slack. If he did that, he would be of no use to his family and his brothers. It was time to step up and do what he'd always done, what he'd promised Avangeline he'd do—and that was to protect them.

He walked down the passage and whipped open the door to Jack's office. His assistant looked up, her face worried. "Jack ran out, I don't know where he is," Irene gabbled. "He looked terrible, is he—"

"He's in the boardroom, he's had some bad news about Avangeline. Call in a helicopter—we need to get to Hatfield as soon as possible. I want that helicopter here ten minutes ago. I'll get the brothers to the roof. Do you have any idea where Peyton is today?"

She thought for a minute. "Jack mentioned that she and Noah were in Hatfield. They are spending the day with her friends Simon and Keane."

"Get hold of Simon, tell him that Avangeline has collapsed and get Peyton to the hospital so that she's there when Jack arrives. They'll look after Noah," Merrick stated. "Soren and Eliot?"

"I'll call them," Irene replied, lifting her phone. "I'll hire a helicopter for them too. I have no idea where Ru is."

Merrick pulled his phone from his pocket and scrolled through his contacts to call Ru. She was in the country; that much he knew. A good thing, because she tended to flit off at a moment's notice. She answered on the first ring and when he asked where she was, told him that she was at her parent's house in Bay Ridge, Brooklyn. She gasped when he told her that Avangeline was desperately ill.

"But I saw her yesterday! I knew she was feeling a little tired, a little unsteady on her feet—"

They could discuss that later so Merrick cut her off. "Irene is arranging a helicopter to take you, Soren and Eliot to Hatfield. She'll call you soon to tell you where the chopper will collect you. Do you have transport to get to where a chopper can land?"

"My father will drive me. You're bringing Fox?"

"And Jack," Merrick confirmed. He heard her sob and gentled his voice. "I've got them, Ru. Trust me. I'm bringing him to Avangeline, and you."

"If she... If anything else happens, he'll need me, Merrick," Ru said, her voice clogged with tears.

"I know, Ru. Just like Jack will need Peyton, and Soren, Eliot. I'm making that happen," Merrick told her before disconnecting. Just as he needed Aly. He needed to hear her voice, to feel her hand in his, grounding him, her shoulder pressing into his bicep, reminding him that he wasn't alone.

He dialed her number but, like the other calls he made to her today, it went straight to voicemail. Hoping for a miracle, he called again as he walked back to the conference room to find Jack and Fox exactly as he left them, both of them staring into space. No answer again. He left her a terse message to contact him urgently. He knew she'd call him soon; she was never out of contact for long.

Merrick stood in the waiting room at Hatfield Hospital and once again, checked his watch. It was nearly six thirty and despite leaving Aly a dozen or so messages over the past seven hours, she'd yet to call him or arrive at Hatfield Hospital. He looked around the waiting room, trying to make sense of the horrible events of the day.

Avangeline, as her doctor informed them earlier, had suffered a stroke, one they doubted she'd recover from. Even if she did survive, the doctors held out very little hope of her leading anything but a bed-bound, immovable and uncommunicative life. From her brain scan, they'd seen that a blood vessel had ruptured in a classic, and fierce, hemorrhagic stroke. They were less common, the doctor solemnly told them, but a great deal more destructive.

They didn't expect her to live through the night.

Merrick rubbed his hands over his face. When he dropped them, he took in his family scattered throughout the waiting room. His mom sat next to Pasco, thigh to thigh. Both his arms were around her slight frame and her face was buried in his neck. He saw the love for his mom on Pasco's face and was glad they'd managed to find their way back to each other. She would need Pasco in the coming weeks and months.

Eliot stood next to Soren at the small window, talking softly, their hands linked. Soren reached out to rub her tummy. Judging by the soft smile Eliot gave him, Merrick suspected that another Grantham would be making its appearance in six or seven months.

Ru and Jack, Peyton and Fox sat on the long bench, with both brothers leaning forward, their forearms on their knees, and their heads dropped. Peyton had her hand on Jack's back, Ru's on Fox's knee. His brothers knew they weren't alone, that they had someone to lean on.

He did not.

And wasn't that so fucking typical of his life, something he'd experienced over and over again? He was the one who stood apart, the one who endured the ups and downs of life alone. Sure, his mom protected him from his dad, but he'd also protected Jace from him, sometimes deliberately goading his dad so that he'd stop beating on his mom, trying to distract him to stop the pain. Sometimes that ended with him being hurt, but that had been the price he'd been prepared to pay, even at so young an age.

When he came to Calcott Manor, he promised Avangeline he'd look after her grandsons and none of them, not even

Avangeline, knew how seriously he'd taken that vow. At thirteen, he'd confronted the bully who'd picked on Soren and made sure everyone understood that Soren was solidly off limits. When it came down to whether to pick Merrick or Jack for their school's basketball team, Merrick faked an ankle injury—despite loving the game—so that Jack would make the team. When Fox crashed his car into that light pole, Merrick told the police he'd been driving, resulting in a lecture from both the patrol officer and being grounded by his mother.

He had done anything and everything he could to look after the Granthams and he couldn't believe—didn't *want* to believe—that the person who'd protected him from his dad, who made sure that they were safe—was leaving him. They'd been, in their way, a team of two and now he was left alone.

He didn't know if he could do it, not on his own.

Aly should be here; he needed Aly.

He turned his back on his family and pulled in a couple of deep breaths, annoyed at how much he wanted and needed her. What more proof did he need that she wasn't someone who would stick around, someone he could rely on? She wasn't even part of the family, not really. She might have part of Malcolm's liver but that meant little if she couldn't make the effort to be with them when they needed her the most, when *he* needed her the most.

What the hell could've kept her out of communication for the best part of the day? He'd left a message at eleven, and it was now after six. Seven hours. Seven long, excruciating hours that he'd been alone, waiting for her, needing her.

He wasn't doing this again, wasn't letting his heart get attached to someone who would just let him down. If he hadn't known better before, he damn well knew it now. It was time to cut her loose, to stop hoping she'd walk through that door, wishing he could hug her, pull in some of her strength. He'd allowed her behind his shields, in too close. Now he wanted too much and felt brutally let down and unbelievably disappointed. He was the one who gave, not the one who received... How stupid of him to forget that.

He'd never give Aly, or any other woman, this much power to hurt him again. He'd never allow himself to need someone so much again.

Of all the days in her life to have a dead phone battery, this was the worst one. Aly stepped off the train onto the platform at Hatfield station, ran up the steps and burst onto the sidewalk, scanning the street for a taxi. After plugging in her phone when she reached Merrick's apartment—a bit disconcerted not to find him waiting for her—she'd been horrified to receive message after message about Avangeline's collapse. There had been Jace's text message asking her to come to Hatfield as soon as she could, and a stack of messages from Ru, Peyton and Eliot. And more, so many more messages from Merrick asking her where she was, telling her he needed her.

Thinking that it would be quicker to take the train than to try to navigate the rush hour traffic out of the city, Aly bolted for the train station and caught the first train to Hatfield. Before leaving, she called Merrick to let him know that she was on her way, concerned when he didn't answer. Knowing there was no point in taking a phone with a dead battery with her, she sent a message to Jace and the others, telling them she was on her way, that she needed to catch a train and she would be with them as soon as possible.

Aly looked for a taxi but couldn't find one. She shoved her hands into her hair and blinked back her tears. Crying wouldn't help anyone. She was about to turn around to ask the first friendly face she saw whether she could use their phone to call for a taxi when a Jeep pulled up beside her and the driver leaned across the seat to open the door. "Aly, remember me? I'm Simon, Peyton's friend."

She nodded and pulled the door open. "Oh, thank God! Can you give me a lift to the hospital?"

He nodded. "That's why I'm here, Peyton sent me. Hop in."

Aly sent Peyton a virtual hug and pulled on her seat belt as Simon pulled away. She turned to face him, pushing her hair out of her eyes. "How is she? My phone is dead, so I haven't been able to check in."

"There hasn't been any change, as far as I know," Simon replied, swinging onto the main road that would take them to the hospital.

Aly closed her eyes, thankful for that small piece of news. She desperately wanted to be with Merrick as his beloved grandmother—and Avangeline *was* his grandmother; their lack of common blood didn't matter—fought the biggest battle of her life.

She'd prayed the train would go faster, prayed that Avangeline would pull through and simply prayed. And wished she was with Merrick, giving him the support she knew he needed. He thought he was so strong, so in control, the guy that everyone leaned on, but she knew that he also needed support of his own. The family, bless them, were so used to him being the steady rock that they forgot to take care of him in turn.

Right now, she knew he'd be checking in on his brothers, and his mom, making sure that they had coffee, that they and their partners were okay. He saw protecting the Grantham family as his job. But who protected him? If he'd let her, she would. For the rest of her life—every day, in every way—she would make sure that he got the emotional support he needed, the love that he'd denied himself for so long. The love he was too scared to accept or didn't believe he deserved. Because, God, she loved him. She'd never known an emotion as powerful, as deep. Aly felt like she could move mountains for Merrick, swim to unheard-of depths and fight monsters for him. There was nothing she wouldn't do for him...

She *loved* him.

Oh, she'd lusted after him from the first moment their eyes met in Simon's bar all those months ago—and she lusted over him in a way that still made her shake. He knew her inside out, and she wondered whether he'd still make her feel squirmy, unsettled and horny, at eighty. She rather suspected he would. Her body was his and would always respond whenever he stepped into the room.

She didn't know how they would make their relationship work but she would, somehow, have that big, bold, beautiful man—inside and out—in her life. Nothing would stand in her way.

"We're here," Simon said, as he swung his Jeep into the entrance of the hospital. "I'll drop you off in front of the entrance. Can you tell Peyton that I've gone home to help Keane with Noah?"

"Sure," Aly said, opening the car door when he came to a stop. "Thanks for the lift, Simon."

She barely heard his "anytime" because she was out of the car and sprinting.

Eleven

When Aly skidded into the private waiting room on the third floor, she looked around, her heart sinking. Only Fox and Jack were there, and they both stood by the window, looking out into the darkness without seeming to see it.

Neither of them needed to say anything, Avangeline's passing was written on their faces.

Aly held out her hands as she walked over them, stepping into first Jack's arms, then Fox's. "I'm so, *so* sorry. When? How?"

Fox wiped the tears from his eyes with the tips of his fingers. "About forty minutes ago. She had another stroke and slipped away," he told her. "We all went in to say goodbye. Merrick is in there now."

Aly looked around. "Where is everyone else?"

"Pasco has taken Jace, Soren and Eliot back to Calcott Manor and Peyton and Ru are waiting for us downstairs. We didn't want to leave Merrick here by himself——we were waiting for you to get here," Fox told her.

"My phone died," she admitted, conscious of the tears streaming down her face. "I'm so, so sorry. I know I didn't know her for long, but I loved her."

Fox ran his hand down her arm. "And she loved you. You brought light to her world, and a connection to Mal, that she badly needed."

She thought about seeing Avangeline and Arthur in the rose garden and her heart jumped in her chest. "Has anyone called Jocelyn and Arthur?" They were both going to be devastated, in a hundred different ways.

"Merrick called Jocelyn," Fox replied. *Of course he did*, Aly thought.

Aly heard the sound of footsteps coming down the passage and recognized them instantly. She slowly turned around and there he was, looking, as she expected, shattered. His olive skin looked pasty, and his eyes held a wealth of sorrow. He looked like someone had sucked the life out of him.

She immediately ran to him, and flung her arms around him, trying to gather up as much of his big body as she could. "I am so sorry," she said, speaking into his hard chest. "So sorry, Mer. I know how much you loved her. She's going to be so missed."

He felt as stiff as a board and Aly frowned. His arms didn't come up to hold her, and he didn't bury his face in her hair. She opened her eyes and saw his clenched fists at his side. *He's had a shock, he just needs time,* she thought, so she stood up on her tiptoes to wind her arms around his neck.

Then Merrick did something she didn't expect. He placed his hands on her hips and bodily pushed her away from him. Aly jerked back and lifted her eyes to slam into his, dark and tumultuous and just a little contemptuous.

What the hell was going on here?

Merrick walked away from her and pulled Jack into a hug, and then Fox. The three big men stood there, taking strength from each other. Aly folded her arms and blinked away the tears blurring her vision. Merrick was doing what he did best, looking after his brothers.

After what seemed like forever but couldn't have been more than a minute, Merrick placed his hand on Fox's face, then Jack's. "Go be with Ru and Peyton, guys."

Jack shook his head. "We need to call an undertaker. We should stay with her until he comes."

Merrick rested his head against Jack's. "I've already called for the undertaker, and I'll stay with her. You guys go now. I just need you to do me one favor, please?"

Fox wiped away his tears with the ball of his hands and nodded, his eyes glued to Merrick's face. "Can you give Alyson a lift back to Calcott Manor?" Merrick asked. "She'll follow you down in a minute."

Alyson. He only called her Alyson when he was trying to make a point. Aly tried to swallow the enormous lump in her throat, somehow knowing that her life was about to flip inside out and then fall apart.

"We need to make funeral arrangements, call people, put out a press release," Jack told him.

"You need to go home, have a whiskey and wait for me," Merrick told him. "I'm going to be maybe an hour behind you. Wait for me, and we'll do it together."

Meaning that he'd take care of it, that he'd make the calls and arrangements so that they wouldn't have to. Fox nodded and the two brothers left the room, leaving Aly on her own with Merrick. He dug his fingers into his eye sockets and eventually lifted his eyes to look at her. "You chose a hell of a day to go AWOL," he told her, his voice missing

all the warmth it had contained moments earlier when he
spoke to Fox and Jack.

"I had a doctor's appointment, he wanted tests done, then
I—"

He held up a hand. "You know what, I just don't give a
shit. The only thing I know, what I can't get past, is that on
the one day I needed you, you weren't here. On the worst
day of my life—and I've had some pretty crappy days, Alyson—you were nowhere to be found."

"The battery on my phone died," she told him. "I would've
been here sooner if I'd known, Merrick."

"It doesn't matter, does it? You weren't here," he said,
his voice a cold monotone. "I can't rely on you, I can't trust
you. I can't depend on you. As you said earlier, maybe it's
better if we call it done."

He was being unfair and she wanted to protest, but she
reminded herself that he'd just lost one of the two most important women in his life. He'd be more like himself tomorrow, the day after. And she could easily forgive him for the
things he said while struck with grief. She knew how pain
could rip you apart, how it made one lash out and say things
they didn't mean.

"I'll wait for you until the undertakers arrive, and then
I'll drive you home," Aly told him, deciding to focus on the
here and now, the practicalities.

Merrick straightened and his eyes were electric lasers on
her skin, burning into her. "You don't understand, I never
want to see you again. There's nothing I want from you,
nothing I need. I can't ban you from any contact with the
rest of the family—I would if I could, but that's beyond
my control. I'll tolerate your presence if and when I have
to, but a few civilities are all you'll ever get from me going
forward."

Wait, he was breaking up with her because her phone died? "I don't understand why you are doing this, Merrick," she said, her voice thin with shock and pain. "I genuinely didn't know that you needed me. I only heard about Avangeline ninety minutes ago—and all I've done since then is rush here as fast as I could."

He shrugged. "I'm glad it happened this way. I needed a wake-up call, a reminder that no one is dependable. The only people I can rely on are my mother and my brothers. I got swept up in the sex, in the romance, but I'm good now. I'm better off alone—I've always known that."

"That's nonsense," she told him. "Neither of us is better off alone—we are far stronger together. I love you, so much, and I think you might be in love with me. We're good together, Merrick."

Dear God, she was arguing about their relationship and down the hallway Avangeline lay, her body not yet cold. Aly lifted her hand. "This isn't the time or place. We can talk about this later."

"We're not going to talk about it at all," Merrick told her, jamming his hands into the pockets of his pants. He stared down at the floor and swallowed. "Please leave. I'd like to cry for my grandmother, and I don't want you witnessing my grief."

There was nothing he could've said that would've driven his words home harder, no statement that could've inflicted more pain than the one he uttered. Being with someone while they mourned was one of the most intensely personal interactions two people could experience and Merrick didn't want to share that with her.

It was over; whatever they had was done. He wanted her to leave the hospital waiting room, and his life.

And Aly loved him enough to do both.

* * *

After Avangeline's lawyer left, the reading of the will hadn't taken too long. Merrick and his family sat in Avangeline's favorite living room at Calcott Manor, the one that led out onto her beloved rose garden. To Merrick, it felt like Avangeline was just down the hallway. He kept expecting her to walk into the room or to hear her calling for Aly.

With Avangeline gone, Calcott Manor felt empty, but without Aly, his life felt doubly so.

Yesterday, he and his brothers had carried Avangeline's coffin into the church in Hatfield. Out of the corner of his eye, he'd seen Aly sitting at the end of a church pew, her face pale and her big eyes awash with tears. When he took his place next to his mom in the front row of the church, it felt wrong that Aly wasn't up there with the rest of the family, that the world would think her to be just another of the hundreds of mourners who'd turned up to pay homage to Avangeline.

He'd been so grateful when Jace and Pasco stood up from their seats, walked down the aisle and pulled her from her seat and sat her down between his mom and Peyton, who immediately took her hand. They'd done what he couldn't...

Jocelyn led the service, and in her inimitable way, she made Avangeline come alive again, telling the congregation stories of her, and mentioning Arthur's long friendship with his grandmother. Arthur read W. H. Auden's "Stop the Clocks" and Peyton did a scripture reading. His brothers asked him to read the eulogy they spent half the night writing, with the help of a bottle and a half of whiskey. His voice cracked but he managed to get through it, keeping his focus off the first row of mourners in case he inadvertently made eye contact with Aly.

He missed her and he regretted the way things ended—

he'd been too harsh, the time hadn't been right—but he still believed he was better off alone. Without a partner, he could give all his focus to the cornerstones of his life: his business, his brothers and his mom. Jace, especially, would need his company as she rattled around this big house she'd just inherited, along with money to maintain it.

But damn, he missed Aly with every breath he took, every beat of his heart.

As he frequently did, Jack picked up on his thoughts.

"We're really happy you inherited Calcott Manor, Jace," his brother said, taking the glass of whiskey Merrick offered him. Jace sat with Noah on her knee, Pasco sitting close to her. His future stepfather—Merrick still couldn't wrap his head around that concept!—hadn't left her side for the past ten days and Merrick was thankful his mom had someone to hold her when grief washed over her. Swimming through it on his own, trying not to drown, was harder than he'd ever imagined it would be.

"It's still going to be your family home," Jace told them, her tone suggesting she wouldn't entertain any arguments on that score. "It will always be your home, you know that."

Soren sent her a warm smile. "Of course we know that, Jace. With you here, it's the place we'll always return to."

Jace waved her hand in front of her face, visibly trying not to cry. "That's such a nice thing to say, Soren."

"It's true," Fox agreed. "We will always be grateful that Avangeline took us in, but you were, and are, our compass point. The one we ran to when we were sick or sore or in trouble."

Noah saw the tears on her face and frowned at Fox. "No cry, Jacy," he said, patting Jace's cheek.

His mom smiled at her baby grandson and kissed his chubby cheek before speaking again. "I'm glad Avangeline wrote a straightforward will. Everything should be easily handled."

He agreed. The major assets had already been settled. For the smaller assets, her art collection was under their joint control, with Peyton named as their adviser, and all her jewelry was to be held in trust by Jace, to be distributed among granddaughters-in-law and great-granddaughters as Jace saw fit. Aly, despite having only known Avangeline for such a short time, was left her favorite ring, a yellow, square-cut diamond, the ring he removed from Avangeline's finger in the hospital.

He could easily imagine it on Aly's elegant hand and knew it belonged there. Avangeline loved her, and so did he.

But was love enough? He still wasn't sure.

Merrick took a big sip of his whiskey and closed his eyes. Hearing a soft rap on the tall door to the sitting room, his eyes flew open and there she stood, dressed in black jeans, a long black sweater and black boots. Peyton, Ru and Eliot surged to their feet and took their turns hugging her. After they let her go, Aly walked over to Jace and hugged his mom for the longest time. Jace's blue eyes met his over his shoulder and she narrowed her eyes at him, a silent command to "*fix this.*"

He didn't know how. He wasn't sure he was brave enough to try.

Aly made her way around the room and greeted his brothers, and Pasco, with kisses on their cheeks. When she was done, she finally looked at him. He couldn't help but notice the dark stripes under her eyes, her gaunt cheeks. She'd lost more weight, and she looked more fragile than he'd ever seen her.

"Hi," she said.

"Are you okay?" he demanded, clutching the marble mantelpiece with too-tight fingers. "You look awful."

He heard a couple of shocked gasps and heard Fox mutter something about him being an idiot, but he didn't care. He needed to know that she was fine. "I saw my doctor the day Avangeline died. I'm *physically* fine."

She put enough emphasis on the word *physically* to insinuate that she was an emotional wreck. Well, fair enough. He was too. But he didn't think there was a way back. Or a way forward. Being with Aly meant taking a chance he wasn't ready to take—not when he'd been let down too many times before.

"Why are you here, Aly?" he asked, sounding immensely tired. He was tired of being by himself, picking up the pieces, and being strong for everyone else. Being alone.

He was so damn tired of being alone. But he didn't know how to be anything else.

Aly pulled her eyes off him and tried to smile. "I have some things to tell you, and maybe we can then, finally, put the past few months behind us."

Being in the same room, breathing the same air as Merrick was hard. Keeping herself from walking over to him and winding her arms around him, was torture. But she knew that if she did that then she'd be rejected again, just as she had been at the hospital. He had made it clear that he didn't think she belonged in this family. It didn't matter how everyone else felt about her. To her way of thinking, his was the only opinion that counted.

She loved Jace with all her heart; she was the mother figure Aly had never expected to find in her late twenties. Peyton, Ru and Eliot were her sisters. This was the family she'd longed for. But after she said what she needed to, explained what she thought she knew about the plane crash, she'd take a little piece of them with her. Thanks to

Malcolm, she'd always have some Grantham DNA in her
system, and she had to be content with that—or at least, accepting of the situation.

After she left Calcott Manor tonight, she was heading
back to Jersey City. She was starting work again at the office in a few days. She planned to bury herself in her work.
Surely her career would, in time, be enough to satisfy her.
Women didn't die of broken hearts; it just felt like it.

"Sit down, darling," Jace instructed her. Fox led her to a
wingback chair and pushed a glass of wine into her hands.
She didn't want alcohol, but it was something to hold, something to anchor onto. *Just get through it and you can leave,*
Aly told herself. *Ten minutes, fifteen, and then you can bawl
your heart out. But only when you get to the end of the drive
and are alone in your car.*

"I have some information about Jesse," she said, annoyed
at her hesitant voice. She was a lawyer, for God's sake; she
could do better than this. She cleared her voice and tried
again. "I didn't want to bother you with this straight after
the funeral, but I am returning to Jersey City so this is my
last chance. Besides, I presumed you'd all be together tonight, and I didn't want to explain more than once."

God, she was rambling, and she never rambled.

"Take a sip of wine, and a deep breath, darling girl," Jace
told her, handing Noah to Jack. Jace sat on the arm of her
chair, and her hand on her back encouraged Aly to speak.

"I think I know what happened on the plane."

Everyone tensed and she held up her hand in a warning.
"Please, *please* remember that I am just speculating, I can't
know for sure."

"Just tell us, Al," Jack said, leaning forward.

She nodded. "So, to backtrack a little. I know you have
all doubted, to varying degrees, my claims about inheriting

Malcolm's traits and likes, and dislikes. Some of you called me a bullshit artist." *I'm talking about you, Merrick.* "Jace and Avangeline believed me instantly, and for that, I'll be forever grateful. I never intend to talk about this again, but I feel the need to tell you that I've been having chest pains over the past six weeks, maybe two months."

Yeah, nobody but Merrick would ever know about her plane-slamming-into-a-mountain visions.

On hearing Jace's horrified gasp, she patted her knee. "I'm fine, Jace, I promise."

She pushed her hand into her hair and wished she could shove away her headache. "The day Avangeline died, I went to see my doctor and he booked me into the hospital for the next six hours. He ran a million tests on me, but he couldn't find anything physically, or medically wrong. I think I know why."

"If it wasn't a physical problem, why did you get chest pains, Al?" Peyton asked her, her eyes wide.

"I realized I only ever got them when I was talking about Malcolm or talking about the plane crash. I've always suspected they are psychosomatic, all in my head," Aly admitted. "And when I tell you what I suspect, then hopefully you'll see the connection to my chest pains."

Jace stroked her hair and Aly felt Merrick's eyes boring into hers. Oh, boy, she now needed to venture into the part of her explanation he wasn't going to buy into at all.

Oh, well.

Aly gathered her courage and looked up at Jace. "You were there at the airport the day of the crash. You drove the twins and their wives to the airfield."

Jace nodded. "Malcolm came with me, he loved planes."

"You told me that he did the preflight check with Jesse

and that Malcolm seemed upset when he returned to you. You said that he looked mad."

Jace frowned. "Yeah, he was. He said something about how his father shouldn't fly with a sore arm and that they should just come home."

There it was, the piece of information she'd been struggling to remember, told to her by Jace months and months ago. "We had that information, about his arm hurting and him seeming sad, confirmed by his flight instructor, who spoke to him shortly before they took off. I think, I *believe*, one of two things happened. Jesse might've had a heart attack mid-flight, a massive one that incapacitated him instantaneously. They were flying in clouds and mist, your dad didn't know how to read the instruments, Soren—"

"Or, to be fair, how to fly," Soren interjected.

Aly nodded. "The second option is that Jesse could've had a panic attack. They can present as heart attacks, and the result would've been the same—the only pilot on board would've been unable to function. I'm leaning toward a heart attack because I think the pain I felt under my ribs was…" Man, she couldn't believe she was about to say this. "I think it was Malcolm trying to tell me that he knew that his dad had a heart attack and that, maybe, he felt guilty for letting them fly."

She didn't need to look at Merrick; she could sense the disbelief on his face.

"He was ten," Soren said, a little hotly. "How could he have stopped them?"

Fair point, Aly conceded. "He couldn't have, of course, but that wouldn't necessarily have stopped him from blaming himself, especially in his twenties when he came to understand more about what his father was going through back then."

"But, as you said, this is conjecture," Merrick stated. "It's not proof. And Jesse was a healthy guy. I mean, we could be saying that he had an aneurysm, and we wouldn't know differently."

"Fair enough," Aly replied. "Except that Jesse did have high-ish cholesterol, he was stressed-out and was, according to his doctor, suffering from depression. All the above can be contributing factors to a heart attack."

Merrick's eyebrows raised. "More conjecture."

He was determined not to believe her, and Aly felt a wave of pain pass through her. Then she remembered that she was here for Jack and Fox, for Soren and not for Merrick. He'd said everything he needed to the day Avangeline died.

"Malcolm went to see his father's doctor. He got the same information I did. I think he put it together to reach the same conclusion. He knew his father had the sore arm that's often a precursor to a heart attack, and he felt dreadfully guilty for letting him fly." Merrick started to speak, and Aly glared at him. "Yes, I know he shouldn't have felt guilty but so much of our childhood affects the here and now...doesn't it?"

Merrick's eyes skittered away as he realized he wasn't only talking about Malcolm. She wasn't here to take pot-shots at Merrick, she reminded herself. She needed to explain the rest and then leave.

But God, this was hard. Being so close to him, seeing the distance in Merrick's eyes, was unadulterated torture. Aly pulled in a deep breath. "I have something else to say that might be hard to hear," she told them, and it took all she had to keep her tone even. "But I think it needs to be said, brought out into the open. Maybe then, Malcolm can fully rest."

And she could get her life, and her liver, back.

"Tell us," Fox instructed her.

"The doctor also told me that Jesse was impotent, and he had been for years, which means he couldn't have taken part in The Basement's activities." She ignored their shocked gasps and kept her eyes on Jack and Fox. "We found a phone of your dad's, one he'd sent in for repair not long before his death. I only showed Merrick a couple of messages your mom and dad exchanged."

She saw interest flicker in their eyes, and shook her head. "I don't recommend you read them," she told Jack and Fox. "You don't want to see them. Trust me on this."

They were smart men and immediately understood her implication that their exchanges had been brutal. "Give us the highlights," Fox demanded.

"Firstly, the sex club was your mom's baby—Jesse wasn't into it at all."

Jack frowned. "But he was involved, his name was all over the documentation."

"I believe he was trying to protect your mom, trying to keep her identity and tastes a secret. His text messages make it clear that he wanted out, out of the club and out of his marriage. Heather was furious and they'd been fighting about it for months. The week of the crash, Jesse instructed his lawyers to initiate divorce proceedings. I think the argument you heard between them, Fox, was about that. Jesse didn't want to go to Martha's Vineyard that weekend. He wanted to stay here with his sons."

Fox ran his hand over his face. "I— *God*. I don't know what to say."

What was there to say? Nothing really. "I think his stress levels were through the roof. I think Malcolm heard him say something about having a sore arm, sensed there was something wrong and told him not to go. Jesse ignored him, and as the years passed, I think Malcolm started to feel guilty about the fact that he didn't stop him. Maybe that's partly why he turned to opioids." Aly shrugged. Like his father, she suspected that Malcolm had fought demons the rest of his family didn't know about.

"Holy shit," Fox said, taking Ru's hand. "Holy, holy shit."

Aly felt the need to caution him again. "Look, as I said, it's conjecture. It's pure speculation."

"But it's conjecture that makes sense," Jack stated. "It makes a *lot* of sense."

It did. Intellectually but, more importantly, it resonated in her soul.

"Girl, drink that wine," Ru told her. "After all that, you need a bottle and a huge slab of chocolate cake."

Without hesitation, she looked at Ru and shook her head. "I don't eat sugar, I don't even like it."

And at that moment, Aly knew Malcolm was gone, that their connection, whatever it had been, was severed. All she had left of him was an organ he once owned. She bit her lip, looked at Merrick and burst into tears.

Wave after wave of emotion rolled over her until strong, familiar arms pulled her against a broad chest. Knowing that she shouldn't, but unable to help herself, Aly buried her face in Merrick's neck, unable to stop the sobs from rising from the deepest place in her.

She cried for all the Granthams had lost, for Avangeline and her twin boys, and for the men who'd been raised without one, or both, their parents. She cried because there was still so much love between them. This was a family that had walked through the deepest levels of hell together and come out the other side, their love stronger and tougher.

She cried for Avangeline, that strong, funny, feisty woman who'd be so graceful and classy while still sporting a huge set of balls. For her mom, who'd achieved so much with so little. For Jace, who'd gone on the run with nothing to save her and Merrick's life, and who had the biggest capacity for love of anyone she'd ever met.

But mostly she cried because she loved Merrick, and she genuinely didn't know how she was going to find the willpower to walk away from him a second time.

Aly felt his hand holding her neck, felt his lips against her temple, his murmured pleas for her to stop crying. "You're killing me, Aly," he muttered. "I can put down a helicopter in a shitstorm, hear the bullets pinging off the fuselage and keep it together but hearing you cry makes me want to jump out of my skin."

She managed to pick up her ten-ton heavy head and glare at him. "Tough," she told him, tears still sliding down her face. "Deal with it."

But having said that, she realized she couldn't sit here, cradled against his chest, couldn't spend another moment in his arms—not for his sake but for her own, because if she did, she might beg him to let her stay.

Love wasn't love when it was demanded, she reminded herself. Trust couldn't be switched on and off. It either burned brightly all the time or didn't exist. There were no half measures, and she wouldn't be able to accept anything less than everything from Merrick.

If she did, resentment might eat her up from the inside out. Aly used the ball of her hands to wipe her tears away. Looking up and around the room, she was surprised to see that it was now empty. Where had everyone gone?

"They thought we needed some privacy," Merrick explained, his hand gripping her thigh.

She forced herself to look at him and took in his sunken eyes and tight mouth. He looked like he'd had even less sleep than she had. Her inner mean girl was glad to know she wasn't the only one who'd been feeling miserable.

Aly tried to pull her thigh out from under his hand but that was like trying to remove a six-ton boulder. "Can you let me go, please?"

Merrick met her hot gaze with steady, oh-so-blue eyes. "No."

Aly made a show of looking at her watch. "I need to get going. I still have a two-hour drive to Jersey City."

Merrick wrapped his arms around her waist and pulled her so that she lay against his chest. "Yeah...that's quite a drive."

Aly released an annoyed sigh. "So let me get up so that I can get on with it," she told him. Her crisp statement was negated by the huge yawn that she tried, and failed, to swallow. Being in Merrick's warm arms, feeling so safe and so protected, made her feel sleepy.

She jerked up and shook her head. She needed to get a grip and leave. Now. Immediately. She turned to look at Merrick and their eyes caught and held. "Please let me go, Merrick."

He lifted a hand to brush his thumb across her lower lip. "Do you really want me to?"

No, of course she didn't! "You made your feelings very clear in the hospital. You refuse to be emotionally attached to me, and I can't have a purely physical affair with you. My affections are too deeply involved."

Merrick nodded and an indescribable emotion flickered in his eyes. "Did you mean what you said that day? That you loved me?"

Aly looked down at her hands. Her fingers were twisted together and were white with pressure. She knew that she could lie and say that she hadn't meant it. Merrick would probably believe her. But she needed to own her truth. She *did* love him, and she wouldn't deny it. "Yes. But it doesn't follow that you have to love me too. It's okay that you don't."

He winced and the flush of embarrassment touched his cheeks. She hadn't thought Merrick could blush. "I was a complete ass that day. I was hurt that you weren't there, and I lashed out because I couldn't deal with the fact that I needed you."

"I know." And for the rest of her life, she'd regret forgetting to charge her phone. "I got there as soon as I could, Merrick," she told him, keeping her tone low. "I wasn't ignoring you."

He placed his hand over hers, separating her hands and linking his fingers in one. "I realized how much I'd come to rely on you. I mean, you were such a part of the Grantham world, but I hadn't realized how deep you'd wiggled your way under my skin. For the first time in my life, I wanted a woman's support, needed someone and you weren't there."

She held her breath, her eyes on the tanned hand covering hers. She knew how hard it was for him to admit that he needed someone. Merrick was the man who gave support, but he didn't take it.

"I looked around and everyone had their someone but I didn't have mine. I felt gutted with grief and angry you weren't there. I used that anger to justify all the reasons I'd formulated over the years as to why I shouldn't be in a relationship, why it was better for me to be alone, and stand alone. Not having you there hurt—and I was already feeling gutted by Avangeline's death."

If she could change the past she would, but there was nothing she could do about it now. Merrick either needed to trust her or not, believe that she wouldn't let him down or not. Love her.

Or not.

Her rested his forehead on her temple and she felt his warm breath on the side of her face. "Will you please forgive me for being a stupid idiot?"

Sure, but...what did it mean? Was this conversation going anywhere or would the hope flickering deep inside her be squashed by a massive reality check?

"I'm so in love with you, Alyson."

Aly felt joy, then fear, invade her body. She couldn't look at him, couldn't move, in case she shattered the moment and reality, horrible and stark, came rushing in and blew her apart.

Merrick gripped her chin and gently moved her head so that she had to look at him. He waited until her eyes met his, frustration and fear warring for dominance. "Did you hear me?"

She nodded. "But I don't know what that means to you. I don't know what you want from me," she murmured.

"It means I want you with me, every day and in every way. It means I want to be able to talk to you, lean on you, seek your advice and have you reassure me when I'm feeling insecure or scared. I want to do that for you."

Aly tipped her head to the side, a little confused. "Do you *ever* feel scared or insecure?" she asked, genuinely curious.

"If you'd seen me this last week you wouldn't ask that question." He gave her a wry smile. "And yes, I know it was my fault because I pushed you away."

She nodded her agreement, not quite ready to let him off the hook.

"The thing is, Aly, you are the only woman, apart from

Jace and Avangeline, to whom I can show my soft belly, one of three I've ever trusted. It's a big deal for me."

It was and she appreciated it. And felt a little honored. "I'll always be there if you allow me to be."

Oh, she knew she should hold out for marriage or a commitment, but this was Merrick, who didn't do either. And the one thing she knew for sure was that she'd take anything he could give her. She just needed him in her life.

He half smiled. "So, I have a couple of suggestions if you're interested in hearing them…"

"Dear God, how *long* is this going to take?"

Fox's voice from behind the closed doors drifted over to them and Merrick rolled his eyes. "Go away!" he yelled at his family.

"You know that they aren't going to budge, right?" Aly whispered.

Merrick brushed her mouth with his. "I know."

Ignoring their audience, Aly placed her hand on Merrick's cheek. "You said you had some ideas and I'm excited to hear what they might be."

"Will you have a child, a few children, with me? Sometime down the road?"

Aly swallowed, her mind going to mini-Merricks running around, causing her to go gray before her time. Then she remembered that Jace raised five boys and thought that if Jace could do it, then so could she. If the kids got to be too much, she'd just dump them on Grandma for an afternoon.

She nodded enthusiastically, emotion clogging her throat.

Merrick lifted one hip and pulled a velvet jewelry box out of his pocket. He flicked it open using his thumb and Aly looked at the ring, her breath catching. She touched the massive stone with her finger, taking in its yellow brilliance. "Avangeline's ring."

"It's yours actually," Merrick told her, his voice low. "She left it to you in her will."

Tears slid down her cheeks. "I loved her so much, Merrick."

"I know you did, sweetheart. She loved you too. But maybe we can keep her close to us if you wear this as your engagement ring. I mean, I'll buy you another if you want something else, but I like the idea of—"

She slammed her mouth on his. "Yes," she said against his lips.

"Yes, to another ring or yes to this one?" Merrick asked, adoringly confused.

"Yes to wearing Avangeline's ring as my engagement ring. And yes to marrying you, although you didn't actually ask," she teased him.

He grinned at her. "I love you, will you marry me?"

She smiled at him, her tears gone. "I love you and yes, I will. Partly because I love you to distraction but mostly because I get Jace as a mother-in-law."

"I heard that!" Jace called from the other side of the tall doors.

"You were meant to," Aly shouted back, laughter in her voice. And as her family trooped back into the room, with Fox carrying champagne and Jack crystal flutes, she looked at Merrick and saw happiness and contentment in his eyes.

She gently kissed his mouth, vowing to keep him looking like that for the rest of their lives.

I am fading and writing this diary takes more energy than I thought I'd need. I think I've managed to hide my waning strength from my family, but it no longer matters. I know Death lurks just around the corner. I'm too tired to be philosophical or pithy so I will take

*the liberty of using another's words: those of Tecum-
seh, Shawnee chief and warrior.*

*"It is my time to die but I will not be afraid, nor will
I weep or pray for a little more time. No, I will sing my
death song, and die like a hero going home."*

Lady Avangeline Forrester-Grantham.

* * * * *

COMING SOON!

We really hope you enjoyed reading this book. If you're looking for more romance be sure to head to the shops when new books are available on

Thursday 14th September

To see which titles are coming soon, please visit

millsandboon.co.uk/nextmonth

MILLS & BOON

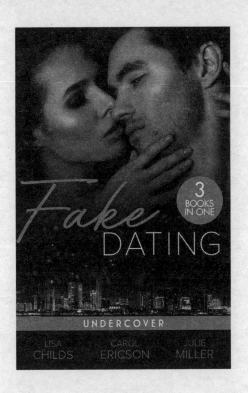

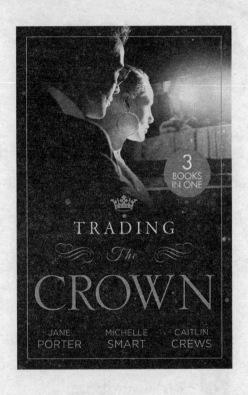

LET'S TALK

Romance

For exclusive extracts, competitions and special offers, find us online:

f MillsandBoon

𝕏 @MillsandBoon

◉ @MillsandBoonUK

♪ @MillsandBoonUK

Get in touch on 01413 063 232

MILLS & BOON

THE HEART OF ROMANCE

A ROMANCE FOR EVERY READER

MODERN

Prepare to be swept off your feet by sophisticated, sexy and seductive heroes, in some of the world's most glamourous and romantic locations, where power and passion collide.

HISTORICAL

Escape with historical heroes from time gone by. Whether your passion is for wicked Regency Rakes, muscled Vikings or rugged Highlanders, awaken the romance of the past.

MEDICAL

Set your pulse racing with dedicated, delectable doctors in the high-pressure world of medicine, where emotions run high and passion, comfort and love are the best medicine.

True Love

Celebrate true love with tender stories of heartfelt romance, from the rush of falling in love to the joy a new baby can bring, and a focus on the emotional heart of a relationship.

Desire

Indulge in secrets and scandal, intense drama and sizzling hot action with heroes who have it all: wealth, status, good looks…everything but the right woman.

HEROES

The excitement of a gripping thriller, with intense romance at its heart. Resourceful, true-to-life women and strong, fearless men face danger and desire - a killer combination!

To see which titles are coming soon, please visit

millsandboon.co.uk/nextmonth